Praise f

Anne and

"Sharp and engaging."

—*Publishers Weekly 2018 Booklife Prize*
(Winner, General Fiction)

"*Anne and Louis* is a masterpiece that paints an extraordinary vision of its times, capturing the facets of a social and political milieu with historical accuracy and vibrant emotional resonance ... satisfying, educational, and hard to put down."

—*Midwest Book Review*

"A dramatically engrossing and historically searching tale about a powerful duchess."

—*Kirkus Reviews*

"A lively, engaging story, rich with historical detail that brings the story of a forgotten queen to life. Reminiscent of Philippa Gregory and Jean Plaidy, *Anne and Louis* gives voice to Anne of Brittany, allowing her to step from the historical shadows and illuminating her as a determined and influential political figure, as well as a bright and devoted woman in her own right."

—Eleanor Brown, *New York Times* bestselling author,
The Light of Paris

"A gripping novel about a larger than life queen, *Anne and Louis* is a smartly written read filled with both passion and wit."

—*InD'tale Magazine*

"A lively narrative filled with strong women."

—Susan Abernethy, *The Freelance History Writer*

Praise for

Anne and Charles

"Gaston's blend of royalty, young love, and the French Renaissance is enchanting."

—*Publishers Weekly*

"A historically sharp and dramatically stirring love story."

—*Kirkus Reviews*

"A delightful read with sparkling dialogue, Gaston puts a human face on these captivating historical personalities from the French Renaissance."

—Susan Abernethy, *The Freelance History Writer*

"A romance for the ages, Ms. Gaston masterfully conveys the passion, heartbreak, and determination of this royal couple."

—*InD'tale Magazine*

"Francophiles, feminists and fans of history and romance alike will delight in *Anne and Charles*."

—Dominique Padurano, Ph.D., *Crimson Coaching LLC*

Praise for

Sense of Touch: Love and Duty at Anne of Brittany's Court

"A romance and an interesting novel about a little-known French queen. It is a story with a strong sense of place and well-drawn characters, a story of heartache and forbidden love, of women in the 15th century French court, who fought with passion and determination for what they wanted. A striking story."

—*Historical Novel Society*

"A fascinating look at a historical time when women fought to find their place in a man's—and a king's—world. Well written, too. Good pacing."

—Jina Bacarr, author of *Cleopatra's Perfume*

"A wonderful read filled with intrigue, adventures, passion and strength, *Sense of Touch* lets the world know more about the much forgotten Anne of Brittany."

—Clarissa Devine, *Quirky Lady Bookworm Blog*

"An enchanting historical romance about a young woman who is determined to marry her one true love. The heroine's quest for self-determination defies the rigid social structure of Medieval Europe as it gives way to the Renaissance. Set in the court of Anne of Brittany, we also learn much about the woman who was twice queen consort of France and her struggle to produce a living heir for the throne...Well-paced with period detail."

—*The Westchester Guardian*

"Well written, well developed characters and accurate historical information make this book a winner."

—*Morning Beans Blog*

ANNE

and

LOUIS

PASSION AND POLITICS IN EARLY RENAISSANCE FRANCE
THE FIRST YEARS OF ANNE OF BRITTANY'S MARRIAGE TO LOUIS XII

ROZSA GASTON

Renaissance Editions

New York

Published by

Renaissance Editions
New York
www.renaissanceeditions.com

Printed in the United States of America

ISBN-13: 978-0-9847906-8-5 (pbk)
ISBN-13: 978-0-9847906-9-2 (ebook)

Author's Note

Anne of Brittany was born in Nantes, Brittany, in 1476 or 1477, the year of her birth disputed. For the purposes of this story, I have chosen 1477 as her birth year. She married Louis XII on January 8, 1499, in Nantes, Brittany. Together they lived at their royal residence in Blois, France, until Anne's death in 1514. Louis joined her less than a year later on January 1, 1515.

Brittany became part of France in 1532, eighteen years after Anne of Brittany's death.

The term '*Brette*' in this story refers to a woman who is from Brittany. It was Louis' term of endearment for Anne.

Coat of Arms of Anne of Brittany
Arms of the king of France (fleur-de-lis) to the left
Arms of the dukes of Brittany (ermine tails) to the right
Courtesy of Wikimedia Commons

Anne of Brittany at her Writing Table
National Library of St. Petersburg
Courtesy of Wikimedia Commons

ANNE OF BRITTANY AND
HER MAIDS OF HONOR

With special thanks to Helen Josephine Sanborn who documented the names of many of Anne of Brittany's maids of honor in her 1917 work *Anne of Brittany: The Story of a Duchess and Twice-Crowned Queen.* Below are those who appear in this book.

Anne de Candale—full name, Anne de Foix-Candale, she came to Anne's household in 1492 at the age of eight. Married Vladislas II, King of Hungary and Bohemia and became queen of Hungary and Bohemia.

Germaine de Foix—Louis XII's niece, the orphaned daughter of his sister, Marie of Orleans. She and her brother Gaston de Foix came to live in Anne's household in 1492. Married Ferdinand II, King of Spain, after the death of his first wife, Queen Isabella.

Charlotte of Naples and Aragon, Princess of Tarente—daughter of King Frederick IV of Naples. Married Nicolas de Laval.

Charlotte d'Albret—daughter of Alain d'Albret, powerful Gascon nobleman. Married Cesare Borgia.

Jeanne de Chabot—full name, Jeanne de Rohan-Chabot, from the Breton House of Rohan.

Blanche de Montberon—a noblewoman from Angoulême.

Anne and Bolandine de Rohan—Breton noblewomen from the House of Rohan.

CONTENTS

To the memory of Christine de Pizan—
How well you captured a woman's struggle

CHAPTER ONE

1498

Entice then Deny

She would return to Brittany. What better way to light a fire under Louis? He was mad to make her his wife. Too bad he already had one.

Anne flicked the insect from her forearm in the July heat of the garden. Ridiculous for him to speak to her of dreams and plans for a future together, when his future was tied to another.

He had an annulment to attempt. She had a country to run. She was itching to see her dear de Montauban again, the only one of her advisors she had truly trusted during those years of uncertainty before Charles had made her his queen. Would her beloved friend and ally of her father's be old and grizzled, worn out by the cares of being Brittany's chancellor once more, since she had reinstated him in the days following her husband's death?

Rising from the marble bench, she paced the wisteria-covered garden of the Hotel d'Etampes, residence of queen-consort widows during the required forty days of mourning after the death of a king of France.

An image from long ago washed over her, making her smile. De Montauban was vaulting off his horse, in search of her specially-made built-up shoe. It had come off as they had fled the outskirts of Nantes to return to Rennes. Their entire entourage stopped until he had retrieved it in the mud some ways behind them on the road. He had known how important it was for his people's sovereign, the eleven-year-old duchess Anne, to be able to stand tall and walk smoothly with an even gait when she greeted her subjects at the gates of Rennes. They would wonder why she was back so soon, and she would have a good story for her men to circulate among the populace.

Just outside Nantes she had narrowly avoided being taken hostage by the marshal de Rieux. He had offered his men to escort her into the city.

Escort her? Hah! The marshal her father had chosen to be her guardian after his death had stipulated that she was to enter the city of her ancestral home under cover of darkness through a minor gate, with only one attendant. Who was marshal de Rieux to tell her, sovereign ruler of Brittany, with whom and how she may enter her birthplace and Brittany's most important city?

Anne had sat tall on her horse, refusing to dismount when the marshal and his men rode out to escort her into Nantes. Dusk was creeping over them; she would act fast before they lost the light so the marshal's men could see her face as she told their commander exactly where to go.

"The duchess of Brittany, sovereign ruler of Brittany, will enter her city by its main gate in daylight with her full entourage, so that her subjects may greet her publicly." Anne's voice rang out sharp and clear, each word clipped so that every man in the marshal's party could hear.

"My lady-duchess, we have made arrangements for your comfort and are here to escort you into the city so that you may rest and greet your subjects on the morrow," Marshal de Rieux's voice oozed. He beckoned to his men to surround her horse.

"Halt!" Anne put up her hand and glared down her nose at the head guard. The man faltered, looking uncertain.

"Brittany's sovereign arranges her own comfort and safety with her own chosen men who will accompany her into her city in full view of her subjects. We will camp here tonight and proceed through the main gate tomorrow after breaking fast," she told the marshal and his men.

"But my lady-duchess, will you not be more comfortable within the city walls tonight?" The marshal's tone rang false. It was unlike him, a man used to barking out orders instead of coaxing recalcitrant counterparties. Anne sensed he was dissembling.

"Men of Brittany, you see your sovereign before you. Will you shame yourselves by dragging her against her will under cover of darkness into the city she and your ancestral rulers have made into Europe's most glorious port?" She might be exaggerating slightly, but she would guess that most of the marshal's men were native Nanteans whose chests would swell to hear their city described so glowingly.

Likewise, they would quake in their boots to lay a hand on a sovereign who had been consecrated by a priest, authorized by God Himself to rule over them. It would be sacrilege.

The marshal's men shifted uncomfortably on their horses and looked at each other.

"Who amongst you will be first to lay hands on your consecrated sovereign?" Anne's voice rang out like a bell.

She had had occasion to use it with authority just months earlier in Rennes, when she had challenged the entire assembly of the Estates-General to answer who among them would marry off their daughter to a man four times her age. That particular speech had resulted in shutting down talk once and for all of her accepting the wretched old Alain d'Albret's marriage suit.

How good it had felt to raise her voice in commanding tones that day. She would never forget the looks of shock, then approval on the faces of the men who made up Brittany's government. Not a single one had challenged her.

"My lady, my men only wish to ensure your safety as escorts for you into Nantes." The marshal's tone dripped honey. It was all she could do not to laugh.

"You see clearly, Monsieur, that I have my own men who will accompany me." Deliberately, she chose not to use his title. He may be his men's marshal, but she was their supreme commander.

"I am afraid they will not, Madame. They will remain here and we will accompany you."

"You are in no position to tell Brittany's anointed ruler what her personal guard will or will not do. I will either enter my own city on my own terms or I will not enter at all."

"*Madame duchesse*, we beg you to enter. Your people are eager to see you."

"On the terms I have stated or not at all." If he thought he would seduce her with words to puff her pride, he was singing to the wind. She was as eager to see her people as they were to see her, but in nothing less than a public entrance with all due pomp and ceremony. Otherwise her subjects would get the wrong idea, thinking de Rieux was in charge instead of her.

"But-but Madame—" the marshal stammered.

Anne turned her mount and commanded her men. "Turn your horses. We return to Rennes."

All in her party did as they were told, preparing themselves in the event that the marshal's men overtook them. The jangle of steel being handled, knives patted in pockets, and spurs clanking informed the marshal's men they wouldn't be welcome should they follow.

None did.

Truth be told, Paris didn't agree with her. It was smelly, there was trash and sewage everywhere, and its inhabitants lived too closely together. She missed Brittany, most of all Nantes, with its fresh ocean breezes, bustling port, and wide open spaces.

She had always required space. She sensed Louis did, too. Having known him almost her entire life, she had heard of his usual dynamic with the ladies with whom he consorted. A hot and heavy start, a period of weeks or months of wildly intense interest, followed by the inevitable denoument: Louis would run off and that would be the end of it.

Two could play that game.

"Entice then deny," her father had frequently advised. As a young girl she had had no idea what use to make of such counsel, but the idea of combining two contrasting actions to achieve one desired outcome intrigued her.

Louis was the perfect candidate for such a technique. She would fan his flame. Then she would disappear. If he wished to marry her, he needed to get an annulment. Such a feat would not be easy, considering his wife was already revered as a living saint by many of Louis' subjects. Already, they were angry that he hadn't named her his queen consort or allowed her to appear by his side a single instance in public since he had unexpectedly become king upon his predecessor's death four months earlier, in April 1498.

Anne loved Louis. To be honest, she had loved him before Charles, then buried that thought for the six and a half years she had spent as the former king's wife. Now those feelings were emerging once more, no longer vague and girlish, but fully formed in the crucible of a woman's heart.

But Louis was married. And Anne loved something else even more dearly than either Charles or Louis.

Brittany was her country. Upon Charles' death, she had become its sole sovereign ruler once again. Was she not her father's daughter, inheritor of the title of Duchess of Brittany, and crowned ruler of Brittany in the cathedral of Rennes in 1489? It had been upon her return to Rennes after her standoff with de Rieux outside the gates of Nantes that she had taken it upon herself to arrange a ceremony of public recognition of her position. It had been well done.

Her heart urged her westward. She longed to see her homeland's granite cliffs, white with ocean-spray exploding against them. She longed to ride in procession amongst her dear Breton subjects, women in tall white headdresses waving in the breeze, men in Breton caps, hardy fishermen and farmers, merchants and traders. She loved them all and she was responsible for them all.

Time to go back.

Besides, Louis was facing a mess on his hands with his bid for an annulment before the court. Not only the tribunal, but the people of France would look askance at a man who asked for an annulment from his wife because she was too ugly to bed. Even if he was king, it was not enough of a reason. Especially from this particular wife, who was as saintly of heart as she was hideous of form.

Anne intended to be far from such a proceeding as it unfolded. Doubtless the people would blame her as well for such scandal if she so much as smiled in Louis' direction while he was casting off his wife like a worn out garment he wished to replace.

Jeanne of France was widely loved by the French people. She was rarely seen, serving to increase her mystique. Stories were rife that she could heal with her touch or even a glance from her limpid brown eyes, welling with mercy and compassion. Her own family members had shown her so little of either.

Anne had never met her, but she had heard of her deformities. It was said that Jeanne of France was both hunchbacked and crippled, Her eyes bulged, her head lolled to one side of her shoulders, and her arms were grotesquely long. At court it was whispered that when her own father, King Louis XI, had seen her on rare occasion he would curse and shout to her governess to take her away. The compassionate lady had taken to hiding the princess royal in the folds of her gown or behind her back whenever the king strode by.

Rejected by her own family, Jeanne of France had embraced her Lord; stories of her good deeds, holiness, and self-sacrifice grew with each passing year.

In short, Louis would have his work cut out for him if he tried to shed himself of such a wife. And what if he didn't succeed?

Anne had given him her terms. Either obtain an annulment within one year or she would withdraw all interest in his marriage offer. What cheek the man had to talk of getting married when he already was! Still, he was her Louis, the Louis of her youth, the Louis who had stood by her side and held the crown of France over her head in 1492 when she had first been crowned as Charles' queen, two months after their wedding.

Charles had gazed at her with adoring eyes in those first months of marriage, but his interest had soon wandered. At her coronation it had been Louis doing the heavy lifting, moving the enormous crown of France up and down as Anne rose and knelt during the ceremony. Already she had been with child.

Now Louis' moment had come. Just as she knew she was the woman of his dreams, so was he the man of hers.

But he was not yet free.

Reaching for a wisteria vine, she brought her face to it, inhaling deeply. After four months she still mourned for Charles, faithless as he had been. He had loved her, in his own fashion, and she him. But he had not allowed her to administer her own duchy, over which he held co-rights with her.

Now Charles was dead and she was sole ruler of Brittany once more. It was her moment to take the reins.

She would return to Brittany and Louis would follow, should he obtain his annulment. She would not consent to become his wife unless a marriage contract was signed that assured her full rights as sole sovereign and administrator of her duchy. Never would she accept the poor terms she had agreed to in her marriage contract with Charles, when her choice had been to become his wife or risk becoming his prisoner, with her country overtaken by his.

This time the man who wooed her was already prisoner of her heart. In return, she would care for his heart tenderly.

At the thought of Louis, a small flame flickered in the pit of Anne's stomach. She smoothed down the front of her gown, her hands moving slowly over her hipbones. Perhaps passionately, too.

Buoyant joy lifted her step as she went inside. She was twenty-one years old and ruler of her own country. The man who adored her wished to make her his queen. It wasn't a bad way to leave behind the sorrow and loss of her years spent with Charles VIII of France. She had given six and a half years to a man who had loved and admired her but had forbidden her to rule over her own inherited lands. This time, the equation would be different.

CHAPTER TWO

1498

Louis XII, King of France

She was making him work for her favors. It was nothing new. Even when she had been Charles' wife, the dynamic they had begun between them when she had been a child of seven and he, Louis, a young man of twenty-one, had continued: feisty, teasing, and, above all, genuine.

When he had leapt too high and danced too gaily at New Year's festivities of the year after her last little prince had died, she had banished him from court. It had only been one year later at the New Year's festivities of earlier that year that Anne had invited him to join them again.

Louis had put on his deep blue doublet and ridden like the wind the six leagues from Blois to Amboise. Leaping from his horse, he had waded through throngs of courtiers, intent only upon finding the one who possessed his heart.

Instead, he spotted her husband at the end of the Great Hall, greeting their guests who would help them welcome in the year of our Lord 1498.

"Your Majesty, it is good to see you again," Louis bowed to his brother-in-law, thinking he looked more frail than the last time he had seen him.

"Louis!" Charles clapped him on the shoulder. "Faith, it is good to see you again. What have you been up to?"

"The usual jesting and jousting. A spot of this, a sport of that." God willing, the new year would prove to be a less empty year for himself than 1497 had been. Louis was powerful, wealthy, not too old, still rashly athletic, and considered to be a looker amongst the ladies. In short, he was bored.

"So you are in form for dancing tonight, then," Charles joked.

Louis twinged. "Sire, I will not make the mistake of leaping toward the rafters as I did last year." He had missed his *belle Brette* for an entire year; how he rued having angered her with his thoughtless gaiety. Why had she not realized he had been trying to cheer her up?

"You may leap from the rafters again, Louis. The queen is blooming once more and has recovered from her sorrows of the year before." The king's face darkened; he put a hand to his chin. Louis guessed it was to hide his mouth.

Who truly recovers from the sorrow of having all of one's children die? Louis averted his eyes to give his brother-in-law a moment. It was almost as bad as being married against one's will to a sterile hunchback, knowing you will never breed at all.

The duke of Orléans scanned the room as he weighed the two situations. He decided his brother-in-law's was worse. Having produced no royal children at all, never mind an heir to the throne, Charles had suffered the shorter end of the stick. Anne even more so. What could be more painful than to lose one's son and the kingdom's dauphin at age three, then to lose two other princes within just days or weeks of their birth?

Truth be told, Louis had had it easier to have known from age fourteen that he would never bear children, at least legitimate ones, for as long as he was married to the old king's second daughter, Jeanne.

"Louis! Where have you been?" a lilting voice called out, curling itself around his heart and squeezing hard.

Her movements were heavier, less buoyant than her usual graceful carriage. As Louis bowed to her, he saw why.

"My lady queen, I have been hiding from you, fearing your wrath and hoping for your forgiveness this past year." He gazed into her beautiful gray eyes and once again felt that familiar twinge: his old friend, desire, tempered by his constant companion, regret. Never would he be able to reveal his true feelings to her.

"Oh, Louis, forget all that. Things have changed around here." Anne's eyes danced.

"I gather they have." His eyes fell to her waist, thicker than usual and making just the smallest of statements. Best not to speak of it until she did. The queen had had many pregnancies. She had no living children.

"Louis, I must speak with you," Anne murmured, leaning toward him. The scent of her under her violet musk perfume ignited him, instantly erasing twelve months of pointless distractions.

His life was to serve her, his place was beside her, but there was someone there already. She had banished him the year before; he knew why. Never would she have been so angry if her feelings hadn't been deeply involved. Sighing, he brushed aside thoughts that had no home, and no point to even bother examining.

His beloved queen appeared to be again with child. Perhaps

this time she would bear a son that lived. Such an outcome would distance him even further from the line of succession and from her.

As a focus for his restless heart, he could rustle up a campaign to Milan to claim his grandmother's rights to the duchy. There he could find a beautiful Italian to offer solace and distraction, while the woman of his dreams raised the dauphin who would replace him.

Louis smiled his wry smile. Over the years lines of irony had carved grooves down either side of his mouth. Life was full of surprises, most of them unhappy jokes played on undeserving innocents such as he had once been. Now he was no longer innocent, only undeserving. Still, a man could dream.

The queen steered him to an alcove next to mullioned windows that looked down upon Amboise Castle's new Italian gardens. She and Charles had spent the better part of the past two years upgrading their home with architects, artists, and artisans Charles had brought back from Italy. In place of gracing France with royal princes and princesses, they were on their way to gracing their kingdom with what was becoming one of Europe's most spectacular royal palaces.

Anne seated herself on the burgundy velvet-cushioned window bench. "You wouldn't believe what has happened to Charles," she began.

"He has lost weight, that much I can see." Louis raised his eyebrows. Not only did his brother-in-law look thin, but he had noticed for the first time how similar the king's bulbous brown eyes were to those of his middle sister, Louis' wife. For the first time Louis wondered if such bulging eyes indicated something more than just unusually unattractive physiognomy. Were they an indication of poor health?

"He grows small as I grow big," Anne jested, her hand

skirting her belly in the eternal gesture of expectant mothers. Her eyes sparkled in the light from the windows. Not for the first time Louis felt his heart ache as he drank in her sweet, lively face.

"When may we expect a new prince or princess for France?" Louis asked, breaking into a smile—this one not ironic. Anne was wan, perhaps even more beautiful in her paleness. Her pregnancies became her. What was it inside her body that thwarted their outcome? Or was it something to do with Charles?

Louis' hand closed tightly at his side. Why had fate doled out all the wrong partners to France's princes and princesses of the blood?

"When the lilies-of-the-valley bloom, God willing." Anne touched a dainty hand to the cross at her throat, bedecked with pearls that resembled the small white blossoms. Everything about her was delicate; everything about her ignited the utmost indelicacy in him.

Louis crossed his long legs to conceal a surge of vitality. His beloved queen had enjoyed only one successful pregnancy thus far in her marriage. Would to God this one would turn out well, too. But he knew nothing about such matters, and never would with the situation he was in. Married for twenty-one years, he had shared a bed with his wife perhaps a dozen times. It had been a dozen times too many.

"*Ma reine-duchesse*, may your dreams come true this year."

"That is precisely what I wish to tell you. Some of my dreams *are* coming true. Imagine, Louis!"

"My fair one, which dreams do you speak of?" Without thinking, he addressed her with easy intimacy. It was all he could do not to imagine certain dreams, none of which would come true for him, ever. Whenever he found himself in tête-a-tête with Anne, they fell back into easy relationship, one that was forged in Anne's ancestral castle in Nantes, in the gay laughing household of her father, Francis II, Duke of Brittany.

"Charles has become a new man," Anne whispered. She tucked a lock of lustrous dark hair back into her headdress. It was all Louis could do to refrain from reaching up and tucking it back in himself.

"How so?" Louis had heard rumors that the king had changed his ways in the past few months. He would like to hear from Anne in which ways before offering comment.

"He has given up his sweethearts."

"No!" That would be quite a feat for Charles de Valois, a king with a philanderer's reputation as large as his long Valois nose.

"Yes! Truly."

"Do you mean he has reduced their number from the hundreds to perhaps a score or so?" Louis couldn't help himself. Whenever he was with Anne they fell to joking between them, with no subject left sacred.

"Be serious!" Anne swatted Louis' knee. "All of them, truly. And he's holding audiences twice a week now for petitioners to present their grievances."

"Ah, what a treat for you." Louis raised his eyebrows, thinking of all the beggars and riffraff such hearings would include.

"It is, Louis. Can you imagine how wonderful it is to sit next to a husband who attends to his duties?"

"A wonder indeed for you, my lady-queen." *And long overdue.*

"I am finally queen-consort to a king worthy of his title."

"Your husband has always been worthy. He has just been a bit remiss." Louis felt a moment of indignation at the queen's swipe at one of his own sex. Always the athlete, as a team player he felt the urge to defend his brother-in-law, however much he wished to take his place.

"Well, he has remedied the remissness and is now in my bed every night." The queen looked satisfied. Blissful, in fact.

Louis' back spasmed. Quickly he twisted his grimace into a smile. His enchanting *Brette* had no idea how painful it was to hear such words from her mouth. "My lady, what did you do to reform him?"

"I prayed, I lit candles."

"In my limited experience, such actions do not accomplish much."

"I spoke with Father de Rély, who counseled him."

"Ahh." Louis knew Jean de Rély. He was a man's man, not the usual bloodless man of the cloth. Charles and he had gone to Italy together. He could imagine that Jean de Rély had managed to knock some sense into his twenty-seven-year-old brother-in-law's head.

"And just before Christmas, he began to stay home and receive his subjects," Anne added.

"Staying home is a good thing." God knew he wished he had reason to stay home. He had spent the past year holed up in his castle in Blois, nobody there other than his staff and himself, with the occasional female visitor. He would give his right arm to come home to a woman like Anne. There he would stay, too, aside from occasional hunting trips limited to game-hunting only.

"It has been a delight." Anne nodded. "Do you know I have always known him to be generous and merciful, but now he is offering largesse to his subjects and not ..."

"Not to sweethearts scattered throughout the Loire Valley."

"Or beyond!" Anne tossed her head, and gave Louis a look that announced she was not to be outfoxed by other vixens. It was something he already knew.

What a resilient woman France's queen was, Louis marveled.

She had suffered through six years of infidelity, the deaths of every one of her children, and here she was making light of her husband's weaknesses and complimenting his strengths. What man wouldn't give his right arm, not to mention his right to carouse, for such a supportive wife? It was about time Charles had come to his senses.

"Why does he look so thin?" Louis asked, as unexpectedly to himself as it was to her. They had always been frank with each other. He had forgotten himself and just blurted out his thoughts, a practice almost unheard of at court.

"Louis, I wonder the same. Why do you think he is so frail?"

"I don't know, my lady-queen. He is young and strong, and I have ever known him to be good at sport, brave in battle."

"He is wasting away, and I worry it is from some pox a *fille de joie* gifted upon him in Naples."

"My lady, take care of him and rejoice in your good fortune: both in him, and in the fruit you will soon bear." He looked at her belly, praying with all his might that this child would live. Then he thought of the *filles de joie* he had passed up in Italy, and felt nothing at all. So many of them had infiltrated the troops' camps, ingratiating themselves with lonely French soldiers, restless and away from their wives and families.

He had not been sorely tempted. Having nothing to return home to, he found himself having lessened desire on the other side of the Alps. It was strange. At age thirty-five he was getting older, but it wasn't just that. As he aged, his true desire became clearer, burnished in the crucible of his mind's eye. Nothing else would do in its place.

He gazed at the woman before him, as ravishing as she was refined, with a sharp widow's peak and a fiery temper. A husband, too. Who was king, no less.

A tender smile was all he could offer her. God forbid that she would guess at the full range of treasures he longed to shower upon her. She had ruined him for life for time spent with *filles de joie* as well as with all other women. All he wanted was her.

"See that the great-chests are aired."

"My lady-duchess, are we moving households?" Françoise de Dinan asked.

"And have them sprinkled with lavender leaves." Anne went to the windows of her receiving room at the Hotel d'Etampes. "I want no vile sickness from this city traveling with us to fresh lands."

"Where are we packing for?" Madame de Dinan tried again.

"We leave for Brittany at dawn, the day after tomorrow."

Anne's former tutor sucked in her breath, then curtseyed and backed out of the room. Within minutes attendants were hurrying in and out, throwing open the grand oak chests they had brought to Paris from Amboise, Madame de Dinan directing them.

"My lady-duchess, is not the king preparing a banquet in your honor for the evening of the day after tomorrow?" Madame de Dinan asked.

"That is precisely the point." Anne flung open the windows. Hot stagnant air wafted in, assaulting her senses. Paris was practically a cesspool in August.

"I'm afraid I'm missing it, then." Madame de Dinan raised both brows.

"We will leave before he realizes we are gone." She couldn't wait to go. She would miss Louis, but certainly not Paris, with plague season bearing down on them.

The next time she saw Louis she wanted to see him with a gift in hand for her: the annulment decree. Without it there was no point in seeing him further, other than on state occasions.

They would bump into each other from time to time as neighboring heads of state if friendly relations continued between Brittany and France.

Anne stifled a laugh. Louis would be eaten alive by desire on such occasions. He already was. Teasing him was a craft she had honed since first meeting him when she had been seven.

"My lady, he will go to some trouble to prepare this dinner in your honor. Will you not offend him by disappearing?"

"Offend him?" Anne moved closer to the woman she had known for as long as she had known Louis. "Another choice of words suits better, Madame." She narrowed her eyes at her beloved advisor as she tilted her head to one side. "Think carefully," she added.

"Do you mean to escape his attentions then?"

"I enjoy his attentions," Anne stated truthfully.

"I thought you did, my lady-duchess. Then what do you mean?

"I mean to fan them further." A slow smile spread across her face.

Madame de Dinan stared thoughtfully until her face broke into a matching smile. "My lady, you are ever one step ahead of the rest of us."

"So my father always said."

"But will the king not be angry once he discovers you are gone?"

"Another choice of words suits better," Anne repeated.

"Then he will be ... he will be ... " Madame de Dinan looked at her sovereign for inspiration. God's breath, what a razor-sharp mind ticked inside that dainty head.

"He will be bereft."

"Exactly. He will be bereft."

"Which will make him work even harder to have me in his presence again."

"Exactly so."

"Which he will do as soon as he travels to Brittany to find me."

"Madame, will he pursue you to Brittany to bring you back to France?"

"If he is free to make me his queen, he will." Anne locked eyes with Madame de Dinan.

"Ah, yes. If he is free."

"Which he is not, at this moment."

"Yes, my lady. I'm afraid you are right. He may be king but the common people know he is married, and they will not stand for a banquet to honor his para—his—"

"Do I look like anyone's paramour to you?" Anne's brows knit together as she faced down her former tutor.

Madame de Dinan broke into a girlish laugh. "My lady-duchess, you most certainly do not."

"I didn't think so."

"Then do I look like anyone's queen to you?"

"You have looked like a queen to me since the moment I first met you." Madame de Dinan put a hand out at waist height. "And you were yea tall at the time."

"But for now and forever I am my people's duchess. I must get back to them. If Louis wishes to make me his queen he will have to prove his case in court."

"Oh, my lady, he has his work cut out for him trying to shake off that saintly cripple." Madame de Dinan crossed herself.

"She is not yet a saint. But she is a good woman, and I am ashamed of what must take place for Louis to free himself from her."

"My thoughts, too, my lady."

"Yet I feel for Louis; he has never had a shot at married happiness, as I have. It isn't fair."

"My lady, you had your shot indeed, and may I say you made the best of it."

"Because I always do. You taught me that."

"Your father taught you that and I supported him. But no one can teach such a skill. You have always known how to make the best of any situation, and God knows you have found yourself in some dark ones." Madame de Dinan averted her eyes, willing away thoughts of the four small souls Anne had buried before her husband.

"So now for a light and joyous one. A change of scenery. As well as mood. What do you think, Madame—is it not time for me to reunite with my subjects?"

"Your Grace, they will be happy to see their duchess in clogs once more!"

"Yes, Madame! I shall wear my sabots and go on procession through all my lands."

"To the west, then?"

"I will take the Tro Breizh."

Madame de Dinan looked pleased at Anne's mention of Brittany's traditional pilgrimage. "Have you given the king a time frame?"

"What do you think, Madame?"

The older woman chuckled. "What is his deadline?"

Anne laughed as merrily as a fourteen-year-old at a May dance. "Don't worry, Madame. It is between him and myself."

"Ahh, my lady-duchess, secrets already between you and the king."

"So many, Madame, including ones from long ago and far away ..."

"In a castle in Nantes ..."

"On a banner-bestrewn drawbridge ..."

"My lady, I can see it now."

"And you will see it again, for we shall cross over it within three weeks' time."

"Bless God, my lady, I have longed to see my lands again for some time." The older woman's face creased into a wistful smile.

"And I long to get out of this fetid city." Anne turned and scooped up a mixture of lavender leaves and sage from a wooden bowl on the table. She held out the bowl to the older woman, who scooped out a handful, too.

"Go now and tell the household to hold their tongues to outsiders while we prepare our departure."

"What fun to sneak out of town!"

"It's time to have some fun, Madame. Beginning now!" Anne tossed the handful of lavender and sage at her dear old friend's gown, sprinkling her with fresh scents of the South.

The older woman laughed and tossed her own handful at her sovereign. She felt a decade younger at the thought of returning to the land of her birth.

"What do you mean she is gone?"

"Her household has left, Sire. There is no one at all at the Hotel d'Etampes, save a stable boy who said they rode west at dawn."

"Where did she go?" Louis stared at the messenger in disbelief.

"Sire, I believe she is on her way to Brittany."

"What do you mean, on her way to Brittany? Without telling me first of her plans?" The king drew himself up, suddenly remembering it wouldn't do to look too entwined with the queen of his heart before his courtiers. Most had not met his wife, but all knew he was married.

"Sire, her mourning period is over and her duchy awaits

her rule," Georges d'Amboise reminded him, dismissing the messenger with a wave. His job was to manage his sovereign at delicate moments. It was one he did with all his heart, springing from the closest of friendships back to when fourteen-year-old Georges had met the twelve-year-old duke d'Orléans.

"She was doing a fine job of that here in Paris." Frustration etched itself on Louis' face.

"She will do a better one back in her lands."

"But how could she not let me know before she left?" Louis' voice rang with anguish.

"Sire, with all due respect, I believe she thought you might try to dissuade her if she alerted you to her plans."

"Of course I would! I want her here, not there!" *I want her anywhere as long as I am next to her* is what he really meant. "How could she spurn my banquet for her tonight in her honor?"

"Sire, she may have felt that the people would find it unseemly to honor the former queen without the present queen being present."

"There is no present queen! That's the whole problem!"

"Begging your pardon, Sire, but I mean the lady Jeanne."

"The lady Jeanne?" Louis looked puzzled.

"Your wife, Sire. The people have been waiting to see her."

"My wife in name only!" Louis roared. "There will be no chance to see her, because she will not be my wife for much longer and she will never be my queen!" The king's face contorted, turning an unpleasant shade of puce.

"Sire, the common people do not see it that way."

"I am their king and they will see it the way I command them to see it!"

Almost imperceptibly the bishop of Rouen shook his head. "I'm afraid not, Sire. You may command their actions, but you cannot command their hearts."

"Then what must I do? Bring a cripple to the throne of France to sit beside me while I long for the woman who is meant to be my true wife?"

"You must address this in the court of law, Sire."

"And so I shall!"

"And may I say, you have a case but you will need to argue it skillfully."

"I will argue it with every fiber of my body. That woman was never my wife!"

Georges d'Amboise looked out the window and sighed. He understood the problem. Not only had his friend never treated his wife of twenty-two years as a wife, but she was constitutionally unsuited to be queen-consort of the king of France.

For one, she was too saintly to be of any help to a ruler in the ways and wiles of managing a royal court, not to mention managing France's position as one of Europe's most powerful countries.

Secondly, Louis couldn't stand the sight of her. They would never create an heir.

At that moment, they were interrupted by an attendant at the door.

"Sire, a letter has arrived from the Hotel d'Etampes." The attendant looked nervous, as if anticipating the king's displeasure at receiving a letter instead of the actual lady of the Hotel d'Etampes, so recently departed.

"Bring it here!" Louis shouted.

The messenger hurried forward, bowed before the king, then held out the missive.

Snatching it, the king quickly scanned its contents.

"Sire?" Georges d'Amboise looked anxiously at his sovereign.

"She is direct, as usual."

"And what has she directed you to do?"

"She says she is on her way home, and when she arrives she will be pleased if she finds that French troops are no longer present on Breton soil."

"Sire, that is a tall order!"

"Is it?"

"Are there not French troops stationed in Brittany now?"

"There are small garrisons in Nantes, Fougères, and St.-Malo. Nothing strategic, just there to maintain the Crown's presence." Louis' brow wrinkled. "In Brest and Conches too, I think."

"And will you withdraw them at her request?"

"I will withdraw them from some, but not all locations."

"You know she will insist on the entirety of her sovereign rights being restored."

"She will. But I must hold onto a few trump cards until she becomes my wife."

"Wise strategy, Your Majesty. Otherwise, she may not be sufficiently motivated."

Louis looked stricken. "My love should suffice."

"Sire, your love burns high partly because the object of it has a strong head on her shoulders," d'Amboise observed.

"Which she uses at all times."

"Indeed, Sire. Would you have it any other way?"

"As a priest, Georges, I command you to withdraw such a question. It is not for your ears to hear under what circumstances I would like her to stop using her head."

"Of course, Sire. My ears would blush as red as a cardinal's hat, should I consider such moments."

"By all means, don't."

"But if you wish to enjoy them with her, you will have to give her something of what she asks."

"Paper and pen!" the king bellowed.

Immediately an attendant withdrew, returning a moment later with writing utensils.

Louis seated himself at his desk and scribbled a hasty note.

> 'To the most gracious Anne, Duchess of Brittany,
> So that you will be pleased upon your homecoming in as many ways as possible, I have ordered the removal of French troops from the Breton towns of St.-Malo, Brest, and Conches. If my affairs proceed to a satisfactory outcome, I will fly to you as soon as possible. Please make me the happiest of men as my wife and queen, *ma reine-duchesse.*
> Louis.'

Springing from his desk, he strode to the door to call for his messenger. Then he would find his head steward to advise him of the change in plans for dinner that evening. After that he would go out for a long ride to cool off.

Anne would be pleased to know he had designated her as the sovereign in charge, to name her own men to decide what to do with the decommissioned French garrison quarters. Perhaps she would have them all turned into Breton defensive posts; if not, then hospitals or almshouses. It would be her decision, and he knew how much she liked making her own decisions.

He hoped she would make another one in the very near future that would make him the happiest of men.

CHAPTER THREE

1498

Brittany

I t was good to be back. Rennes had not changed overmuch in the almost seven years since she had left. How far away that December of 1491 seemed to her now, when she had left Brittany for France to marry its king.

She and her entourage of men at arms, maids of honor, and ladies-in-waiting were met by her chancellor and old friend, Philippe de Montauban, at Rennes' main city gate. They proceeded directly to the cathedral of St. Pierre where she had been crowned duchess of Brittany in February 1489, just after her twelfth birthday.

In the square before the cathedral entrance, Anne dismounted and was greeted by Brittany's administrator, her cousin Jean de Chalon, Prince of Orange. Anne had appointed both de Montauban and de Chalon to their roles in the days following Charles' death, when she had risen from mourning and seized control of her duchy's administration. Again taking control of her country had been her only bright spot in the sea of grief and loss she had swum in following that fateful day in April 1498, when Charles had hit his head on a low door lintel and died ten hours later. Only three weeks earlier she had lost their fourth child the same day she was born.

"Your Grace," Jean de Chalon greeted her. Bowing deeply, he kissed her extended hand then placed it on his forehead.

"I'm back." She smiled. "How goes it here?"

"My lady-duchess, the people are overjoyed to have you among us once more." The warmth of de Chalon's smile reminded her he had once aspired to her hand.

"As I am overjoyed to see my subjects again." Anne thought of how much she looked forward to making a royal progress throughout the duchy, reconnecting with her countrymen and shaking off the confines of court life. Soon again she would wear her wooden sabots; soon again the common folk of her realm would cheer her on as their *duchesse aux sabots*, their duchess in clogs.

She glided to the steps of the cathedral entrance with the regal dignity known only to those raised to rule, her trusted chancellor following. She would hear Mass to thank God for her chance to reunite with her people and to show her subjects that their duchess was again among them, as sole ruler of their lands.

"Madame, my condolences on the loss of your husband," de Montauban murmured.

"Thank you, Philippe. He was a good man and on his way to becoming a better one when he died."

"So I had heard, Your Grace."

"Did you receive my missives?" Anne changed the subject, wishing to focus on the here and now. God knew she had had enough of death in the six and a half years she had spent with Charles.

"Your Grace, I received your instructions to convene the Estates General. Some are here already and we have set the meeting for three days' hence."

"Philippe, what would I do without you?" She was warmed and relieved to have at her side the man who had protected her from age eleven to fourteen after her father had died and before her marriage to Charles.

"*Madame duchesse,* it seems that you have done very well indeed without me around. And word has it that you will resume your court in France and expand it even more gloriously in the near future." His gaze held in it a question.

"So you have been listening to gossip, Philippe, is that it?"

"Your Grace, Brittany is abuzz with rumors that the new king of France seeks your favor. Every one of your subjects remembers what a good friend to Brittany he was."

"As well as a great friend to my father," Anne added. Memories warmed her of the affectionate badinage that had flowed between her father and Louis.

"And hoping to be an even greater friend to you, my lady." De Montauban's eyes twinkled.

"If he plays his cards right, he will." Anne tilted her chin upward, her nose pointed heavenward, to the delight of the fast-gathering crowd, who huzzah'd and cheered their regal duchess. She would show them how well she had polished her poise as queen of France for the past almost seven years.

"My lady, I can only imagine the strenuous conditions you will lay on him."

"You shall do more than imagine them, Sire de Montauban. If the king of France obtains his annulment, you will help me craft the marriage contract I will hand him once he arrives."

"My lady, your advantage is clear this time." De Montauban squelched a chuckle to think how supremely advantaged his duchess would be in her second marriage. He had been present when the young duke d'Orléans had first visited Anne's father in Nantes when the duchess was only seven years old. Soon after his arrival, a spark between the young girl and the twenty-one-year-old duke had been evident. Louis had admired her greatly, and Anne had preened with pride at his attentions. Now that small spark had a chance to burst into a great flame that would warm all of Brittany and France should the two old friends become husband and wife.

"Unlike the last time, Philippe."

"Well I remember. But you made the most of it. All of Europe admires your ladies' court," de Montauban observed.

"As well they should," Anne sniffed, to de Montauban's apparent delight.

Moving off, she began to prepare her remarks before the Estates General to be assembled a few days' hence. Brittany's governing body was comprised of two-thirds Breton noblemen, the remaining third split between clergy and representative burghers from the duchy's forty-two towns.

Before them she would announce the change in regime, reminding them all that with the king of France now dead, she was again their sole sovereign ruler. She would watch closely as they paid obeisance, one by one, knowing there would be factions interested in wresting power from her or holding on to what they had already gained under the administration of her late husband.

Most notably, she would keep an eye on members of the House of Rohan, who had sided with the royal Penthièvre faction that Anne's own royal line, the dukes of Dreux-Montfort, had ousted late in the century before. It was time to remind all factions of Breton society that the House of Dreux-Montfort was still in charge, with her at its head.

Three days later, Anne addressed the Estates General in the great room of Rennes' town hall, the Hôtel de Ville, opposite the cathedral on the main square.

"My beloved Breton subjects," she began. At that, a roar went up from the assembled gathering of over two hundred men.

As the members of the Estates General cheered, her gaze swept the gallery. For many before her she felt true affection: Philippe de Montauban was one, her dearest companion Françoise de Dinan another. Then there were those she knew but didn't entirely trust, foremost among them the marshal de Rieux of the House of Rohan.

She would include all in her address, as well as in the largesse she would distribute afterward. Brittany was too small a realm for discontented outsiders to be left to their own devices.

In her heart Anne admired the countess Jeanne de Penthièvre, who had been duchess of Brittany the century before and had led the Penthièvre faction in the war of succession against Anne's own Montfort ancestors. Jeanne de Penthièvre had been a great and powerful lady about whom many stories had been passed down. Anne had listened to them with avid interest as a child, eager to gain insight into the ways and means of female leadership.

"As you will recall, it was here in February of 1486 that my father, Francis II, hereditary Duke of Brittany of the House of Dreux-Montfort, recognized me before this body as his successor and heir to the ducal throne of Brittany," she reminded the assembly.

Philippe de Montauban's cheer rang out over the others as the room filled to its vaulted ceilings with hurrahs and applause.

"And it was here in Rennes in February of the year of our Lord 1489 that I was crowned Duchess of Brittany," she continued as she searched for the marshal de Rieux. He had sought to wrest control from her as acting regent after the death of her father.

Spotting his bulky form, she cast him a gimlet gaze. Should he try to push forward ancestral claims he would not get far, now that she was back in her lands.

"I bid you to salute and support the good work of our duchy's administrator, Jean de Chalon, Prince of Orange, and of my appointed chancellor, Philippe de Montauban."

The crowd clapped and shouted out its support, although less resounding than its cheers had been for the duchess.

"You will find me at your disposal, both here in Rennes and then in Nantes, where I will travel next to return to my ancestral seat. And at the end of proceedings today, I will greet each of you individually," she finished, putting them on notice that each man present would be expected to pay obeisance to her as hereditary ruler of Brittany. If they did not, their absence would be noted.

The hush that swept through the room was not unfriendly. Rather, it was an indication that each individual present was absorbing the news that homage must be paid; some with joy in their hearts, others preparing to dissemble skillfully within the hour.

"You may be assured that I intend to go on royal progress throughout my realm and if you wish me to visit your parts at a special time or for a special occasion, you may grant me this request today or by missive or private audience in the near future."

"Your Grace, will you visit as far as Brest, then?" one of the burghers asked.

"Not only will I visit Brest, Monsieur, but I will appoint a man of ability from Brest to take over the French garrison quarters there."

Confusion registered on the burgher's face. "*Madame-duchesse*, do you mean to say that the French have been cleared from our town?"

"I do, Monsieur, and they will not return. At this moment they are on their way back to France. You may think on who you might recommend to me to take charge of the site they occupied and to what good use the people of Brest might make of it."

"Your Grace, on behalf of the people of Brest, we thank you from the bottom of our hearts!" The burgher's heartfelt appreciation and astonishment at his ruler's routing the French from his town rippled through the room. Brest was one of Brittany's most important port towns. It was no small feat that the duchess had cleared out the French troops stationed there.

"And the same for the burghers of St.-Malo and Conches. I charge you with presenting to me a plan for the repurposing of the garrison quarters in your towns that have now been vacated by the French."

"Hurrah, *Madame la duchesse*!" rose in tumultuous roars all around.

Anne went down a short list of recognition of administrators she had approved over the past few months for management of the ports, the fishing and maritime industries and the lace-makers' guild in Quimper to the far west of Brittany. Soon she would visit all of these places and see if they were doing their job, or if she needed to make changes.

"That will be all the business for this convocation today. On my sacred duty as your duchess and heir to the ancestral dukes of Brittany, I promise to protect you and the people you represent, each of you my subjects, whom I hold dear to my heart."

She paused, then raised her voice. "May peace and prosperity reign in Brittany under my rule," she rang out, her tone as commanding as any leader Brittany had known.

The room went wild with cheers. Anne swept from the dais to take up her position on the ducal throne. For the next three-quarters of an hour she received obeisance from close to two-hundred men and women who filed by. Not one failed to greet her and offer homage. If any had, their absence would have been carefully noted by the scribe and two assistants Philippe de Montauban had set up at a desk behind the duchess.

Within the hour it was over. Anne rose, exited the hall, and swept out onto Rennes' main square.

The cheers of the crowd that went up at her appearance were thrice as loud and heartfelt as any that had filled the Hôtel de Ville behind her.

Anne had given instructions to distribute largesse in the form of new coinage she had ordered to be minted in the days after King Charles' death the April before. With a flick of her wrist to the left and right, she bade her attendants to begin showering the crowd.

Brittany's new coins showed an image of Anne of Brittany on one side wearing Brittany's crown of gold, and an image of Duke Francis II of Brittany on the other with the same *couronne d'or* on his head. Its value was not only monetary, but in the symbolic reinforcement of the line of succession of the dukes of Brittany. There would be no doubt in anyone's mind, either nobleman or commoner, that Anne, Duchess of Brittany, was back on the power seat, actively administering and overseeing her duchy.

Mounting a large white palfrey, Anne rode slowly through

the throng, ears sharpened to discern the tone and mood of her people.

"Huzzah, *Madame la duchesse*! By the grace of God you are back!"

Anne turned to the townswoman who had shouted such a fine greeting. With a gesture she bid an attendant to throw the woman a handful of coins.

"Cheers to our duchess! May she be queen again!" a man's voice called out.

Bidding her men to throw another handful of coins in the direction of the voice, she giggled as two children dove for the gilt, scrabbling on the well-scrubbed pavement of the town square.

Would she be queen again? God knew she missed Louis. A frisson coursed through her to think of the thirty-six-year-old king back in France, pining for her. Charles had been twenty-one when she married him, barely past youth. Would it not be delightful to savor the adoration of a full-grown man, one who had not yet known the full measure of happiness of marriage and family?

Nor had she, God knew. She had suffered a grown woman's sorrows, bearing the continued infidelities of a roving husband, forever in need of approval from an endless parade of women. She had known even worse suffering than most other women with the deaths of every one of her children. Seven souls in all had flown Heavenward. Three she had miscarried, three she had buried within hours, days, or weeks of their birth, and one—the most heartbreaking of all, her beloved Charles-Orland—had been carried off by measles at age three.

The warm August sunlight poured onto her head and shoulders like a balm, healing and caressing her. Buoyed by the joyful shouts of the crowd, she felt herself coming to life

again. Girlish high spirits bubbled inside her, tempered by
the dignity and regal carriage she had practiced from the age
of four and burnished in her six and a half years as queen of
France.

Soon it would be harvest time and she would reap the full
bounty of what her losses had left her: sole control over her
country, no distractions of wifehood or motherhood, and the
revenues from her ducal inheritance, wealth passed down to her
from her father, plus a generous widow's pension. Not bad for
a twenty-one-year-old.

Waving at a beaming matron wearing a Breton white lace
shawl, she reveled in the attention of the crowd. Never in her
life had she been stingy; never had she been frugal. The last
time she had lived in Rennes the town had been under siege
by the French. That summer and early fall of 1491 her people
had been starving, her mercenaries unpaid and looting. To pay
them, she had sold every stone in her gem collection left to her
by her mother. Never had she skimped on any human being
under her charge. Nor would she now.

"*Madame la duchesse*, will you marry the king of France?" a
woman's voice cut through the noise of the crowd.

Anne raised a hand to her mouth to conceal a giggle.
Memories washed over her of a procession she had made ten
years earlier at that same time of year. She had followed the
casket of her father, Duke Francis, from Couëron, where he had
breathed his last, back to Nantes where he had been buried.
Along the way the crowds had saluted her as their new ruler;
but, as crowds were wont to do, exclamations of respect soon
turned to rowdy excitement and pointed questions regarding
her future.

"Who will you marry, *duchesse?*" she remembered one
woman calling out.

Anne had teasingly asked her younger sister riding behind her for advice.

"Marry someone like Father," Isabeau had advised.

Yet Anne hadn't. She had married Charles de Valois, King of France, who had been as unlike her father as night was to day, except in one ignoble regard. Both rulers had exercised their sovereign rights to rove. It had been something that Anne had not liked about Charles, but it had not stopped her from loving him. She had told herself his predilection for dalliances was simply a bad habit, a king's prerogative. Frankly, it had angered her, but as a queen it was unseemly to show traits of commoners such as jealousy, anger, and fishwifely behavior.

Instead, she had poured her energies into the education and formation of the young noblewomen she had invited to court. At least she could control their behavior, unlike that of her own husband.

Now, seven years later, she had the opportunity to marry the man most like her father of any she had ever met.

She had brought peace to Brittany by marrying Charles VIII in 1491. Would she bring peace to her own heart by marrying his successor?

Eying the crowd, she dazzled the throngs to either side with smiles that rooted their recipients to the spot, spellbound by her radiance. Each time a child appeared, she bade her attendants to toss a shower of coins. Some of the children were so overcome by the sight of their grand and beautiful duchess that they stood open-mouthed in wonderment instead of diving for coins.

Anne smiled to herself. She had that effect on people. God knew she had that effect on men; most of all on Louis.

Nothing could bring her more happiness than marrying a man like her father. Tall and handsome Louis was as refined, charming, and cultured as Duke Francis II of Brittany had been. Like two peas in a pod, they had cavorted and carried on at her father's castle in Nantes. Anne had known exactly how to handle her father, who had turned to her in all matters of his realm and household after his wife died in 1486. Anne had practiced and refined her skills on him as a sort of surrogate spouse in the years following her mother's death. Well she knew how easily she could transfer such skills to management of Louis, now king of France. She sensed he would be as delighted to be in her capable hands as she would be to have another man in her life much like her father to look after, coddle, and direct.

Anne of Brittany held high her chin and remained silent to the probing questions of the crowd. They had a right to ask about her future plans. They would affect Brittany. But which did her subjects value more: independence from all encroachers but vulnerable to attack or peace at the price of continued vassal status with France?

This was the question she would seek to answer while on progress that fall. By Advent she would be back in Nantes, ready with an answer for Louis should he obtain his annulment and appear. She would search her heart and decide whether the wishes of her people would take precedence over her own wishes for future happiness. If she were very lucky, perhaps they would coincide.

Her goals in Rennes accomplished, Anne and her entourage rode south to Brittany's largest port city of Nantes. There they were joyously greeted by its inhabitants. How sweet it was to ride through the main city gates of her birthplace, surrounded by cheering crowds.

"Madame, will you accompany me west on my Tro Breizh?" Anne asked Madame de Dinan one morning soon after their arrival. It was said that Bretons who failed to make the traditional tour of Brittany, which linked the towns of its seven founding saints, were destined to walk it as phantoms once every seven years in the afterlife. Anne had no intention of failing her obligations in the here and now, especially as sovereign of her realm.

They sat on a bench of the walled garden of Anne's castle in Nantes, the ancestral seat of the dukes of Brittany. Her beloved advisor was looking frailer. Perhaps their journey from Paris to Rennes, then to Nantes, had tired her.

"My dear *duchesse*. I would so like to be at your side, but I have not seen my family for so long and I am—I am—"

"Tired, Madame. I know." Anne studied her old friend more closely. Françoise de Dinan was almost sixty-two years old. The clear blue-gray eyes in which Anne had found so much understanding and affection were beginning to cloud over with the film that only those who had attained a great age acquired. It was not a time for one of her years to suffer the indignities of the road, especially in Brittany's rough western parts, where sabots, the wooden clogs of the common people, were worn to protect from the mud-covered roads devoid of paving stones in all but the centers of the largest towns.

"We have just come from Paris, Your Grace. Forgive me, but I must rest awhile until I recover my energies." The older woman's smile was tender. "I am not like you, dear one—nor was I ever."

"What do you mean? Of course you are like me. Or, rather, I should say I am like you, since you are as a mother to me!"

"No, dear one. You have the boundless energy of youth, yet something more."

"Something more?"

"My duchess and sovereign, you have ever been the most determined and energetic woman I have ever met."

"Come now, Madame." Anne's look was severe. "Neither tease nor flatter me."

"Far from it, Your Grace. You are at the age your husband was when, God rest his soul, he married you."

"Oh, Charles!" Anne's tone was sweet, a hint of longing in it. He hadn't been an ideal husband, but she missed him. He had been her peer, and she missed having someone of her own rank to talk with and more.

"Remember how active he was." Inwardly, the older woman rolled her eyes.

"How could I forget?" Inwardly, Anne rolled hers.

"Forever ready to hunt, to wage war, to renovate your castle. He never stopped until—"

"Until a low stone doorway stopped him." Anne shut her eyes, batting away memories of that day. At least the end had been quick. Still, it had been the longest day of her life, worse than any of her childbirth deliveries, since she had known and loved the man for six and a half years, despite his failings.

"God rest his soul." Madame de Dinan crossed herself. She was sorry for her duchess' loss, but frankly she had always thought that her beloved sovereign was largely wasted on so unlettered and uncultured a man. Courtiers were seldom frank if they knew their job, so she had said nothing.

The future ahead looked far brighter for her Anne, especially if Louis wrapped up business in Paris and spurred his horse to the west. The present king of France possessed the refinement of Anne's father, Duke Francis of Brittany, who had engaged her a lifetime ago to be his elder daughter's tutor. At age thirty-six, Louis XII mayhap had sown his wild oats and would settle into marriage without bringing to it the bad habits his predecessor had.

"'Tis true. Charles was like a caged animal most of the

time." *Except at moments when I tamed him.* Anne smiled a secret smile to herself, remembering how very majestic that animal had been at certain moments that no one but she and a few thousand other women scattered throughout France and Italy had witnessed. Thank God she hadn't known any of the others. She would have clawed their eyes out.

"Well, you possess the same energy." The older woman smiled at the younger one, grateful that she no longer needed to keep up with her. Now that they were back in Brittany, her intuition told her that her time on Earth was drawing to a close. She had done her job well and she was not unhappy. If only she might see her sovereign married to a man truly suited to her.

"Do I, Madame?" Anne asked. "Then I hope I shall use it to better application than he did, God rest him." Between her and her closest friend there had been few secrets concerning Charles.

"Your Grace, I am sure you will." Madame de Dinan had known when Charles VIII of France had visited his wife nights and when he had disappeared for days on end. She had kept her own counsel concerning his waywardness, knowing it never served to criticize a king's behavior, especially when his wife might be angry with him one minute and madly in love the next. Anne had been both in the time she had spent with him. *God grant her a better husband the next time around,* Madame de Dinan prayed as she eyed the capable girl she had raised, mature beyond her years at age twenty-one.

"I shall observe the industry of each town I visit, then confer with my counselors before I make changes or appointments."

"You will be magnificent, *ma duchesse.*" Madame de Dinan spoke with all her heart. She knew how good her sovereign was at making decisions. She herself had been charged by Duke Francis to school his chosen successor in how to make decisions then to deliver them well as a female ruler.

Madame de Dinan had understood the nuances and had drilled her student in the grace, charm, and ceremony that a woman armed herself with to convey effective leadership. Anne had already possessed the qualities necessary to absorb such lessons, charm being her innate gift, and attention to pomp and ceremony her hallmark.

It had not been difficult to school the young duchess in techniques of leadership. The main requirement Anne already possessed: she enjoyed making decisions. She was unlike her younger sister Isabeau, who had felt uncomfortable when asked to make up her own mind about most matters. Royal princesses were traditionally not encouraged to make decisions. They were expected to obey the ones their parents made on their behalf and then their husbands one day.

Not Anne.

Once Duke Francis had been informed by his court physician that his wife would bear no more children, he had engaged Madame de Dinan to instruct his elder daughter in the skills she would need to succeed him as his heir. Salic law prevailed only in France, where it was unheard of for females to rule. But in Brittany, as in England and in Spain, in the absence of sons succession to the throne went to the eldest daughter.

"Teach her to think for herself, Madame. Above all, teach her not to fear making a wrong decision, but only to fear not making a decision at all. My Anne will be my successor one day. She must learn how to lead."

"Your Grace, she leads us all already. But I will do my best to shape the qualities she already possesses."

"Madame, you have noted my daughter's temperament. Have I not chosen my successor well?" Duke Francis' face shone with pride.

In that moment Madame de Dinan vowed she would spend

the rest of her life advising and protecting her sovereign's beloved elder daughter. Such love between a father and daughter
was rare to witness. She felt honored to play a part in shaping
the young girl who would grow up to rule Brittany.

"Your Grace, you most certainly have," Madame de Dinan
wholeheartedly agreed, thinking that the duke's daughter
would make an even better ruler than he had.

At age eight, Princess Anne had both energy and intelligence, but also showed signs of a natural rigor to her tastes
and temperament, something her father had never possessed.
She would not be careless in the execution of orders and she
would not forgive her enemies as the duke had done far too
many times, in Madame de Dinan's opinion. Duke Francis' elder daughter hid a coat of steel under her girlish exterior. Well
she would need it on the road she traveled ahead, as ruler of her
duchy then as queen of France.

"Who should I rely on most on my progress, without you
at my side?" Anne looked closely at the older woman. She knew
very well who she would rely on, but she wished to hear what
her dear friend would say. She would not forget that the woman
she loved best after her long-dead mother had advised her to
marry her younger half-brother, the ghastly Alain d'Albrecht.
Four times Anne's age, he had been as unsuited to Anne's refined
tastes as a wild boar was to sharing a cage with a baby bird.

"Listen to all, answer as little as possible, and rely on your-
self to make your own decisions," Madame de Dinan replied.
Her words could have come straight from Duke Francis' mouth.
He had advised his daughter similarly more than once.

Anne sighed with relief. Her advisor had counseled well.
No longer did she show signs of representing the interests of
the House of Rohan, from whence her mother, Catherine de
Rohan, came. How the mother of such a refined and learned

woman as Françoise de Dinan had also borne such a coarse son as Alain d'Albrecht, Anne had no idea.

"I shall miss you, Madame."

"I shall miss you more, *ma duchesse.*"

"You will see me back here by Advent, Madame."

"I shall gladly celebrate the season with you," the older woman replied. *If I am still alive,* she thought.

"Perhaps we will have good news by then." Anne's eyes were veiled, but the hint of a smile revealed her thoughts.

"Undoubtedly we will, Your Grace." *And when it comes I shall have accomplished my full duty to my sovereign and to her father,* Madame de Dinan thought with great satisfaction.

Anne rose to take leave of her former tutor. She sensed the older woman needed to rest. Perhaps her counselor and friend had been right when she observed that she had more energy than any other woman she had ever known. God knew she was bursting with plans she wished to get started on that moment.

She would allow her advisor to rest while she toured her duchy with others who were young and keen to accompany her. Some would become her trusted counselors. But none could take the place of the few she had known since childhood who shared her memories of her father, her mother, and Isabeau.

Of those, only three were left: Madame de Dinan, Philippe de Montauban, and Louis back in France. Would there be others she would meet on her progress who had known her parents and sister?

If so, she was eager to find them; to talk, to reminisce, to hear stories of those she had loved and lost but whose legacy she must carry forward to fulfill the royal mandate of the House of Dreux-Montfort. Anne couldn't wait to begin her journey, to mingle again with the people of her ancestors' realm, her beloved Brittany.

She hurried off to find her chancellor.

CHAPTER FOUR

August–December 1498

Disgraceful Proceedings

I f only her character were as horrible as her body; yet it was just the opposite. Louis studied the packed courtroom, maintaining the most serene of kingly demeanors while his insides quaked.

It wasn't so much the opinions of the noblemen and justices present that he feared. God knew they were all master dissemblers, and, no matter what judgment the justices passed down, Louis' back channels in Rome would use every measure to influence the pope to sign the annulment bull.

Fortunately for the king, Pope Alexander VI , the former Rodrigo Borgia, was thoroughly corrupt of character, possessing the lusty temperament of a breeding bull. Before ascending to the papacy he had fathered at least eight children by different mistresses, claiming them as his nieces and nephews. He was eager to see his eldest son Cesare awarded lands and a title, married to a French princess, and settled with a sizeable annuity. All this was manageable for Louis as king of France.

What was less manageable was the opinion of his common subjects. The second Louis exited the courtroom into the bright glare of public opinion, they would let him know exactly what they thought of their king casting off his saintly wife on trumped-up grounds that everyone knew boiled down to his desire to marry the beautiful young duchess of Brittany.

Another king, such as Jeanne's father, Louis XI, would not have cared. But Louis did care. He wanted to be a good king. Could he help it if he also wanted a chance at happiness?

Jeanne of France, princess of the blood of the royal Valois line, sat in one corner of the room, crumpled in on herself, looking more like a pile of rags than a daughter of a former king of France and wife of the present one. Her ghostly-white face was cocked to one side, her ear meeting her shoulder. Her small, misshapen body was covered by her usual shapeless black cloak. Everything about her was hideous, save for her eyes. Those large, limpid brown eyes were alive with righteousness; Louis knew only too well that whatever truths swam in them were founded on firm ground.

Shooting her a glance, he shuddered. The one time that Louis thought he could count on Jeanne to be her usual mousy, self-deprecating self, she had instead come blazingly alive, on fire and fully capable of defending herself in no uncertain terms when questioned as to the validity of their marriage. What rotten luck.

In a flash, he thought of how the English must have felt when questioning the maid of Orleans. They must have sensed they were wrong and she was right, yet they had soldiered on, right up to the moment they lit the first bundle of straw at the base of the stake they had burned her upon. Little good it had done them to destroy her body. Her legend had grown with each passing year until it had chased the English from France altogether. In comparison, all he was doing was trying to get his wife to quietly go away, found a convent or an order somewhere, and live on the sizeable annuity he was offering her. Why couldn't she just be reasonable? And why couldn't he stop himself from feeling like an utter knave? As king, was he not entitled to a full life, including a wife he found attractive and children, one of whom would be heir to the throne of France?

"I swear upon my Savior's cross that I am my lord's lawful and fully-wedded wife," Jeanne's voice rang out, as clear as cut-crystal glass in response to her examiner's question.

"Have you had marital relations with your lord the king?" the examiner pressed.

"Yes, I have." For once his wife sat up straight, managing to lift her head off her shoulder as she stared down the courtroom.

"And in the twenty-two years you have been married, how many times have you had relations with your husband?" the justice drilled down.

"Monsieur, I would not be able to say with exact certainty, but at least a dozen times," Jeanne of France replied with confidence.

Louis felt his face blanch. He turned to one side to hide it. She had hit the nail on the head, coming up with the same number he had, although he wasn't admitting to it. He couldn't even curse her; it would be like cursing the Son of God himself. She was a damnably good woman; honest, pious, and self-sacrificial. She had even saved his life, begging her brother to spring him from the prison that her eldest sister, France's regent Anne de Beaujeu, had put him in for taking Brittany's side against France in 1488.

"Madame, your husband has stated that you have not

engaged in conjugal relations. What say you to the statement of your lord and king?"

"I say that he knows full well what has passed between us as husband and wife. And I know full well that I am not a woman fair of face or form, but there are others like me who have been loyal and good wives to their husbands and have not been cast aside for lack of grace or beauty." The tiny woman's voice rang out through the courtroom, capturing the heart of every wronged wife present.

Murmurs drifted from the gallery. Apparently, some common folk had found their way inside. A chill breeze of disapproval swept down onto the heads of those on the main floor, all from the higher classes, where money and influence was used to make unwanted wives go away. No such methods were available to commoners. Untrammeled by any hope of being able to cast off their own spouses, men and women of non-noble stock were at liberty to disapprove of the distasteful methods of their superiors to cast off unwanted partners. It was as bad as the pope in Rome fathering children.

No man or woman would state their disapproval face to face with the king, certainly. Such criticism would amount to lèse-majesté, a crime punishable by death.

But safe within a crowd of hundreds, common men and women were free to murmur and whisper their dissatisfaction with the disgrace of casting off a wife who behaved like a saint and whose rightful place was as queen-consort of the king. What matter that she was hideously ugly? So had been many kings and queens, including the one who had recently died, with his long nose, bulbous eyes, and spindly legs. It was no crime to be ugly. But was it not a crime against God to cast off a saintly wife, who had served her husband as well as she could?

"Sire, do not let them trick you into admitting anything

other than what you have already stated," a familiar voice whispered into Louis' ear.

Louis stared numbly at his friend and confessor, Georges d'Amboise. He felt like a rat, but he knew he must maintain his kingly demeanor. He was being closely watched at that moment.

Turning away from the room, he propped his left hand on his armrest, resting his face in his hand, so that none but Georges could catch his words or see his expression.

"Georges, what if—"

"Sire, you are king; she is not. The word of an anointed king prevails over the word of any other."

"Even if it is—"

"It is your word, Sire. By definition, it trumps the word of any other witness."

"Then I must—"

"Yes, you must, Sire, if you wish to gain your annulment as well as your future happiness."

"But I will—"

"Sire, that is between you and your Maker. I beg you to stop making my job harder than it already is and not tell me anything more."

"But Georges, you are my confessor." The king looked at his lifelong friend, the smallest of ironic lines appearing at each corner of his mouth.

"And I confess I have been your friend first and always shall be, but I'm telling you as a friend that I don't need to hear any confessions that shouldn't be stated aloud."

Louis studied his friend's face as he absorbed his words. There had never been secrets between them. But he was king now. It seemed Georges was telling him to start acting like one. Life at the top was lonely and if he didn't obtain his annulment his lovely *Brette* would never take her place at his side to chase away his loneliness and replace it with wedded bliss, the kind he had never known before.

"Then, Georges, what about our Lord? Will He not punish me for putting away this saintly woman, much as I cannot stand the sight of her?"

"Louis, I mean, Sire—"

"I'm Louis to you at this moment. What do you think God will do to me for all that I have done and am about to do to a woman who is as unblemished in soul as she is blemished in body?"

"Louis, you were forced to marry her against your will. You have not had a moment of marital happiness with her and you will never beget heirs if you keep her as your wife. As your subject I ask you, is it not your duty as king of France to produce heirs? And as your friend, I tell you that I am sick of seeing you rootless and without family, year after year. It was unbecoming to you as duke, and even less becoming for you to remain so unanchored as king. Do your duty to yourself, and to your subjects, and follow your heart. You will never be happy otherwise, and you will disappoint your subjects if you remain unhappy and childless."

"That's quite a speech, friend."

"I wish to see you happy, Sire. Don't you think your Maker does, too?"

"Do you counsel me as priest, then?"

Georges chuckled. "Never mind all that, Sire. I counsel you as a friend who wants to see you settled."

"And what do you know about being settled, man of the cloth?"

"Not much, Sire, but I'd settle for a red cap from Rome one day."

"We'll work on it, then." Louis reached behind Georges'

back and gave the midpoint of his black stole a jesting tug. It was good to be able to talk to someone in confidence. Even if the counsel Georges had given him was to not put into words what must remain hidden in his heart. It wasn't Louis' style, but it was prudent advice. He would follow it.

Turning back to the room at large, he waited to hear what next would come out of his unwanted wife's mouth. Whatever it was, he was king and she was not.

One week later, the proceedings were at an impasse. Jeanne of France had stood her ground; Louis had stood his. One was lying, the other was not. One was king, the other was not.

After conferring with his legal team, it was decided that an examination would be requested to determine if Jeanne of France could bear children. It was distasteful but unavoidable, as the king's two strongest arguments thus far had both been dismissed.

Firstly, his legal team had argued that the marriage had taken place without his consent; secondly, that they had not had conjugal relations.

Yet he had been fourteen, the minimum marriage age for a male, and no witnesses remained alive who had attended the wedding and had remembered Louis' violent objections, as well as his mother's tears. Would to God his father had been alive to object, but Charles d'Orléans had died when Louis was four years old.

Louis' mother, Marie of Cleves, had had a difficult time raising her son and daughter in a style appropriate to their rank. She was forever low on funds and was rumored to have relied on the affections of her chief steward after the death of her husband, in her struggle to raise her children alone. She was in no position to object to the king of France's offer of a princess of France to join hands in marriage with her only son.

All involved suspected the old king knew that his second daughter was sterile and would not be able to beget heirs for the House of Orléans. With Louis d'Orléans the sole male heir, his lands and holdings would revert to the crown of France upon his death. It had been an ingenious method to increase the holdings of the crown and diminish those of France's most powerful noblemen, precisely the sort of machinations the old king excelled at. He wasn't known as the spider king for nothing.

Then there was the conjugal relations point. That hadn't gone well at all. It wasn't as if Louis had ever wanted to have conjugal relations with the woman he had been forced to marry, but her tyrant of a father had all but posted witnesses in their bedchamber to ensure that their unwanted union was fully consummated.

It had been distasteful to the fourteen-year-old youth. Not having vast experience with which to compare his bride's body to that of another woman's, he could see for himself that she was hideous to look at and repulsive to touch. He had made the best of the situation by snuffing out the candles and proceeding in utter darkness.

Yet with the blithe thoughtlessness of youth he had boasted of his prowess to a few friends the following day, one or two of whom were still alive, and whose signed statements had been obtained by the court.

The chief examiner had delicately passed the signed statements to the king's chief counsel, who had privately shown them to the king.

Curses.

Then there had been his jailer and his wife in Bourges, who had welcomed Jeanne as an overnight visitor to Louis on several occasions during his three-years' captivity after the battle of St.-Aubin. The former king's oldest sister had been regent of France at the time and had had him locked up to punish him, ostensibly, for aiding Brittany against France. The real reason was that she had harbored an infatuation for him that he had never returned, increasing her fury against him tenfold. The other French noblemen who had fought on Brittany's side she had chastised then released. Louis she had imprisoned.

Louis scowled. God, how he wished he could rid himself of both of the former king's sisters once and for all. Anne de Beaujeu seemed to have finally resigned herself to leading a quiet life in the countryside with her husband and daughter. But to be rid of Jeanne he would have to think of something other than swearing under oath he had never had conjugal relations with her. Technically, his word would prevail over hers. But the sticky point of signed statements by those who knew conjugal relations had indeed taken place would be discussed ad infinitum by his subjects should he not come up with a more compelling reason to put her away.

"Madame, the court requests you to undergo examination to determine if you are able to bear children, at the request of the king's counselors," the chief examiner addressed the tiny creature taking up only half of the chair she sat on.

"I will do no such thing," Jeanne of France replied, holding high her birdlike head.

"Madame, there is no other way to determine if you are able to beget heirs for France."

"I am a princess of the blood and will undergo no personal invasion of my body."

"Madame, with all due respect to one who is a princess of the blood, the court requests an examination so the point can be clarified."

"The point needs no clarification. I am as capable as any woman in France of bearing children, should my lord and husband wish it." Jeanne raised her head again and looked around the courtroom with eyes as bright and on fire as any healthy woman of childbearing years. She was thirty-five years old but looked younger, perhaps due to her clear conscience and pure life.

Louis shuddered, hiding his face. He couldn't stand it when she referred to him as her lord and husband. God knew he had never wished to be either. If only she would rail at him, hate and berate him, accuse him of being a neglectful husband at the very least. Anything but the eternal patience, loving devotion, and charity she consistently showed him. It was subversive, serving to steer the hearts of all who heard her to her side, to plead her case. How could a simple man, even if he was king, argue with a saint?

Frustrated, Louis curled his fingers around the edge of his chair seat and raked it with his nails.

"Madame, in the absence of a physical examination, the point shall not fall in your favor that you are capable of bearing children," the chief examiner declared.

"So be it. I will not have myself subjected to an examination by strangers." Again, Jeanne de France held high her head, looking queenly for perhaps one of the few moments of her life.

Murmurs rustled throughout the room. Louis looked at Georges d'Amboise, who shot him a reassuring glance. Was this the breakthrough they had sought? Who would have thought, after Jeanne had stood strong through endless grilling on the state of their conjugal affairs, as well as his embarrassingly detailed description of her physical deformities, that she would refuse a simple physical examination?

The chief justice of the commission conferred with the

examiner for a moment, then motioned to the court referee. Whispering something to him, the court referee then raised his staff and struck the floor twice.

All fell silent.

"We will break for the midday meal," the court referee bellowed.

The courtroom broke out into discussion, a higher current of tension running beneath the general tone at the unexpected refusal of the king's wife to comply with the court's request. After two full months, it was the first time Jeanne of France had categorically refused to cooperate with a request from the judicial commission.

Now was the moment Louis dreaded most of each day of the proceedings. He must hold his head high and block his ears. Not before the noblemen and courtiers, but once he got outside and the common people of Paris let him know what they thought of their new king.

Rising from his chair on the dais, he descended the few steps and strode down the length of the courtroom. On either side noblemen and courtiers bowed as he passed, a human wave of courtesy and respect; some heartfelt, others professionally executed.

It would be otherwise outside. Steeling himself, he caught his friend's low voice behind him.

"Steady on, Sire, we will get through this."

The doors of the courtroom opened before him, and in another few steps he was out the door.

Glaring sunlight on the cold, clear December day streamed down on him, highlighting every expression, every furrow, every movement of his face.

"All hail the king!" rang out on both sides. Hundreds of commoners stood in the noonday chill, eager for a glimpse of their sovereign, ready to evaluate every aspect of his demeanor, his carriage, and bearing so they could discuss it at home, then in the marketplace. Paris would be abuzz with whether the king looked guilty or innocent in his quest to divest himself of his wife.

Louis was not a dishonest man. Neither was he an unfeeling one. He cared about what his subjects thought of him. If it was anything similar to what he thought of himself at the moment, he hoped they would keep it to themselves. So far so good.

Slowly he made his way to the royal carriage, knowing that if he hurried it would seem as if he had something to hide.

Well he knew it was a ruler's job to dissemble. He would have to get used to it, although it wasn't his natural modus operandi, as it had been for Louis XI, two kings before him. The late King Charles had not been much of a dissembler either, something Louis had always liked about his brother-in-law. But it was Louis' duty now to conceal his true feelings to maintain control over his kingdom.

"Long live the king!"

"All hail the king!"

It did his heart good to hear his subjects support him.

"Long live Queen Jeanne!"

Oh, God.

"Long live the king's wife!" another voice rang out.

"God's blessings on good Queen Jeanne!" a woman cried.

And hell's bells to bad King Louis. Picking up his stride, Louis kept his eyes straight ahead on the now-opening door of the carriage.

"May God bless the king and queen!"

Which queen? The one forced on him against his will, or the true queen of his heart?

"All hail the king!" Another vote of support.

Suddenly the crowd's roar swelled. Was he finally getting some sympathy? God's mercy, couldn't a man get a little understanding for wanting to untie himself from twenty-two years of marriage to a deformed cripple he had never wanted to wed in the first place?

"Huzzah, the queen!" rang out behind him.

"Huzzah, Madame Jeanne!"

"Herod, Caiphas, and Pilate will be judged as they have judged you, good Madame."

Louis' heart stung.

"Heal me, Madame Jeanne!"

"Heal my child, Madame Jeanne; one touch from you will heal him!" a woman's voice pleaded.

The throngs were abandoning him. Aside from some stragglers, the crowd was streaming back to Jeanne behind him.

God, it was humiliating. He felt as if he was Judas Iscariot followed by Jesus in a procession.

Getting into the carriage, he beckoned Georges behind him to hurry up.

Heaving his hefty bulk into the coach, the bishop slammed the door shut and rapped sharply to the driver to take off.

Within minutes they were back at the royal residence in Paris, only a few streets away from the Hotel d'Etampes where Louis had last laid eyes on his true love. Good God, how would he ever get through this?

"Sire, do not worry about the crowds."

"Why should I not? They are my subjects and I want their goodwill."

"Sire, the prevailing wind will change."

"Not likely, considering that woman back there is regarded as a saint by my subjects."

"Then let us fan the flame of her sanctity."

"Why so?" He had always found her saintliness annoying, truth be told. But maybe because what he wanted was a wife, not a saint, for a partner. Someone who would challenge him, like the feisty *Brette* he couldn't stop thinking about.

"Because the people will hold you in higher regard if they see you recognize her goodness."

"I do. I just can't stand it."

"Nor could any man married to a saint," d'Amboise dryly observed.

"There you have it, Georges. That's it in a nutshell!"

"Sire, if you put her away nicely, with all due respect and generosity, the people will come 'round to you. No man anywhere would wish to be married to a woman with looks like hers, and no wife anywhere would wish to be compared with a woman as saintly as she."

"Do you think, then, that our desired outcome will come to pass?"

"I do, Sire. Just show patience and, above all, give her her full due so that she may give you your freedom."

"You heard her! She will never give me my freedom."

"No worries, Sire. The court is appointed by the pope, and the pope is in need of a favor from you."

"I am ready to grant it." Louis was generally frugal, a habit maintained from his penurious childhood. But this time he would open his purse, even if it meant emptying the treasury of France to attain his objective.

"Just remember to also grant the largest of favors to the woman you wish to resign to sainthood. Thereby you will gain not only your annulment but also the forgiveness of the people."

"Forgiveness? Do you think so?"

"Forgetfulness first, forgiveness will follow. In a few years' time this will all be over, and in a decade a new generation will be springing up that knows nothing of what took place here."

"Thank God."

"Thank God, indeed." Georges d'Amboise crossed himself, giving his friend and sovereign a reassuring nod.

Louis slumped back against the plush seat of the carriage and put a hand to his brow. It was tough work being king. He needed a queen at his side to help him. Not a saint, but a woman who knew how to rule, so he wouldn't have to do the job alone.

Glancing out the window he stared west, in the direction of Brittany. *Soon, my love. Soon.*

He wouldn't bother to send her a letter when he got back to the palace. Knowing his *Brette,* she would return it unopened, with a short note scrawled on top.

"Don't bother me until you've achieved your goal."

CHAPTER FIVE

Fall 1498

Back in Nantes

"I wish to have a history of our people written," Anne told her chancellor. Back in her ancestral castle in Nantes, she was filled with emotion to be surrounded by memories of her parents and sister, even Louis. As usual, when overcome with emotion she sought to gain mastery over her feelings by pursuing a practical intent.

"Your Grace, do you mean a history of Brittany's noble houses?"

"I do not, Sire de Montauban, although I am well aware that yours is one of the oldest among us." She paused. "I mean a history of Armorica." She used the ancient name for Brittany which the Gauls had called it before settlers from Wales and Cornwall arrived in the late sixth century. 'Armorica' meant 'place by the sea.'

"Of the origins of the Breton people," she continued. "All of us. Whence we came and what sets us apart from others." "From the French, you mean, Your Grace?" De Montauban's eyes twinkled. "Of course. God knows they admire us. Let us toss them something to feed on as to the reasons why." She straightened herself up, shaking out the folds of her gown as if to shake off French court dust now that she was back in the bracing, fresh air of her own lands.

"Shall I find a scholar amongst your court, or should we look elsewhere?"

"I would like to find one who is not biased in his account. Let us look for a scholar who is not from too prominent a family, so that he will write a fair account without pushing forward the glorious accomplishments of his own house."

"Then the Rohans are out, Madame?"

"Quite."

"Or the Penthièvres?"

"The puppets of my husband, the late king?" sniffed Anne. "Certainly not." She had been angered that Charles had appointed a Penthièvre to manage affairs in Brittany after their marriage. The Penthièvre family had sold their claim to Brittany's rule to his father the old king, Louis XI, in 1480. Their alliance with France had been bought before, so Charles had secured it again. Why, oh why had her late husband not allowed her to manage her own duchy's affairs?

Balling her fist in the folds of her gown, she vowed not to allow her ducal rights to be lost again should she choose to marry Louis. Therein was the crux of it: she had had no choice but to marry Charles—it was that or watch her duchy be overrun and plundered by France. But now France and Brittany were at peace, and she could marry Louis or not.

"Not even the Montforts?" de Montauban asked delicately, referring to Anne's own family.

"No, not the Montforts. I do not seek to set one noble house above another. This is to be a serious scholarly work, not some panegyric to please me—although I wish to be pleased with the result."

"Then I shall keep my eyes and ears open to find your man."

"Or woman," Anne added.

"A woman, Madame?" de Montauban's eyes widened. It was unusual for a woman to author a scholarly work.

"Someone such as the one who wrote the biography of Charles V of France," Anne said.

"Do you mean Madame de Pizan?" de Montauban asked. The author, Christine de Pizan, earlier that century had produced an astonishing body of work in her time. Most libraries of Europe's princes were stocked with the Parisian-Venetian's books, ranging from her political and biographical ones to her widely read love ballads.

"Yes, someone like her," Anne said. "If she could do it, then a Breton woman among us might be up to the job, too."

"Madame, I will make inquiries."

"Do. And bring me Madame de Pizan's biography of Charles V from my library. I wish to use it as an example to whomever I select."

"Very good, Your Grace," de Montauban murmured.

"I know," Anne agreed.

De Montauban hid his smile with a bow and backed from the room. His duchess was exactly as she had been before leaving Brittany for France seven years earlier: imperious, and sure of herself. This time she had maturity, experience, and vast wealth to add to her quiver. Brittany was again in good hands.

Within one week of arriving in Nantes, Anne had made a

dizzying number of decisions. She had appointed one hundred Breton archers to positions as her personal corps of guardsmen. If the king of France could have his corps of Scottish guards, why should she not have her own retinue of personal guards? With revenues from her duchy added to her ancestral wealth, as well as her widow's pension from Charles, she was now one of the richest women in Europe. With no husband interfering, she would dispose of her resources in her usual magnanimous style.

Anne's vision was large, her pockets deep. She would seize her moment before she succumbed to the marital bed of her beloved Louis, perfect in almost every way except in his frugalness. Soon enough she would change even that.

Already she had seen that Louis could dig deep into his pockets when he needed to. He had paid for the entirety of funeral expenses for the late king. At Louis' request Anne had organized it, ensuring it to be as magnificent as it had been costly. Why had he made such a generous gesture? He had wished to impress her. Indeed, he had succeeded.

Once she had recovered from the grief of losing her husband, Anne allowed feelings to surface that she had held for Louis all her life, not only as a protector and friend, but as the first adult male for whom she had felt womanly stirrings as a young girl. She was ready to deepen those feelings into something more if he could meet her terms.

Thus far, he was delivering.

In the second week of her arrival home, Anne formalized the status of her growing number of maids of honor. She founded an order for them to encourage them in pious behavior and to secure their futures as Europe's most sought after brides. The order of the Cordelières, or the order of the Ladies of the Cord, was the first order for noblewomen in all of Europe's royal

courts. Anne chose the symbol of the knotted cord to honor St.
Francis, whose followers had worn knotted rope belts, as well as
to honor her father, Duke Francis II of Brittany.

"Shall we wear rope belts then?" Anne de Candale had whispered to Charlotte of Naples as the two girls rose from their
investiture in early November 1498, in the great hall of the
duchess's castle. Both young women had been raised at Anne
of Brittany's court after losing their mothers: Anne de Candale
from the age of eight and Charlotte of Naples at age twelve.

"Do you really think that our queen-duchess will have us
wear rope cords like fishermen?" Charlotte scoffed. Of all of
Anne's maids of honor, she was the most highly born. The eldest daughter of the king of Naples, she was a princess born,
with her own retinue of attendants at court. "She is no longer
queen, Charlotte," Anne de Candale corrected her. Fed up with
the older girl constantly trumping her, she couldn't help but
admire the way Charlotte was always so sure of herself, just like
their mistress.

"Wait and see. Our sovereign mistress will soon be queen
again. It suits her, and she will accept no lesser role than the
one she has already fulfilled so well." Charlotte's expression was
smug, as it frequently was.

"Then do you think she will forego rope belts?"

"I think she will offer us belts that will dazzle your eyes,
and slide gracefully in your hands, little one."

As usual, Charlotte was right. At the close of the investiture of sixteen ladies-in-waiting and eighteen maids of honor,
Anne, Duchess of Brittany, presented each, one by one, a silken
cord shot through with gold thread and knotted with a gleam-
ing thick gold knot at each end.

The effect was as elegant as it was striking. Perhaps not
what Francis of Assisi had had in mind when taking a vow of

poverty, but Anne of Brittany's vows were more on the order of impressing all of Europe with the highest standards of refinement and comportment of her Cordelières. She would be mindful to instruct them in largesse to the poor and downtrodden, but she would insist that they be well-dressed while carrying out their mandate.

"With this belt I gird you with the knot of chastity, which you will strictly guard until such time as I choose a suitable lord for you," Anne intoned to each of her maids of honor as she tied the golden belt around their waists, one by one.

"Why may I not decide what to do with my own chastity? Does it not belong to me alone?" Anne de Candale whispered to Charlotte the moment their sovereign moved past.

The older girl narrowed her eyes at the younger one. "Because the duchess will banish you from court if you take it into your head to dally with any man other than the one she chooses for you."

"But what if her choice is not mine?" Anne de Candale asked, not unreasonably.

"Little one, you don't have a choice. You will do what she says, as will I, when the time comes."

"But what if I wish to choose my own husband?" Anne de Candale's fresh young face beamed a question mark.

"It doesn't matter what you wish or what any of us wishes. She has given us these silken cords to wear to remind us we are bound to her in service."

"But even if I try to obey, my heart may go elsewhere all on its own," Anne de Candale pointed out.

"You must not let that happen." Charlotte of Naples frowned at the younger girl.

"But what if it does?" Anne de Candale pressed.

"Don't be ridiculous. It's out of the question." Over the

shorter girl's head, Charlotte of Naples rolled her eyes then stopped.

Across the room a handsome and well-built youth was gazing at her, a fixed look on his face. She hadn't seen him before.

Stunned, she returned his regard for a brief second, just long enough to realize that her younger colleague's observation was perhaps not so out of the question.

"Who is he?"

"Who is who?" Blanche de Montberon asked. From the region of Angoulême in the south, Blanche was known for both her beauty and her quiet grace. Alone with the other maids of honor her beauty withstood, while her manner became somewhat less restrained.

"The one with the chestnut-brown hair." Charlotte of Naples pointed. "There."

She moved to one side of the window. In the courtyard below stood three young gallants, all waiting upon their lords, who were finishing up a meeting of the duchess of Brittany's counselors inside in her privy council chambers.

"Do you mean the tall one?" Blanche peered out the window.

"Not him. The handsome one." Charlotte took another peek at the young man who had caught her eye at the investiture ceremony the week before.

"The fair-haired one to his left?"

"No. The one on his other side; who is he?"

"Whoever he is, he is not the most handsome of the group," Blanche remarked.

"You are no help at all, and blind besides." Charlotte swatted Blanche's arm then pushed her aside to see better. "He is clearly the handsomest of them all."

"My sister Cordelière, Cupid has shot his arrow deep into your heart, compromising your vision as well as your sense."

"I'm going to the kitchen so I can find out who he is."

"No." Blanche stopped Charlotte with a swat of her own. "Better let me do the job. They will know you are lovestruck in a minute and your secret will be out."

"What secret? I simply want to know who he is." Charlotte looked cross for a moment then took another peek out the window.

Energy poured off the trio below, crackling in the air around them. Suddenly the chestnut-haired one looked up and Charlotte felt a similar energy pouring off of her, jumping and dancing in the air and raising the hairs on the back of her neck.

"I'll be back in a minute," Blanche Montberon sang out.

"Take your time," Charlotte called back, eyes riveted to the window. Grateful to have Blanche gone, she could study the unfolding situation in private.

The chestnut-haired youth had broken away from the group and was strolling closer to the window. Had someone told him it was the window to the room she shared with Blanche and Anne de Candale?

She pulled back to ensure she was concealed. At the same time, another instinct within her asked if the youth below was searching for her or perhaps another. She would like very much to know.

As if he had heard her thoughts, the youth looked up to the window with yearning eyes.

Propelled by a force she had never felt before, Charlotte moved into the center of the window and gazed down at him.

The youth's face instantly lit up, causing roses to spring into Charlotte's cheeks. It was she he sought, after all.

Shivers ran down her spine as golden knots of obedience

and chastity came undone then slipped away. Her heart rushed
to his, just as Anne de Candale had said might happen.

In the end it was not a woman at all that Anne selected to write
Brittany's history, but her court treasurer, Pierre Le Baud. He
had presented her with a historical work he had begun a few
years earlier, and she had found it satisfying enough to commission him to finish it.

Then she had begun preparations for her tour of Brittany—
the Tro Breizh, as it was called in Breton dialect. She would
begin in Vannes to the northwest, then return to her royal residence in Nantes in time for the start of the Advent season.

"Who shall I select to accompany me, if you are not coming?" Anne asked Madame de Dinan, after concluding her
meeting with Sire Le Baud. She had had enough of appointments and meetings. It was time to ride out into the countryside, breathe deeply of Brittany's crisp late harvest air, and wear
her sabots. She had already instructed Sire de Montauban to
have a pair specially made with a built-up sole in the left one so
that she would not limp before her subjects. They loved their
good duchess, their *bonne duchesse*, for her perfection. She would
give them nothing less.

"Bring the hardiest among your maids, Your Grace. You
do not want to be encumbered by fragile flowers who wilt
at the first splash of mud on their skirts," Madame de Dinan
counseled.

"Then both Charlottes are out."

Madame de Dinan nodded. Charlotte of Naples and
Charlotte d'Albret were both rare flowers. The former was not
so frail, but too highborn to risk bringing on a journey to the
rugged west, and the latter was as fragile and delicate as her
powerful warrior toad of a father was not.

"I would suggest Anne de Candale and the lively little one," Madame de Dinan advised.

"Do you mean Bolandine?" Bolandine was somewhat headstrong, but hardy. She and her sister were Rohans, like Madame de Dinan.

"Yes. Bolandine and her sister Anne, too. They will prove good reminders to the House of Rohan that they are receiving an exceptional education under your care at court."

"Well-stated, my Rohan friend," Anne approved.

"You know my loyalty is always to you and no other," Madame de Dinan said, giving her sovereign a loving look.

Anne made no reply but smiled at her former tutor. From what Anne could see, her older friend did not have many more seasons to enjoy until Heaven snatched her home. The older woman had been delighted to return to Brittany in October, but had become increasingly frail in the weeks since they had arrived. Perhaps she knew she had achieved her life's work and now she could rest.

Anne's heart ached to think of how many of her loved ones already rested in eternity's arms. Who would be next?

"And Germaine too." Anne held a soft spot for Louis' niece Germaine de Foix, a sturdy and bright young girl who did not hesitate to voice her opinions.

"Will you bring Nicolas de Laval with you?" Madame de Dinan asked. "He was such a help to you in Rennes during the siege."

"'Tis true, but I think not." Anne could imagine what mischief her lively maids of honor would get up to with the handsome and gallant Nicolas riding amongst them. She would arrange to have her Breton archers accompany her personal entourage. All married men, they would not dare to rustle amongst her maids of honor, as would the young unmarried gallants of her court.

"We shall make for Vannes then head to Quimper," Anne announced.

"Will you stop by the church of Sainte-Anne-d'Auray, Your Grace?" Madame de Dinan asked.

Anne eyed her. St. Anne, the mother of the Virgin Mary, was Brittany's patron saint of childbirth. God knew she needed her help should she choose to marry Louis. "It is on the route, so I might." Frankly, she had planned to.

"Oh, good. Then I shall give you something from your childhood that I have saved for you to have blessed there," Madame de Dinan declared.

"What is it, Madame?"

The older woman's eyes twinkled. "Your Grace, grant me the favor of surprising you. I will give it to you wrapped and you can see for yourself when you unwrap it and ask for St. Anne's blessing."

Anne looked at her curiously. "Something from my childhood, Madame?"

Madame de Dinan's mouth formed a line. "I will say no more, but don't leave until I've given you the packet."

"Madame, do not part with something valuable. Already I plan to make a nice gift to the church there."

"*Ma reine-duchesse*, it is something your father gave me before he departed this Earth, and it is my prerogative now to part with my worldly goods as I see fit. Do you not agree?"

"Madame, what say you? Do not speak that way!" Anne's heart throbbed. She could see that her dear friend was loosening the ties that held her to this world.

"Your Grace, I have always taught you to face life with clear eyes and a mind unclouded by sentiment." Madame de Dinan gave Anne a stern look.

"Indeed you have, Madame, but—"

"But nothing. My moment is done and yours is upon you. My child, you have ever reached for the sun, the moon and the stars—and why shouldn't you? Seek all with France's new king and let nothing stop you." Warmth and love poured from the older woman's voice.

"What say you, sweet lady?" Anne clutched at her former tutor's hand. She had lost so many loved ones in her short life. Must she lose another soon?

"I say that I wish for you to allow me to put my house in order, Your Grace. Do you not see the sense of it?" Madame de Dinan asked.

"I do, Madame." Her heart protested but her head approved.

"Then let me request from the mother of the blessed Virgin my dearest wish for my dearest sovereign." Madame de Dinan knelt at Anne's feet and took a fold of her gown in her hand.

"Stop that, Madame! Off the floor and about your business! No need for all that," Anne ordered her. Frightened by the serious turn her dear friend had taken, Anne wished to steer her back to lighter thoughts. But the approach of something as unfathomable as it was inevitable was upon the older woman.

"Thank you, *ma reine-duchesse*; you have made me very happy. Now let me go and find what I wish to give you." On creaky knees Madame de Dinan rose with some difficulty and bowed, then backed from the room.

Anne sensed what her lifelong companion's dearest wish was for her. It was precisely the same wish she had for herself, which was why she needed St. Anne's help.

At age twenty-one, she had achieved exclusive sovereignty over her duchy, immense wealth, and the love of the man she had admired and loved since childhood. If only she could create a child with him; one that she could keep alive.

At the entrance to the church of Sainte-Anne-d'Auray, Anne paused.

"Wait here for me," she bade her attendants, then entered the ancient church. She wished to pray, but she also wished to unwrap in private the packet her dear Françoise de Dinan had given her, so that she could scan its contents alone.

As she undid the strings of the packet, she prepared herself for what she knew must come. Her trusted former tutor, wise counselor, and close confidante would leave her soon. Louis would replace her in her affections, but well she knew how different the love of a man was from the love of a woman. Anne had relied on the older woman as a mother, since Anne's own mother had died when she was nine.

It was now time to stand on her own without her. If God and St. Anne smiled upon her, the next time she became a mother she prayed she would get a chance to raise her child instead of burying it.

Kneeling before the statue of the Virgin's mother, Anne undid the packet. Inside lay a filmy, frothy garment laced with pink ribbon. Anne unfolded it, recognizing her own christening gown. Her father must have found it among her mother's things after she died, then passed it on to Françoise de Dinan for safekeeping until such time as Anne would need it.

She lifted the fine lace garment to her face and buried her nose in it. Lavender scent enveloped her in memories of happy childhood days in Nantes, frolicking in the courtyard of their castle with her dear Isabeau and their older half-siblings: Francis d'Avaugour, that rascal, and his sister Françoise.

Laying it carefully on the altar before St. Anne's statue, she silently asked the saint to bless the babe who would one day be dressed in this garment. *Above all, Madame, keep alive the child who will wear this.*

She rose and called for the priest to come bless the garment. While she waited, she looked up at the face of the statue.

St. Anne's eyes stared back with an expression both compassionate and sad.

A chill ran down Anne's spine. She had seen someone wear that expression before, but who?

Searching her mind, she thought back. It had been a member of the clergy, she recalled. Not her confessor, nor her late husband's. Nor had it been the bishop who had married them.

Then it struck her. Francis de Paule, founder of the Minims and a great friend of Charles, who had baptized their darling dauphin, had worn a similar expression when they had stopped outside Amboise on the day after their sweet prince had died. Charles had asked the holy man how his son fared before galloping the final stretch from Lyon to Amboise. The holy man had said nothing, only pointed a finger toward the castle on the hill where the boy lay, already dead, unbeknownst to Charles and her. The holy man's face had worn the exact same blend of compassion mingled with terrible sadness.

No, my lady. Don't tell me my children will all die. No, Madame, I beg of you, Anne silently begged the effigy with eyes closed, her hands tightly clasped.

After a moment she looked up.

The statue's expression had softened. It seemed to be reassuring her that not all her children would die. Yet it was still sad. What was the saint telling her?

"Your Grace, I am here," the priest called out behind her.

She turned and got down to business, explaining to him that she wanted the garment she held out blessed, then asking him what the most pressing needs of the church and parish were, in order to offer a suitable bequest.

The priest blessed the christening gown, then lay it across

Anne's outstretched arms as if placing a newborn babe into them.

Anne looked down at the gown, her eye immediately going to the pink ribbon laced through the eyelets of its borders. Looking back up at St. Anne's effigy, she saw the same compassionate yet sad expression there.

Then it struck her.

The mother of the mother of God was telling her that she, too, would be the mother of a mother. Inescapably, it was a christening gown for a girl.

"I am Nicolas. Nicolas de Laval," the young man said, moving a step closer.

"Are you the son of the count of Laval, then?" Charlotte asked, mindful of rank as befit a princess born.

"I am his nephew and heir," Nicolas replied, his eyes moving over her face almost as immediately as if his hand were.

Charlotte sucked in her breath. "And why did you not accompany the duchess on her Tro Breizh?" Her thoughts leapt ahead like frolicking fawns, bounding through weeks, months, and years to a fine fantasy of a life made with the handsome chevalier gazing at her. Her father would be pleased to hear he was the heir of the count of Laval, should the young man seek him out.

"I had wanted to, but now ..." His eyes remained fixed on hers, careful not to descend below her face. He was well raised, she could see. Yet a gallant all the same. *Beware, beware* a warning voice sounded in her head.

She batted it away. "But now—what?" she demanded.

"But now, not so much," he replied, bowing to her.

"You do not need to bow before me," Charlotte chided him.

"To a princess born, a count-in-waiting must bow," Nicolas de Laval disagreed.

"Let us put aside all that stuff and nonsense while the court is away," Charlotte suggested, surprising herself. Usually it was she reminding those around her of attention to protocol. "How may I put aside my manners in the presence of a princess?" Nicolas de Laval asked. "My mother would slap me if I did any such thing."

"Then your mother is a noble lady," Charlotte replied, pleased to hear the man before her mention his mother. The thought of anyone's mother lurking nearby should serve to clear the heady air between them, just a few arms' lengths apart.

"She is, my lady. But perhaps not so noble as your mother," Nicolas gallantly replied.

"My mother is dead."

"I am sorry to hear it, lady Charlotte."

"You know my name?"

"Everyone at the duchess' court knows the name of her most highborn Cordelière."

God's breath, why had he mentioned the Cordelières? The golden chastity knot that she had felt loosening tightened around her once more. "Then you know who my father is?"

"I have heard of King Frederick but never met him."

"He is away in Naples now."

"So you are alone."

"So I am." The air between them thickened, no amount of mention of parents nor musings on chastity knots succeeding in clearing it.

"So I see." Nicolas looked away, then back again. "I am charged by the duchess with looking after her household in Nantes in her absence."

"Are you really?" Charlotte tried but failed to keep the teasing tone from her voice.

"Well—more or less. She asked me to keep an eye on things

around here while she is gone, and so I am." His eyes trapped her in their gaze.

"Why would our *reine-duchesse* charge a youth with looking after her affairs?" Charlotte scoffed, desperate to maintain the upper hand. The mystery that was transpiring between them was completely new to her; except that she had been dreaming about it for weeks.

"What do you mean 'a youth'? Do you see a mere youth before you?" Nicolas straightened, a scowl marring his handsome features.

"I know not what I see before me, but if you tell me your age I will know what to think," Charlotte fumbled, thinking her words had come out wrong.

"I am one year older than the duchess herself, long past the age of a youth."

Charlotte breathed a sigh of relief. He was twenty-two to her eighteen, a perfect age difference.

"I apologize; I mistook you for a younger man."

"And if I am not mistaken, you are younger than I."

"Yes."

"Will you tell me your years, fair lady?"

"For what reason?"

Nicolas' face colored slightly. "None really. I just wish to know."

"I am eighteen."

"A good age."

"Indeed. As is twenty-two."

"What is it good for, then?" Nicolas asked, as if reading her thoughts.

It was Charlotte's turn to color. "Well, it is good for enjoying life before responsibilities crowd out pleasures."

"Pleasures such as what?" His light brown eyes flashed gold in the mid-afternoon sun.

"I don't know, I'm sure. Just having time to chat, I suppose, as we are chatting now." *Beware, beware* the voice inside Charlotte's head chanted again. She ignored it.

"I agree. And have you time to take a walk, too?"

"A walk? A walk where?" Charlotte's blood raced. She had read about walks in some of Christine de Pizan's works. The walks mentioned in her book *One Hundred Ballads of a Lover and His Lady* had been especially interesting.

"In the garden, perhaps?"

"Which garden?" Walks in gardens were almost the most interesting of all, topped only by walks in the forest.

"The one of your choosing."

Charlotte thought fast. Not the herb garden, certainly. Cook might be out there, or one of her assistants. If they weren't, they would be watching from a window.

"Perhaps the flower garden by the moat," she suggested. Near the tennis courts?"

"Yes."

"Shall we?"

"I must let my attendants know."

Nicolas de Laval's face fell. "Of course. I will wait for you here."

Charlotte glided off. She had no intention of letting any of her attendants know. If she bumped into any of them, she would put them off her trail by telling them she would be lying down for a nap, just as her chaperone was doing at that moment. Charlotte congratulated herself on recommending a second helping of venison at the midday meal. The older woman had eaten well; she would sleep deeply.

Charlotte hurried down the hall that led to the duchess'

rooms, where the Venetian mirror hung on the wall. She needed to consult it. Then she would take another route back to where Nicolas waited.

Back in the courtyard, Nicolas moved into the shadows of the entryway into which the princess of Naples had disappeared. The last thing he wished was for one of his roisterous friends to come along and ask what he was doing there.

From the moment he had spotted Charlotte the day of her arrival in Nantes with the duchess' entourage he had felt himself less a gallant and more a man. Something about the haughty princess reminded him of his sovereign, Anne. Well did he remember how brave she had been all those years ago in Rennes, standing up to the king of France until Charles VIII had bent the knee to her and asked her to become his queen.

His thoughts ajumble, he felt outside of himself looking in and not quite recognizing what he saw. Up to the day he had first laid eyes on Charlotte he had enjoyed his freedom, focusing his attentions on laundry maids, scullery wenches, and the like. But when the cool young woman at the head of the duchess' maids of honor had glided behind her sovereign into the receiving room of the great hall in Nantes, he had followed as if mesmerized. The tall maid of honor had a sort of self-possession about her he couldn't help wanting to take away.

Confused, he spit on his leather boots, then wiped them clean. His chivalrous nature urged him to perform valorous deeds for this fair lady. Yet he wanted to kiss her at the same time. But there could be no stealing of kisses from a princess. Was he ready for the challenge?

When he looked up, Charlotte of Naples and Aragon was floating toward him in the full glory of beauty and youth. He felt himself in the presence of a goddess. One day such a ravishing creature would grow into a woman like his mother or the duchess Anne. For such a woman, an offer of marriage must follow a kiss. But first, a kiss.

Her father would kill her; her mother would roll over in her grave. She had allowed him to take her hand. He held it in his as they strolled in the far corners of the garden, hidden from view by the late afternoon shadows. November days were short; soon it would be dark. She must return to the castle before her chaperone sent out the entire household in search of her. Soon Charlotte would.

Soon.

The warmth of Nicolas' hand seemed to promise her own hand something true. She had heard of such promises made in secret between maidens and gallants. Without exception, everyone said they were false.

But this was different. Nicolas' hand was attached to a man with the truest gaze she had ever felt upon her.

Yet it was just a gaze. Would not Christine de Pizan have scoffed at such wisps, offering nothing more than the moment they occurred in? Yet why had she written a full one hundred love ballads describing such meaningless gestures, devoid of context or future security? Had the author not lingered over each of them, choosing every word carefully, imagining scenes and scenarios that she would spend the greater part of her more didactic works disparaging?

There seemed to be an innate contradiction contained in the wide breadth of Madame de Pizan's works. Had the author uncovered an innate contradiction hidden in the hearts of most men and women? No wonder her works were so wildly popular, Charlotte thought, trying to focus on something other than Nicolas' hand clasping hers.

Her tutor had told her students that de Pizan's books were

widely read at royal courts across Europe. Even Charlotte's father in Naples had a complete collection of her works. How had de Pizan arrived at her censorious conclusions on the dangers of courtly love? Had she come to such a stern verdict through scholarly reflection, or after wandering down the shaded paths of experience?

Charlotte felt the squeeze of Nicolas' hand then the soft brush of his thumb on the back of her own.

Instantly, the hairs on her arm stood at attention, waving wildly with a message that shrieked so loudly she couldn't make it out. Was it 'beware', or was it 'proceed'?

"Mademoiselle! Mademoiselle Charlotte! Where are you?" a voice called out.

Charlotte dropped Nicolas' hand and ran behind a plane tree for cover. It was the kitchen maid calling, a sprightly young thing who would find her in no time.

Smoothing her headdress, Charlotte pushed back the strands of hair that had escaped from under its edge. She had wanted Nicolas to catch a glimpse of her chataine locks: half blonde, half brown. Now she pushed them out of sight along with her highly-charged feelings.

The kitchen maid appeared on the path.

"Do you know where Mademoiselle Charlotte is?" she addressed Nicolas.

"Who is Mademoiselle Charlotte?" he asked.

Charlotte reeled. How dare he renounce her? Then she realized he was protecting her. Still, her heart hurt to hear him so glibly deny knowing her. It was like Peter telling the servant girl that he had no idea who Jesus was.

"Never mind. What are *you* doing here?" The kitchen maid's tone was unpleasantly familiar.

"Just strolling."

"You? Just strolling? Hah! What are you really doing?"

At the sound of the kitchen maid's knowing laugh Charlotte's blood ran cold. How well did the girl know Nicolas? Did he escort young women on unchaperoned strolls around the castle grounds on a regular basis?

"Nothing, Blanchette, nothing at all."

Charlotte's cheeks flamed to hear the sound of the girl's name in Nicolas' mouth. How dare he address a kitchen maid with the same familiarity he had addressed her, only moments earlier?

Instantly the sweetness and magic of the past few hours vanished, swept away in a maelstrom of humiliation. Nicolas knew this kitchen maid too well. Charlotte, a princess born, would never give him a single thought again.

A whispered exchange ensued. Sick with disappointment, Charlotte suffered the further indignity of fury at her own slip in self-control. God knew if the kitchen maid hadn't come along, she might very well be doing whatever it was Blanchette was now doing with Nicolas de Laval. Whatever it was, Charlotte couldn't see or catch a word of it. But well she knew that a whispered conversation between a gallant and a maid alone in a garden meant they were very close together. Too close for comfort, especially for her.

"... so you say," Blanchette's words ended in a titter, followed by Nicolas' laugh.

"Really. Go see for yourself. I think she's the one you mean."

Heaven's breath, was he now slandering her reputation even further in his attempt to get the kitchen maid to leave? Charlotte peeked out from behind the tree to see the back of Blanchette's skirts disappearing up the path. She waited a moment then stepped out of her hiding place, her back to Nicolas.

"Charlotte, you are safe. She is gone," he murmured behind her.

Charlotte turned and slapped Nicolas de Laval across the face as hard as she could.

"And since you are *not* gone, I am not safe at all," she hissed.

Nicolas stumbled backward, his hand to his cheek. "My lady, you misunderstand."

"I understand perfectly. You know her, she knows you, and I don't want to know anymore."

"She is just a kitchen maid, Charlotte—"

"Do not speak my name with the same voice you used to speak hers," Charlotte cut him off, feeling sick to her stomach.

"My lady, I only wished to divert her from finding you," he protested.

"Ahh, and how well you did. Now she thinks I am further down the path, no doubt trysting with one of your colleagues," Charlotte snapped.

"I did not say that at all," Nicolas defended himself.

"No, but you implied it," Charlotte railed. Gathering up her skirts she began to run back to the castle.

"I did not mean to, lady fair. I was trying to get rid of her before she spotted you," Nicolas protested, coming up behind her.

"Do not bother me with further defenses. I am no longer interested."

"But my lady, I am very much interested," Nicolas countered.

"In me, or in a bit of fun?" Bile rose in her throat.

"In you! In you, Charlotte!" Nicolas' voice throbbed.

She couldn't stand it. Stopping dead in her tracks, she slapped him again with the back of the same hand. "Never speak my name again," she spit out, hot tears welling in her eyes.

Grabbing her wrist, Nicolas pulled her to him.

"Stop!" she protested.

"Then stop me," Nicolas said simply.

Inches from his face, she felt faint. His scent, bracingly fresh, stole over her, befuddling her thoughts.

"You disgust me," she hissed, feeling just the opposite.

"I am sorry."

"You are—you are what?" Startled, she couldn't think of how to respond to the simplicity of his words.

"I am sorry." Nicolas' eyes held the same fire in them that they had the first time she had locked eyes with him from the window of her room.

"For what?"

"For knowing the kitchen maid's name."

"What else do you know about her?"

"Not much, but as much as I want to know."

"And what else do you know about me?"

"Not as much as I'd like to know."

"And if I gave you a chance to find out, you would one day say the same of me." Her stomach churned.

"Never."

"Such light lies you breathe. So effortlessly they flow from your lips." Maddeningly, those lips were extremely close, distracting her from her wish to be done with him.

"My lips, Charlotte?" His eyes flamed, consuming her reason.

"Yes, your lips!" God's breath, if only they weren't so close, his scent all around, overpowering her in every way.

"Then seal them."

And so she did.

She rushed into the castle and up the stairs to her bedchamber. Thankfully her chaperone was not there, no doubt out on the grounds at that moment trying to find her.

Charlotte flung herself onto her bed and went over the past

few hours second by second. She had slapped the knave twice, then kissed him. It was horrible. Not only had she disgraced herself, but she still couldn't quite hate him.

Instead, all she could think of was of how good he had smelled when she had touched her lips to his and of how muscular his arms had been when he had wrapped them around her.

Worst of all, it had been she who kissed him, not he who had kissed her. He had responded in full, but it had been she who had decided the moment.

Punching her pillow, she beat it for several long moments. Then she buried her face in it. Why had she allowed herself to be so misled? And why did she not feel fully certain that Nicolas de Laval was a despicable knave?

Suddenly she understood de Pizan's vehement passages warning of the perils of courtly love. She had engaged in behavior outside the bounds of propriety. Thus, there was no one she could confide in. She, Princess of Naples and Aragon, head Cordelière of the duchess of Brittany's maids of honor, had no one to turn to for advice or counsel.

Absolutely no one must know what she had allowed to transpire—no, worse—what she had caused to transpire.

There had been a kiss. She had given it. After suffering humiliation by the one she had offered it to. What had happened to her? Even worse, what had she caused to happen?

Rising from her bed, she moved to the basin on the washstand and splashed cold water on her face. Then drying her hands, she went to find her chaperone, telling herself she would put the afternoon behind her now that she realized the pitfalls of succumbing to a gallant's call with no promises attached. Infinitely more experienced a woman than she had been that morning, she didn't feel any wiser at all.

Instead, she felt utterly confused. Whose call had she

succumbed to after all: a gallant's entreaties or the yearning of her own senses propelling her in his direction? Her heart was now hopelessly and utterly in the hands of Nicolas de Laval, a knave who dallied with kitchen maids.

Reaching for the knot of her Cordelière belt, she yanked it. But the silky fabric betrayed her, slipping from her grasp. What could she count on, having failed the test of her own resolve?

Along the corridor, down the wide staircase leading to the castle's main entryway, Charlotte took stock. What exactly had happened between Nicolas and the kitchen maid back in the garden? She hadn't actually seen anything, only heard whispers then silence that her imagination had filled in.

But the kitchen maid's tone had been unmistakably familiar. And Nicolas had responded to her by name. They knew each other. Yet how well?

At the thought of their mingled laughter Charlotte's blood boiled once more. Then she put herself in his shoes.

Who else was a young gallant to dally with than kitchen maids and the like, when the noble maidens of the court all held themselves apart wearing golden cords tied with chastity knots? It wasn't the kitchen maid who was the problem. It was between Nicolas and herself.

Shivering, she hugged herself. What would she do when next she bumped into the future young count of Laval? Before him she would maintain impeccable composure and reveal no sign of what had transpired between them. But secretly, her heart would rush to him, just as Anne de Candale had described, without anyone's permission but its own.

At the bottom of the staircase Charlotte turned in to the library instead of going to find her chaperone. She needed to consult further the works of Madame de Pizan. Was there a passage somewhere that offered an antidote to the helpless situation she was now in?

Searching through the books of de Pizan's works on the shelf Anne de Candale had pointed out, she found the one she was looking for. She leafed through it blindly, unable to focus with the imprint of Nicolas' lips still fresh on her own. No matter how many times she washed her face, she would feel them there forever.

"My lady Charlotte!"

Slamming shut *One Hundred Ballads of a Lover and His Lady*, Charlotte jumped at the sound of her chaperone's voice.

"My lady, I have been looking for you everywhere." The older woman heaved in the doorway, trying to catch her breath.

"I was just here looking at the readings we were working on before the duchess left," Charlotte told her. Was it possible that a trace of Nicolas' lips showed on her mouth?

"*The Book of the City of Ladies?*" her chaperone asked.

"Something like that." Coolly, Charlotte placed the volume back on the shelf then strolled toward the door.

CHAPTER SIX

December 1498

Sweet Release

"Sire, a missive from the West has arrived for you." At the entrance to the king's personal chambers in his Paris-St.-Pol residence, the messenger bowed, a courier's leather pouch in his hand.

"Come." Louis beckoned him to enter. Was it a message from his Breton dove? The one who had flown the coop to breathe the fresh air of her lands, while he was left behind in Paris to clean up the mess he had made in order to capture her? Perhaps she preferred not to be captured at all. If so, he knew the feeling.

Trying to conceal the trembling of his hands, he reached out to untie the laces that bound the leather satchel.

"Whence did this come?" Georges d'Amboise asked, coming up behind Louis to read the missive over his shoulder.

"From the Loire Valley, Your Excellency," the messenger addressed the bishop. "Here is the stamp on the bag."

Louis glanced at the embossed device on the satchel. It was the device of Plessis-lez-Tours, favorite royal residence of the former king's father, Louis XI. He was long dead, so what was this? "God, don't tell me another signed statement has surfaced swearing I slept with that woman." Louis shot his friend and confessor a pained look as he pulled out a thick sheath of papers.

D'Amboise coughed to conceal a chuckle as he skimmed the top page of the satchel's contents.

"May I, Sire?" he asked the king.

"Take it. It's not from the one I wish to hear from, so what does it matter?" Louis wasn't in the mood to act kingly. Fortunately, in front of Georges he could relax from his duties. He rose and paced restlessly to the window, dismissing the messenger, who backed out of the room.

Peering down into the courtyard he imagined his *Brette* in her royal carriage, about to enter through its main gates.

His vision vanished. She would never return to visit him here, or anywhere else, unless he mopped up the mess at hand with a satisfying outcome.

"Sire!" Excitement shimmered in d'Amboise's voice.

"What?"

"This is it!"

"This is what?"

"This is just what you need!"

"How so?"

"It's a signed letter all right, but from the old king, boasting to his grand master that he's marrying you off to his daughter because he fancies it won't cost much to rear your children."

"Meaning?" Louis scratched his head. Louis XI had been a nasty man. A deviously effective king, but without a single friend other than his eldest daughter. Anne de Beaujeu, as scheming and controlling as her father, had revered him.

"Meaning you're in luck, Sire! This is just what you need to prove that you were forced against your will into a marriage that would prevent you from producing heirs."

D'Amboise waved one of the papers at the king. "'Tis right here, Sire, in the king's own handwriting!"

"Where?" Louis strode to Georges and snatched the paper from his hand.

"Read here, Sire, where it says 'I fancy that the children they will have together will not cost them much to rear.' It's clear he knows your union will produce no children at all."

"The fiend!" What an evil schemer the old spider king had been. No surprise at all that he knew his daughter was sterile. Here he was, boasting of such foreknowledge in his own handwriting. "That's what I told the court all along!"

"Yes, Sire, it was your word, a powerful thing indeed coming from the king's mouth, but this is a signed original document."

"Evidence beyond all question?"

"Exactly, Sire. The note accompanying this says this letter was found amongst the grand master's possessions by his son, who had heard from his father before his death, that the old king had boasted to him of his plan to acquire the lands of the House of Orléans by insisting on this union."

"Just what I said!"

"Indeed, Sire. And once this is entered into evidence with the court, there will be solid grounds that you were forced into your marriage, rendering it unlawful."

"This is the missing link we need!" the king exclaimed.

"Let us present it to your legal counsel today."

"Guard!" Louis shouted. "Go to the court chambers and summon my head counsel here."

"Yes, Sire!" The guard rushed off as the king and the priest bent heads together over the old, yellowed letter written in the old king's hand himself.

"Sire, does it not give you satisfaction that you will finally undo the web he bound you in twenty-two years ago?"

"Undone by his own boasting, as most of us are," Louis observed, wishing he hadn't bragged about bedding Jeanne the morning after his wedding.

"Pride goeth before a fall, does it not, Sire?"

"It does indeed. So I shall not take pride in waving this evidence in the face of the daughter of the man who wrote it."

Guilt overcame him as he thought of Jeanne. Not because he was setting her aside so much as because he had found it so hard to be nice to her in every one of their rare exchanges over the twenty-two years of their marriage. It wasn't just her horrid looks. Much worse was her unfailing devotion to him despite his unkind and ungallant abhorrence of her. The woman made him feel like a monster each time they met.

"Wise words, Your Majesty. You must put on a sorrowful face and let her know that you wish to release her from Earthly bonds so that she may serve Heavenly interests more closely."

"What if she says she wishes to serve Heaven's interests as my wife?" Louis' heart sank. It would be just like her to respond with the utmost in wifely duty, maddening him as she gained even more sympathy from the common people.

"It doesn't matter, Sire. With this letter, your case is strong. It is clear that her father forced your union for unlawful reasons."

"Shall I bequeath her a castle, then?"

"Sire, I would not stop at a castle. Give her her own lands, a title, and a generous annuity."

"What lands?"

"Lands that you hold and are free to dispose of."

"The estate in Bourges, then?" He shuddered, dark

memories of the three years he had spent locked up there flooding him. He had been in the prime of his manhood, from age twenty-six to twenty-nine, chafing like a lion to be confined to its grim dark rooms, forced to sleep in an iron cage at night. The only nights he had been allowed to sleep in a bed had been the ones when Jeanne had visited. The sister he had refused to bed had forced him to bed her younger sister, his undesired wife, if he wished to sleep in a bed at all.

It had been a cruel punishment meted out by a daughter cut from the same cloth as her father. Louis would be glad to rid himself of the estate and property forever. If only he could shed his memories of the three long years he had spent there, too.

"Sire, why not award her a title, as well, so that she may live out her days in a rank befitting a princess born?"

"She does not care for worldly titles or goods." Too saintly to be bought off, Jeanne of France had outmaneuvered him at every route of escape from her.

"Well I know, Sire," d'Amboise agreed.

"But she cares to do good, and for that one needs money, power, and land," the king mused.

"Then may I suggest you offer her a duchy and name her as its head?"

"What an idea!" Louis didn't sound entirely happy. He was careful in his spending habits—not stingy, but not expansive—unlike the high-living woman of his dreams.

"Sire, were you to name her Duchess of Berry, where Bourges is located, you would be viewed by all as offering generous largesse."

"Must I be that generous?" The king eyed his friend peevishly.

"To save your reputation? Think on it, Sire. You must make the case that you hold the woman you have never been lawfully wed to in the highest esteem; therefore you wish to award her a position that enables her to offer her good works to as many in need as possible. Otherwise, it will look as if you are just trying to rid yourself of an unwanted wife."

"But an entire duchy?" Louis frowned.

"Which will revert to the crown once she dies, of course." D'Amboise narrowed his eyes at Louis.

"Ahh. I hadn't thought of that." The king's face relaxed.

"Because you are not the scoundrel the old king was."

"No, Georges, I am not. Just a man who has found what he wants and wants it as soon as possible."

"Remember, Sire. The woman of your dreams is a woman of lavish tastes."

"So she is, Georges. For her, I will relax my stinginess."

"Sire, it is not stinginess born of meanness. You are stingy because you grew up fatherless, with your mother doing the best she could."

"She struggled, Georges. It was not easy for her." Louis thought back on his beautiful mother and winced. She had been widowed at a young age then had fallen in love with a commoner, the head steward of his father's estate. No one in their social circle would accept such a match, so Marie of Cleves had lived a circumspect life away from court, bereft of the income and status a remarriage to a wealthy nobleman might have afforded.

"I know well, Louis. You have walked through shadow and light, and now it is time for you to enjoy the full measure of happiness that has escaped you all these years. But you need to impress the one you wish to wed, and you will do so by show-ing generosity to the one you are casting off."

"Do you mean she will take offense if I am not generous in settling a good position on Jeanne?"

"I do, Sire."

"Why should she care?" Louis studied his friend's face, puzzled.

"A woman who considers becoming your wife will consider your treatment of any other wife you have had."

"Do you think so?"

"Sire, what do you think? Did you yourself not note what good care the duchess Anne took of her husband before he died?"

"While he dallied non-stop with any female over the age of twelve." Louis' nostrils flared. How Charles could have even thought to look at other women when he already had the most ravishing, intelligent wife in Europe was beyond his comprehension.

"Yet she never reviled him."

"I will never serve her so."

"I am sure you will not, Sire. But you must be impressed with how she honored him at the funeral and all through her mourning period."

"Charles was a good man. A flawed one, but good."

"Sire, may I be frank?"

"You know already that when we're alone I insist on frankness."

"Charles' weakness was women. Yours is stinginess. I know the source of it, but others don't."

"Your point?"

"Do not allow any woman important to you to perceive you as stingy. Neither the one you wish to marry nor the one you were forced to marry."

"Are you telling me my subjects will dislike me if they think me stingy?"

"No, Sire. Your female subjects will dislike you if you appear stingy to the women in your life."

"What's the distinction, then?"

"To your male subjects you will appear shrewd, practical, keeping a tight hand on the coffers. Not so to the women."

"They're different, aren't they?"

"Very different, Sire. They do not take well to a man being mean, especially not their king."

"They certainly flocked to Charles."

"And hated his father."

"I see your point." Louis XI had been as mean-spirited as he had been clever. Keeping tight control on everything he oversaw, generosity and largesse had not been part of his make-up. On the other hand, Charles had possessed an expansive and generous nature. Unfortunately, he had mostly squandered it on the pursuit of women other than his wife.

"Sire, you will do fine. Just lavish the ladies with whatever it is they need."

"Georges, as a priest, how is it you know so much about women?"

"I grew up watching my father and mother fight and make up, then fight and make up again."

"They were at odds with each other?"

"They loved each other with all their hearts." Georges smiled, a tender smile Louis had never before seen on his friend's face.

The king peered at Georges. He hadn't grown up with loving parents. He had no idea how it worked. "Are you saying this is what I look forward to?"

"By all means, Sire. And when you've run out of steam, just give her what she wants."

"But what if the thing she wants is the very thing I don't want?" Louis frowned. He'd never thought about any of this, having enjoyed a life free from marital demands.

"Then lavish her with other things. Whatever it is she enjoys, needs, or thinks she needs—give it to her!"

"Is this sound policy for managing a wife?"

"Sire, essentially wives are unmanageable, but to give it your best try you must serve them generously. Surround them with luxury and lavish them with love."

"That I will gladly do." He burned to think of the one he wished to lavish with love. Apparently, there would be a lot of catching up to do to learn how to live with a wife. It was a good joke that he would rely primarily on his most trusted advisor, a priest, to counsel him on how to proceed.

The head of Louis' legal team approached the table where the members of the committee of investigation sat. In his hand he held the missive from Plessis-lez-Tours, the letter from Louis XI to Antoine de Chabannes, Lord Grand Master of France.

Clearing his throat, the counsel read:

"'My Lord Grand Master, Antoine de Chabannes, Count de Dammartin,

I have decided to go on with the marriage of my little daughter Jeanne with the little duke of Orléans, because I fancy that the children they will have together will not cost them much to rear. I advise you that I hope to accomplish this marriage, otherwise those who go contrary to me will have no assurance of life in my realm, where I am minded to carry out the whole according to my intention ...

Louis'"

A stir swept the room as the committee absorbed the full import of the letter's contents. Handing the document to the head of the committee, Louis' counsel retreated to a corner while the paper was passed amongst its members. Low murmuring and muted expressions of surprise filled the room as the letter was read and re-read.

"It is our contention that with the words 'the children they will have together will not cost them much to rear,' it is evident that our former king, Louis XI of France, deliberately arranged the union of his sterile daughter Jeanne of France with Louis, Duke d'Orléans, now His Majesty Louis XII, our present king, knowing full well that no heirs would result from such a union," Louis' chief counsel stated.

The chief of the committee nodded, motioning him to continue.

"Furthermore, King Louis XI states that anyone who opposes such a union "will have no assurance of life in his realm," thereby threatening with death or banishment any subject who would object to said union," the king's counsel went on.

"Though I did object, none present moved to prevent this unlawful union from taking place," the king broke in.

"Yes, Your Majesty." The chief investigator's tone was gentle.

For the first time since proceedings began, Louis sensed that the committee members appeared moved to hear of his plight as a boy of fourteen. It would seem that none of them would have wished to find themselves in similar circumstances on their own wedding day.

"We contend from this letter that no one defended the wishes of the bridegroom, for fear of death or banishment from the realm on direct order of the king," Louis' legal counsel continued.

The sound of his mother's muffled sobs in a corner of the room came to Louis as memories assailed him of that bleak

September day in 1478. The old king had disliked him from
the moment he had assisted at Louis' christening as godfather.
Louis d'Orléans had heard from his mother that he had peed
on the old king as he held him for the priest to christen him.
Louis' mother had told him that the king had grumbled afterward that her son had ruined his new outer coat, and that she
should have seen to it that the babe had been more securely
swaddled. Ever since that moment, it had been all downhill
between the spider king and the young duke d'Orléans.

Louis had been angry, and had been forcibly marched into
the room where the wedding was to take place. He had objected loudly to what was about to take place. But no one lifted
a finger to prevent the wedding from proceeding.

"You will marry my daughter or you will enter a monastery,
where God knows what will happen to you!" the old king had
shouted at him.

"But I want neither, Sire! I wish to be free until I am old
enough to make my own choice," Louis had cried.

"You will do as I say!"

"Then I will enter a monastery!" *And soon run away.*

"Where an accident may well befall you," the old king had
hissed at the boy.

His mother's gasp was audible from where she stood at the
back of the room.

"Talk some sense into your son, Madame!" the king shouted
at her.

"Sire, would you have my boy marry one who is—who cannot—who ..." What could she say with the princess Jeanne
there in the room with them: so young, so fragile, and so grotesquely deformed? Marie of Cleves quaked in fear to think
of what the king might arrange to have done to her son in
a monastery. It was said that unwilling novices sometimes

disappeared at the behest of powerful lords who had them sent to monasteries to be rid of them.

"Do you say something against a princess of France, daughter of your king, who stands before you?" Louis XI had demanded.

"No, Sire, of course not," Marie de Cleves sobbed. What could she say? Who would dare to cross a king?

"Then keep silent while we proceed," the king spat out.

It had been done. Then, even worse, it had been consummated that night. The king had had the bride and groom locked into their bedchamber and stationed spies at keyholes to ensure that the union was fully executed.

It had been more like Louis himself who felt himself to be fully executed, his life over before it had begun, at the very dawn of his adulthood.

"Sire, may my committee members and I have a word with you privately?" the chief investigator asked, breaking into the king's thoughts.

"Clear the room," Louis commanded. Was this the moment he had waited for all these months?

In a moment his legal team was gone, as well as his attendants. The chief investigator bowed low before the king, then looked up at him with grave eyes.

"We will examine the origins of this document, and if it is authenticated it shall be entered as evidence that the union was forced upon you," the man spelled out.

"Then may this nightmare finally come to an end," the king said.

"Not entirely, Sire. We also need a second ground to ensure that the annulment is granted in the event that the grounds of lack of consent are not accepted by the pope, due to you being at the age of consent when it took place."

"I tell you there was no consent!" Louis raged.

"Yes, Sire. But those who were in the room with you on the day of your wedding are now dead. And it is documented that you were past your fourteenth birthday, thereby of the age of consent to marry."

"Then what else do you need, man?" God, how he wished Georges was there. Thinking of what his friend would counsel, he remembered the bishop advising him not to confess too much.

"We need a second ground on which to establish that your marriage is invalid," the committee head went on.

"Such as?"

"Your word, Sire, that your union was not consummated." The investigator narrowed his eyes.

"Have we not been through all that? I told you before, must I tell you again? All who have followed proceedings know very well that I did what I had to do whether I wanted to or not."

"And do you mean to say, then, that you did have marital relations with this woman or that you did not?"

Louis paused; he was within reach of his goal. Praying God would not strike him down, he spoke.

"I did not." Louis hated himself at that moment, but reasoned he was embracing a larger good: the chance to produce an heir to the throne of France.

"And do you solemnly swear this statement to be true in the presence of these two witnesses?"

There was nothing else to be done for it. One party in the proceeding must take the part of a saint and the other party the part of the opposite. It was clear Jeanne would play the part of the saint, as she was seen as such already.

"I do," Louis breathed out.

"Then it shall be entered into the records." The investigator turned to his colleagues. "See that it is done today."

Louis heaved a sigh of relief. Thank God the examiner hadn't forced him to spit out the entire statement. Although he knew that his word as consecrated king would be held as incontestable, he was relieved that he had not been asked to state the entirety of the statement he had just been asked to make. It would have rankled afterwards, even worse than it already did.

"When may I expect a decision?" he asked.

"Sire, you may expect to hear from us within the next few days."

"I await your ruling with impatience," the king pressed.

"Thank you, Your Majesty. We will confer now amongst ourselves, with your leave."

"You will have it." *And I will have my annulment,* Louis told himself, blocking out all other thoughts.

The fifteenth of December dawned gray and grim. By midmorning a sharp chill bit the crowds outside, muffled in their wool capes. Word had gotten around that a ruling was about to be announced. The courtroom was as packed as the streets outside. Those inside the courtroom wore fur-lined mantles over their doublets. The committee took their seats and the court referee stood to deliver their decision.

The room went silent as the referee cleared his throat. "May it be known that the Committee of Investigation appointed by His Holiness Pope Alexander VI has reached a decision concerning the marriage between Jeanne de Valois, Princess of France, and Louis, Duke d'Orléans, now His Majesty, King Louis XII of France," he intoned.

Georges d'Amboise tensed as he prepared to hear the news he must deliver to the king, waiting at his royal residence in Chinon.

Louis had decided to clear out of Paris before the decision

was announced. Better not to hear the comments and fallout from the crowds, nor to be assailed with mocking ditties made up by Sorbonne students in the taverns and cafés of Paris on how the king had rid himself of his crippled wife.

"It has been determined that such marriage taking place on the day of our Lord, September 8, 1476, is declared invalid on the grounds of lack of consent and of non-consummation."

A stir rippled through the crowd. Tones of relief and disbelief seasoned the snippets and mutterings heard. Georges was glad his sovereign wasn't there to hear it.

His heart leapt for joy for his lifelong friend, but he maintained a solemn face as he prepared to pay his respects to the lady Jeanne. He would handle her with the utmost care now that the court had ruled in the king's favor.

Moving toward the tiny figure seated on a chair in the corner, he rehearsed his remarks. In his hand he held the document the king had dictated, in hopes of a favorable outcome, granting Jeanne de Valois the title of Duchess of Berry, the estate of Bourges, and an annuity that would enable her to expand the scope of her charitable works or even found a religious order. Whatever she did, Louis wanted her out of his hair for the rest of his life.

Arriving before her, Georges d'Amboise, Bishop of Rouen and Prime Minister of France, bowed low.

"Lady Jeanne de Valois, Princess of France, I offer you the most distinguished regards of the king, who begs you to understand his difficult position and to concur with the decision of the court."

A silence ensued, during which time Georges prayed that Jeanne would make no further trouble. It was best for all for her to accept the inevitable; it was no longer subject to debate.

A ruling had been made. The annulment would be granted,

as Louis'offer of a title, land, and a stipend to the pope for his purported nephew Cesare had been accepted. There was nothing more Jeanne could do to change the outcome, but God knew she could still protest the court's decision, if she chose. *Please, dear lady, show your high breeding and accept your passage to your next role in life.*

Looking up, Georges watched as the fragile bird of a woman raised her head and regarded him with eyes full of sacrifice, but also of burning zeal.

"I will pray for my lord and former husband the king," Jeanne of France said clearly and loudly enough for all in the courtroom to hear.

Hurrah, my lady, you have done the right thing, Georges thought, heaving a sigh of relief.

"The king will welcome your prayers, my lady. He, in turn, wishes you all success in continuing your good works, and wishes to grant you the means by which to expand them." He handed the tiny noblewoman the document from the king outlining his parting gifts to her. They were generous.

Georges had drafted the document himself to ensure that the king set the right tone with his settlement gift to the woman who was now no longer his wife. God knew each and every point of his offer would be hashed over in the court of public opinion outside.

Without a glance at the document the lady Jeanne of France looked heavenward then crossed herself and rose, wrapping her crooked body in her shapeless black cloak. Slowly, she exited the courtroom as all bent a knee to her, a sudden stillness descending upon the room.

Georges mused as he watched the retreating back of the tiny figure. Something about Jeanne de Valois, Princess of France, was so holy that every subject of France inside and outside the courtroom felt it from her presence when she passed. For the first time, he felt as happy for her as he did for his friend and sovereign back at Chinon in the Touraine.

Whether Jeanne of France, the new duchess of Berry, knew it or not, the king had just set her up in a position to embark upon the mission she was born to fulfill. Anyone could see she was not well-suited to be queen-consort of France. The idea of it was almost as laughable as the idea of Louis being suited to be a good husband to her. They were both better off free of each other.

Exiting the courtroom, Georges noted that the sun had come out. What a great day it was for his sovereign. Hoisting his bulky frame into the carriage that brought him, he thought with joy of his friend's imminent future.

Christmas had come ten days early for the king of France.

CHAPTER SEVEN

November 1498

Progress

Continuing on her progress through Brittany, Anne's thoughts turned to the welfare and prosperity of her people. After spending a few days in Quimper, second stop after Vannes on the path of the Tro Breizh, she veered off to make a visit to the duchy's west coast port city of Brest.

Wending her way north from Quimper to Brest, she stopped overnight in the small town of Locronan. She expected to tour the traditional lace-making workshops of local textile-makers. Instead, she was surprised to be taken to visit workshops for the town's new and thriving industry: the manufacture of sailcloth from locally-grown hemp and flax.

"Where do you sell this cloth?" Anne asked the mayor, who had paid obeisance to her in Rennes the month before. She picked up a section of sailcloth and brought it to her face, inhaling the sea-infused scent of L ower Brittany as she admired its fine weave.

"Your Grace, we bring the sailcloth to Brest, where you are headed," he told her.

"And then what happens? Is it used to rig Breton ships or sent abroad?"

"My lady-duchess, that is the heart of the matter." The light in the eyes of Locronan's mayor told Anne she had hit upon something important for the future of the town.

"The shipbuilders of Brest have always used it for their own rigs," he explained, "but we are now discovering markets abroad where demand is great for sailcloth." The mayor's eyebrows rose, apparently in hopes that his sovereign would put her energies toward expanding the new industry from which his town was prospering.

Anne thought back to her conversation in Rennes with the burgher from Brest. She had asked him to recommend someone to take charge of the site of the former French garrison there. Would it not make a useful location at which to store sailcloth for export abroad?

"I will look into it when I arrive in Brest," she advised the mayor, noting how proud and industrious the sail-makers in the workshops had been, intent upon their craft and producing as fine a product as the lace-makers of Quimper were renowned for.

It struck her that expanding export markets to the Flemish Lowlands and beyond would serve as an excellent way to keep Brittany's economy firmly separate from France's. She might soon be queen of France again, but her ancestral mandate as Brittany's ruler remained first in her heart. She would do whatever she could to maintain her country's independence.

At the entrance to the main gate of Brest, Anne was met by

the mayor. He was the same burgher who had addressed her at the Estates General meeting in Rennes in October.

"Monsieur, I look forward to you showing me the vacated French garrison quarters, so that I may confer with you on how best to repurpose it," Anne returned his greeting.

"With pleasure, *ma duchesse*." The mayor of Brest turned and whispered some orders to one of his attendants.

Within hours, Anne had made a complete tour of the site of the former French garrison. Located on the port itself, it made a perfect location for the storage and loading of sailcloth for export abroad.

"Who are the leading export merchants of sailcloth here?" she asked.

"Your Grace, there are three. They are—"

She cut him off. " I wish to meet with all three of them tomorrow at this time, so that I may decide which of them I will appoint to oversee the use of this site for storage and loading of sailcloth to be shipped abroad."

"Your Grace, what an excellent idea." Immediately, the mayor sent his men to notify all three merchants.

By the following day's midday meal, Anne had made up her mind. All three men had struck her as capable, but two had taken great pains to stress their ties with local feudal houses.

Anne chose the third merchant, the one who had not mentioned any ties. He would be her emissary abroad to seek out new markets for Breton sailcloth. She would send him in her name, commissioned by her alone. The last thing she wanted was for local feudal lords such as the Penthièvres or Rohans to make inroads, both abroad and within the rising merchant class, while she was away in France, as she guessed she soon would be.

As she rode from the garrison site to the city gates to depart

Brest, the cries of the common people lining the street gave her food for thought.

"Long live the duchess!"

"*Vive la bonne duchesse!*"

"She looks to the future and not to the past," she heard as she rode past.

In that instant, she realized that was exactly what she had begun to do from the moment she had stepped out into the sunlight from the church of Sainte-Anne-d'Auray.

The past had been her father's world, of feudal lords warring with each other. They had impeded Brittany's prosperity by destroying its peace in their constant struggles against each other or with France.

The past had also been Anne's own anguished record of losing every one of her children by the late king of France.

Now a new era was dawning, a new alliance with France's new king, and a new way of ruling her duchy by appointing administrators from the ranks of the emerging middle class instead of the nobility.

No longer was the world divided into nobility, clergy, and peasantry. She had heard of the emergence of a new class populating the towns and cities of Italy from Charles' account. Now she saw it with her own eyes in the far western reaches of her duchy. Untitled merchants and craftsmen who lived in Brittany's towns and were not tied to the lands of feudal lords were busy spinning, weaving, and selling fine textiles across the realm. Soon, with her support, they would also be selling Brittany's products abroad. She would see to it that their interests were served so that her duchy prospered.

The next stop of the Tro Breizh was St.-Pol-de Léon, on Brittany's rugged northwest coast.

"Your Grace, will you tour the site of the battle your ancestors of the House of Montfort won against the French here?"
Philippe de Montauban asked, riding up alongside her as they
approached St.-Pol.

"Of course I will pay my respects to my ancestors. But it
is not just the house of Montfort I serve; it is all the people of
Brittany."

"You are wise, *ma duchesse*. No wonder the people call you
their good duchess."

"And in the years ahead, as it was in my years with Charles,
I will not seek to fester wounds that must heal, so that Brittany
can enjoy its prosperity now that there is peace with France."

"Yet it is due to the superior forces of the Montforts, with
the English, that your own house prevailed over the French
here."

"Philippe, I can guess what their victory was due to, and it
was not superiority of forces but rather superiority of tactics."

"In what sense, *ma duchesse?*" Hs heart warmed to hear her
address him familiarly. Their best conversations always ensued
after.

"As you and I both know, to France's great tragedy at
Agincourt, the French did not recognize the superiority of the
English longbowmen nor of the English chain of command."

"I beg you tell me more of this chain of command, as I,
along with all Europe, know the woeful tale of French unpre-
paredness before the English longbowmen." De Montauban
looked grave.

"The French as well as the Bretons have spent far too long
trapped in outdated notions of rank when it comes to fighting
battles," Anne observed.

"My lady, it comes as a surprise to hear you, of all people,
criticize those who pay due respect to rank."

"At court, it is important to respect rank. On battlefields, it is important to obey orders from one's commander no matter what his rank."

"Then say you the House of Montfort was better at obeying its commander than the French army was under Charles de Blois?" de Montauban asked.

"It was not due to the Montforts at all that our side won. It was due to the English, led by a common man-at-arms and not a nobleman."

"Say you it was the Englishman Dagworth who won the battle that caused the Montforts to emerge as Brittany's rulers?"

"It was indeed," Anne agreed. "If it had not been for the English troops strictly obeying their General Dagworth, with not a drop of noble blood in his veins, my own house would not have prevailed and I would not be duchess of Brittany now."

"My duchess, what lessons do you derive from this tale?"

"What I see is that we speak of chivalry now giving way to modern ways, but modern means to fight battles were being used by the English over a century ago. We must open our eyes to the reality of a new order and conduct ourselves accordingly so that our lands can thrive."

"My duchess, you have always been one to stand for tradition and custom, protocol and deference to rank. Are you telling me now that you are part of the new order, or of the old?" de Montauban's eyebrows rose in amusement.

"My friend, I am Brittany's sovereign ruler. Therefore I have no choice but to bring my duchy into the new order. I see my subjects thirst to better their lives, their willingness to work hard and to produce fine goods for export abroad. It is this new class of people whom I must first of all understand, then support, so they in turn will support me."

"And will they?"

"I, who have kept them exempt from France's salt tax all these years under Charles' reign? What do you think?" Anne glared down her nose at her chancellor.

"You are right, Your Grace. You have maintained your duchy's separate status and privileges with France. And now you will see to it that your towns prosper and that Brittany's wealth derives from its cloth industries rather than agriculture."

"Because wealth stems from trade, not from peasant produce; although God knows I love every one of my peasant subjects who till the land."

"My duchess, I have ever admired you but never knew you to be so thoughtful as to the waves of change now upon us."

"This very progress has opened my eyes."

"My lady, you do a great service to your subjects by recognizing their needs and serving them in new ways."

"It was at St.-Anne-d'Auray that I felt a voice as if from Heaven tell me to look to the future and not to the past."

"'Tis exactly what I heard a man in Brest shout to you as you rode by two days ago."

"I heard him, too. And when he spoke, I felt as if our Lord Himself was speaking to me."

"So our good duchess is no longer the traditionalist she has always presented herself as?"

"I will always be a traditionalist, Philippe. 'Tis my nature to pay obeisance to the old ways and to uphold ancestral customs. But inside I will strive to understand the new ways and work within new frameworks to bring wealth to my realm. Do you understand?"

"I admire your complexity, Your Grace. I have seen it in you since you were four years old. You are a natural for the role God and your ancestors have bequeathed you."

"So I am." Anne of Brittany kicked her horse and cantered ahead, spraying her chancellor with a fine coating of dust.

Philippe de Montauban laughed aloud. It wasn't the first time his sovereign had ended a conversation in such a way. She knew what she was about.

He wiped the dust from his face and spurred his horse to follow. Brittany's duchess was imperious, demanding, and keenly competent. He would follow her anywhere.

Anne traveled to Tréguier next, then to St.-Brieuc, spending a day in each town. Then it was on to St.-Malo, Brittany's most important port on its northern coast.

Louis had freed St.-Malo, too, of French troops garrisoned there. His sweetener to Anne to ensure her affections was proving a boon on her progress. Everywhere she was enthusiastically received as the ruler who rid Brittany of French troops, something her father had not been able to do.

Anne had heard much of St.-Malo from childhood days. The large rough town could barely be called Breton. Its history had been sharply re-routed in 1144 by the bishop Jean de Châtillon, who granted rights of asylum to any who entered St.-Malo from other parts. This special status had the unintended consequence of attracting criminals and thieves as well as rogues who had been banished elsewhere. The port town faced the Sea of Brittany, also known as the English Channel, and soon enterprising and dishonest seafaring men were busy exacting tribute from English ships in the channel. This unlawful practice had transformed St.-Malo into a corsair stronghold.

It was especially important to Anne to stage a ceremonial royal entry, a *joyeuse entrée,* to let its inhabitants know its rightful ruler had arrived and intended to keep a close eye on its activities, however difficult this had been for Brittany's rulers since 1144.

The *joyeuse entrée* of her entourage through the main city gate of St. Vincent was greeted by a boisterous crowd, noisy and brimming with wild approval of their sovereign.

Eyeing the preponderance of rough-hewn men amongst the inhabitants lining the streets to greet her, Anne turned to the head of her men-at-arms, who rode just behind her.

"See to it that my maids of honor are strictly chaperoned while we are here. I will not have them going about town, with so many men of doubtful background about."

"My lady, I will see to it that they are escorted at all times," her man said.

"Better yet, have them taken to the guesthouse of the convent here, so that the local sisters can keep them occupied and out of sight." Glancing around, she did not care for some of the impertinent glances she saw on the faces of men here and there in the crowd.

"Yes, Your Grace." The head of her guards trotted off to make arrangements.

After visiting the cathedral of St. Vincent to pay homage to St. Malo of Aleth, the sixth-century priest who had founded the town after landing on Brittany's northern coast from Wales, Anne accompanied the ladies of her entourage to the convent attached to the cathedral. Relieved to deliver them into safe hands, she then hurried off to tour the site of the recently vacated French garrison, as she had done in Brest.

There was much to oversee, with many decisions to make. At the sound of a seagull's squawk overhead, she laughed out loud. As the sea air filled her lungs, energy coursed through her. Anne loved every minute of her journey through her realm.

CHAPTER EIGHT

November 1498

The Tale of the Nightingale

"I pray you, tell my maids of honor somewhat of history and local lore," the duchess of Brittany instructed the head of the convent of St. Vincent.

The Mother Superior nodded eagerly then turned to her brightest novice, charging her with keeping their noble young guests occupied. Sister Celestine had been given responsibility for the library after the Mother Superior had noted her zeal for books and learning. She was a perfect choice to entertain their guests and make the best possible impression on them so that they would report back favorably to their sovereign.

The duchess of Brittany's reputation of generosity to churches, convents, and lay houses was well-known. The Mother Superior hurried away to consult with her senior staff on what they might ask for, should the duchess wish to make a bequest at the end of her visit.

Sister Celestine took the girls to the convent refectory to
refresh them with food and drink after their long, dusty journey. Then she led them to the library where a roaring fire had
been set in the hearth. Her favorite room in all the convent, she
looked forward to sharing its magic and charm with the four
young noblewomen before her.

"*Mes demoiselles,* which do you prefer me to start with: the
legends of the local saints who lived near St.-Malo, or some local lore?" She would give the young ladies of the duchess' court
the best entertainment possible, so that they would tell their
sovereign what a good time they had enjoyed during their stay
at the convent. Their satisfaction would undoubtedly influence
the duchess to make a generous bequest.

"Some local lore, please," Anne de Candale replied, brimming with curiosity.

"Then shall I decide on a story to start with, or would
you like to choose one yourselves?" Sister Celestine was young
enough to remember how she had loved to be given a choice
when she was a girl. It was rare that girls were ever given
choices, especially girls raised at court. She could see from the
sparkling eyes and high spirits of the four girls before her that
they might like some say in how they would pass their day in
new surroundings.

"Oh, Sister, do let us choose for ourselves!" Bolandine cried out.

"Yes, Sister, what a lovely idea!" Anne, Bolandine's sister,
chimed in.

"Shall we draw straws?" Anne de Candale asked.

"No, little doves, I have another idea." She paused, a twin-
kle in her eye. "Who is the oldest among you?"

Anne de Candale's hand shot up. "'Tis I!"

"Fine. We will blindfold you, then the second oldest will
lead you to the library shelves."

The girls looked wildly interested. Already the day was shaping up to be fun, with a game involving a blindfold and the pleasures of perusing a new library.

"There you shall run your hand over the books on the shelf devoted to local lore and choose one," Sister Celestine continued.

"Then what?" Anne de Rohan asked.

"You, my dear, will take the book that the oldest has chosen. Then this one here—" she gestured to Bolandine.

"That's my sister!" Anne de Rohan interrupted.

"Your sister will blindfold you and you will open the book to a page somewhere in the middle, and whatever story is on that page will be the one we shall read together."

"But what will the final one of us do?" Germaine de Foix asked plaintively, fed up with always being the youngest in the group.

"The youngest one of you will have the most important job of all," Sister Celestine declared, joy swelling in her heart to see how excited her young guests were. Mother Superior would be pleased to hear how well she had entertained them.

"What will I do?" Germaine de Foix cried, hopping up and down.

"You will read the title and first page of the story."

"Oh my!" Germaine burst out.

"And we will take turns reading until it is done."

"Then will you explain it to us?"

"If it's a good story, it will need no explanation," Sister Celestine told her.

Anne de Candale took in her remark, thinking of some of the tales she had secretly read since coming to court. How much she had enjoyed them despite almost never fully understanding what she had read.

"Now, let us get started," Sister Celestine ordered. She gestured to Anne de Candale to stand. From the folds of her habit the nun produced a white silk scarf. She tied it around the young woman's head, covering her eyes.

Bolandine took her hand, and following the nun, led Anne de Candale several steps to the library shelves that lined the walls.

Sister Celestine moved down the room until she reached the shelf she was looking for. Bolandine followed, the blindfolded Anne taking tentative steps beside her. The younger girls trailed behind, giggling and chattering. This St. Malouine holy sister was proving to be more fun than their tutor, Madame Leroux, back at court.

"Here is the shelf of books of lore from the region of St.-Malo." She reached for Anne de Candale's hand and, taking it in hers, ran it along the length of the books she would choose from. "This is all of them; no more, no less. Take your time and choose one among them."

"Nothing boring," Bolandine urged.

"I never choose to read anything boring," Anne de Candale retorted, her hand moving from one volume to the next.

"Nothing on the lives of saints, please," Anne de Rohan advised.

"Don't worry, those are on another shelf," Sister Celestine reassured her.

"Take care," Germaine de Foix piped up. "Our education is in your hands."

At that all four girls burst out laughing, as did Sister Celestine, making Germaine's head swell with pride at her bon mot.

"I take no responsibility for my choice as I can't see what I'm doing," Anne de Candale replied.

"My dove, you have just described the human condition, for which you must take your share of responsibility, just as the rest of us must," Sister Celestine said, none too gravely. "But I can't see what I'm choosing!" Anne de Candale protested. "Nor can any of us; for seeing the results of what you choose would mean seeing into the future, which none of us can do," Sister Celestine pointed out. "Fine. Then I shan't worry and shall choose ... this one." Anne de Candale pulled out a thin volume and waved it in the air before her. "Give it here." Anne de Foix grabbed for the deep blue vellum-covered book with no title on its cover.

Anne de Candale relinquished the book, then pulled off her blindfold and handed it to Bolandine, who blindfolded her younger sister. She had done so at times before, always with great satisfaction.

"There. You may open the book, and when your finger has found the page it wishes to rest on, hold it out," Sister Celestine instructed.

Anne de Rohan made a show of turning to one page then another, running her finger up and down its smooth surface, then deciding against it and turning to another.

"That's enough; choose one and let me do my part!" Germaine de Foix cried.

"Then I will stop ... here." Anne de Rohan's finger came to rest on a particular page. She held out the book and Germaine de Foix snatched it from her.

"Easy, little dove," Sister Celestine cautioned, as she took in the words on the page. They were ones she had read many times before.

"Is it a poem, then?" Germaine de Foix asked as she leafed backward to find the start of the story.

"'Tis, my little one. A famous poem set in St.-Malo.'"

"I hope it's not about fighting men and war," Anne de Candale remarked, looking over Bolandine's shoulder to see better.

"The Nightingale; it's called The Nightingale!" Germaine de Foix called out excitedly, thrilled that the title wasn't something beyond her reading comprehension.

"'Tis one of Marie de France's most well-known *lais*," Sister Celestine told them.

"What's a *lai?*" Germaine asked.

"It's a poem," Anne de Candale said.

"Not just any poem but a Celtic poem, this one set in Brittany," Sister Celestine explained.

"Like King Arthur and his Knights of the Round Table?" Anne de Rohan asked.

"Something like that," Sister Celestine replied.

"But not about war and fighting, I hope." Anne de Candale pouted, the light in her eyes dimming.

"No, dear girl, not this *lai* at all. You will find it is about knights fighting, but not in a war."

"Who wants to read about knights fighting?" Germaine de Foix asked, her tone disgusted.

"Whoever wishes to read about knights fighting over a lady, that's who," Sister Celestine retorted.

"Now, that's more like it!" Bolandine cried, trying to wrest the book from Germaine. The younger girl held onto it like a dog with a bone.

"Let's take our seats so Germaine can read the first page," Sister Celestine ordered.

The girls trooped back to their seats and Germaine began.

"'The Nightingale, by Marie de France ...

The story that I'll tell today
the Bretons made into a *lai*:
Laüstic they called the tale
French *rossignol*–or nightingale.
By Saint Malo there was a town
famed far and wide, of great renown.
Two knights lived there in luxury:
fine houses, servants, horses, money.
One had married a lady fair
wise, discreet, and debonair
(she kept her temper wonderfully
considering her company)."

"You may continue, Anne," Sister Celestine
said, pointing to Anne de Rohan.

"'The other was a bachelor
well known among the townsfolk there
for his courage and his courtesy
and for treating people honourably.
He went to all the tournaments,
(neglecting solider investments)
and loved the wife of his neighbour.'"

A sharp intake of breath ensued around the room.

"'He begged so many boons from her
she felt he *had* to be deserving
and loved him more than anything–
as much for the good he'd done before
as for the fact he lived next door.
Wisely and well they loved each other,

avoiding undue fuss and bother
by keeping everything discreet.
This was the way they managed it:
because their houses stood side by side
there wasn't much they couldn't hide
behind those solid walls of stone.
The lady, when she was alone,
would go to the window of her room'"

"My turn now!" cried Bolandine, taking the book from her sister's hand.

'"and lean across to talk to him.
They swapped small tokens of their love:
he from below, she from above.
Nothing interfered with them.
No one noticed, or poked blame.
However, they could not aspire
to reach the peak of their desire
because there was so strict a guard
on all her movements. It was hard,
but still they had the consolation
of leaning out in any season
to exchange sighs across the gap.
No one could stop *that* access up.
They loved each other for so long
that summer came–green buds, birdsong:
the orchards waxed into full bloom
bringing amorous airs with them,'"

"Amorous airs! What's that?" Germaine de Foix's eyes goggled.

Bolandine put an arm around the younger girl and rolled her
eyes at Anne de Candale while Anne de Rohan put a hand to
her mouth.

> "'and little birds carolled their joy
> from the tip of every spray.
> The knight and lady of whom I speak
> felt their resistance growing weak—
> when love wafts out from every flower
> it's no surprise you feel it more!
> At night, when the moon shone outside,
> she'd leave her husband sleeping, glide
> wrapped only in a mantle, till
> she fetched up at the window sill.
> Her lover did the selfsame thing,
> sat by his window pondering,
> and there he'd watch her half the night.
> This simple act gave them delight.
> So often did she do it that
> her husband started to smell a rat.'"

"A rat? Not a real one, I hope," Germaine de Foix cried at
which the others snickered.

"Bolandine, your turn," Sister Celestine directed.

> "'He asked her where she went at night
> and why she rose before first light.
> "Sir," the lady said to him,
> "It's more than just a passing whim.
> I hear the nightingale sing
> and have to sit here listening.
> So sweet his voice is in the night

to hear it is supreme delight,
the joy it gives me is so deep
I can't just close my eyes and sleep."
Her husband heard this glib reply
and laughed once: coarsely, angrily.
He thought at once of thwarting her
by catching the bird in a snare.
His serving men were rounded up
and put to work on net and trap
to hang on every single tree
in his entire property.
They wove so many strings and glue
the bird was caught without ado.'"

"Now Anne the elder," Sister Celestine said.

"'When the nightingale was caught
they brought it living to the knight.
This exploit pleased him mightily;
he went at once to see his lady.
"Lady," said he, "where are you?
Come here; this concerns you too.
I've snared that little bird, whose song
has been keeping you awake so long.
Now you can sleep the whole night through,
Rest easy: he won't bother you."
When the lady heard him speak,
she felt crestfallen and heart-sick.
She asked a favour of her lord,
if she could have the little bird.
At that he did something macabre,
snapped its neck in front of her,

and threw the body at her dress
to bloody it above the breast.
Then he stalked out of her door.'"

"Anne the younger, you may read again," Sister Celestine said,
to Anne de Rohan's great satisfaction.

"'The lady picked it from the floor,
and sobbing, called a living curse
on those who'd made her prison worse
by hanging nets in every tree
to snare the bird who set her free.
"Alas," said she, "I am undone!
I can no longer rise alone
and sit by the window every night
to watch my lover, my sweet knight.
There is one thing I'm certain of:
He will believe he's lost my love
unless I tell him what's occurred.
By sending him the little bird
I'll warn him what's befallen me."
She wrapped it in embroidery
and cloth of gold, and asked a page
to deliver this last little package
to her friend who lived next door.'"

"And now Germaine, as you began the tale, you may end it,"
Sister Celestine directed.

"'The page walked over to their neighbour,
saluted him on her behalf,
and gave what he'd been asked to give:

the bird's body, the lady's message.
When he understood the damage
his love had done to this lady
the young man did not take it lightly.
He had a cup made out of gold,
studded with precious stones, and sealed
against the corrosive outer air.
He put the nightingale in there,
then shut it in its little tomb
and took it everywhere with him.
The tale could not be hidden long
so it was made into a song.
Breton poets tell the tale;
they call it "The Nightingale.'"

A moment of silence ensued as the girls absorbed the meaning of the poem, each lost in private thoughts.

"So, my little ones, what do you make of that?" Sister Celestine asked, gazing from one stunned face to the next. "You, Anne. What are your thoughts?"

"I—I hardly know what to make of it at all," Anne de Rohan stammered. She looked at her big sister, who usually jumped in and cut her off when she tried to express any opinion at all. This time she was strangely silent.

"Bolandine? What about you?" Sister Celestine's eyes followed Anne's to her older sister.

"I know what I make of it, but I cannot say in front of the others." Bolandine's face flushed, but her eyes shone as if they held some secret.

Sister Celestine turned to Anne de Candale. "You are the oldest. What do you say?"

"Do you ask what lesson I think it imparts?" Anne de

Candale asked, thinking she could not care less about whatever lessons the poem held, but could hardly wait to read it again in private.

"No, little doves." Sister Celestine leaned in and lowered her voice. "Let us leave aside lessons for the moment and talk about how this *lai* makes us feel."

"It makes me feel very grown up!" Germaine de Foix blurted out. A flame in the hearth behind her leapt up as if in agreement.

"And so it should, little one. 'Tis a very grown-up poem," Sister Celestine remarked, looking mysterious and not very nun-like at all. "Try again, Anne. Tell us what you think, and let no one interrupt her." Her eyes swept the rest of them, lingering on the older girls with a warning glance.

"I like the way I don't understand everything in it, but there seems to be far more to it than just the words the poet wrote," Anne de Rohan offered haltingly.

"My dear, you have grasped the essence of good poetry!" Sister Celestine reached out and squeezed the girl's shoulder.

"Have I?" Anne de Rohan beamed, then stole a glance at her older sister. *So there, you know-it-all. 'Tis I who gave the right answer.*

"Now what about you, Bolandine? How does this poem make you feel?" Sister Celestine continued.

"I–I am afraid to tell you how it makes me feel." Bolandine's voice was hushed.

"Bolandine, this is not a lesson and I am not reporting back to your mistress. Do you understand that?" Sister Celestine's voice was gentle.

"Yes, but our mistress says that as Cordelières we are to set an example to each other, especially the older to the younger ones."

"My dear good Cordelière you will set the example by your actions, but no one can dictate your feelings to you." Sister Celestine's smile was sage. She reached out and smoothed Bolandine's headdress.

"That's just what I always say!" Anne de Candale cried. It was as if Sister Celestine had read her mind.

"Does it not feel nice to be in the company of like-minded friends?" Sister Celestine asked.

"Yes, it is so much fun. Far more fun than I would have thought for a ... for a ..."

"For a visit to a convent and a conversation with a nun," Sister Celestine finished for her.

"Well, um, something like that," Anne de Candale admitted.

"Exactly like that." Sister Celestine's smile was radiant, devoid of judgment.

Anne de Candale mirrored her smile and in that moment all the scruples and careful responses of the girls dissolved into animated talk and laughter. Sister Celestine was proving to be a special nun indeed. Freed from their usual surroundings in her stimulating company, the small group of Cordelières was having a very good time indeed.

"Can you believe her husband broke the bird's neck right in front of her?" Germaine de Foix remarked. "What a horrid man!"

"Didn't you already know he would be horrid?" Anne de Rohan responded, buoyed by the nun's encouragement to express her thoughts. "Remember, the poet said the lady kept her temper wonderfully, considering her company!"

"Is not that an example of saying more with less?" Sister Celestine asked.

"Oh, how well this Marie de France does that!" Anne de Rohan agreed.

"And where else does she say more with less?" Sister Celestine probed.

"What about where she called a living curse on those who'd made her prison worse—" Anne de Candale was interrupted.

"By hanging nets in every tree to snare the bird who set her free," broke in Bolandine. She and Anne de Candale exchanged sympathetic glances.

"But was it the bird who set her free?" Germaine de Foix asked, her face screwed up in puzzlement.

"What an excellent question, little dove. How clever you young ladies are!" Sister Celestine exclaimed, giving Germaine a chuck under the chin.

"But I should like to know the answer," Germaine pressed. "It didn't seem to me the bird set the lady free. In fact, she wasn't free at all, was she?"

"What do you think, *mes demoiselles?*" Sister Celestine looked around, her eyes bright. "How is it that the bird set her free?"

"The bird is a symbol of her feelings for the knight. The one next door, I mean," Anne de Rohan offered gravely.

"Oh, my dear, you have again captured the essence of the tale. One day you will grow up to be a fine scholar—perhaps a poet yourself!" Sister Celestine enthused.

"Do you think so?" Anne de Rohan had never had a better day in her life. She snuck a glance at her older sister, whose face was strangely flushed. Bolandine seemed to be keeping her thoughts to herself for once, to Anne's delight. Finally, she could get a word in edgewise, and how wonderfully well-received her words were proving today. Smiling at Sister Celestine she shifted closer, warmed by the magic spell of the unusual nun's charm.

"What is going on here?" a voice rang out, as jarring as steel dropped on stone.

"Nothing, Sister, we are just finishing up a *lai* of Breton lore," Sister Celestine replied, giving the girls a wink.

"Then when you are done, bring our guests to the court-yard so that our Reverend Mother may give them a tour." The owner of the voice appeared in the doorway, an older sister whose businesslike style was no match for the incomparable Sister Celestine.

"Tell them we will be there in a moment. I am just finishing up now," Sister Celestine called back in dulcet tones, causing the girls to break out into giggles.

As soon as the older nun disappeared Sister Celestine put a hand on Anne de Rohan and Germaine de Foix's shoulders. The nun gazed into the faces of each of the four girls, one by one.

"Let us make a pact between us, shall we?" she asked, her voice low and intimate.

All four drew closer.

"A secret one, right?" Germaine de Foix whispered, looking wildly excited.

"Exactly right, little dove. A secret pact that we alone shall share forever. Are we agreed?"

"What's the pact, then?" Anne de Candale asked. She was ready to agree to anything Sister Celestine suggested, but her sensible nature urged her to ask what she was agreeing to.

"Let us agree not to mention that we read this *lai* together to anyone outside this room once we leave," Sister Celestine proposed.

"But it's such a good story. What if I want to talk about it with someone else?" Germaine de Foix protested.

"My dove, I agree it is a good story. And you should talk about it with someone else one day when you reach a certain age. Just don't mention you heard the tale of "The Nightingale" here from me."

"But why not? You helped us understand it!" Germaine de Foix cried.

"All I did was help you to unlock your own thoughts about it." Sister Celestine looked levelly at Germaine.

"And our feelings. Don't forget our feelings," Anne de Rohan pointed out.

"Especially our feelings, Anne. You are right. Let us never forget that our feelings are our own to possess and no one can take them away from us, no matter what lessons we must learn." Sister Celestine paused then added, "And, of course, we must learn our lessons to grow up to be good women one day, no?"

"Of course! But we will never forget such a good time we have had here with you!" Anne de Candale cried, sad to think that the moment they had shared was about to end.

"Then I hope you let our good duchess know how well you enjoyed yourselves. But don't divulge the secret of what tale we read."

"Then what do we tell our duchess if she asks what we did?" Anne de Candale asked.

"Tell her you heard a tale of Breton lore, the name of which you forget." Sister Celestine half closed her eyes, an irresistible gesture that made her look much like a magical and mysterious lady similar to the one in "The Nightingale", and not much like a nun at all.

"I will *never* forget "The Nightingale", Germaine de Foix proclaimed, puffing up her chest as befit the more grown-up person she had become over the past few hours.

"Nor I. Nor will I ever forget you, Sister." Anne de Rohan gazed at the nun with adoring eyes.

"Nor I you, wise and delightful girls." Sister Celestine's voice was warm. "Now let us share a secret together forever and ever and promise me you won't mention you heard the tale of "The Nightingale" here. Will you?"

"I promise," Anne de Candale said, putting her hand over her heart.

"Sister, I would swear to anything you asked from me," Anne de Rohan followed.

"Sister, you have my troth," Bolandine offered.

"Sister, you are the most exciting nun I have ever met," Germaine de Foix exclaimed.

"Thank you, but do you swear to keep our secret?" The thin line of Sister Celestine's mouth looked ready to erupt into a smile.

"Yes!" Germaine de Foix broke into giggles and flung herself into Sister Celestine's outstretched arms.

"Ladies!"

"Coming!"

CHAPTER NINE

December 1498

Final Stop of the Tro Breizh

The seventh and final town of the Tro Breizh was Dol-de-Bretagne, a short ways past St.-Malo and due north of Rennes. Here it was that the great Breton warrior Nominoe had been crowned Brittany's first duke in 846.

From the moment her party entered through the main gate, Anne sensed the town was as spiritually significant as St.-Malo was not. Situated on marshy lowlands leading to the Bay of Mont St. Michel, Dol-de-Bretagne possessed an ancient quality, with its stone and timbered houses and Romanesque arches.

It was a fitting final destination for the Tro Breizh. Neither commerce nor piracy reigned here, but the weight of history: both of the origins of the Breton people and of the line of the dukes of Brittany of which Anne was the present successor.

Dismounting in the town square, she then entered the

cathedral, bidding her attendants to wait at the entryway. Proceeding down the long, dimly-lit nave, she stopped at the spot where Nominoe was said to have been crowned. There she kneeled and prayed to carry out the ancestral mandate to which the dukes of Brittany, through her father, had entrusted her.

As she rose, she thought of all she had seen on her progress. Her mind wandered back to her years as queen of France and lingered on Charles' tales of Italy. How was the feudal rule of the dukes of Brittany consistent with the industry and activity that was occurring now in her duchy amongst a class of men and women that hadn't existed until recent times?

Emerging into the square from the dim recesses of the cathedral, a ray of sun beamed directly on her as if offering an epiphany. The future of her subjects would depart from the old ways. She could see that the rule of feudal lords was ending. Yet she was the latest in a long line of them. The changes in the organization and industries of the towns that she had noted every step of the way on her Tro Breizh needed to be addressed. She, as Brittany's ruler, must address them. She would uphold the traditions and customs of the dukes of old, but the winds of change whispered to her that the days of feudal rule were over.

Shrugging off her thoughts, she mounted her horse and informed the town officials she wished to pay her respects to St. Samson at this final stop of the Tro Breizh.

"Your Grace, shall we visit Mont Dol on our way back? You can see the Mor Breizh on a day like today," the official suggested, using the Breton name for the Sea of Brittany that lay between Brittany and England.

"As it is a fine day, why not?" Anne beckoned to her head man-at-arms. "I will bring my maids of honor; it will be a treat for them."

"My lady, no worries here as you had in St.-Malo?" her man asked.

"None at all. This town breathes the spirit of Brittany, and I would have my maidens view its surroundings for a final memory of our Tro Breizh."

"Very good, Your Grace. I will assign two of my men to each of them, as well as to your ladies-in-waiting."

On their way to Mont Dol, less than a league from town, Anne's party stopped at the tomb of St. Samson, seventh and final founding saint of Brittany. He had journeyed to Armorica in 548, settling in Dol and transforming it into Brittany's spiritual center of that era.

"It is said that when Samson arrived, the ruling lord of these parts was devastated by problems of his wife and daughter," one of the local officials told the group.

"I wonder what kinds of problems his wife had," Bolandine whispered to Anne de Candale beside her.

"Maybe it was he who was the problem," Anne de Candale speculated.

"Ladies, quiet!" one of the ladies-in-waiting shushed them.

"It was said that his wife was ill with leprosy and his daughter possessed by a demon," the official continued.

A sharp intake of breath from the group of girls ensued as they tried to imagine a wife and daughter with such problems.

Anne de Candale told herself perhaps the wife had pretended to have leprosy in order to keep her husband at arms' length, her affections engaged elsewhere like the lady of "The Nightingale."

Bolandine wondered if the daughter might not simply have been possessed by the high spirits of youth that her parents had despaired of curbing. Was it not a common problem?

"And what happened?" the duchess of Brittany asked.

"Samson cured them both and in thanks the lord granted him the land that is now Dol," the official told her.

Anne nodded then turned to the girls. "Do you feel a special atmosphere here, *mes demoiselles?*" she asked, her mood lightening as the end of their progress neared.

"In comparison to what?" Anne de Candale asked, always the questioning one.

"In comparison to St.-Malo, for example," Anne replied.

A slight tittering rose amongst the four girls.

"Your Grace, I feel a special atmosphere here, but we did as well back in St.-Malo," Anne de Candale answered.

At that, it seemed to Anne that the tittering amongst the girls increased.

"And what was so special about St.-Malo then?" she asked.

"Madame, the nun at the convent there was such wondrous fun. Not like a nun at all!" Germaine de Foix declared.

Anne of Brittany breathed a sigh of relief. Thankfully they had enjoyed their time at the convent and not wandering the dubious waterfront of the port city. Even heavily escorted, men's eyes would have followed them everywhere. That would not do in her opinion.

"Then, if you had so wonderful a time we shall make an even greater bequest than I planned," she told them.

"Oh yes, Your Grace. And please mention Sister Celestine for special recognition," Anne de Rohan cried.

"I believe that nuns in convents are not allowed to be singled out, to set one above another," Anne of Brittany pointed out.

"Then would you make your bequest for her to add to the library she is in charge of?"

"She was such a wonderful host and showed us the most interesting book!" Germaine de Foix added.

"Books, you mean." Anne de Candale shoved an elbow into Germaine's side.

"Books. Yes! Please help her build her library so there are even more interesting books there next time we visit," Germaine elbowed Anne de Candale back, followed by a a furious exchange of amused faces and giggling. Meanwhile, the duchess had moved off with two officials in the direction of Mont Dol.

"Your Grace, it is said that here St. Michael fought the devil and won," one of the officials remarked.

"'Tis good to win one's battles over such a one," Anne of Brittany observed, thinking of the endless battles Charles had fought with himself in the final months of his life. He had truly wanted to change; he had in the end. But it had been a struggle, and there were times when Anne wondered if that struggle hadn't worn him out.

"Do you see those striped markings on the cliffs there?" The official pointed to one side of the hill as they began to climb its slope.

"Yes. What are they?"

"Local lore has it that they are markings left by the Evil One's claws." The official crossed himself.

"Oh tell us more. We love local lore!" Anne de Rohan enthused.

"What do you know of local lore, *mes demoiselles?*" The duchess of Brittany eyed them sharply.

"Nothing much. Just what the lovely sister back in St.-Malo shared with us," Anne de Rohan answered, looking rather catlike.

Satisfied with her response, Anne of Brittany turned her back on her high-spirited charges to climb the final steps to the summit. At the top the flat marshy countryside spread out before her.

In the late morning sunlight the bay of Mont-St.-Michel shimmered in the distance like a beckoning jewel. Beyond lay the Mor Breizh, which some called the Channel, the body of water over which Brittany's settlers had traveled from Wales and Cornwall. She drank in the view and knew she would never forget it.

Soon she would return to Nantes and then perhaps to France. But she would hold dear all that she had seen and heard on her Tro Breizh. It was her duty to advance the prosperity of her people, whose ancestors had crossed the Channel to settle here.

She let out a sigh then turned to begin her descent. Her Breton subjects loved her and she loved them. Even were she to wear the crown of Queen of France for a second time, the people of Brittany would remain foremost in her heart.

CHAPTER TEN

Cesare Borgia Delivers

A horrific rainstorm deluged Amboise on the day the annulment was announced.

When word reached the town that surrounded the royal residence of Anne of Brittany and Charles VIII of France for the duration of their marriage, its inhabitants eyed each other and made the sign of the cross, whispering that the heavens had cried for the saintly Jeanne of France on the day she was legally set aside by the new king.

Old gossip bubbled to the surface again, that Anne and Charles had been punished by God with the death of every one of their children because they both had broken their marriage vows to others in order to marry. Had the new king also offended God by putting aside his wife to marry another?

Back in Chinon, Louis paced the floor. The annulment had

come through; thanks be to God for the discovery of the old king's letter to his grand master. The spider king's devilish web had finally become unwound, giving Louis back his life and a chance for happiness, too.

His heart's desire lay due west, only a few days' ride, but he would not go to her until the papal papers were in his hand. Couriers had been sent from Paris to Rome by Georges d'Amboise at the king's pre-arranged request. The dispensation and annulment bull were to be delivered directly to Chinon. Louis envisioned it would take at least two weeks by fast courier.

On the final day of the year, a page burst breathlessly into the great hall of Chinon. "Sire, a party of riders approaches!" he cried, before remembering to bow.

Louis hurried to the window overlooking the town gate. In the valley below, a large group of horsemen approached. As Louis made ready to question his head sentry, the man himself appeared in the doorway.

"Sire, a missive has been delivered, requesting permission to enter Chinon."

Louis took the ornate gold and crimson pouch that lay upon the silver platter the man held out. The pouch was emblazoned with a coat of arms. One side depicted a red bull, the other black and yellow stripes. Underneath were inscribed the Latin words '*Aut Caesar aut nihil.*'

Staring at the words, Louis struggled to make sense of them: "Either a Caesar or nothing." For an instant he was reminded of Anne telling him in Rennes back in 1491 that she would marry no one less than a king. "Either a king or no one," she had declared. He had taken her message to Charles and he had followed through. There was nothing like a woman who knew how to state her mind.

But "Either a Caesar or nothing"? Who would have the

audacity to use such an arrogant motto? Louis tore open the envelope.

'Your Majesty, Louis XII, King of France,
I have what you need. Do you have what I need?
In anticipation of our meeting,
Cesare Borgia,
Servant of His Most High Holiness, Pope Alexander
    VI of Rome'

Louis crumpled the paper into a ball and threw it into the hearth. Never had he imagined that the pope's son himself would deliver the necessary documents.

"Bid them enter!" Louis shouted to the sentry, who hurried from the room.

Louis strode to his personal quarters, calling for his valet to dress him in more formal attire. As he waited, he peered out the window to view the travelers as they approached.

Dozens of riders dressed in lavish splendor from head to toe greeted his eye. Even more astonishing was the attire of the horses they rode. Their mounts were caparisoned with what looked like silver trappings that shone in the sun, dazzling the eye. It might have been the entry of the Ottoman sultan or a Middle-Eastern potentate instead of the illegitimate second son of a pope.

Louis descended to the courtyard, Georges d'Amboise huffing and puffing behind, his well-padded frame no match for the long-legged king.

As the first riders entered the castle courtyard, Louis saw that the horses were shod in silver to match their trappings. Never had he seen such an extravagant sight.

Maintaining a cool demeanor he vowed to pull out all stops

to welcome his unexpected guest, then get rid of him as soon as possible. Never mind the extravagance of the party's appearance; the number of horses and men in the party would cost him a fortune to put up at Chinon. And how was he to address his visitor? Cesare Borgia was no longer a man of the cloth and had never been a nobleman. With what title then was he to address the pope's bastard son?

Stifling a sigh, he readied himself to greet his guest of honor. Already, Louis had agreed to bestow upon the pope's son an annuity of 20,000 écus yearly. And that was in addition to a title, lands, royal subsidy, and a French noblewoman to marry. He reminded himself that he had left behind the frugality of the duke of Orleans to embrace the largesse of the king of France. His soon-to-be wife would show him how. In the meantime he would fake it as best he could. Putting a linen handkerchief to his forehead, he mopped his brow.

Cesare Borgia rode into the courtyard and stopped, remaining on his horse a moment as if to allow all present to admire him. Dressed from head to toe in silver and gold, the young nobody wore headgear sporting gold and crimson feather plumes, adding another three hand-breadths to his youthfully imposing figure.

Louis watched as the pope's son grandly dismounted, the plumes of his headdress appearing to wave to the assembled crowd. Those in the courtyard stood stunned at such a magnificent sight on the final day of a year filled with unexpected events.

The visitor moved regally toward Louis as if he were emperor of Europe.

Louis stifled the laugh he felt welling up inside. Whatever ensued, he must receive the documents from the pope's brat then treat him well before seeing him off. Louis had plans in

Italy and he would need His Holiness's future help to see them come to fruition. Perhaps the ridiculous young man would prove useful as an ally.

God knew he was rumored to be dangerous as a foe. All of Europe had heard stories that the second eldest Borgia son had arranged the murder of his older brother two years earlier. Cesare had not wished for the traditional ecclesiastical path offered to second sons. He had coveted his eldest brother Juan's lands and title, determined to take his place: and so he had.

Louis would proceed with caution.

"Your Majesty, I am your most humble servant," Cesare Borgia greeted him, offering only the most cursory of knee bends. Apparently, the young Italian, half-Spanish on his father's side, was not well versed in court protocol.

"Welcome to the court of France and to Chinon," Louis greeted him in return, omitting any address at all. "Hail Caesar" was definitely out. He eyed the jeweled rings over Borgia's gloves as the strapping young man removed his plumed headdress, which appeared to wave in protest at being lowered from its lofty perch.

"Let us go inside where you and your party will find refreshment," the king suggested.

"And I may give you the important item you have requested from my uncle, His Holiness."

"You are prompt to deliver it, Monsieur." Louis shifted nervously. He required two items from the pope before he could go to Anne. One was the annulment, the other the papal dispensation. Pray God the young tiger cub before him had brought both.

"I am eager to assume my new responsibilities," Borgia said amiably.

"I am sure you are and we shall be pleased to invest you with them." *As soon as you hand over the papers.*

Behind Borgia stood a priest in his party, deep in conversation with Georges d'Amboise.

"Yes, he has them," Louis overheard before leading his guests into the great hall of Chinon castle.

Food and drink was brought as Borgia occupied himself with ogling the noblewomen present, reminding Louis, to his distaste, that he had promised his father to award him with a highborn French bride.

"And so you have something for me," Louis finally said, eager to get the papers into his own hands as quickly as possible.

"Ah yes, Your Majesty. And I understand from my uncle that you have something for me as well." The young Italian's eyes glittered.

Vainglory, ambition, and cunning all swam there in a mix that alarmed Louis; especially as it was packaged in a youth brimming with vitality and charm and untrammeled by the moral trappings of chivalric values. Louis shivered, aware that he did not fully know who he was dealing with; his instincts told him he was dangerous.

"You will receive the title of Duke of Valentinois, as well as income from two deeded estates, when I receive what you have brought me from His Holiness." As unholy a pope as ever there was, he thought, but in the circumstances it had been a good thing that the highest representative of the church on Earth had been open to suggestion in order to grant the annulment Louis sought.

"Remind me, Your Majesty, of the income that entails." Borgia's expression was smug, astonishingly self-confident in light of his youth and lack of background.

"Twenty-thousand écus yearly." Louis squirmed inside with distaste. Here he was, talking like a shopkeeper with a youth from the street who didn't know any better. The world had shifted and Louis hadn't yet found his bearings in the new order of things, largely streaming out of Italy.

Like Charles before him, he couldn't help being drawn to the wonders of the boot-shaped peninsula. But danger lurked there, too: popes who fathered children, beautiful women who shared ugly diseases with their lovers, and sophisticated poisons traceable to no one that ended the lives of hapless souls

"Ahh, my dear uncle, His Holiness, had mentioned a figure of forty-thousand écus now that I recall."

"You will receive in addition a royal subsidy of twenty-thousand, bringing the figure to the one His Holiness your uncle referred to." Uncle, God's breath. No one but a father would have fought as hard as the pope had for favorable terms for his unsettled son. And what a son this was, bargaining like the shrewdest of merchants at an age barely older than that of Louis' intended bride.

"And what of the princess I have been promised in marriage?" Borgia gazed around the room, apparently not finding any female present quite what he had in mind.

"As I told your uncle, I cannot bind and hand over any candidate of your choosing, but we will look for a maiden of the court to your liking, who may agree to become your bride."

"I had in mind the princess of Naples. Is she here?"

"She is not here, but she will be consulted." Charlotte of Naples was one of the most refined maids of honor at Anne's court, now in Nantes. He couldn't imagine her accepting this young valiant from the streets of Rome as a husband, but he would leave the affair to Anne to manage. Matchmaking was not his forte.

"I should like to consult with her in person." Cesare Borgia pressed his point, unaware that it was not a courtier's place to argue with a monarch.

"It is our custom in France to consult with the parents of the maiden in question before an introduction is made. My intended wife will see to it that you wed the Frenchwoman of your dreams as soon as you deliver the papal papers."

"Papers? I have only one paper." Borgia pulled out a rolled-up parchment bound with a silken cord. At its end dangled the wax imprint of the papal emblem.

Inside, Louis froze. Trying not to show surprise, he took the rolled up parchment, opened it, and read the short statement of annulment with a wax imprint of the pope's signet ring stamp below his signature.

"And the dispensation?"

"The dispensation will come shortly."

"What do you mean by shortly? Have you not both documents in your possession now?" Icy fury gripped Louis' insides. Who did this arrogant youth think he was, withholding the document upon which hung Louis' plan to wed his *Brette* as soon as possible?

"Upon my introduction to the princess Charlotte of Naples."

"There will be no introduction until I hold the dispensation for my marriage to the duchess of Brittany in my hands. The princess of Naples is a member of her court and under her protection. I can do nothing further for you until the duchess of Brittany is my wife." Louis raised his voice so that it could be heard by all in the room. "Now, where is the dispensation?"

"Your Majesty, I have it here." A priest from Borgia's party stepped forward, a scroll in his hand.

As Louis took it from him, Borgia scowled fiercely at the man. The priest recoiled at the sight of the displeasure on his patron's face.

"And my red cardinal's hat has arrived, too," Georges

d'Amboise added, coming forward to stand between the priest and Borgia, who was staring at his underling as if he would eat him for dinner.

"I am happy for you, Georges," Louis remarked as he unrolled the second document. Silently, he exhaled. Indeed, it was the dispensation, granting him permission to marry Anne. Relieved to have both documents in his possession he wondered at the wiles of the peacock-like man standing before him, as filled with pride and self-importance as any prince of the blood might be. Louis had never comported himself in such a way, but he had not needed to prove himself, having been born into the lesser Orléans line of France's most noble house of Valois.

Eying the young Cesare it occurred to Louis that this youth had everything to prove, as well as the natural intelligence and powerful backing with which to do it. He would need to keep a close eye on this unpredictable new player on Europe's stage.

"Rest now and we shall meet again at dinner where I will invest you as duke of Valentinois before my court," the king said.

"So be it, Sire. I look forward to dining with the king of France."

"As I look forward to dining with the new duke of Valentinois."

Cesare Borgia bent a knee, somewhat more deeply than before, and left the room. Louis watched as he paused at the doorway to hiss something into the ear of the priest who had handed him the dispensation.

The priest's shoulders drooped as he mumbled something back. Whatever trick the pope's bastard son had intended to play by withholding the dispensation had been spoiled by the honesty of the upright man of the cloth.

Louis shuddered. He would not wish to be in the position of displeasing the young man the pope in Rome had sent to him. He would have Georges order the priest back to Avignon to get him away from Borgia as soon as possible.

The next few days passed in a blur of hunting, entertainments, and banqueting. Louis refrained from organizing a tourney, as he doubted the young Cesare had been trained in knightly skills. He feared the young man might go at a jousting opponent with the aim to harm him, not simply to unseat him, unschooled as he was in chivalric rules of engagement.

On the third day of his visit, with the new duke of Valentinois showing no signs of leaving, Louis let his guest know that he had business in Nantes.

"Perhaps you would like to visit your lands," the king suggested, at wits' end to get rid of him.

"I am in no hurry, Your Majesty. It is pleasant enough here and the company is sweet." He glanced in the direction of a gaggle of noblewomen. The older ones disdained him, but one or two of the young maidens, not yet fully aware of the importance of background, returned his smiles with their own.

"Then by all means, stay and enjoy my wine cellars and hunting forests," Louis urged disingenuously. He was fast learning the endless feints and dissimulations it took to effectively rule.

"You are altogether too kind, Sire. My uncle and I will not forget your welcome when you visit us in Italy."

Precisely the point, thought Louis, as he beamed at the young man determined to carve out his own position in life at the highest level possible. Could he blame him? He laid a hand on the strapping Borgia's shoulder and told him to enjoy his stay for as long as he wished until his new duties in Valentinois called him there.

Early the next morning, the king and his party gathered in the courtyard to ride out to Nantes. He had hoped to avoid his cocky guest altogether, but the young man hurried down the steps and rushed to Louis' side.

"Please let the princess of Naples know I send my warmest regards," he pressed the king.

"If I see her, I will pass on your message," Louis answered, thinking that Charlotte of Naples would refuse the regards of any man from common stock, never mind one who showed no sign of understanding how France's social order worked. The princess' hereditary title traced through her father, Frederick of Naples, but Charlotte herself was French-born and raised, the great granddaughter of Charles VII of France through her mother, Anne of Savoy. She would not suffer the aspirations of a man of no background, however handsome or ambitious he was.

Cesare embraced the king, a gesture unheard of at court between a commoner and a monarch. As Louis suffered the indignity, his senses assaulted by an unwelcome strong male scent mixed with spiced perfume, his eyes caught Georges d'Amboise behind Borgia receiving a note from the head steward of Chinon.

The king and his party rode out into the clear, not overly-cold January day. As Louis sank into the rhythm of his mount, he berated himself for thinking ill of such a determined young man. Perhaps he had misjudged him. Coming from a different land and culture, with both Italian and Spanish blood running through his veins, Louis could not place the young Borgia in the social order with the same expertise that the French nobility used to size each other up.

"A word, Sire?" d'Amboise broke into his thoughts, his horse coming up alongside the king.

"Georges, is it not a fine day—what is it, man?" Louis broke off, startled by the grim look on his friend's face.

"Some news, Sire, from the steward back in Chinon."

"Speak, man. Is there a problem?"

"A discovery made this morning."

"What happened?"

"The priest, Sire—the one who accompanied the duke of Valentinois from Avignon."

"What of him?" Louis peered into his friend's eyes. They were troubled.

"He is no more, Sire."

"What do you mean?"

"The valet assigned to our guests found him this morning in his bed, unconscious."

"What happened?"

"The court doctor was called, but it was too late. The steward said black foam ran from his mouth; his body was rigid."

"Did the doctor know what it was?"

"He suspects poison, Sire, although he could not say for sure." Georges' voice was a whisper. "The doctor served under the former king in Italy. He had seen such cases there. "

Louis locked eyes with his friend. "Are your thoughts mine?"

"I'm afraid so, Sire."

"Let us not delay in getting our guest fully occupied with the administration of his own lands."

"Shall I write to the bishop in Avignon to let him know what happened?"

Louis shook his head. "Have the steward back in Chinon send word to Avignon. Tell him to say the king's party was already gone when His Majesty was told." Louis shook his head in the cool morning air. "Let us clear our heads of the detritus left in them from our unusual houseguest." *Dangerous, too.*

"Your Majesty, he is one we must watch closely while he tarries in France."

"Then I task you with the job of arranging his return to Italy soon."

"He won't go until he has gotten what he came here for."

"He has his title, his lands. See to it that the first annuity payment is sent to him."

"His wife, Sire. We will not be rid of him until he has been given the highest born princess we can find."

Louis shuddered. How could he in good faith arrange a match between such a cold-blooded killer and any fair young flower of France or Brittany? If the Borgia had his own brother murdered for standing in his way, and his priest poisoned for spoiling a trick he had intended to play, what would he do to a wife the first time she displeased him?

Louis rubbed his forehead with his hand, suddenly tired although the day was fresh. God save him from having to arrange a bride for such a man. He would turn over the whole affair to Anne and let her decide who amongst her maids of honor would make a good choice. He had a sense it would not be Charlotte of Naples. The princess of Naples and Aragon was too fine a bloom to be sacrificed to a man as ruthless as the new duke of Valentinois.

CHAPTER ELEVEN

December 1498

Advent in Brittany

C hristmas had been sweet. It had been sweet the year before, too, under completely different circumstances. She had been with child, and Charles had finally turned a corner and reformed his ways. Who would think that, just one year later, her entire life would have changed? It was scarcely imaginable that she was now preparing to marry the man who had captured her heart as a young girl.

Sweetest of all was that she was reunited with her people, at home in the ancestral palace where she had been born in January 1477. Soon she would be twenty-two, ready to take on the world. Frankly, she already was.

The dispatch from Louis had arrived the afternoon of December eighteenth. Couriers had ridden for two days and nights from Chinon to Nantes to deliver the king's Christmas gift to her.

'My esteemed duchess and beloved *Brette*,' it had begun. Anne's heart beat faster at Louis' intimate tone. She blushed and turned away from Madame de Dinan and the others to savor her suitor's news in private.

'The court has ruled in my favor, and the annulment will be granted. I will set out for Nantes the moment I have the pope's bull in hand, as well as the dispensation for our marriage. Prepare now, my heart's desire, to celebrate the new year together with whatever wedding ceremony pleases you most. For me it is all the same, for all I want is you. No greater joy has ever come to me, including becoming king, than to make you my wife and queen. Louis.'

Anne's heart swelled. But her head swam with plans. This time things would be different. She would not make the same mistake she had with Charles by relinquishing control over her lands. She had been in no position to argue, although she had. But Charles had insisted on administering her duchy over the course of their six years together. She had had little choice in the matter, as the terms of their marriage contract had stated that he and she were to hold co-rulership over Brittany. She had married him as a vanquished ruler in December 1491. Her country overrun by French troops, reduced to rubble and starvation by endless war with France, her situation had been desperate.

This time would be different. She would not be traveling to France to be married as a war bride, a supreme spoils-of-war.

Louis would travel to her and they would marry in her own lands. More to the point, they would not marry at all unless they both agreed to a contract which ensured her sole control over her duchy.

Anne clapped her hands in delight. Thank God Louis wasn't there. If he were, he would distract her from careful drafting of their marriage contract. Above all, she needed to ensure that her duchy remained independent from France.

Once Louis showed up it would seem that he was putty in her hands, but in her heart she knew she would also be putty in his. The king of France had been her very first crush, the handsome and refined duke of Orléans who had left an indelible impression on her from the moment she had met him as a child. A frisson ran through her as she imagined finally being in his arms.

"Prepare my writing table and implements," she bade an attendant then turned to Madame de Dinan. "Summon Sire de Montauban and tell him to bring my notary. We have business to attend to."

"My lady, will you share your news from Paris?"

"Read my face, old friend, and tell me yourself what your guess is."

"The annulment has come through?" Madame de Dinan's eyes widened.

"The king will come to me as soon as the documents arrive from Rome."

"My duchess, congratulations!" Her old tutor's eyes sparkled. Knowing her sovereign as well as she did, she couldn't see Anne as anything less than a queen.

"No congratulations yet, Madame. Wait until there is a reason."

"But you will be queen of France once more!"

"Will I?" Anne gave her a shrewd look. "That depends on the king."

"Of course the king will crown you queen. He is mad about you, as anyone with eyes can see," Madame de Dinan sang out, her face beaming.

"Yes. But if he does not succeed in making me his wife, he cannot make me his queen."

"My lady, what do you say? Why should he not succeed in making you his wife? Do you not love him with all your heart?'"

"I love him as much as I love my country. And if he agrees to allow me to continue as sole ruler of Brittany, I will agree to become his wife."

"And if not?"

"I will refuse his offer."

"My lady! You would refuse the chance to become queen of France again?"

"If it means no longer ruling over my own country, then yes." Her firm tone hid her true feelings. She hoped not to be put to the test of her ultimatum. But if she was, she knew which she would choose.

"But will the king allow you to administer your own lands? Remember the late king ..." Madame de Dinan crossed herself at the mention of Charles VIII. Less than a year since his death, they were still in mourning.

"I will never forget him, God rest his soul. He did not allow me to administer Brittany, and I was not in a position to object."

"And this time, my lady?"

Anne's smile was as sweet as it was astute.

"This time I will prepare the marriage contract myself, with the help of Sire de Montauban."

"My lady, I can imagine what your terms might be." Inwardly, the older woman rolled her eyes. The king of France would be lucky if Anne allowed him any say in anything at all.

"Yes. And to get them down on paper precisely and fully, I need to begin drafting it now."

"I will go find Sire de Montauban."

"And don't forget the notary."

"Yes, Your Grace. Right away." Madame de Dinan curtseyed and swept from the room.

Looking out the window into the vast courtyard of the chateau of the dukes of Brittany, Anne laughed for joy. All was in order. She was a woman in love, as well as ruler of her own lands. For her to fully give her heart to Louis, she first must use her head to hammer out terms that would satisfy her sovereign mandate.

Louis would understand. He had been close friends with her father and would know how important it was for her as his successor to carry out his charge to maintain Brittany's independence.

"My lady-duchess, I hear good news comes from Paris." Philippe de Montauban bent his knee then rose, smiling broadly at his sovereign.

"The king has cleared his final hurdle, and if I can clear mine then good news indeed."

"And what is your final hurdle, Your Grace?"

"It is that I will not marry him unless the marriage contract states that I am to enjoy full and sole sovereignty over Brittany, as I do now."

De Montauban sucked in his breath. The girl he had protected at age eleven had grown into a magnificent woman, fully capable of ruling over her lands as well as the king of France's heart. He didn't doubt that the king would sign whatever she put before him in order to marry her. But his advisors would balk at overly onerous terms, so the contract needed to be drafted well.

"Then let us draw up the contract now, so that when he arrives it is ready for him," he said.

"Precisely, Monsieur. It will be another two weeks before he gets here, so let us take our time and ensure that this contract includes more favorable terms than the one I signed with the former king did."

"Madame, you may be sure of it!"

"I will. Or I will not sign."

"Shall I call in your other advisors to begin on it?"

"No. Let us review my old contract with Charles. We can go over it point by point, then correct it."

"As I recall, it was the present king of France who drafted your previous marriage contract."

Anne's laugh rippled through the air. To hear her sound so joyful after all the deaths she had suffered in her young life made de Montauban's heart swell.

"Indeed, he will be familiar with the text." Anne's tone was merry. "Who knows? Perhaps he won't even read it, knowing it as well as he does, and will just skip to the end and sign."

"I'm afraid his counselors will read every word, so let us ensure that all is in order and completely reasonable."

"Am I not always completely reasonable, Monsieur?"

Sire de Montauban cleared his throat then raised his eyes Heavenward for inspiration as to how to answer. It would not do to flatter his sovereign, whom he had protected and advised from the moment she had taken the reins of her duchy upon her father's death in 1488. She had been eleven years old at the time. He knew her too well to think that she would be pleased with a courtier's fawning assent.

"My lady, may I say that you are the most reasonable of women when you are on the path to getting what you want." *And the most stubborn of mules when you are not.*

"Why should I not get what I want in this situation, Philippe?"

Ah, she had dropped her formality. It was a good sign for him to continue in all frankness.

"You should, *ma duchesse*. You are now in a position to receive the terms you ask for, unlike before, when French troops invaded our land and the king could as well have made you his prisoner rather than his wife."

"I would have made a very bad prisoner."

"Madame, no doubt you would." De Montauban turned his head slightly to hide his grin. God's bells, what a demanding prisoner she would have made. Any jailer charged with guarding her would have been outwitted by her before the end of his first day of duty.

"Louis, on the other hand, likely made a good prisoner." Anne wondered at those three lost years of her dear friend's life. She remembered well how magnificent Louis had been as the young duke d'Orléans. With long limbs and an extraordinary athleticism, he was further gifted with a handsome chiseled face, strong jaw, and straight nose, somewhat long as was typical of the House of Valois. How had such an active and athletic man survived three years of imprisonment at the peak of his manhood?

"Madame, he chafed at the bit." De Montauban had heard that it had been Charles, Anne's late husband, who had sprung Louis, at the pleading of his middle sister, Jeanne, that unfortunate creature whom the king of France had just set aside. He could well imagine how guilty the king must feel that Advent season to have cast aside a wife of twenty-two years who had been responsible for his release from prison, restoring his life to him.

"So he must have." Remembering her wedding to Charles,

Anne thought of how much Louis had changed when he had parlayed with her in Rennes in November of 1491 to make the case for peace with France by marrying his brother-in-law, its king.

The duke d'Orléans had still been handsome, witty, and debonair. But there had been a sadness to his countenance, a droop to his eyelids that hinted to Anne of unknown horrors he had escaped, but which had left an imprint on his soul. He had only been twenty-nine when she had married Charles. But Louis, at times had worn the careworn expression of one far older in years.

When he had danced with her at her wedding reception, she had longed to reach out and smooth away the premature furrows that ran down each side of his face. Now, seven years later, she planned to do exactly that in a few short weeks.

"Have you thought of what the points are that you wish to modify in this new contract?" De Montauban eyed his duchess.

"What do you think, Philippe?"

"I'm sure you have, Your Grace. How many, and what are they?"

"There are two. The first is that it is to be fully spelled out that I am to continue sole reign over my duchy, which is to remain independent from France."

"Although in vassal status."

"But as the ancestral dukes of Brittany have never done, neither will we bend the knee nor kiss the ring of the king of France." Anne referred to the ancient custom of the dukes of Brittany who had greeted the king of France standing, with sword at side, and not on bended knee as had rulers of other vassal territories to France.

"Indeed not, Your Grace." Soon enough, his sovereign duchess would be kissing most other parts of France's king, but that was between him and her and not between France and Brittany.

"The second is the point that I had wanted inserted in my contract with Charles, but which never was."

"My lady?"

"About the succession. I want my duchy to go to our second prince, should we have more than one, not to the dauphin."

"And should no princes be forthcoming?"

"Then to my eldest daughter or whichever daughter I choose, so long as she does not become the wife of the next king of France."

"Should you not have sons."

"Yes." God, if only she and Louis could have sons. Many of them. Had she truly left behind the horrors of her childbearing losses with Charles? Soon enough she would know if the reason for their deaths lay with her or with her dead husband. The late king of France had been rumored to have been sickly. With a short, misshapen body, he had been far from handsome. But she had loved him for his chivalric nature and his desire to better himself.

With Louis, she would have a far easier time desiring him, with his comely face and fine physique. But most of all, she would love him for his adoration of her. Finally, she would be the consort of a man whose love for her burned as brightly as her father's had.

A quiver of anticipation ran up her spine as she contemplated how different her future with Louis would be from her past with Charles. Louis commanded admiration, unlike Charles, who had had to work hard to earn it. Louis, on the other hand, possessed a natural nobility in his graceful carriage, with his long lithe legs, charming conversation, and refined tastes.

Stifling a smile at the thought of him, her heart danced. Finally, she would have a true peer at her side. Now, if only she could beget an heir.

CHAPTER TWELVE

January 1499

Wedding in Nantes

Louis' party clattered into the courtyard of Anne's ancestral home. They had ridden hard from Chinon, the typically two and a half days' journey taking them just under two.

How vividly he remembered the times he had visited the vast castle of the dukes of Brittany. He had been awestruck the first time he had crossed the three-spanned bridge over its moat, then ridden under its raised portcullis in 1484 at age twenty-one.

Seven seven-story towers punctuated the white limestone walls of the enormous castle, easily dwarfing Louis' own ancestral home back in Blois. Duke Francis II had stood in the courtyard, greeting him with a refined charm that told Louis he was in the company of a kindred spirit.

At dinner that evening, the duke's daughter had descended the grand staircase to be introduced to him. With her amethyst purple gown billowing out behind her, the little girl had descended slowly with head held high, her gaze fixed at a point just above the heads of the guests gathered in the great hall below. At the age of seven, the duke's elder daughter had possessed all the gravitas and refinement of a grown woman.

"My wife and younger daughter will not be joining us. They are both indisposed. But may I present my eldest daughter, Anne?" Duke Francis' eyes shone with pride.

As the tiny princess made a deep and unhurried curtsey, Louis marveled at the young girl's self-possession. Then Anne lifted her eyes to him and for one startling moment the duke of Orléans, one of France's most suave young princes of the blood, lost every ounce of his own self-possession.

Deep-violet eyes fringed by thick lashes studied him. He felt as if he were being assessed by a mature woman, as stunningly beautiful as she was royal.

Sucking in his breath, he bent over the princess Anne's extended hand and kissed it with all the dignity he felt the little figure before him required.

"*Mademoiselle la princesse*, I am deeply honored to meet you."

"I, too, Monsieur," she stated simply, her serious eyes evaluating him. As she turned he realized they were not violet, but a clear and lucid gray.

All he could think of for the duration of the dinner was how to coax a smile or giggle from the rosebud mouth of the grave young girl seated across from him.

It took him until the end of the following day and only after great effort. He had finally pulled out all stops and sung the refrain of a bawdy Breton sailors' song, the only one he knew.

It was highly inappropriate, but with a meaning that would be missed by a child.

For his pains, the princess Anne indulged him with the ghost of a smile.

By the end of two days, he had succeeded in eliciting a giggle from her, and by the third day, if he was not dreaming, he thought he detected a growing warmth from the regal tiny princess.

Now he was again in the same home where he had experienced such exhilaration and happiness. But where was his intended bride?

A party of attendants stood in the courtyard, a few noblemen scattered among them. Brittany's chancellor, Philippe de Montauban, stepped forward.

"Your Majesty, welcome to Nantes."

"Thank you, Sire de Montauban. I had rather hoped to be greeted by my host, but perhaps that was too much to ask," Louis joked, tossing his reins to his squire.

"Your Majesty, the duchess of Brittany awaits you inside. She is mourning the loss of her companion, Madame de Dinan, who passed into eternal rest just a few days ago."

"Ahh. I am grieved to hear this." Louis' heart rushed toward Anne. She would be distraught to have lost her lifelong companion. Thank God he was there to comfort her. God knew his *Brette* had suffered enough loss in the past twelve months.

"She died peacefully, Sire. But it is a great blow to the duchess, and—"

"Take me to her." Under his riding cape Louis smoothed down his doublet. Anne was fastidious. She would not wish to receive a dusty, tired man straight from the roads. But he sensed that she needed him urgently in the wake of her loss.

Hurrying up one of the two grand staircases, Louis admired

the castle's opulent gothic style. Unapologetically grand, there were no pretensions to modesty in this edifice erected for the use of Brittany's ancestral leaders. His future wife, if she would have him, had been raised in sumptuous style; he intended to keep her there. Not being a sumptuous sort, himself, he had no idea how, but he was certain his *Brette* would direct him. For her and her alone, he would find it within himself to spend freely. It was the only way she knew how to be, and Louis had admired her firm nature long enough to know he would never change her.

Philippe de Montauban hurried down the grand passage-way, but Louis overtook him with his long strides. Putting a hand on his shoulder, he stopped the chancellor.

"Monsieur, allow me to announce my own entrance."

"Your Majesty, the duchess is one for protocol; I will announce you."

"Sire de Montauban, she knows my arrival is imminent. Grant me the favor of being first to discern her expression when she spots me."

De Montauban locked eyes with the king. "Sire, your request is a command in France, but this is Brittany."

"Know that I would never command one so senior as my duchess' chancellor." Louis smiled warmly at de Montauban. The man was one of Anne's closest and most long-time friends. Louis both liked and respected him; he had been a strong friend and protector of the duchess since her father's death. "I ask you as a man pressing my suit to let me find my way to her privately, so that I may have the favor of seeing her face the moment she sees me."

"Your Majesty may assume her reaction will be favorable." De Montauban's mouth twitched.

"I should like to judge for myself."

"Sire, I cannot deny you such a request." De Montauban

grinned and pointed down the hall to the room where the duchess could be found.

"Good man." Louis whipped off his dusty riding mantle and handed it to the chancellor with a clap on the back, then strode toward the doorway.

As he entered the room, Anne looked up. Her face was as somber as the stark black velvet gown she wore. A black head-dress covered her dark-auburn hair except where her widow's peak showed. Surrounded by her ladies in waiting, a deep still-ness cloaked the room.

His heart contracting, he rushed toward her then fell to one knee.

"Louis! No need for all that." She touched his shoulder with her hand, its warmth igniting him.

He grasped it, kissing it reverently, and placed it on his forehead. Inside his doublet he felt the hard scroll of the annul-ment document against his chest.

"My duchess, my heart grieves to hear you have lost your dear Françoise."

"Oh, Louis." Anne's head went to his shoulder.

He embraced her, oblivious to the attendants present. God, how good it felt to be needed by her.

"My dear, you are no longer alone."

"That is just how I've felt." Her muffled voice vibrated against the crook of his shoulder.

He pressed her tighter to him. The only woman who would have objected to such familiarity was now gone. But Françoise de Dinan had done her job well, and within seconds Anne re-covered the self-possession she was known for.

Drawing back, she gazed at him through her tears.

"Was she in pain?" he asked gently.

"No." Anne shook her head, her lips drawn into a tight

smile. "She died in her sleep and when I saw her in final rest she was at peace, her face content."

"She had much to be proud of, *ma duchesse*. You are her finest work."

"Do you remember, Louis, when Sire de Dunois died on the way to Langeais all those years ago?"

"How could I forget?"

"He, too, knew he had done his job well."

"His soul was ready to rest."

"Exactly as my dear companion felt."

Louis' heart leapt to hear her draw such a parallel. The count de Dunois had made it his final project to see the duchess of Brittany marry the king of France. So, too, it appeared that Françoise de Dinan had labored to see her duchess marry another king of France. Himself.

"My dearest *duchesse*, I have here something I hope will please you."

Anne smiled, saying nothing. She gestured to an attendant to draw up a chair and table so Louis, King of France and a peer, could take a seat beside her.

Pulling out the document from his doublet, he unrolled the parchment and lay it flat on the table. Anne placed a marble paperweight on one end as Louis held the other.

Carefully, she read the Latin words. Thanks to Madame de Dinan's tutelage, she had studied the language thoroughly enough to make out the two reasons given for the annulment: lack of consent and lack of marital relations.

The former she knew was true; the latter might not be, but with the old king, Charles' father, the cruel Louis XI, overseeing the union, she knew Louis would have had no choice in the matter. Well aware of what it was to make hard choices, Anne knew no ruler escaped having to make them. Her own had been to break off her proxy marriage to the archduke of Austria to marry Charles, allowing him co-rights over her duchy. Both actions had made her conscience squirm.

Now Louis would have to live with his own troubled conscience. Such was the fate of rulers faced with difficult choices. How wonderful it would be to have a peer to share such burdens with once more.

"Have I not kept my promise, *ma duchesse?*" Louis asked, his voice low as his eyes searched hers.

"And the dispensation?"

"Here." Louis drew out the other document.

"And have you considered the draft of the contract I sent you?"

"I have, *duchesse.* I have considered all."

"And are you satisfied?"

"I will only be satisfied if my future wife is satisfied with the terms of our marriage."

"You know that my sole and sovereign leadership of my country is my requirement." Her clear gray eyes bored into his. This time, she was no longer desperate. No mistakes in the wording of the marriage contract had been made. Not only had her father and mother frequently observed, but Madame de Dinan as well, Anne's head ruled her heart. She loved Louis. But she was not willing to lose control of her country for the sake of becoming his wife.

"You are your father's daughter, Anne. You will not be satisfied unless you are able to carry out the mandate with which he entrusted you," Louis observed, taking her hand.

"That is true." How good of Louis to point it out, instead of her.

"I know it is. And I will not be satisfied until my *Brette* becomes my queen."

"Then if you sign, I will say yes." She peered at him from under a thick forest of lashes; already he was lost in them. "Where's the pen?"

On the afternoon of January 8, 1499, Louis XII, King of France, entered the great hall of the chateau of the dukes of Nantes. Georges d'Amboise followed behind, newly minted as cardinal of Rouen since receiving his cardinal's hat from Cesare Borgia just weeks earlier.

The king of France strode the length of the hall and took a seat on the raised dais at the far end. A deep blue canopy enveloped it, embroidered with four royal coats of arms. Two represented France and two represented Brittany.

What was about to take place would be a marriage of equals. And although it would be the uniting of two hearts, it would not be the uniting of two countries. Every bit of decor and symbolism surrounding their wedding ceremony attested to the new politique they would bring to their union, different from the one Anne had had with Charles.

Anne, Duchess of Brittany, and Louis XII, King of France, would enter into a separate but equal union. It suited both of them.

In point of fact, the duchess of Brittany had ruled over her own lands longer than Louis had ruled over France. Already he was learning from her the power of pageantry, something to which he had never paid much attention. He had taken the utmost care to have the blue canopy draping the dais bear the coats of arms of both countries: gold fleur-de-lis on a royal blue background for France; black ermine tails on a white background for Brittany.

When his bride appeared in the doorway, he hoped she would be pleased. He knew that all present would report to the four corners of both France and Brittany that the king had received his bride under the escutcheons of both countries, equal in size.

But where was she?

At that moment, a stir swept the room. All eyes turned to the door.

There stood Anne de Dreux-Montfort, Duchess of Brittany and former Queen of France. In a damask gown of blue and gold she moved gracefully into the room, as regal and as radiant as she had ever looked to Louis. Seven years earlier in France, he had witnessed her make her entrance into the great hall of Langeais on the day she married Charles. Today she looked even more beautiful and more in command of herself.

This time the royal bride would not marry in a foreign country but in her own lands, in the castle in which she had been born. She had let Louis know she would marry him only on her own terms and in her own lands. He had willingly conceded. What did he care where they married or what the details were? All he cared was that they marry, so that finally he could know the joys and comforts of making a life with the woman he loved.

As the duchess of Brittany made her way toward him, Louis' heart swelled. What was it about this diminutive woman that proved larger than life? She had led her own father around by his bejeweled little finger. She had captured Charles VIII of France's heart from the moment he first laid eyes on her. As for Louis?

It was the same. Rarely did a queen exercise authority in her own right, but the duchess of Brittany had exercised it every day of her six and a half years as queen of France. Louis guessed it was because she had been raised to assume the mantle of leadership: first as her father's companion after her mother had died, then as his successor, when Anne was eleven. Once she ascended the throne of France, she had taught Charles how to behave like a king. God knew no one else had, least of all that other commanding figure in his life, his eldest sister.

A shadow slid over Louis' heart as he pushed away memories of Anne de Beaujeu. She had pursued him for years. Ultimately, she imprisoned his body when she realized she would never capture his heart.

He shook off his thoughts. No dark clouds would sully this day for him. He had waited thirty-six years for happiness. The woman walking toward him was on her way to deliver it to him. His heart belonged to her and her alone.

Anne looked up at Louis as they stood before the altar. A frisson swept through her as she thought of how different this wedding day was from her first. This time she was marrying a man she had known and admired since childhood, both handsome of face and graceful of figure. The only mark of his age were the deep furrows running down either side of his nose, from nostril to mouth.

Louis was thirty six years old. Along with her marriage vows, Anne vowed secretly to herself that she would do all within her power to soften her new husband's furrows and see to it that they deepened only from the passing of years and not due to pain.

The cardinal de Rouen cleared his throat to get the bride and groom's attention. They appeared to be lost in each other. Sprinkling each with holy water, his eyes twinkled as he met those of the king.

Anne's heart warmed. She was happy for Louis that his best friend was there to play a role in officiating their union. God knew Louis had given her free rein to decide every other detail of the ceremony. At the very least, her husband should have a close friend play a role in the history they were about to make that day for both Brittany and France.

As the cardinal de Rouen stepped back Jean d'Espinay, the bishop of Nantes, stepped forward. His father had been chamberlain to Anne's father. Both Anne and Louis felt Duke Francis' presence there with them, offering his blessing and joking that it was about time they had finally found their way to each other.

The bishop held high a simple gold ring and blessed it, then handed it to Louis.

"In the name of the Father," the bishop intoned and Louis repeated as he placed the ring on Anne's thumb.

"In the name of the Son," the bishop continued as Louis removed the ring from her thumb and slipped it onto her index finger.

"In the name of the Holy Spirit," the bishop continued as Louis took the ring off Anne's index finger and put it on her middle one.

"I marry you, wife," the bishop prompted him. Louis removed the ring from Anne's middle finger and slipped it onto her ring finger. "I marry you, wife," he pronounced in a clear, firm voice.

Anne gazed straight into Louis' eyes and smiled. "I marry you, husband," she said back to him, in a voice as clear as his.

The bishop of Nantes took their hands and blessed them as the cardinal of Rouen held a veil over their heads, cloaking them together for all eternity.

Mass was said, then the cardinal of Rouen raised one arm to bless the couple with a final benediction.

It was done.

"*Ma Brette*, are you happy?" Seated next to her at the wedding banquet table, Louis' eyes sought hers. Large and heavy-lidded, warmth poured out of them, making Anne feel as if spring had begun that day despite the January chill.

"I am happy to be sole ruler of my country again. And I am happy to be your wife for the first time, my lord." A current ran up her insides, from the pit of her stomach to her throat. The valiant chevalier she had admired for almost all her life was now her husband. Thoughts she had forever batted away she could now indulge.

"As I am happy to be husband for the first time to a woman I adore." His voice low, he leaned in toward her.

"And as I am happy to be wife for the first time to a man it will be easy to love," she whispered back, breathing in the cloves and lavender that mingled with his musky male scent. Under her gold-threaded snood, the hairs on the back of her neck stood up.

"What if I prove difficult?" Louis' eyes twinkled.

"Louis, I have known you far too long for you to give me a problem." Her confident tone masked a growing awareness of just how little she knew Louis in ways that had been whispered about by women in the kitchen and laundry rooms, as well as among ladies of the court. Women had found Louis d'Orléans irresistible in his younger days. Would she feel the same way that night?

"And I have known you long enough to know that you will always endeavor to get your way." Louis' smile was forgiving, like a doting father to a favorite daughter.

"My lord, it is good to be understood." Her father had adored her. She was used to being that indulged daughter. How very well that dynamic would work for her in her new marriage to a man fifteen years her senior who had been witness to the esteem in which her father had held her.

Louis placed a hand on her thigh under the table.

"I am eager to understand you further." His eyes narrowed, the heavy lids half closing.

"Soon you will, my lord." How sweet it would be to pass her first night as wife to the man of her dreams within the walls of the home in which she was born.

"I enjoyed so many gay times here with your father."

"And with Isabeau and me, Louis."

"It took me two full days to coax a smile from you, *ma Brette*." Louis' laugh was throaty. Hidden from sight, his hand traveled to her waist; he squeezed tightly.

"Such a man as you receives smiles from the ladies far too easily." Anne pried off his hand under the table.

"And so you challenged me."

"I considered it my duty, lest you become spoiled."

"Dear one, life has far from spoiled me." Louis' eyes dimmed as the furrows in his face deepened.

Her heart contracting, Anne lifted her hand to his face. With one finger she traced one of the lines that ran from nostril to mouth. "Nay, Louis, all that is changed now."

"Will you spoil me now, little one?" He grasped her wrist.

"'Tis my duty as your wife, my lord." *After I have bent you to my will.*

"Lady, when may we retire from our wedding table?"

"When I say so." Impishly, Anne smiled at him. Then her heart twinged at the thought that her dear Madame de Dinan would not be ushering her to her wedding night bedchamber, offering advice and support as she had done so ably on the night she married Charles seven years earlier.

"Then say so now, *ma Brette*." Louis' voice was barely a whisper as he brought his face to hers.

Locking eyes with him, Anne pushed him away. *Entice then deny.*

Turning, she raised a finger to her closest lady-in-waiting. After some whispered instructions, she rose and leaned toward Louis' ear.

"Give me an hour, then find me in my bedchamber."

"My lady, it will be an hour too long."

With one final liquid velvet gaze into his eyes, she turned and swept from the banquet hall.

As Anne and her attendants glided down the corridor to her quarters, she thought of the advice her beloved tutor had given her on her wedding night with Charles.

Seven years later, she was far less in need of advice. Not only did she know and enjoy the hidden pleasures of husband and wife, but she looked forward to discovering the lines of her husband's lithe, athletic body. That night she would not extinguish the candles, as Charles had ever been quick to do, self-conscious about his ugly face and form.

She floated into her bedchamber, anticipation coursing through her. That night she would see the entirety of the man she had admired from childhood. He had been magnificent then. He was both magnificent and seasoned now, no stranger to suffering and eager to suffer no more. She would endeavor to see that he did not.

"My lady, you look like a young maid." Her senior lady-in-waiting broke into her thoughts as she removed the gold mesh snood that had bound Anne's hair for the wedding ceremony.

"Ah, but I don't feel like one." Anne grinned mischievously.

The tinkle of her lady-in-waiting's laugh brought the attention of two of Anne's maids of honor, Anne de Candale and Germaine de Foix.

"That is just as well, my lady, for the work that lies ahead," the older lady-in-waiting offered slyly.

Anne broke into laughter. "It will not be work tonight, Madame."

"You are right, Your Grace. Only pleasure with such a

handsome husband to tame!" The older woman's eyes sparkled in the light of the candelabra.

"Your Grace, will you teach us how to tame our husbands one day?" Anne de Candale was a maid of sixteen, spirited and intelligent. Eager to learn the secrets of womanhood and married life, she was already old on the marriage market. Anne was grooming her for a special match.

"I will teach you all you need to know when the time comes." She gave the girl's flowing hair a soft tug. "Now help me get this off so I may bathe."

"*Ma duchesse*, will it be the violet musk or the rose de Provence to scent your bath tonight?"

Anne thought for a moment. Both were her favorites. But she had bathed in violet musk the night of her wedding to Charles.

"The rose de Provence." She stretched like a cat as the folds of her blue and gold wedding gown fell to the floor. Stepping out of her finery, she moved to a nearby table and took a sip of warm spiced wine. Then she stepped into the steaming hot bath, scented with rose petals from the South.

Leaning back in the bath, she sighed languorously as her two maids of honor began to brush out her hair. How much better it was to embark upon one's wedding night with a firm idea of what was to come.

Charles had done his utmost to make her introduction to the marital bed a good one. Humor had been his foremost weapon. He had not been a pleasure to look at, but he had disarmed her fears with a great many jokes at his own expense. Ultimately his humility had charmed her.

With Louis, it would be different. Closing her eyes, she imagined just how different it might be. Tall, refined and dashing, Louis d'Orléans had occupied a secret room in her heart for most of her life. Until the summer past, she had kept the door shut. That night she would open it and walk through.

Moving from hair to arms Anne de Candale smoothed a wet linen cloth over Anne's lily-white skin, as Germaine de Foix took the other arm. Would her new husband serve her in such a way?

A laugh bubbled from her lips, making the girls giggle.

"Your Grace, what joy to see you so happy!" the older one cried.

"*Mes demoiselles*, you have no idea yet how happy a woman can be," Anne teased. Even she had no idea. Charles and she had met only weeks before they married. He had desired her, but this was much more. Beyond doubt, Louis loved her. His was the deep regard of a man who had watched her grow up and was finally able to shower her with the pent-up passion of a lifetime. She looked forward to discovering the difference.

Germaine looked at Anne across the bath, her eyes wide. She had just passed her twelfth birthday and was now of marriageable age.

"Really, Madame? Can you tell us what it is you hint at?"

"No, my darlings. I cannot!" Her laughter swelled into a full blown chortle, joined by her lady-in-waiting behind.

"Why is that, *ma reine-duchesse*? I would so like to know what the ladies speak of when they laugh and make eyes amongst themselves," Germaine protested, looking at Anne with brimming curiosity.

"Some things can be understood by words. Others only fathomed by experience." Anne made an inscrutable face to her young maid of honor. She shook with mirth, thinking of the boundless imagination she herself had possessed at age twelve.

"Oh, Madame, I should so like to know what you hint at!"

"And so you shall one day, but not until I have arranged a

match for you that you are worthy of. So, until then, be sure you do not seek from experience what I hint at or you will ruin my plans for you."

"Plans for me, Your Grace?" The young girl's eyes sparkled as she bounced up and down with excitement. "What are they?"

"They are secret until such time as I choose to reveal them. Meanwhile, do not eavesdrop when the ladies talk amongst themselves." Gazing at the long waves of Germaine's reddish golden locks, Anne indeed had plans. No minor nobleman for Louis' niece would do. She would find a prince or a king for the niece of the king of France. How satisfying it would be to honor the memory of Louis' dead sister Marie of Orléans, who had grown up fatherless and struggling, as had Louis himself.

"But Your Grace, I don't understand any of what they say," Germaine wailed.

"May it remain that way for some time longer, *ma chère*." Anne tossed a handful of rose petals at her, spraying the girl with scented water. "Do you want your future husband to think he has married a scullery maid on your wedding night?"

"But, Your Grace, is it not helpful to know a few facts before embarking on one's wedding night?" Anne de Candale piped up from the other side of the bath. The older girl looked mischievously at her duchess, whose body was now as rosy and pink as the delicate petals floating around her.

"My dear, what you need to know is that it will be a shock that very first night, then turn into a shock of a different nature once you have taught your husband to give you pleasure."

"But how can I teach a husband something I do not know myself?"

"We will help you when the time comes." Anne exchanged looks with her senior lady-in-waiting, who narrowed her eyes, the thin line of her mouth curving into a private smile.

"Do you mean the ladies will share with us what they whisper about?" Germaine asked hopefully.

"Yes, my dove. That is precisely what I mean. And we will make sure you receive your due."

"But how can the ladies influence another lady's husband?"

"They will speak to their own husbands and see to it that they offer helpful advice to the chevalier you marry."

"Ahh," Anne de Candale exhaled. "So that's how it works!"

"No, my dear, that is not exactly how it works. That is how one gains instruction, but without practice there is no result."

"What is the result you speak of, Madame?" Germaine de Foix's eyes opened wide.

"It's a baby, silly. Even girls younger than you know that," scoffed Anne de Candale, looking down the length of her short nose at her colleague.

"No, my dove," Anne of Brittany corrected her. "It is not a baby I speak of, although that result comes in time, assuredly." Anne crossed herself underneath the surface of the bath. Pray God that that result would assuredly come to her and Louis, with a better outcome than it ever had for her and Charles.

"Then what result do you mean, Your Grace?" Germaine was not to be put off.

It is pleasure I speak of." Anne half-closed her eyes, glancing from one girl to the other as they both stared at her with wide eyes.

"Pleasure?" Anne de Candale asked. "Such as the pleasure of taking a warm bath?"

"Far more than that." Anne leaned back against the tub and closed her eyes.

"The pleasure of cuddling Fantôme?" Germaine referred to the duchess' little dog who sat in one corner of the room, as far

as he could get from the tub and the hated water droplets. At
the sound of his name, his pointed black ears perked up.

"Not even close." Anne's smile was sly.

"Of having your hair brushed?" Anne de Candale guessed.

"Leagues beyond." Anne closed her eyes, then threw her
head back and let out a sparkling laugh that danced through
the room. Anne's senior lady-in-waiting joined in, along with
the other married attendants.

The girls looked at each other across the bath and burst into
giggles. Neither had any idea what their sovereign was referring to, but both looked forward to whatever it was.

"Get my lingerie," Anne ordered.

"Right away, *ma duchesse.*"

"And take care not to rip it."

"No, Your Grace, it would be a crime to rip such fine
workmanship."

"No, my doves. Not a crime, but an honor reserved for husbands on wedding nights."

"Really, Madame?" Anne de Candale looked as intrigued as
she did confused.

"Really, Mademoiselle."

"Will you tell us more tomorrow?" Germaine eagerly asked.

"I will tell you nothing at all." Anne splashed them both,
then rose like Venus emerging from the sea: pink, white, and
glowing.

"Then how shall we gain understanding?"

"You will read my face."

"Will it glow with joy?"

"You shall know tomorrow. Now dress me."

Laughing and smiling, the two young noblewomen dried
off their admirable sovereign and wondered to themselves at
mysteries and joys to come.

Slipping into the bedchamber, Louis' form threw a tall, slender shadow against the tapestried wall.

The bed curtains were drawn. Where was his bride?

Padding across the room, he took a deep breath and parted the deep blue velour drapes shot through with gold and silver thread that surrounded the marriage bed.

Not there.

Peering around the room, he wondered if she had not yet arrived. Sniffing the air, he scented roses. He studied the table laid out before the fireplace; two goblets and a plate of delicacies were set upon it. No flowers were in the room at all, unsurprising for early January.

That scent.

"*Ma Brette?*" he called.

No answer.

"*M'amie?*" For the first time, he used the endearment with which husbands and wives commonly addressed each other. He had never used it with Jeanne of France.

The scent of roses remained strong. He sensed she was there, but where?

Going to the table, he filled the two goblets with wine. Picking up one, he sipped. As the spiced liquid hit his stomach, an idea formed. He began to hum the tune he had enjoyed teasing Anne with when she was a young girl.

Was that a rustle? Eyeing the deep gold brocade curtain drawn over the window, he continued to hum.

The warm, richly upholstered room seemed to vibrate; a sort of shimmering presence hung in the air. Whence did it come?

Knowing his *Brette*, she was hiding somewhere, shaking with laughter. The words of the ditty he hummed were highly coarse. It had always made her laugh to hear him hum it. Where was she?

Taking another sip of wine, he began to sing the words to the tune.

"En baisant m'amie,
J'ai cueilli la fleur..."

It had been a favorite of Anne's father's, as well as her older half-brother François d'Avaugour.

"La cuisse bien faite,
Le tétin bien rond..."

A silvery laugh floated to his ears.

Louis strolled to the window. Within seconds he stood in front of a slight bulge in the deep gold curtain at one end. He could pull it aside and claim his prize.

Or not.

Would it not be more pleasurable to tease the one who was now teasing him?

Running his hand up and down the edge of the thick brocade curtain, he let her know he was there.

The ripest of silences informed him she knew.

Slowly he slipped his hand around the curtain's edge. He was in no rush. Was not the prize he came to capture already his? Carefully and deliberately he reached further around the curtain, almost able to hear his *Brette* holding her breath. Within seconds his hand closed upon his goal.

"Ahh," a muffled shriek escaped the curtain.

"Ahh," Louis echoed, his hand moving over the firm but pliant landscape, covered in what felt like fine lace. Languorously, he drew his fingers down the length of her torso and around to her back where his bride's well-made *cuisse* quivered beneath his touch.

There would be no escape.

Silently he listened as her breathing changed to short, fast breaths. Neither she nor he moved from where they stood, the curtain blocking sight of each other. Soon they would see treasures in the other wondered at but never gazed upon by either. For now, his hand would continue its mission of calming and igniting his *Brette* at the same time. It was pleasant work.

She guessed what Louis was up to. He would not claim what was his by force. Instead, he would drive her out of hiding. How well she knew him. But she had not trained in the arts of self-possession for her entire life for nothing. To honor the careful tutelage of her dear friend who had so recently gone home to God, she would take her time before parting the curtain.

She took his proffered hand in hers, brushing her body against it. Languidly, she shifted, sliding his hand over her haunches. At the slight squeeze he attempted, she tossed him off.

What rush was there anyway? Louis was hers. He was signaling to her that she would be the one to remove the final barrier between them. How like him to offer the moment to her, giving her the power to decide when to pull away the curtain and proceed. Once she did, they would know each other in a way they never had before. Would it deepen their regard for each other? Or ruin their longstanding friendship?

Within seconds his hand rose again, this time with palm upward, inviting her to guide it. With no aggression, no indication of force, the gesture was gallant. How could she refuse his invitation to let her lead his hand where she may?

She put her own hand under his upturned palm and stroked its center with her thumb. Instantly, she felt it tremble. With her forefinger she caressed the knuckles, her senses attuned to every tremor of the body on the other side. Power surged through her: the power of a woman over a man's desire that eclipsed both force and size.

Smiling to herself she brought his hand up to her throat. Slowly she slid it over her neck then up to her jawline.

His fingers curled over its contours as he supported her face in his hand. Had he not always supported her?

Softly, she kissed the palm of his hand as she thought back to her coronation day in 1492. It had been he who had held the enormous crown of France over her head, too heavy for her to wear. He had patiently moved it up and down as she repeatedly knelt then rose throughout the long ceremony.

He had stood behind her, out of her range of vision. But she had known it was him by his scent and by the assurance that it could be no other than Louis, the man who had always supported her: through joyful times and difficult ones.

Marrying Charles VIII of France had been a difficult one, but with her duchy overrun by the French her choice had been to be the king of France's prisoner or his wife. She wondered how hard it must have been for Louis to have been tasked with the job of convincing her to marry Charles. Had not Louis felt the pain of knowing he was destroying any chance for himself of making her his bride?

Then Charles had died unexpectedly and Louis had come to the throne. She had been greatly sorrowed, but the moment for sorrow had passed.

She took Louis' hand and moved it down to her heart..

On the other side of the curtain the king gasped.

She thrust his hand away. Pushing aside the curtain, she stepped into the room. Candlelight flickered all around, dazzling her for a moment. Then she lifted her eyes and met those of Louis.

"Well?"

"Well and truly." His eyes shone down on her.

"Well and truly what?" What pleasure to gaze on Louis'

well-made features. She was unused to admiring male beauty, except from a distance, as befit a proper and pious woman. But this was her husband.

"Well and truly made, *ma Brette*." He sucked in his breath.

"Ravishing," he murmured, reverence lowering his voice.

"You are not so bad a sight yourself, my lord." God, what a noble knight he looked in the golden light, his fine straight hair framing his handsome face.

"*M'amie*." He held out both arms to her.

She fell into them, feeling for a moment as if she were in her father's arms again, realizing the next that indeed she was not, nor did she want to be.

Her senses on fire, she melted, letting Louis lift her and carry her to the bed.

Drinking in the face of the man she had admired for almost her entire life, she allowed her eyes to wander over his form as he threw off his clothes.

Silence tightened between them as she took in his broad, well-defined shoulders and long, lean limbs, his tawny-brown torso. Never had she had the opportunity to admire a man in all his natural magnificence. Charles had taken great pains to hide in darkness when they came together, so lacking in male comeliness had he been. She had taken it as her due that all focus had been on her.

But now she was in an altogether different position, one that sharpened her senses and tightened the pit of her stomach. Her husband's form was breathtaking. For the first time in her life she felt the pleasure of desiring her husband's body and not just desiring what he could do to hers.

Falling back on the bed, she gazed up at him, spellbound. She was used to being the one to dazzle. For the first time in the marital chamber, it was she who was dazzled.

Louis leaned over her and as his lips closed upon hers she felt the sweet fulfillment of a long-held dream that she had never dared to dwell on. Louis d'Orléans was completely hers. How fitting that he was king of France, too.

The next morning the newly wedded couple lingered in bed. Louis' delight in his bride was something he had never experienced before. Not only was she ravishing to behold and to possess, but her lively admiration energized him again and again. He knew he had been handsome in his day. He felt as if his day had returned again, thanks to his ardent *Brette*.

After a final rapturous engagement Anne reminded him that their guests waited downstairs, eager to congratulate them and learn of their plans so they could make their own.

Descending the stairs to the magnificent great hall of his wife's ancestral home, Louis stood back as his bride received her maids of honor in a chorus of girlish congratulations. The view was splendid, but his days of bird-hunting were over. He had found his heart's desire after having lived his youth as a royal pawn. Anne was more than enough for him.

"Your Majesty, have you slept well?" Anne de Candale cried. Curiosity shimmered in her eyes.

"How very much you would like to know, little dove," the queen whispered, just loud enough for Louis to overhear. She pinched the sixteen-year-old's shoulder then embraced her. Raised in Anne's household since the age of eight, Anne de Candale was like a younger sister to her.

Over the shoulders of Anne and her maid of honor, Louis spotted a young noblewoman with eyes fixed upon a group of young men, talking and laughing in one corner. As Louis wondered which of the group she was intent upon, she turned and glided toward him and Anne, her face as serene as it had been distracted a moment earlier.

"Your Majesty, I wish you the happiest and longest of years with your lord husband the king." The young beauty curtseyed deeply.

"Have I introduced you, my lord, to my maid of honor, Charlotte of Aragon and Naples?" Anne asked Louis.

He shook his head slightly as Charlotte curtseyed again and murmured, "Your Majesty." When she stood, she held high her head in the sort of chin-tilting stance usually adopted by royals. Louis greeted her, noting the dignity of her bearing.

As she moved away Anne leaned toward him, her mouth brushing his ear.

"She is the second cousin of Ferdinand of Aragon, descended from Charlemagne," she whispered.

"Ahh, so that is why she tilted her chin almost as high as you do when she rose from greeting us," Louis jested.

"It is I who trained her to do so."

Is she from Naples or Aragon?" Louis asked.

"She has never stepped foot outside of France save to accompany me here to Brittany."

"And so?"

"Her father is Frederick, King of Naples, but before that he lived in France with his wife Anne of Savoy, God rest her soul." Anne put her hand to the cross that hung from her neck.

"Ah yes, the granddaughter of Charles VII," Louis mused. "So, her mother is dead?"

"Long dead, my lord, since shortly after Charlotte was born. I brought her to my court the year I married Charles, and she has been with me ever since."

"You value her highly, my lady." Louis didn't need to ask. He could see with his own eyes.

"She will prove an important match when the time comes."

"How old is she?"

"Nineteen, my lord."

"Has the time not yet come, my lady?" Knowing Anne, he was surprised she hadn't married off her prized maid of honor already. Was there hope, then, for Cesare Borgia? Charlotte of Aragon and Naples would be just the feather in his cap the pope's son needed to don the cloak of respectability and assume a royal lineage through marriage. Perhaps she could even get him to tone down his flamboyant court attire.

"I have plans for her."

"What are they?"

About to reply, Anne was cut off.

"Your Majesties," the countess of Angoulême greeted them. Her red hair peeked out from under her high headdress as she curtseyed then prodded her young son forward to bend the knee.

Louis could sense his bride tense beside him. One advantage to having known and observed Anne all his life was that he was not hard put to discern her moods.

He had known for five full years that she disliked Louise of Savoy, ever since she had borne a son to his cousin and close friend, Charles d'Angoulême. Why did his *Brette* dislike her? The answer was evident in the striking young boy who stepped forward and gave as graceful a bend of the knee as the most seasoned of courtiers.

"Your Majesties," little Francis's voice piped up. The boy looked at them with large round eyes that swam with curiosity. Louis imagined that even Cesare Borgia could not have held a candle to such a fine boy in his own childhood. Chuckling to himself, he thought of the nickname he had often overheard Louise de Savoy use to address her only son: she called him her little Cesar.

"We are honored to be here, Your Majesty. We wish you all health and happiness in the years to come," Louise de Savoy purred, her tone as sophisticated as its owner.

But did Charles d'Angoulême's widow wish for sons for them? Eyeing the red-headed noblewoman, only a year older than Anne, Louis doubted it. Charles' son and heir, Francis d'Angoulême, stood next in line to the throne should Louis produce no sons with Anne. All present knew this fact, except perhaps the little boy, who was busy examining the fleur-de-lis pattern on the king's cape.

"Thank you, Countess. Will you be staying with us long?" Anne asked, frost icing her tone.

"We are here at the king's disposal. And at yours, too, Your Majesty. We will stay for as long as you need us."

"The king and I plan to go on progress to tour my duchy," Anne said curtly, glancing at the bright-eyed, handsome boy. Louis could feel the tight tension of her body next to his as she held herself tall.

He could guess at her private thoughts. Undoubtedly she was thinking of her own dead prince Charles-Orland. The boy would have been just a few years older than the one who stood before them now. Doubtless, he would have been just as fine a young man. How it must hurt; how well his wife hid her sorrows. Hidden in the folds of her gown, Louis squeezed Anne's hand.

"Ah, then we shall return to Amboise where we will await the king's pleasure—and yours," Louise said, including Anne after a small hesitation.

"It is a good plan. God speed you on your journey home," Anne replied, making it clear that returning to France soon was her preference for Louise de Savoy and her precious son. Anne turned to greet the next guest, dispatching the countess with a twist of a fur-clad shoulder.

When Charles d'Angoulême died on the first day of 1496, he had just returned from paying his respects to Anne and Charles in the weeks after their son Charles-Orland's death. The count had had a slight cold when he set out. In the deep winter chill of his ride, it worsened to pneumonia. Within three days of his return he was dead, and Louis had taken his dear friend's wife and children under his wing. Louise de Savoy was ambitious for both her children; she was educating them well.

Now that Louis was king, with no son yet, five-year-old Francis was France's dauphin. As such, Louis took a special interest in the boy's formation. With Anne's past losses, there was more than just a distant chance that the young boy under his care would one day become king of France after him. If such an eventuality came to pass, the boy already showed kingly qualities.

Reaching out, Louis squeezed the boy's shoulder. "You must practice your lessons and listen to your mother until I return to Blois. Then you will come to me, and if you have minded her we shall have a game of tennis."

"But lessons are for girls! I will practice my tennis and my sword-thrusts and I shall beat you at tennis and dueling both!"

"Is that so, Monsieur *mon garçon?*" Louis had almost said *mon dauphin*, but had caught himself. It would displease Anne to overhear him call the boy by such a term. Besides, by the time he and Anne returned to Blois a new dauphin might be on the way. Yet studying the sturdy form and noble bearing of the boy before him, he couldn't help but think that France would be graced with such a one as he as its next king.

Straightening up, Louis exchanged a sympathetic look with Louise de Savoy, giving a slight shrug of his shoulders as if to say, 'What's to do?', then turned to his next guest. There was something about his friend's widow that put him off. Everything about her was commendable, yet she left him cold. Comely and of good lineage, at the age of twenty-three, she should be looking for a remarriage match. Yet the woman seemed entirely consumed with raising her children, especially her son. It appeared she had no other interests than seeing her little Cesar on the throne of France one day. Perhaps he could put Anne up to finding a husband for her. But first he would put his bride up to creating a dauphin of their own.

Tomb of Louis XII and Anne of Brittany
Basilica of Saint-Denis
Saint-Denis, France
Courtesy of Wikimedia Commons

Brittany and France in 1477
Courtesy of Wikipedia

Statue of Anne of Brittany
Chateau of the Dukes of Brittany, Nantes, France
Courtesy of Nantes Art Blog, Wikimedia Commons

Anne of Brittany and Louis d'Orléans, 1491
Gravure from Secrets of History: Anne of Brittany
Courtesy of Stephane Bern

Anne of Brittany as Prudence at her parents' tomb
By Michel Colomb, Cathedral of Peter and Paul, Nantes
Courtesy of Wikimedia Commons

Close up of Anne of Brittany as Prudence at her parents' tomb
By Michel Colomb, Cathedral of Peter and Paul, Nantes
Courtesy of Wikimedia Commons

Beggar's Meeting with Anne of Brittany and Louis XII
By Adrien Thibault
Courtesy of Wikimedia Commons

Portrait of Louis XII, King of France
Courtesy of Wikimedia Commons

Portrait of Louis XII, King of France
By Jean Perréal, c. 1500
Courtesy of Wikimedia Commons

The Unicorn is Killed and Brought to the Castle
From The Unicorn Tapestries thought to be commissioned by
Anne of Brittany for Louis XII, c. 1495-1505
Gift of John D. Rockefeller to The Met Cloisters
Metropolitan Museum of Art, New York
Photo by R. Gaston

Detail from The Unicorn is Killed and Brought to the Castle
From The Unicorn Tapestries thought to be commissioned by
Anne of Brittany for Louis XII, c. 1495-1505
The Met Cloisters, Metropolitan Museum of Art, New York
Photo by R. Gaston

Louis XII, King of France
Stained glass of Louis XII by Jean Perréal
Walters Art Museum , Baltimore, Maryland
Courtesy of Wikimedia Commons

Sepulchre of Cesare Borgia
By Victoriano Juaristi, 1934, Viana, Italy
Courtesy of elsborja.cat

Cesare Borgia coat of arms
Courtesy of Wendy Fortune on Pinterest

Cesare Borgia (1475-1507)
Portrait of a Gentleman Thought to be Cesare Borgia
by Meloni Altobello (1490-1543)
Museum Accademia Carrara, Italy
Courtesy of Wikimedia Commons

Statue of Louis XII over front doorway of Chateau Royal de Blois

Royal residence of Anne of Brittany and Louis XII of France
Courtesy of Wikimedia Commons

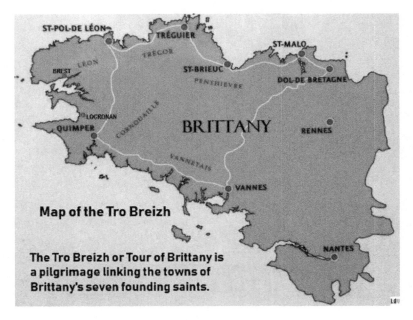

Map of the Tro Breizh

The Tro Breizh or Tour of Brittany is a pilgrimage linking the towns of Brittany's seven founding saints.

Map of the Tro Breizh (Tour of Brittany)
from Editions Coop Breizh, courtesy of Google Images

Nominoe, first Duke of Brittany, crowned 846
By Jeanne Malivel,
Courtesy of Wikimedia Commons

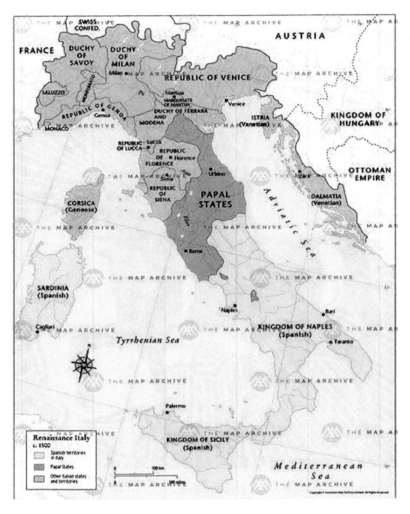

Map of Italy, 1500
Courtesy of The Map Archive

Niccolò Machiavelli (1469-1527)
Close-up from portrait by Santi di Tito
Courtesy of Wikimedia Commons

Germaine de Foix (1488-1538)
Niece of Louis XII,
maid of honor at Anne of Brittany's court
Queen-consort of Aragon (1506-1538)
Courtesy of Hilde van den Bergh, Hemmahoshilde Blog

Anne de Candale (1484-1506)
Cousin of Anne of Brittany and maid of honor at her court
Queen of Hungary and Bohemia (1502-1506)
Artist unknown, courtesy of Wikimedia Commons

Vladislas II, King of Hungary and Bohemia
By João do Cró - Arquivo Nacional Torre do Tombo
Courtesy of Wikipedia Organization

Marie de France (1160-1215)
From an illuminated manuscript
Courtesy of Bibliothèque Nationale de France (© public domain)

Christine de Pizan (1365-c. 1429)
Courtesy of Wikimedia Commons

Statue of Anne of Brittany
Nantes, France
Courtesy of Wikipedia

Claude de France (1499-1524)
Daughter of Anne of Brittany and Louis XII
Portrait by Corneille de Lyon
Courtesy of Wikimedia Commons

CHAPTER THIRTEEN

Winter–Spring 1499

Wedding Trip

That winter Anne traveled with Louis throughout Brittany. She was overjoyed to visit her people again so soon, checking on the councilors she had appointed on her progress of the fall before and hearing from town leaders on whether they were capably carrying out their mandates.

Louis hunted to his heart's delight and took a contented back seat to his wife as she went about her duties. He was not in the habit of feeling so satisfied. Having spent most of his adult life avoiding women he was tied to, notably his former wife and his former sister-in-law, he was surprised to find himself not trying to get away from the woman at his side.

Perhaps it was because he was away from France and all the duties and encumbrances of his responsibilities there. Or perhaps because the sweetest memories of his youth were linked to this land, first from his visits to Anne's father in Nantes, and then in the final years of the Mad War, when he had joined the Breton noblemen in fighting to oust the French from Brittany. It had been known as such because some Bretons had fought on the side of the French, and certain French noblemen such as Louis had allied themselves with Brittany.

Anne de Beaujeu had been at the head of the French plan to overtake Brittany. He had been infuriated to have such a one try to dominate him, and had sympathized with Brittany's desire not to be taken over by its powerful neighbor.

To escape her clutches he had galloped west, straight across the border into Brittany. There he had taken up arms with Francis II, Duke of Brittany, joined by other Breton and French noblemen to throw off the chains, bribes, and machinations of Madame la Grande, as France's regent in her brother Charles' minority, had been known.

Louis had not succeeded, but it had felt good to fight for freedom, both for Brittany and for himself. He had flexed the muscle of his youth and carved out his own path, rather than fall into the arms of France's most powerful woman. Forced like a helpless puppet into a repellent marriage by Anne de Beaujeu's father, he was determined never to be used again in such a fashion.

"My lord, you must wind this around your neck before we go out into the cold." Anne held out a thick wool scarf to him, of the sort Breton fishermen and farmers wrapped around their necks and faces in winter weather.

God's breath, she was bossy. Besides he hated scarves. He always felt bound and restricted in them, as if he were being tied up with a rope.

"My lady, I have no need of one. 'Tis not my way to be bundled up like a dowager aunt when we greet your subjects. What will they think?"

"They will think that you pay them great honor to wear the scarf woven by the good women of Fougères and delivered to us by messenger yesterday." They were on the second leg of their wedding trip, traveling from Nantes to Rennes, then northeast from Rennes to the small but fast-growing textile center of Fougères.

"Why does it matter?" Louis looked doubtfully at the thick, mouse-brown length of cloth. It looked well-made. He ran a hand over the densely woven material, surprised at how smooth it was.

"My lord, one of the main industries here is weaving and textiles. It has been so for over a century, since the count de Laval saw the benefit of exporting cloth and wool abroad. I must show my support of the weavers here, as last fall I appointed a local trader to arrange new lines of export to Flanders and the Lowlands."

"My lady, you have a motive to your request."

"When do I not have a motive to my requests, my lord?" Anne looked at him shrewdly.

"Good point. Yet why do you not wear this garment yourself?"

"You do not know the Breton people if you do not know that they would not like to see their sovereign duchess in such rough attire."

"I know you well enough to know that you would not allow any such common cloth to touch your skin."

"Quite. But the people desire to see their sovereign in dress that befits her station."

"Ahh, so it is left to the king of France to wear the rough-hewn fisherman's wear."

"But Louis, you look so good in common dress." Gaily, she wound the scarf around his neck and kissed him on the nose as she tucked both ends into his doublet.

"I am happy to wear what the common people wear. I just
don't like feeling bound up like a prisoner." His father Charles
had been held captive in England for twenty-five years after
being captured at the battle of Agincourt. A strain coursed
through Louis' bloodline that chafed against being restrained
or trammeled.

"I remember when you came to me just before the battle of
St.-Aubin in peasant gear."

"Do you, *m'amie*? Did I frighten you then?"

"When have you seen me frightened of you, my lord?"
Anne scoffed, poking him in the chest. "But I remember how
well you looked in the clothes of the common people."

"Ahh, perhaps it was my expression." Louis pulled a comic face.

Anne lightly cuffed his cheek. "No, Louis. It was your un-
fair gifts. Long legs, strong shoulders, height, and bearing."
Her eyes wandered over him, warming his vitals. His sturdy
Brette was as ardent privately as she was decorous in public. The
contrast set him on fire.

"You wore it well, and so you shall wear this scarf well to
honor those who labor to turn Fougères into an important textile center."

"As for the count de Laval, why should you support the
industry of a town begun as the fief of your enemy?" He referred to the House of Laval, one of Brittany's most noble
houses which had challenged the power of Anne's own House
of Dreux-Montfort in centuries past.

Anne drew herself up to her full height, coming up to the
second from the top hook of Louis' doublet. "My duchy is a rich
but small realm. Only a handful of great families live here, the
House of Laval among them. We are all intermarried and inter-
mixed; I would be a foolish ruler not to bind them all closer to
me, so that I can keep my eye on what they are up to."

"My lady, I see that your wits outstrip those of your father, God rest his soul." Duke Francis had not been especially adept at binding his noblemen together. He had been quick to forgive them, but not so wily in knitting them to him in alliances.

"My father was a great man." Anne's temper flared as red as her face. "If I asked him to wear this scarf, he would have worn it." She slapped Louis hard and stormed from the room.

Down at the inn's stables, the horses were ready to be mounted. They would enter the town gates of Fougères in grand ceremony, as befit her visit to one of Brittany's more important eastern towns. If her husband appeared without his scarf on, she would wear it herself. But it would ruin her outfit. That, she knew, the people wouldn't like, especially the women, who would grumble and ask amongst themselves why their duchess was playing the peasant.

Anne tapped her foot impatiently, the built-up wooden sole of her shoe making a sharp sound against the paving stones of the courtyard. She loved Louis, but he had ruled France for only eight months. She had been ruler of Brittany for eleven years, although Charles had interfered for six and a half of them. She had a long trail of experience with handling her noblemen, as well as sad lessons learned from watching them betray her father for French bribes and pensions. They were an unruly bunch, as ready to turn on each other as they had been to turn on the House of Dreux-Montfort when Duke Francis died in 1488.

The only way she could control them was to support them, intermarry her own people with the other great families, and keep a close eye on them. She would also ensure that the common people knew their good fortune and prosperity came from her, and not just from their feudal lords. To make that point today she must ride through the gates of Fougères in splendid

style, offering largesse and showing her support of their growing cloth and wool trade industry. The perfect touch would be
to have the king of France at her side, wearing a locally-made,
homespun garment.

The clatter of clanking metal sounded behind her. She
turned to see Louis striding toward her. Without a word, he
narrowed his eyes at her and swung himself up on his horse, the
dung-colored scarf around his neck.

"*Allons-y*, let's go!" he shouted, spurring his mount.

Anne rode out behind him. Just before the gates of the town
she would overtake him and ride in first. The people would see
her and be dazzled. Then they would spot the king of France
behind her, wearing a scarf from their town, and their hearts
would be filled with gratitude as well as continued goodwill
toward France. It was a rather new emotion in Brittany. The
peace that had come with Anne's marriage to Charles VIII had
restored stability to the duchy, laying the groundwork for trade
and commerce to grow. It was a good plan, she knew, worthy of
the nickname the people had shouted at her along the road on
her progress of the fall before.

"*Vive la bonne duchesse!* Long live the good duchess!" they
had cried. Deeply feeling her duty, she had vowed to rise to
her people's regard for her. She would be their good duchess.
She would be a good wife, too, but today it was the turn of her
people, and not her husband, to receive her bounty.

Eyeing Louis' long, straight back, she mused to herself on
how she would manage his complicated personality. He had
told her he couldn't bear to be shackled but she had already
known, having seen it in him over the years. She must some-
how make it up to him for forcing him to wear that scarf.

Knowing how teeming with game the forests outside
Fougères were, she decided to speak with the count of Laval

personally to ask him to take her husband off her hands on a day's hunting expedition. Louis could bond with Guy de Laval and escape further demands from her while engaging in one of his favorite pastimes.

She, in turn, could spend the day meeting with her trade appointee of the fall before, assessing how exports were faring and signing letters of introduction to send further appointees abroad to seek out markets for Fougères cloth.

Spurring her horse, she rode up alongside Louis. Looking over, she batted her eyelashes at him.

"How well you look today, my lord."

"How well you know how to bend me to your will, Madame," he replied, attempting a scowl.

"And me to yours, my lord. I look forward to whatever punishment you wish to carry out on me tonight." Leaning over, she flicked her riding whip against his thigh.

Instantly he flexed, his long hard muscles outlined against his leggings. Then he leaned toward her. "It will be severe, *ma Brette*. You have taxed me with your demands," he scolded, his tone low and gruff.

At that moment, Louis' horse nipped the neck of Anne's mount. Both Louis and Anne looked to see the reaction of Anne's horse, who whinnied, then rubbed her head along the neck of her admirer. At that, the royal couple looked at each other and laughed.

As they progressed through her lands on their wedding trip that winter, Anne saw that her subjects were not unhappy to see her allied with the new king of France. With peace prevailing between France and Brittany, her people were content as long as their businesses continued to flourish and grow.

Anne took pains to bond with her subjects They loved her

for having saved Brittany from the salt tax levied on France when she was married to Charles, as well as for clearing the French garrisons out of their land thanks to her influence with her new husband.

By April she and Louis had circled back to Nantes from Brittany's west coast, and Anne knew it wasn't just the support of her people that warmed her. Just as in the early months of her first marriage she felt as if a fire were lit in her belly, heating her day and night and keeping away the early spring chill.

It was time to return to France and take up the reins of establishing her royal ladies' court in Blois. It would keep her occupied while she awaited the birth of her first child with Louis.

"She's taken the place of the rightful queen," the woman watching the royal procession grumbled. On their way to Blois, Anne of Brittany and Louis XII were stopping in Amboise, the town along the Loire where Anne had last lived as queen of France with the late king.

"She *is* the rightful queen," the woman's husband disagreed.

"Jeanne of France is our rightful queen. Not the Breton minx."

"She is indeed, truth be—"

"Hold your tongue and watch what you say about our queen!" The woman jabbed an elbow into her husband's side.

"You see? She was our queen and so she is again. Why is that not as it should be?"

"Because she took the place of another. One who is a saint, no less."

"And would you really want a saint for your queen? How would she give her husband any brats?" The old man smiled wickedly at his wife.

"If the maid of Orleans could be a soldier, then why couldn't Jeanne of France be queen?"

"Because she's a cripple, fool wife. She would never produce an heir for the king. Can you blame him if he wants one?" He gave Anne of Brittany, sitting tall astride her white palfrey, another admiring glance. What a vixen. Smart too, they said. Who could blame the king?

"You think this one will have any better luck, with every one of her babes dying?"

"At least she is able to bear them. Who knows, maybe her luck will change with the new king."

"You may be right. But will Jeanne of France curse her for taking her place?"

"You would, wife, but not her. She's a saint, as you said."

"I don't curse the Breton, but maybe our Lord has." She eyed the regal duchess as she rode by, drinking in the rich brocade of her deep pink gown. Shot through with gold thread, it caught the sun as she passed, dazzling the crowd. Jeanne of France would never have dressed so lavishly. God's bells, it was fine. With a sigh, she imagined having a gown of her own like that but more suited to her station. She could wear it to church on feast days, while her women friends ate their hearts out at the sight of her.

"She doesn't look so cursed to me," the old man observed, receiving another jab for his remark.

"Do you not remember the storm on the day the king's annulment was announced?" The woman glowered at her husband. "The skies turned black as night at midday, just as happened on the day of our Lord's death."

"The good Lord was showing He thought of his saintly daughter at that moment. As he shows now that He's thinking of our new queen. Thinking highly of her too, I'd say." He crossed himself just in case he had said something irreverent. He hadn't meant to, but the glorious good looks of the old queen, now the new one, were firing his vitals. With the glow on her face, he guessed the king had already gotten busy.

"Shut it, old man. And take a good look at her gown because I want a bolt of something like that next time you see the cloth merchant."

"I don't need to study it since I'm sure you'll describe every detail when the time comes." God's bells, the king's choice was fine. Her cheeks were as rosy as a maiden's, although with two husbands notched on her belt, she was anything but.

"Put your eyes back in your head," his wife scolded. "It's disrespectful to stare at the queen like that."

"Oh, so she *is* the rightful queen now, is she?"

"Only if you promise me a bolt of cloth something like that of her gown."

"Anything to shut you up, woman."

"Take a breather, old man. You'll drop dead from excitement if you keep imagining whatever is now in your head."

"Go on with you." He poked her.

"Get on with you." She prodded him back.

The crowd began to stir again as the new old queen passed from sight. Someone else important was coming along.

"'Tis the king!" a man called out.

"*Vive le roi!*" rose from the crowd.

"Why is he riding so far behind the queen?" a nearby voice asked.

"He doesn't want to steal her thunder," another voice answered.

"As it should be, husband," the woman whispered into her husband's ear.

"Get on with you, woman!" her husband roared back as his

wife's face split into a grin as wide as the Loire River next to which they stood.

It was as mild an April day in Amboise as any there ever was. Judging by the king's smile lighting up his face, his mood matched the bright spring weather.

"*Vive le roi!*" the man's wife called out.

"Long live King Louis" *and well done, Sire.* No question why the king had fought for his annulment. What man with eyes in his head wouldn't fight to win a wife like the one who had just passed by?

"Come on, husband. Let's move ahead so we can see where the queen's going."

"So she's still your queen, eh?"

"I want to see what her bodice looks like when she takes off her mantle."

"I'd like to see what's under her bodice."

"Enough!" The woman smacked his arm and hurried off in the direction the queen had gone. Most of the crowd was moving with her.

In a minute they stopped before an enormous pavilion that had been set up next to the Loire. Pennants fluttered at each of its four corners, two with the gold on blue background of France, and two with the black on white of Brittany.

As the crowd drank her in, Anne of Brittany gracefully dismounted her horse, then climbed the few steps to the dais of the pavilion. Slowly she removed her mantle before taking a seat.

A high feminine hum was heard as the full splendor of the queen's gown was revealed. Her bodice was patterned with pink and purple peonies, outlined in silver thread that sparkled in the sunlight, and edged with ermine. Glorious.

"Tell you one thing, your saintly Jeanne of France wouldn't

have worn a bodice like that one," the man whispered to his wife. "Nor filled it the way this queen does." He crossed himself again, just to be safe. Was it a sin to compliment a queen?

"My people, I am here today to be among you again as I was in the years of our great King Charles' reign," Anne of Brittany's voice rang out.

"'Great' is not the word I'd use to describe the late king, God rest him," the woman murmured.

"Great at certain kinds of sport would be more like it," the old man agreed.

"Despite that misshapen body," the wife added.

"Not misshapen on all counts, as far as the ladies were concerned," her husband added.

"When a man's a king, strumpets overlook his flaws," the wife observed.

"And would you have, given the chance?" Her husband nudged her with an elbow to the ribs.

"God's judgment, I would rather disport with one as ugly as you, than have fallen into the arms of that dwarf."

"And that's as fine a compliment as any I'll get from you," her husband jested.

"Shut it, she's saying something." The woman gazed toward the regal woman on the dais, drinking in every detail. She had to admit, Jeanne of France would have seemed out of place there. She was saintly, as humble as a servant of the Lord should be, whereas the one addressing the crowd now, with her head held high, was as queenly as they come. Maybe she should drop it with her man. But not before she got her bolt of cloth.

CHAPTER FOURTEEN

Summer 1499

A Bride for Cesare Borgia

"Men and their stupid dreams!" Anne railed. "Are they all like this, Your Grace?" Anne de Candale's forehead creased into worry lines.

"All the ones I've married, unfortunately. I thought Louis had better sense than ... than others." She had almost said "Charles", but it wouldn't do to speak ill of the dead. He had been so misguided to try to claim Naples for France. Why couldn't either of her husbands leave well enough alone in Italy, and enjoy the peace and bounty of the kingdom they already ruled?

"Most of them, I think. But not the one I plan to marry." Charlotte of Naples looked disdainfully down her nose at an imagined bevy of suitors she was not planning on marrying.

"*Ma chère,* your plan is to marry the one I select for you.

That is the only plan you should have, along with your plan to obey me in all matters." Anne of Brittany frowned at her star maid of honor. Charlotte of Naples outranked the other young noblewomen at her court, but she needed to be reminded at times that she would never outrank her queen.

The mouth of Charlotte of Naples twisted into a moue. "Your Grace, did not you yourself tell us the story of how you shouted down the entire assembly of your country's Estates General when you were only twelve to let them know you would not marry the old man that had been chosen for you?"

"He was four times my age and hideous," Anne sniffed, remembering those desperate days.

"Then how can you tell me that I should have no say in who I am to marry, when I am a princess no less than you were, before you became duchess then queen?" Charlotte dropped a quick curtsey. "Begging your pardon, Your Grace."

Anne of Brittany eyed the nineteen-year-old princess she had raised at her court. Indeed, she was caught in a bind at that moment. Louis was eager for Charlotte of Naples to accept Cesare Borgia's marriage offer. Anne found the idea repugnant, but she knew well why Louis was pressing for it.

As with so many other bad ideas, it all boiled down to the men's plans in Italy. What was it about that seductive, sinister land that turned the heads of the kings of France and made them want to leave their already perfectly well-balanced kingdom? She kicked the pillow next to the one her small dog lay on, sending him running to the far corner of the room.

"That was then and this is now. I know better what you need and want than you do." Or Louis does, she thought.

"*Ma reine-duchesse,* I know very well what I need and want, and what I do not need is a bastard son of a pope for a husband who wishes to marry me for my title so he can pretend he is not from the streets of Rome." Charlotte tilted her nose to the ceiling and rolled her eyes.

"Calm yourself, Charlotte. I know your concerns." God's breath, did she ever know her charge's concerns. The whole idea of her highest ranking maid of honor being married off to the vulgar Cesare Borgia was outrageous. Especially as Anne could see that the Borgia had impressed Louis with his wily charm, athleticism, and jovial good nature. Did Louis see a bit of his younger self in that posturing half-Italian, half-Spanish rogue?

If so, he was mistaken. Her husband was refined, moderate, and temperate in his tastes, none of which Cesare Borgia appeared to be. The young braggadocio had taken up residence nearby and wouldn't leave France until he had gotten what he came for: a noble French bride, preferably a princess. Who did that arriviste think he was?

"What is the king's stupid dream, Your Grace? I mean the dream, of course, not the king," Anne de Candale bumbled.

"I know what you mean, and it is indeed stupid." Anne pursed her lips. "He plans to go to Milan to claim it for France."

"When does the king plan to go?" Anne de Candale asked, peering fretfully at her queen. There was no doubt the court ran much more peacefully without the men around. God knew she and her maids of honor could focus better on the lessons the queen led them in, but where was the fun in it? The queen wouldn't allow any of them near any of the youths of the court, yet there were many exchanges of looks as well as occasional brushes with the young gallants as the queen's ladies' court went about its daily routines.

"To Milan, to claim it for France through his grandmother's line," a new voice added. Charlotte d'Albret stood behind Anne de Candale, looking serene. Hers was a subdued beauty, one that didn't shout from the rooftops but pleased the eye more every time it returned to her. She was another of Anne of Brittany's brightest stars in her growing court of Cordelières.

"When did you join us?" the queen asked, trying to remember if she had used Charlotte's father's name when she had mentioned the lecherous old man she had refused to marry at age twelve. He was as powerful as he was loathsome; it would not do to offend his daughter. At court it did not do to offend anyone and, as queen, Anne was a master of dissembling, careful not to show her hand.

"As I came in, Your Majesty, you were saying you know better what Charlotte needs and wants than she does, and I'm sure that's true." Charlotte d'Albret cold-shouldered her rival, the other Charlotte, as she gracefully curtseyed to the queen.

Inside, Anne sighed with relief. She detested Charlotte d'Albret's father, but he was a powerful and wealthy nobleman from the south, and his continued support of her intent to keep Brittany independent from France was essential. No need to remember the horrors of ten years' past when the old toad had sued for her affections and she had had to deliver a verbal trouncing before Brittany's parliament to get him to back off once and for all.

Yet, who was she fooling? She never forgot a slight nor forgave one. But it was unwise to humiliate a powerful foe. Better to gain the advantage over a close enemy than pretend as if no bad blood had been spilled.

Peering at Charlotte d'Albret, she bid her come closer.

"Your Majesty?"

"My dear, have you remained true to my teachings and not allowed your heart to be diverted by some unsuitable young man?" This quiet beauty amongst her Cordelières always seemed in possession of her feelings. She outshone the others in exemplifying the qualities of reserve and self-control that Anne had endeavored to instill in her charges.

"Of course, Your Grace. I will wait for you to choose some-one for me, and when you do I will try my hardest to consider him."

Anne eyed her approvingly. Charlotte d'Albret was mallea-ble, as unlike herself as night is to day. But the young woman's pliant nature served her purposes. She would make a match for her maid of honor and avenge herself on her overbearing father in a single strike.

"Your Majesty, the king asks that you join him," an atten-dant broke in at the doorway.

"Where is he?" Anne asked.

"He is in the courtyard, talking with the duke de Valentinois, but he is on his way to his chambers and bid me ask you to meet him there in ten minutes."

"With or without our guest?"

"Without, Your Grace. The duke de Valentinois is about to ride out on the new mount the king has given him."

It was highly unusual for Louis to shower gifts upon anyone other than her. She could see that the young Borgia was having an effect upon her husband, turning his head and making him see everything around him in bolder, more vivid shades. Anne sniffed.

"Tell the king I will be there," she bade the attendant. Turning to her maids of honor, she gave them strict instructions. "You will continue the reading until the end of the passage we have begun. Do not get up until you have finished, and do not whisper and talk amongst yourselves. Do you understand?"

"Yes, Your Grace," Anne de Candale said brightly.

"We will try, Your Grace," Germaine de Foix chimed in.

"Of course, Your Majesty." Charlotte of Naples eyed the others with irritation. They were so unruly, unlike herself.

Charlotte d'Albret nodded, pressing her lips together, hands folded in her lap.

The queen shot them one last glance. What paragons of virtue she had created. Her maids of honor were the toast of Europe under her rigorous discipline. With a swish of her skirts she glided from the room, her heart full to think of how well she had trained her young charges.

Immediately the rigorously trained maidens rushed to the window.

"Do you see him?"

"Ooh, he is mounting now."

"Look at those tights!"

"Look at his legs!"

"Look at those leg muscles!"

"They say he killed eight bulls in one day on horseback in Spain," Charlotte d'Albret gushed. She had overheard her father saying so to his men.

"Is he not dashing?" Germaine de Foix sighed.

"And that accent!" Anne de Candale added.

"Is he not ridiculous in all that fluff?" Charlotte of Naples injected a sour note, her eyes glued to the man now seated on his horse in the courtyard.

"Mayhap he needs a wife to show him how to dress at court," Charlotte d'Albret suggested.

"No doubt, *ma chère,* he needs a wife to show him more than that!" Anne de Candale added.

They broke into laughter, pushing each other out of the way to gain a better view of the new duke of Valentinois. Everyone at court knew he was looking for a French bride.

Then Anne de Candale let out a low whistle. "Can you imagine?"

With wide eyes, Germaine de Foix stared at her. "Can you imagine what?"

"You know what, goose." Anne de Candale rolled her eyes.

"I can imagine," Charlotte of Naples broke in. "But not with a commoner such as he." Her heart flew to the one she had pushed from her thoughts. But like a bee to a flower, his image returned to her mind's eye.

"Have we not just noted how very uncommon he is?" Anne de Candale protested.

"That does not excuse his lack of background," Charlotte of Naples protested.

"There may be some who would excuse such a man for not having what he had no power to determine," Anne de Candale pointed out, ever reasoned in her thinking.

"In any case, it looks as if he is correcting his lack of background by his friendship with the king," Charlotte d'Albret observed.

"Is he not enormous?" Anne de Candale cooed.

"Enormously handsome, too!" added Germaine de Foix.

"Look at his chest!"

"What about his shoulders?"

"His hands are huge!"

"And you know what that means." Anne de Candale eyed Charlotte of Naples.

"No. What does it mean?" Germaine de Foix asked.

A moment of whispering ensued, followed by gales of laughter between the two older girls. Only Charlotte d'Albret remained silent, continuing to stare out the window.

"What does it mean?" Germaine de Foix persisted.

"Ask the scullery girls. They'll tell you." Anne de Candale gave Germaine a sideways glance.

"Why don't *you* tell me? Now!"

"We may not say, lest our queen be angered with us teaching you lessons outside the lesson plan," Charlotte of Naples said primly.

"Oh, come now. Tell me!"

"Can you guess, little goose?" Anne de Candale fluffed the hair of her younger comrade.

"His, um, his feet?"

"No, little love, not his feet!"

"His, er, parts under his clothes?"

"Now you're warming up."

"His buttocks?"

"Ooh!" Anne de Candale jabbed Charlotte of Naples in the ribs. "No, but good guess!" Massive giggling broke out as everyone jockeyed for position to see just how much of the outline of Cesare Borgia's buttocks in his multi-colored tights was visible below his doublet. Agreeably, a well-defined muscular outline greeted their eyes.

"The parts on the other side, then?" Germaine asked brightly.

"I cannot say, but what a clever girl you are!" Anne de Candale wickedly complimented her.

"So that's it, then!" Germaine crowed. Her face reddened as further thoughts sank in.

"*Mes demoiselles*, get away from that window!" a voice rang out.

The young women scattered like geese, pushing each other out of the way to be first to dive back into their seats on the floor cushions.

"Have you finished the passage the queen asked you to read?" Their tutor, Madame Leroux, moved into the room, looking cross, her back ramrod straight.

"Almost, Madame," Anne de Candale fibbed, wondering where their tutor had been. Usually she began the lessons earlier, but that day she was late.

"Not quite, my lady," Germaine de Foix hedged.

"We are almost there, Madame." Charlotte of Naples rummaged in the floor cushions for the discarded book from which the queen had bid them read.

"Which passage?" Germaine de Foix piped up, causing the others to flash her sour glances.

"What were you looking at, *mes demoiselles?*" Madame Leroux glared at them.

"Nothing, Madame!" Anne de Candale exclaimed. The older woman's color was high, her cheeks unusually flushed with a rosiness that became her. Perhaps it wasn't a bad thing to get worked up at times.

"Just a horse!" Charlotte of Naples put in.

"With a man on it," Germaine de Foix added.

"What man?" Madame Leroux asked.

"No one special."

"Exactly who is this no one special?" The dignified woman marched to the window. She was of the lesser nobility, the daughter of a widow without means. How well she knew what it was to be no one special. All she had was her education and her carriage; she made efforts to maximize both.

"Just one of the king's guests," Charlotte of Naples spoke up.

The head tutor peered out the window. The guest in question was now riding out of the courtyard. She caught her breath as the plume on his hat waved in the March breeze. In the wee hours before dawn, when court rules relaxed and deeds done in the dark were blotted out by rosy dawn, she had blissfully lost herself in those arms, her fingers digging into that magnificent back.

He had left her satisfied, sated, and ravished. Would the memory of those moments recompense her for a lifetime of service? It was as close an encounter with a duke as she was ever likely to have.

Exhaling a long sigh, she took one last look then turned back to her students.

"*Ma Brette*, you know I must go. The moment is right. With the pope's support I will sweep Milan clean of Sforza and claim my inheritance for France," Louis reasoned to Anne. As usual, she was not having it.

"Why must you fall into the same trap that Charles did? Do you really think there is something on the other side of the Alps so much better than what we have here?" Anne balled her fists at her side, containing the urge to beat some sense into her husband's head. What was with these men and their hare-brained dreams of conquest in foreign lands?

"'Tis not the same trap at all. Milan is mine through my father's mother. And Borgia has given his word that he will support me in sweeping Sforza from the city. His son will ride at my side as soon as I can wrap up his affairs here." Louis looked frustrated. He was no matchmaker like his wife and without her support Cesare's marriage aspirations were going nowhere.

"Get rid of him as soon as possible, then stay here and wait for the birth of your child, husband. Is not your duty to manage the affairs of your country and not interfere in the affairs of another?"

"This is an opportunity ripe for the picking. And you know the Borgia won't leave unless I personally accompany him over the border." Louis rolled his eyes. "We just need to get your princess to agree to marry him."

"She will never agree."

Louis looked closely at his wife. Usually Anne didn't put too fine a point on whether her maids of honor agreed with her marriage choices for them or not. She just insisted on their obedience. What his *Brette* really meant was that she herself would never agree to handing over Charlotte of Naples to such a man.

Louis sighed, wondering how he could get her to change her mind. His wife's motto was '*Non mudera,* I will not change.' Well did he know.

"I have arranged for Cesare to come to dinner tonight. Have Charlotte come, too, and we will excuse ourselves so that they may dine alone and get to know one another." Louis tried to sound authoritative. He was king, but he had never arranged a private dinner for two unmarried people to meet. He had no idea how to manage it.

"Why should a princess of Naples and Aragon get to know a man with no title and no lineage, other than one he cannot claim?" The accepted story was that Cesare was the pope's nephew. Not a single soul in Europe believed it.

"Wife, do you not understand that the Borgia's support is vital for me to claim Milan?"

"Husband, do you not understand that claiming Milan gains you and your kingdom nothing?"

"Of course, it does. It would be a gem in the crown of France."

"A gem that will fall out at the first push. The moment you leave Milan you know what will happen, just as it did with Charles in Naples. The Italians will re-form their alliances and push you out. Do you not know them well enough by now after suffering so horribly at Fornovo?" Louis and his troops had endured terrible losses in 1495 at the battle of Fornovo, due to the treachery of Ludovico Sforza. Initially France's ally, Milan's powerful ruler had switched sides to the League of Venice at the last moment.

"It was a terrible time, but this will be different."

"Men! When will any of you understand that war is never different? It always ends badly, and none of you ever learn that it is best not to go where one is not invited."

"And that is precisely the difference. The pope has made it clear that the people of Milan want Sforza out. They've had enough of him. With the pope's help, and his son at my side, they will welcome the king of France, great grandson of Giangalezzo Visconti, their very first duke!" Louis pulled himself up, looking almost Italian for a moment, handsome and glowering.

"For how long do you think they will welcome you? You will be greeted in glory, welcomed for a month or two, then slowly resented and ultimately booted out. Has not recent history taught you this, husband?"

"I know that if ever there was a chance to claim Milan for France, it is now. Bid the princess of Naples to join us for dinner, so that Cesare can work his magic and we can wrap up this marriage business so I can get to Milan."

"Husband, you are in a dream, and I would have you wake from it soon."

"Wife, I am in a hurry. Deliver the princess tonight and I will write to her father to request permission for Cesare to proceed with his suit."

"I will not deliver Charlotte into the hands of such a ruffian."

"This is dinner, m'amie. Not an engagement."

"I will never deliver her to such a man."

"Then he will never leave France."

Anne paused a moment, looking as if she had swallowed a bag of lemons. Finally, she spoke. "If her father says no, this cannot proceed."

"Of course, m'amie. Just dinner is all I ask." Borgia was enjoying a certain degree of success with the maidens of the court he had already met. It reminded Louis of his own easy successes with the ladies in the days he had been married to Jeanne, but living apart from her. He didn't doubt Cesare would make an impression on any woman with whom he spent time alone.

Yet the princess of Naples would be a tough nut to crack. His wife had educated her well. She would not suffer fools gladly. Cesare was no fool, but neither was he a nobleman born and raised. Louis could see that he was a quick learner, but Charlotte would immediately spot where his deficits in up-bringing lay. The question was, would she fall for him, too?

"I will deliver her for dinner. If he lays a single finger on her I will have him sent over the border, back to Italy or Spain or wherever he is from." Anne's eyes shot daggers.

"*M'amie*, you are magnificent. Let us make the introductions then slip away. The rest is in God's hands," Louis reassured her. He knew perfectly well that the rest was not only in God's hands but the hands of his wife, as well as Charlotte's father, Frederick, King of Naples.

Yet Louis had confidence in the young Borgia. Let the man have his moment. At the very worst, he would try and fail. Louis had done that, too, in Italy the last time around, with Charles in 1495. This time he would succeed. Perhaps Cesare would too.

He grabbed his wife around the waist. After a long kiss then a teasing swat from her hand, he set off in search of the young Borgia to give him the good news. As he exited the room, he whistled Anne's favorite Breton sailor's tune.

He was vital, larger than life. Vulgarly handsome, Charlotte thought—with the accent on vulgar. His face and muscular frame seemed painted in broad brushstrokes, unlike the smaller more fine-boned French and Breton noblemen she had grown up amongst. Eyeing his orange and royal blue dagger-slashed sleeves, she noted the sauce stain at the end of one of them.

Revolting. If he wiped his hands again on the loaf of bread from which he had just offered her a piece, she would get up and leave. Already she had lost her appetite, although it looked as if her dining partner was just getting started.

"*Princesse*, are you enjoying the duck?" Cesare Borgia leaned toward her, the grease from the sauce in which he had dipped his bread glistening in his moustache.

"I—I have had enough." *Of you.* She took a sip of wine, anything to avoid further eye contact with the handsome foreigner who sat uncomfortably close. A moment earlier he had brushed his knee against hers, making her feel as if she were being untrue to the one with whom she was still angry. Utterly confused, her thoughts were leagues away from the man sitting next to her.

Where was her queen when she needed her? Anne, Duchess of Brittany and Queen of France, would have stomped on the man's foot under the table to let him know what she thought. But this one might take it as a sign of interest, an invitation to a subsequent skirmish.

Wistfully, she thought of Nicolas. He would never have taken such liberties as the ones the ruffian beside her was now attempting. Thinking back to her hand in his, she admitted to herself it had been she who had offered it. As for the kiss, she knew very well whose lips had sought whose. Perhaps she had judged him overly harshly.

"Try the rabbit instead," Cesare interrupted her thoughts. "I bagged it myself this morning with the king." He held out a morsel of meat to her, brown sauce dripping onto the table. Did he really think she would deign to lean toward him and take the morsel into her mouth from the end of his knife?

"Thank you, I will serve myself when I am ready." Instantly

she regretted her rebuff. Was it his fault that he had no manners, no upbringing, no skills whatsoever in conversing at table with a princess royal?

"Do you not wish me to serve you then, *ma princesse?*" The slight edge to his voice warned her that she had no idea who she was dealing with. Already she knew this man was not gently raised. But was he dangerous?

Rumors from Rome had floated to her ears. She would proceed carefully.

"You may serve me some more wine, if you please, Monsieur." Anything, just to give him something to do with his hands other than try to touch her. Despite his undeniable good looks, she froze at the thought of a man with no background and no breeding putting his body anywhere near her own. Who knew if he was familiar with basic rules of cleanliness? Had he washed his hands before coming to table? He appeared to have washed his body; he smelled strongly of some spiced oriental scent. But the fact that she could smell him at all warned her he was too close for comfort.

Her queen should never have allowed this. Yet it had been her sovereign herself who had insisted on her joining them for dinner that evening. How could her own beloved mistress and queen have sold her out like this? There was only one reason Charlotte could guess at.

The king.

His Majesty must have some goal in mind to insist on her dining privately with this man. That night she would write to her father and let him know what was afoot. Frederick of Naples would never allow his only daughter to wed the bastard son of a pope. The king would have to find someone else to marry Cesare Borgia. It was all she could do to get through dinner with him.

"Let us drink to your happiness and mine," Cesare Borgia purred, picking up her goblet. His hand covered the entire stem. To take it from him would require touching his fingers.

"Let us drink twice, then." Charlotte used both hands at either side of the balloon of the goblet to take it. It was not the correct way to hold a drinking cup, but under no circumstances did she wish to touch any part of the arriviste before her.

Cesare put his other hand over one of Charlotte's before she could lift the goblet to her lips. "Let my happiness be to make you happy."

"I'm afraid I cannot," Charlotte replied. Her skin crawled as his hand touched hers.

"And why is that?" Cesare Borgia asked, his dark eyes boring into hers. Overpowering male beauty flooded her senses then rolled off her like water off a duck's back as Nicolas de Laval's image came to her. She was mad at him, it was true. But stubbornly he would not leave her thoughts, blocking the efforts of the man now trying to make inroads with her.

"My father would forbid it." *And you would never make me happy under any circumstances.*

"The king will ensure that your father give his permission," Cesare argued, his eyes moving to the neckline of her bodice.

"My father is a king, too. He will not be dictated to by a peer." And I will not be raked over by a peasant, she thought, wanting to slap him. Instead she balled her hand at her side and shifted her leg farther from his under the table. It was infuriating that he had pulled his chair next to hers instead of sitting across from her, as any well-born chevalier in a first encounter would do.

"Of course not, my lady. The king of France will suggest and your father will find his suggestions agreeable."

"I'm afraid he will not," Charlotte demurred. *In fact, I will be delighted if he is utterly appalled.*

"And why is that?" Cesare demanded.

"Because ... because ..." she must tread carefully not to crush the pride of the potentially dangerous man before her.

"Because what?"

"Because I am taken by another."

Anger flashed in the Italian's eyes. "No word of this has reached my ear from the king and queen."

"It has not yet been announced." And perhaps never would be, but she couldn't imagine her sovereign mistress allowing her to be delivered into the hands of a street ruffian, no matter how powerful his father was.

"Then, until it is, you are free to entertain another attachment." Cesare took a gulp of wine then smacked his lips.

"I'm afraid I'm not," Charlotte said. And certainly not with a man who smacks his lips, she thought.

"And why is that?"

"Monsieur, is it the custom in your country to press a lady on private matters?" Charlotte drew herself up. The sooner she could end this conversation the better.

"If the lady is receptive, then yes."

"Then you have my answer, Monsieur."

"That you will give me a chance?"

"That my heart is already taken." She didn't know why she felt herself already attached, but she did.

Cesare Borgia looked indignant. "Will you not at least allow me to try to change your mind?"

Charlotte shook her head. "You have my answer."

"Then you have wasted my time." Borgia scowled.

"This was not my idea, Monsieur." How dare this swaggering man turn the tables on her? It was she who had had her time wasted but it would not do to say so, as it had been the king and queen who had insisted on this dinner. She must disengage the foreigner's interest delicately. Word had traveled to her ears that back in Rome he had had his older brother's throat slit in order to claim his inheritance. She would not like to earn the enmity of a man capable of such an act.

As she rose from the table, she sensed it would not do to leave him angry. Leaning ever so slightly toward him so that he would be distracted by the bounty of her décolletage, she bade him good evening. "Sire de Valentinois, I wish you all the happiness in the world with a bride dazzled to be the wife of such a powerful and handsome man." *And who will most certainly not be me* she didn't say.

With a ravishing smile she flicked back her headdress and swept from the room, leaving Cesare Borgia speechless.

"I must have Charlotte!" he shouted, as petulant as a five-year-old.

"We shall see what we can do." Louis shifted uncomfortably in his seat. A message from King Frederick, delivered by envoy from Naples just minutes earlier, was tucked into his sleeve.

"But she won't have me!" Cesare raged.

And neither would her father, Louis thought but didn't say. The note had been blunt: 'I would never give my legitimate daughter to a bastard son of a pope.'

"We shall see what the queen says," Louis hedged, praying she would soon appear. He was no good in situations like this. Matchmaking was his wife's forte, not his.

Hidden behind the arras concealing the alcove adjoining the room, Anne pricked up her ears. Catching every word, she sensed she must act. The young Borgia must be appeased. Her husband had promised him a noble French bride and they must deliver one. But God forbid it be her prize maid of honor, the highborn princess of Naples. Yet this upstart needed as highborn a wife as possible to manage the social leap from no-body to somebody.

Who could she offer amongst her beloved maids of honor to serve the social bounder's needs? And who amongst her maids of honor would not find Cesare Borgia as unsuitable as the prin-cess of Naples had? The gifted Anne de Candale?

The queen froze. Never. She had other plans for her: a royal match, to raise the girl's rank as befit her intelligence and great promise under her tutelage at court. A man like Cesare Borgia would feel threatened by such a woman for a wife.

The sweet Germaine de Foix? A shudder ran through her. The king would forbid his own niece being married off to a bastard, no matter how charming he was or helpful to Louis' aims in Italy.

The exquisite Charlotte d'Albret?

Anne paused. The young woman was as fine as her father was not. Yet she had grown up in his household. She would know how to handle a coarse man. Furthermore, her father would leap at the chance to increase his power by aligning his family with the pope's. Alain d'Albret was ambitious, not squeamish. She sensed he would not hesitate to marry off his daughter to a bastard as long as he received financial gain from it, as well as an important friend in Rome.

Besides, it was payback time for Anne to take her revenge on the coarse Gascon, who had leered at her on every occasion they had met in the years after her father had died. She had spurned him before the entire Estates General of Brittany just to get him off her back. Was it possible that he would see as a social advantage precisely the play that would offer her the sweetest revenge on him for his unwanted suit for her hand?

She would deliver a Charlotte. Just not the one Cesare Borgia thought he wanted. If her second Charlotte, the daintiest, most

delicate of all her Cordelières, was agreeable, she would likely make
Borgia forget all about the first Charlotte in a matter of seconds.

Sailing into the room, Anne glided up to their raging
guest. "Did you say you must have Charlotte?" Her smile was
the most beguiling one she had offered him yet.

"I am here to take Charlotte for my wife and I will have
her!" Borgia shouted. A slight prod from the courtier behind
him reminded him to dip one knee at the entrance of the queen.
Clumsily, he did so, adding, "Your Majesty."

"Shall I call her now?" Anne's tone dripped honey.

"She has changed her mind, then?" he asked, startled. Back
in Italy and before that, in Spain, the ladies had dropped like
flies for him. Since arriving in France, scullery and laundry
maids had, too, even a most charming tutor, but amongst the
ranks of noblewomen he had met at court he was finding himself a tougher sell. Self-consciously he put a hand to his face.
God forbid that cursed rash had come back.

Anne studied the man, wondering why he was hiding his
face. Did he have a weak spot? It was hard to find one, but did
not every man, beginning with Achilles?

There was only one way to deal with the likes of Cesare
Borgia, she decided. Only one quality could prevail against
such unbridled masculinity: supreme femininity. No one possessed such a quality more than the candidate she had in mind.

Anne clapped her hands.

An attendant appeared. The queen whispered to her briefly
and the woman hurried from the room.

Louis bid Cesare come to him and together the men went to
a nearby table, where the king unfolded a map of Italy. Within
seconds they were deep in conversation, Borgia's full dark head
of hair close to Louis' lighter head, his lank straight hair thin-
ning somewhat with age.

Anne glanced at them, thinking what fools men were with their grand plans for conquest in places far from home. Putting her hand to her belly, she felt the warm comfort of life inside. Her work was at home and she was now intent upon it. If it came to fruition she would deliver in October, the same month her beloved Charles-Orland had been born. God grant her one to replace him. How sure she had been that she would have a son when she had carried him, seven long years ago.

But now, seven dead babes later, at age twenty-two, she no longer felt the certainty of youthful optimism. All she was sure of now was that the child was still alive inside her, judging by the heat she felt throughout her body.

A rustling sound at the door interrupted her thoughts.

"Oh, there you are, Charlotte," she called out. "Come in, I have someone for you to meet."

"I have already met her, Your Majesty," Cesare Borgia grunted, without lifting his head from the map on the table. Worried that his rash had returned, he did not wish to show his face too closely to anyone until he had examined it himself in the Venetian mirror he always traveled with. Besides, he would not rush to be scorned once more by the princess of Naples. She would be his, but first he would teach her a lesson for treating him so disdainfully at dinner the week before.

"I don't believe we have," a musical voice floated toward him, along with the scent of lemon verbena.

Cesare's senses sprang to attention. Was it possible that the woman who had been so cold to him before was now so sweetened that even her voice and scent were different? It had all been an act, perhaps. What woman could resist such a man as he? Careful to angle away the side of his face upon which the rash had last appeared, he lifted his eyes.

At the sight that met him, his mouth fell open. The

delicate beauty before him was not the tall, imperious princess of Naples at all. Thoughts of the other Charlotte fell from him like dust shaken from a doublet. Who was this fairylike new creature?

"Your Majesties." The young noblewoman curtseyed gracefully, her head bowed. When she rose, she lifted an exquisitely fine-featured face to the queen. Perfectly trained, she did not attempt even a glance at the chevalier in the room with them. She would wait until the queen directed her further.

"Monsieur le duc de Valentinois, I present to you one of my maids of honor—Charlotte d'Albret."

Cesare Borgia bowed to the new Charlotte. "Enchanted, Mademoiselle."

"Mademoiselle d'Albret is the daughter of Alain d'Albret, Count of Gavre," the queen continued.

"I have heard of him," Borgia remarked, his eyes fastened on the face of the sloe-eyed gentlewoman before him. The princess of Naples was beautiful in a grand sort of way. This one was a beauty in a more exquisite vein. It was one he wished to mine. His heart beat faster.

"Is he not known as Sire le Grand d'Albret?" he continued. He had heard of this powerful Gascon from the south. He, too, was from the south, and thought of himself as rather grand. Perhaps he could make more headway with the father of this enchanting woman than with the father of the princess of Naples, who, as far as he knew, had not yet sent a response to his request for his daughter's hand.

"Indeed he is, Monsieur," Louis said, folding up the map of Italy. There would be other occasions to study it with the young Borgia. At the moment it appeared that his guest only had eyes for the maiden who stood before him. It was a wonder indeed that a woman with such elegant features could actually have been sired by the coarse man who had tried to marry his *Brette* in the troubled days before she had wed Charles.

Knowing his wife, he had a feeling this was her way of paying back d'Albret for his unwanted pursuit of her. Let him feel the pain now of seeing his dainty daughter in the hands of a brute cut from the same cloth as he.

But as Louis glanced closer at Charlotte d'Albret, he saw that his wife's maid of honor was not shrinking from the bold gaze of his guest. Instead, she was gazing back.

Perhaps this match might not prove a sacrifice at all.

CHAPTER FIFTEEN

Fall 1499

The Wisdom of Christine de Pizan

In the wake of a mild spring, summer arrived in Blois, and with it the plague. Anne and Louis wished to take no chances while they awaited the birth of their first child together. Louis insisted that Anne join Louise de Savoy, in Romorantin, a day's ride to the south. Until Anne produced a male child, Louise's son, Francis d'Angoulême was France's dauphin; as such, their position was high at court.

"She wishes me only daughters," Anne complained as Louis laid out his reasoning.

"*M'amie*, you know how she looks after her son. You are better protected from the plague with her than you would be locked up in a fortress deep in the woods."

"It makes me sick the way she calls him her little Cesar. Am I to be surrounded by Cesars my entire life?" Anne made a prunish face.

"At least I am taking the big Cesare off your hands. He rides out with me in two weeks, and you are going to Romorantin if I have to escort you there personally before I leave."

"Of course you must escort me there personally. You must make it clear to Louise that if I join her household temporarily I am still queen and must be accommodated as such."

Louis' sigh was deep. Why couldn't the two women closest to him get along? His cousin Charles' widow was as conscientious and prudent a woman as they come. She lacked Anne's fire, but he wished that his wife could appreciate Louise de Savoy's many admirable qualities. If only the two women could make peace and enjoy each other's company, he wouldn't feel so guilty about leaving Anne behind.

"Sire, you are wanted in the great gallery. An envoy is here from Milan with a message for you," Louis' squire bellowed, his young face full of importance at being asked to fetch the king.

"Tell them I will be there shortly," Louis commanded him. Turning to Anne, he kissed her then leaned over and kissed her growing belly. "I will make sure Louise knows your needs while you stay with her till the babe arrives. But rest assured, *m'amie*, you could not be in better hands than with Francis' mother. She will guard her home, indeed the entire town, from the plague so carefully that you will be in the safest spot in all of France while you await our prince's birth.

"Don't say that, husband. I said it too many times myself in the past and was wrong."

"I would be perfectly happy with a princess."

"The throne of France needs a dauphin."

"It has one in Francis." Louis was extremely fond of the boy. France could do worse than have a king one day like the man the boy promised to grow into. Only the week before, the young chevalier had held his own in a game of tennis against him.

"No more Cesars, please!"

"*M'amie,* I must go. Bid your attendants to begin packing and bring all you need for several months. No more traveling, once you are there, until after the babe is born."

Louis strode from the room. Thank God he had business on the other side of the Alps. Never mind the heat of summer, it was the hothouse atmosphere of his sparring womenfolk he was desperate to escape. Anything would be preferable to staying at home watching Anne grow larger and more irritable each day then having to listen to her complain about Louise every night.

Two weeks later, the king escorted Anne to Romorantin then turned east toward Lyon. He would rest his men there a few days, then proceed to Grenoble and across the Alps to Milan. It would be the same path Charles had taken five years earlier. He told himself it would not be the same outcome.

Anne was as sorry to see Louis go as she was delighted to see Cesare Borgia leave. There was no point to try to convince her husband to tarry. He had something to prove across the Alps and, God knew, she needed to let him prove it. Having managed her father in the years after her mother's death, then Charles, she knew enough about men to know Louis would feel less of one if she prevented him from attempting to fulfill his mission in Milan.

While he was away, she would pray he did not disport himself the way Charles had in Naples. By the time the bedraggled remnants of his army had returned sixteen months' later, at least a third of them carried the 'mal de Naples' back to their wives and sweethearts in France.

But with Louis she felt reassured that it would not be the same scenario. Louis' more mature age would temper him. More importantly, their deeper love for each other would curb his appetites and steer him to pursuits that could withstand the light of day. She knew her second husband. He was hers through and through, in a way that Charles had never been.

Charles VIII of France had been unsure of himself and in need of constant reassurance. Twenty-one when they married, he had been twenty-seven and a half when he died. In his final five months he had begun to settle down; who knew what kind of king he would have matured into if he had lived?

Louis, on the other hand, was sure of who he was at the age of thirty-seven. His love for her was mingled with his love of freedom, the bracing scent of Brittany and the sea, his desire to avoid the clutches of Anne de Beaujeu, daughter of France, and the responsibilities of being a prince of the blood of the land he was born in. It was much to manage; at times he needed to escape.

Anne understood. She was having her moment, too, cultivating a circle of artists around her, as well as her ladies' court, as her belly grew. She ruled herself not to think of the birth or the days thereafter. It would not do to dwell on the past, so she turned her mind to the present. With her husband gone and that ridiculous Italian peacock with him, she turned her attention to her maids of honor.

Charlotte of Naples had been adamant in her refusal of Cesare Borgia for a husband. Anne had agreed with her. Why should a princess born and bred marry a parvenu, no matter how ambitious or able? God knew the Borgia possessed considerable assets. He put to shade any man standing next to him. Fortunately, Charlotte d'Albret had noticed and her father had been sufficiently sweetened to grant his permission for the match.

August passed quickly and pleasantly, spent mostly in the

garden reading to and with the handful of her maids of honor she had chosen to accompany her to Romorantin. Her host's daughter, little Marguerite d'Angoulême, had joined them at the age of seven. She was bright and quick, and reminded Anne of herself at that age. As much as she disliked Louise de Savoy, she could see the noblewoman raised her children well. She ran her household strictly, but with sophisticated touches and a large library. Frankly, Anne knew in her heart of hearts that the real reason she disliked her was because Louise had two beautiful intelligent children, whereas Anne had none. All that might change in a few months, but then again it might not.

Anne's school for young noblewomen was growing in prestige. She was strict with them; both in their education, exposing them to classical works, and in their comportment, insisting on no dalliances. Her young ladies were gaining a reputation as the most eligible crop of noble maids in Europe. She would harvest them well, one by one, matching each with a man worthy of the training and education she had given them. The kings, princes, and great lords she married them to would be tied to the French and Breton courts through them, thereby strengthening Louis' and her power throughout Europe.

"Your Grace, do you think that our Charlotte will marry soon?" Anne de Candale asked, one hot August afternoon in the garden. They rested after finishing a strenuous chapter from Madame de Pizan's most acclaimed work, *The Treasure of the City of Ladies.* The girls had each read the part of a female character in the book representing one of the three virtues: reason, justice, and rectitude. The queen had chosen her to read the part of Reason. It seemed only reasonable that Charlotte should marry soon, since she was already nineteen, Anne de Candale told herself. She was next in line to have a marriage partner selected for her by her sovereign queen.

"I think that she will marry when I am ready to give my permission for her to do so," the queen told her cheeky charge.

"And who do you think will make a fitting prince for her?" Germaine de Foix asked. She had just read the part of Justice. It seemed just to her that Charlotte should be allowed to marry the man of her choice.

"I have not yet decided." It was a good question. Who indeed was worthy to marry her most highly ranked maid of honor, whose father was king of Naples?

"Will it be a foreign prince, or one from home?" Anne de Candale asked, her eyes wide and dreamy.

"It will be one most suited to handle her," the queen told her in a practical tone.

"Then I daresay one from home," Anne de Candale remarked.

"Not that it is your concern, but what is your reason?" the queen asked. She had been mulling over the question of finding a match for Charlotte, but no princes of Europe's royal houses were of marrying age at the moment.

"Our Charlotte is like a finely bred horse. She will do best with a lord who knows her well. How could a foreign prince understand her as well as a French or Breton one?" Anne de Candale-Foix was descended from the queen's mother's side, the daughter of Marguerite de Foix's younger sister.

The queen said nothing, but thought to herself that she had observed the same of the princess of Naples.

"Should he not be a man of rectitude?" Little Marguerite d'Angoulême asked. She had just read the lines of Rectitude from Christine de Pizan's well-known book, and was eager to use the important word right away.

The queen looked at her, impressed. Louise de Savoy's daughter was precociously intelligent. "Little one, he must indeed be filled with rectitude."

"He must be a great lord but he must also have the finest sensitivity toward his wife, so that Charlotte's gifts will be drawn out and not trampled upon," Anne de Candale observed.

"It is time to get back to our reading," the queen directed her, thinking how astute her young kinswoman was. She was worthy of a great lord for a husband, perhaps a king or emperor. Anne would look carefully to find the best possible match for her most clever Cordelière.

"Your Grace, doesn't Madame de Pizan say that married love is the surest way to achieve the virtues we have just read about?" Germaine de Foix asked.

"Yes, my dove. For that reason I asked Anne to find this book in the library here for you to read today. But now I have letters to write, so you must finish up yourselves, and Madame Leroux will quiz you tomorrow on what you have learned."

Anne de Candale squirmed in her seat. She had found quite a few works by the most famous female author of the times in the library of their host. In particular, one had caught her eye, but not the one from which they had just read. The second book was now hidden under the cushion on which she sat. It was fitting that the queen had given her the part of Reason to play. Was it not reasonable that the girls should examine other works by noteworthy authors, in order to understand the full scope of their thoughts?

Anne of Brittany got up and bade one of her ladies-in-waiting to find Madame Leroux, then re-entered the house. She would send off a letter to Charlotte's father, Frederick of Naples, once she had decided on a few candidates for his daughter. God knew an alliance with one of France or Brittany's noblest families would please him more than the suit of Cesare Borgia. Most fortunately, Alain d'Albret had relinquished his daughter in exchange for the handsome sum of 200,000 écus, paid to him by the pope, as well as a red cardinal's hat for d'Albret's son, Amanieu.

Cesare and Charlotte had married in May in the queen's own chambers in Blois. Rumor had it that the radiant bride was already with child.

The moment the swish of the queen's gown was no longer heard, Marguerite d'Angoulême jumped to her feet. "Let's play!" she cried, hopping up and down for sheer high spirits.

"No, little one. Let's read some more." Anne de Candale patted the cushion next to her for Marguerite to sit down.

"But the virtues are so dull! I've had enough," Germaine de Foix protested.

"I have another book here by the same author that's more interesting." Anne de Candale's eyes glittered.

"What is it?" The girls clamored around as she pulled out the volume from beneath where she sat.

"It is a book of poetry by Madame de Pizan. Now, who would like to read the first stanza of one of her poems?"

"Will it be more dullness on virtue and rectitude, then?" Germaine de Foix sighed unhappily.

"Not from what I saw when I leafed through it in the countess' library," Anne de Candale replied, pulling the littlest one closer to her. "Marguerite, why don't you open the book to a page and we will read the poem on it from the beginning."

The little girl, pleased to be given an important role, closed her eyes then opened the slim book to a random page in the center. It fell open there easily, apparently having been opened to that section numerous times before. The poem on the page before them was titled 'The Lady'.

Anne de Candale took a deep breath and began to read.

'Come to me, sweetest friend, at the usual hour,
do not fail to come, for the gossip mongers want
to attack our love, which makes me tremble with fear.
Beware of them, be wise, for they are
determined to hurt us, I am sure of it. We have
to be very careful, I have heard all about their
ways. They will harm us, may hell fire burn them!'

The girls fell silent, their eyes wide, as Germaine de Foix continued.

'And don't make the mistake of coming too late or
too early, for I will not fall asleep. God help
me, I desire you with the loyal heart of a lover.
And if you feel the same desire put on a brown
habit and cloak to disguise yourself, I beg you,
so that you will deceive the guard they have put
around me, this is not a joke. They will harm us,
may hell fire burn them!'

"My turn now," little Marguerite piped up, eager to display her
reading skills.

"No, little one. This poem must be read by a woman, not a
girl," Anne de Candale declared. "I will continue."

'I am so impatient, sweet friend, that I am crying.
May I be with you in an hour and a half, I know
and ask for no other good, without you I feel
dazed. Watch out for what 'they' do before you
leave, for my reputation will suffer if one sees
you, and so, though I am impatient, I am afraid
of being found out by them. They will harm us,
may hell fire burn them!'

"I am thirteen now, a woman for a year already, so I shall read next." Germaine de Foix pulled the book from Anne de Candale's lap and read the final stanza.

'Oh, sweet friend, I would be so reassured if I were in your arms. I am such a coward in face of the gossip mongers and their false designs. They will harm us, may hell fire burn them!'

A long pause ensued as the girls absorbed as much as they could of the words they had just read.

Finally, Anne de Candale broke the stillness. "So what do you make of that?" Her face was flushed, although not from the heat of the day, as they sat in the shade.

"I don't understand it at all, but it is very... very..." Marguerite d'Angoulême looked from one girl's face to the other. Whatever it was, it seemed to be a poem about a big secret between two adults who desired something urgently, but she knew not what.

"It is very exciting! Is this the way grown up ladies act?" Germaine de Foix asked, unknown delights firing her thoughts.

"I'm not sure, but this is definitely the way some of them think," Anne de Candale answered.

"I think this is the way they act, too," Germaine de Foix declared.

"Why say you that?"

"Because one of the ladies of our court in Blois bid me go to bed when I tried to help her one night when I got up to get some water from the kitchen."

"What do you mean?"

"I mean, I could tell she was waiting for someone,"

Germaine de Foix whispered. But when I asked if I could help her, she shushed me and bid me go back to my room."

"Are we not all waiting for someone, *ma chère?*" Anne de Candale asked, rather philosophically.

"Or something," a new voice put in.

The girls gasped as the face of Madame Leroux above them looked down at the book Anne held.

"Give me that," she ordered.

"Oh, Madame, please don't take it from us. It is so very interesting to read such words," Anne de Candale pleaded, holding the book tight in her hands and hugging it to her chest.

"I'm sure it is, little goose." Madame Leroux's tone was stern, but something else swam in her eyes; a softer, gauzy look that wasn't stern at all.

"Even more precious to feel such feelings, don't you think?" Germaine de Foix asked.

Madame Leroux's smile was tight. How well she knew the cruel caprices of illicit passion. Could the memory of a few nights of joy override the pain she would feel forever on having been discarded the same day her dark friend met Charlotte d'Albret? Yet, given the choice again, would she not still have flown into his arms?

"*Mes demoiselles,* I can only advise you to marry well," she told her charges.

"What does that have to do with anything?" Anne de Candale asked, puzzled. Why wouldn't any of the noblewomen who watched over them reveal the real mysteries of the adult world they would soon enter?

"Because once passion's flame has arced and returned to Earth, you will have nothing left if you don't," the tutor replied.

"But, Madame, this story has nothing at all to do with marrying well."

"No, *ma chère*. You are entirely correct. It has to do with secret passion that leaves nothing but memories: some sweet, and some sorrowful, in its wake."

"Then where is the connection?" Anne de Candale demanded.

"When you marry well, and I hope for all of you that you do, you will be subject to the same laws of nature everyone else is."

"Which laws?"

"The arc of passion's arrow."

"Meaning?" It was exciting to hear her tutor talk in such terms. Never before had Anne de Candale heard the older slightly faded noblewoman speak of passion before. Suddenly, she seemed younger, more vivid, as if she'd burst into color.

"Meaning what goes up to Heaven returns again to Earth," Madame Leroux explained. "But for the lady who marries well, Earth is filled with bounty; children and homes to manage, staff to oversee, charities and churches to give alms to, and many more pursuits that will occupy a woman's hours richly, to fill the time before passion's arrow shoots Heavenward again."

"And what if one does not marry well, but has watched passion's arrow fall back to Earth?" Anne de Candale asked, her quick mind moving to the corollary of her tutor's mysterious words.

"Then one suffers in silence, dependent on others to provide a place or position, and if one is terribly unlucky a babe arrives with no father to claim it." Madame Leroux's eyes wandered to the window as a collective gasp filled the room.

"How sad, Madame!" Anne de Candale exclaimed. Finally, they were learning something real rather than passing dull hours perusing texts on virtue and rectitude.

"How shocking!" one of the older girls cried.

"Yes, my dears. And that is why so many convents are located deep in the woods, far from prying eyes."

"Is it a place for ladies in a certain condition to go?" Anne de Candale had heard of unlucky ladies of the court who had found themselves in dire straits. Invariably, they would be called away by a far-off kinsman. Some returned to court months later, more subdued, less jolly and gay. Most of those who returned married soon after. Others were said to have taken the veil, having suddenly received a religious calling. Those were the ones never seen or heard from again.

"Yes, my dear. As well as a refuge for many other women who may not hear God calling them, but need a place to turn to for lack of any other." Madame Leroux had already begun counting her days. So far she was not worried.

"Then it is a solution for a woman in need," Anne de Candale summed up.

"A solution that falls far short of marrying well and building one's own happy and full life."

"How do you know all this?" Anne de Candale asked, cocking her head and scrutinizing her tutor.

Because, if I am unlucky, it might well be my story, the older woman did not say. "All I know is that if you read more of Madame de Pizan's books, you will see that her conclusion is the same as the one I've given you: marry well, so that you may enjoy passion's caprices with a safe place to land when you fall back to Earth."

"Madame, I had no idea you were so wise!" Anne de Candale exclaimed. Their tutor seemed like an entirely different person, one who knew far more than just knowledge taught from books.

"Madame, may we read another of Madame de Pizan's poems for tomorrow's lesson?" Germaine de Foix asked. Her tutor's importance had risen in her eyes, too. What more might she have to teach them?

"You may give me that book now, and I will see if there's anything suitable in there for you to read." She held out her hand.

Reluctantly, Anne de Candale relinquished the delightful book of poems.

"Now you may go inside and put on your smocks. We will continue our lessons in the herb garden, where you can put courtly love poems out of your head and learn something useful for the households you will be running one day."

With a smart crack Madame Leroux snapped the book shut She would at least have the consolation of reliving her feelings that night before sleep overtook her. God knew she was well acquainted with the fire that burned inside her at the thought of Cesare's hands on her. Every night she relived the bliss then pain of remembering his touch again and again, knowing he had abandoned her for a woman of higher rank. And now that he had departed France for Italy, who knew but he might abandon his new wife as well?

But Charlotte d'Albret, even if left abandoned and with child, was now the duchess de Valentinois, with land, holdings, and the yearly pension of her husband the duke. She had married well, unlike herself, who, most likely, would never marry at all.

Hurrying from the room, she counted her days again on one hand and realized she had missed a few.

She crossed herself as her eyes wandered to the window again.

On the night of October twelfth, Anne felt her first birth pang. Nothing about the experience was easy. The pains themselves were the easiest to bear, far easier than dark memories of three times before when she had delivered a babe, only to die within hours, days, or weeks. She tried to focus on happy thoughts as she rested between contractions.

Only the day before she had heard via courier that Louis had entered Milan to a resounding welcome. The duchy's previous duke, Ludovico Sforza, the man known as *il Moro*, had fled. It had been an auspicious entry for Louis.

Yet she remembered the same sort of welcome given to Charles when he and his army entered Naples in February of 1495. How happy she had been for him and for herself at that time, their young prince a strapping two-year-old and another babe on the way.

But all three joys had disappeared by year's end. Anne had lost her unborn child the following month. Charles had returned from Italy in November, having lost Naples and gaining a scurrilous pox carried home by many of his men. The 'mal de Naples' slowly disfigured them, often with a telltale rash, then eating away at noses and lips, causing their wives and sweethearts back in France to shrink from them. Worst of all had been that December of 1495 when, just days after their fourth wedding anniversary, Anne and Charles' precious dauphin succumbed to measles.

"Madame, the countess of Angoulême wishes to assist you," one of Anne's attending midwives interrupted her thoughts.

"Not until I have delivered my babe!" Anne cried. She grit her teeth as the next contraction began. Whatever magic arts Louise de Savoy knew, Anne didn't doubt she would use them to ensure the coming babe was not a boy, so that her precious Cesare would remain dauphin.

"Yes, Your Grace." The midwife kept her tone neutral and placed a lavender-scented cloth between the queen's teeth for her to bite when the next contraction came. The midwife knew all about superstitions surfacing during the birth process. It was every woman's due to exhibit every sort of unreasonable behavior during her hours of travail before delivering a child. Was not the birth process itself utterly unreasonable to women, supposedly frailer than men, yet made to suffer a hundredfold worse when it came to monthly courses and the agony of childbirth?

The midwife fussed over Anne, stroking her abdomen and easing the child down the birth canal in between bathing the queen's sweat-soaked face and massaging her shoulders and neck.

Hours passed in the companionable silence of women waiting together, suffering as one when one suffered. They ministered even more attentively, as not only was Anne of Brittany their sovereign queen but she had had no success with keeping any of her children alive. It was time for the queen's luck to change, the midwife told herself. Perhaps with a new husband siring this child, it would.

Just as dawn's light broke through the window, the babe's head crowned.

"Get it out!" Anne shrieked, no longer caring about anything other than deliverance from pain.

"A deep breath, Madame, then one final push," the midwife advised, grasping the head firmly.

"Shut up!" the queen screamed, thinking of all that had gone before and of how it needed to be different this time. What could she do to make the difference? Whatever it was, she would do it to her utmost.

"Now, Madame. As hard as you can! Out! Out! Out with you, babe!"

Anne screamed a sound as unholy as any ever heard. The pain of the babe's enormous head in her birth canal was unbearable.

She pushed. All that had gone before with her children was unbearable.

She pushed harder. Louis leaving her alone and trotting off to Italy was unbearable.

She pushed as if she were pushing an Italian vixen off a cliff. Bastard knave husband! She would kill him when he returned.

With a final thrust, it was done.

"Yes, Madame, yes! Your child is born, Madame; the babe is delivered!" the midwife exulted, catching the infant in both hands.

"Thank God," Anne exhaled, then waited to hear the news. Sounds of bathing the newborn, oohing and aahing, and a faint mewling cry that thrilled her heart filled the next few moments. Dear God, why hadn't anyone in the room said anything yet?

Already she could guess why not, but she clung to the brief blissful moment, before someone spoke, when she could imagine that she had delivered a dauphin for France.

"Congratulations, Your Majesty. You have a beautiful princess!" the midwife crowed.

Exactly the words she had expected to hear, but not the ones she wanted.

"Give her to me," Anne ordered weakly. She held out her arms and the midwife placed France's newest princess of the blood royal into them.

Peering into her daughter's face, her first thought was that she was so much smaller and more delicate than her Charles-Orland had been. This babe was tiny, almost doll-like, not a lusty screamer as Anne's ruddy boy had been. But alive, nonetheless.

She unwrapped the babe to see it's form. Perhaps in protest against the cold, the newborn princess batted the air with her fists. Anne laughed, all worries flying from her head. Her daughter was born, and she would do everything within her power to keep her alive.

"I shall call her Claude, for Claude of Besançon," she announced, referring to a popular saint to whom she had prayed some months earlier for the safe delivery of her child.

"Princess Claude is a beauty, Your Grace," the midwife exclaimed.

Anne studied her tiny daughter's face. In any case, she was alive. The image of her last princess, who had died the same day she had been born, filled her head. She remembered thinking the babe had been too quiet when she had arrived, as if unsure if she wanted to stay. As Claude squirmed again, Anne laughed with delight.

This princess would live. It was her duty, just as it was her mother's duty to control fearful thoughts and steel herself to meet her public, all of whom would congratulate her then whisper amongst themselves that the queen once again had failed to deliver a dauphin for France.

Anne would meet their glances with fierce ones of her own. The princess in her arms would one day be Duchess of Brittany. She had delivered an heir to her own country's ducal throne. France's loss, with its ancient Salic laws forbidding female succession, would be Brittany's gain. She smiled to think of it.

"Madame, the countess d'Angoulême is asking after you," an attendant whispered to her.

"Tell her I am sleeping." Anne turned her face to the wall to hide her grimace. No doubt Louise de Savoy would go directly to her chapel, where she would light a candle to whichever saint she had been praying to over the past months and thank him or her that no rival to her son had entered the world that day.

"I will take the child so you may rest, Your Grace." The babe's nurse came forward.

"No. I will hold her awhile longer." Anne looked into her daughter's face, unwilling to relinquish her even for a moment.

What if she fell asleep then woke to sad faces and glum voices informing her that her daughter had died? Thoughts crowded into her mind of that March day only a year and a half earlier, when she had slept after the birth of her princess only to learn, upon awakening, that her babe had returned to God.

Claude began to wail, a thin high-pitched cry. She sounded as if she were protesting her mother's thoughts: *That was her, not me. I am here now and not planning on going anywhere.*

Anne gave a weak laugh and hugged her tiny bundle closer.

"Your Grace, may I nurse the princess?"

"Yes, but bring her back to me when you're done." Anne allowed the nurse to take the child from her arms. As she fell back on her pillows, she prayed to St. Claude to keep her daughter alive.

The princess lived, and her father returned home within a week of her birth to meet her. Anne was warmed that Louis would cross the Alps again, mid-campaign, just to see his newborn daughter. God knew Charles had not been willing to leave Italy for a full eighteen months, despite Anne's miscarriage and her repeated pleas for him to return as soon as possible so they could reunite with their son in Amboise.

Instead the king had tarried in Italy, then again in Lyon after crossing the Alps. After weeks of delay, news arrived that their dauphin was gravely ill.

They had torn across France back to Amboise. But before they could reach home the boy's soul had flown Heavenward. Anne had never been able to forgive Charles his delays after the death of their son.

But Louis was showing her what a different sort of man he was. It had not taken the birth of a son to compel him to rush to her bedside. He was here now, glowing with pride and refusing to relinquish his little princess until she bawled with outrage at not being fed. The moment she had drunk her fill, the king insisted on holding her again, bringing tears of joy to Anne's eyes.

A rustle outside the door announced a visitor.

"The countess of Angoulême requests an audience," an attendant said in a low voice, anticipating the queen's expected response.

"Louise, come in!" Louis heartily bade the figure at the door.

Anne steeled herself. Louise de Savoy was her host. She had offered safety and hospitality to her and select members of her court. As queen, she must compose her face and be civil to the mother of France's dauphin. Putting on her most gracious expression, Anne beamed regally as the countess of Angoulême sailed into the room.

"Your Majesties, congratulations!" Louise sang out, her eyes moving to the babe.

"Behold your daughter-in-law, Madame!" Louis jested as he moved toward her to show her the princess Claude.

Anne bit her tongue in dismay. What was Louis thinking to say such a thing? Her daughter was heir to the duchy of Brittany. The last thing Anne wanted was for her to sit on the throne of France as Francis' queen. If such an eventuality came to pass, Brittany would be forever entwined with France, and all her efforts to maintain its independence would go up in smoke.

"How delightful!" Louise de Savoy exclaimed, clasping her hands and bringing them to her mouth as if in rapture.

Louis turned to his wife, realizing his *faux pas* by the pained expression on her face. He hurried to her side and placed the babe in her arms, hoping to placate her with the delicious warmth and scent of their squirming bundle. "Do not fault me for my jest," he murmured as he bent over her.

Anne gave him a warning look as she took Claude in her arms. Was it a jest? If so, it was at her expense. She would make him pay for it afterwards, although not too dearly. He had shown his manliness by rushing back to France the moment he had received word his daughter had been born. Anne knew her father, Duke Francis, would have done the same. Charles? Probably not.

"Your Majesties, shall I bring the children to see their little cousin?" Louise de Savoy asked.

"Yes," Louis said with a smile.

"No," Anne snapped at the same instant. An awkward pause ensued.

"Not now, my dear Louise," Anne broke the silence. "Let us wait until she is a little larger and then we shall introduce her to your children." She did not like the way Louise had referred to her children as "the children," as if they were the royal children. Only Claude was royal, and Francis would only be royal one day if Anne failed to give Claude a brother.

She told herself it would come to pass. But doubts plagued her on all sides. Best to thank God for the daughter she had and not dwell on the sons that she didn't.

Offering her husband a radiant smile, Anne continued. "Let us name Madame de Bouchage as Claude's godmother."

Louis looked startled, but quickly recovered. It seemed he was trying to remember who Madame de Bouchage was.

"My dear, what an excellent idea."

"Thank you." There. It was decided, however clumsy it had been to name another than Louise de Savoy as godmother to Claude with Louise standing right there. She had only done so because of Louis' jest. God knew what else he might offer Louise in the next moment. Anne sensed that if she hadn't spoken up he would have suggested the countess of Angoulême be

Claude's godmother as well as her future mother-in-law before she left the room.

Anne wasn't having it.

Back in Blois before Christmas, the queen's mood was expansive that Advent season. Her daughter, although small, was thriving. She had passed the two-month mark, under the care of a large, attentive staff. Anne relaxed her fears of losing yet another child in the first months of life.

To celebrate the joys the year 1499 had brought them, Anne invited a dozen noble families with daughters between the ages of seven and twelve to join her and the king for the New Year's festivities.

She would expand the number of her maids of honor, inviting the new ones into her order of the Cordelières to join the thirty-six already in her care. Anne knew that the heads of France's leading families thought of her as an upholder of traditional values of piety and decorum. They admired her combined qualities of refinement and rigor and had heard wondrous tales of the excellent education she gave her maids of honor, including instruction in Latin and the classics.

The king, for his part, reduced taxes as a gift to his subjects to celebrate the new century upon them. Louis, being a fiscally prudent man, decided to make up for the loss of revenue by reducing pensions and annuities so lavishly given out to members of the nobility in the previous century.

Louis reckoned that it was better to free up the income of his common subjects than line the pockets of noblemen who might gain too much power then use it against him. By reducing their tax burden the peasants would love him more, and the rising middle class of merchants and tradespeople would have more means by which to buy and sell goods and expand

French trade with nearby countries. His reasoning as king had transformed from the days when he had been duke of Orléans. No longer focused on merely holding on to his own family's wealth, he was now intent on increasing the wealth of every one of his subjects.

Louis was seeing the world with new eyes. He was the happiest of men to have Anne beside him. Her unchanging nature provided an anchor for him in the new times they were entering.

That New Year's Eve mass he thanked God for his stubborn *Brette*. Now that she had produced a daughter, why should she not produce a son? And if she didn't, there was the dauphin Francis d'Angoulême at the ready, as fine and promising a boy as any he had ever laid eyes on.

With much to be grateful for, King Louis XII of France rested during that momentous New Year's season. The old century passed to the new, and with it the dawn of a new era.

CHAPTER SIXTEEN

The Marriage of Charlotte of Naples

Within weeks their respite was over.

By mid-January, word had reached Blois that Ludovico Sforza had raised an army to retake Milan. "I must return," Louis told Anne.

"Your duty is to rule your country, not fight battles in foreign places," Anne protested.

"Milan is the ducal territory of the father of my grandmother, Valentina Visconti." The furrows running down either side of Louis' face deepened. "It is not a foreign land, it is my family's land by ancestral right. I must claim it for our daughter."

It was as if Charles' ghost paced the room, putting words into Louis' mouth. How well Anne remembered the same conversation, the same arguments before Charles had departed for Naples in August 1494.

"What will Claude care if she holds Milan or not? She will be Duchess of Brittany, busy on France's other border and at least ruling over a manageable population," Anne argued.

"My lady, what do you know of the Italian people?"

"Enough to know it's a land where popes father children and enemies poison each other instead of fighting fairly in the light of day." *And a land for which your own moderate temperament is far from suited.*

Louis shook his head sadly. "*M'amie*, the times are changing and chivalry no longer anchors men's behavior as it did when we were born."

"Truth to that, husband. And the winds of change blow most fiercely out of Italy. Look at that peacock who came to us last year with his lawless, uncourtly ways."

"Cesare was a big help to me in taking Milan."

"And I am sure he will prove a big help to someone else when it pleases him to change sides for a better offer elsewhere." Anne's tone was sharp.

"Many are like that, *m'amie.* Your father knew only too well what it was to have men loyal to him switch sides then switch back again. A ruler must be quick to forgive and forget when he needs what's before him done."

"And what's before you is your kingdom to guide into this new century, with its new ways and a new class of subjects emerging. If chivalry is over, then what's to take its place?"

"Don't leap too far ahead," Louis protested. "I must maintain the gains I have already made in Milan. Sforza will be dealt with once and for all."

"Then hire more Swiss soldiers and let your commander do his job."

Louis studied her. On both counts, not a bad idea. "At the very least I must go to Lyon, where I can direct operations."

"Then let us go to Lyon," Anne agreed. As long as he was somewhere where she could keep an eye on him.

The royal court moved to Lyon near France's border with the duchy of Savoy. Milan lay just beyond. By the first of February 1500, the French army, under the Italian commander that Louis had appointed, Gian Giacomo Trivulzio, had been forced to retreat to positions west of Milan. Four days later Ludovico Sforza entered the city, to joyous acclaim from its inhabitants.

It all seemed so treacherously familiar to Anne, the riotous welcome both Charles and Louis had initially received in Italy, then a complete reversal of support by the locals soon after.

But Louis was determined. Since lowering taxes he had found great favor among his French subjects, who had largely forgotten about his disgraceful annulment proceedings of the year before. In no time at all he raised a second army and put Louis de la Tremoille in charge, much to Anne's dismay.

"How can you appoint that man to lead your army, when he led the French against you and my father at St. Aubin?" Anne shrieked when she learned of his choice.

"My lady, the king of France must put aside the grievances of the duke of Orléans," Louis replied stoically.

"How can you possibly promote the man who invaded my city of Nantes at the head of Charles' army, then laid siege to my people in Rennes?" Anne railed at him.

"Madame, talent is talent. De la Tremoille is a top military commander. He is the man to do the job in Milan and clear my duchy of *il Moro* once and for all." Louis reached out and squeezed the side of Anne's neck.

"I don't understand how you can just forget the past and reward a man who was responsible for putting you in prison for three years!" Anne stormed.

"Madame, just as it was La Beaujeu who sent the French

army to invade Brittany, so it was she who had me locked up those three long years." Louis' face darkened, the light fleeing from his eyes as he thought of those lost years with which France's regent had punished him, not only for fighting on the side of the Bretons against France, but for spurning her affections. He would keep that memory far from his wife's inquisitive ears. Best if she didn't know, although he guessed she might have heard something of it, as had most at the French and Breton courts. "It is not de la Tremoille's fault that he ably carried out the mandate she charged him with."

"God's bells, husband, I will never be the man you are," Anne harrumphed, looking somewhat mollified by Louis' hand caressing her shoulder.

"*M'amie,* I am grateful you are not." He kneaded her tense shoulders, feeling her anger dissolve under his fingers. His fiery *Brette* required careful management. Having known her for sixteen years, he had an instinct for how to calm her when the occasion arose.

Within a few short weeks, the French army led by Louis de la Tremoille marched over the Alps. On the other side they would join Trivulzio's men to chase Sforza out of Milan once and for all, and reinstate the king of France on its ducal throne.

The battle came down to a decision by the government of the Swiss Confederation. Both the French and Sforza's army had hired Swiss mercenaries to do a large part of their job for them. But the Swiss Confederation had been informed of the battle about to take place, and to preclude Swiss killing Swiss they issued a proclamation forbidding any Swiss soldier from fighting against a fellow Swiss.

Obediently, the Swiss marched home, leaving the French and Italian armies to their own devices, both with greatly reduced numbers, as ineffective as they were effete.

Sforza's side had held the greatest number of Swiss mercenaries. With their numbers drastically reduced, *il Moro* dropped his battle plans and secretly fled Milan to retrench. Accompanied by a select group of men, Tremoille pursued him and, finally, in April, Sforza was captured. Louis took no chances and had him brought back to France as a prisoner.

With the people of Milan, however, Louis dealt less harshly. Its inhabitants were pawns in the hands of their rulers, he reasoned. They had seen a neverending parade of them in the past few decades. Who could blame them if they appeared to welcome one, then just months later, welcome the previous one's sworn enemy? They were trying to stay alive, just as every mortal creature strove to do.

Louis used the same politique he had used in France at year's end. Instead of punishing them, he reduced taxes. In addition, he offered something practical that Sforza had not. *Il Moro* had forbidden the export of grain from Milan during his rule.

But Louis knew that, at heart, Milan's rising merchant class cared more about personal prosperity than allegiance to whichever ruler might occupy the ducal throne at the moment. He passed laws allowing grain to be exported for the first time since 1494, when Sforza had come to power. Within months the king of France's popularity as the new duke of Milan had risen, along with economic conditions.

Anne was overjoyed to have Louis conduct Italian affairs from Lyon rather than Italy, not just for his safety but for his companionship. Her courses had not returned since giving birth to Claude. But the fire had resumed at the bottom of her stomach, informing her that new life grew inside once more.

She was determined not to dwell on the two miscarriages she had suffered the last time she had held court in Lyon while Charles had been in Italy. Instead she focused on commissioning works of art, responding to missives from within France and abroad, and finding a suitable match for her star maid of honor.

The news from Queen Isabella in Spain was especially interesting. Her daughter Joanna of Castile had given birth to her first son in Ghent at the end of February, a boy named Charles, whose father, Philip, was the son of Anne's first husband by proxy, Maximilian I of Austria. Should the boy survive, he would one day become Holy Roman Emperor, as his grandfather was now.

The infant Charles was heir to three of Europe's most powerful dynastic houses: Habsburg of Austria through his father, Trastámara through his maternal grandparents Ferdinand and Isabella of Spain, and Valois-Burgundy through his paternal grandmother Marie of Burgundy, whose father was Charles the Bold, the powerful duke of Burgundy, brother to Louis' grandfather. Would not such a prince make a good match for her daughter?

Anne was determined not to see Claude married off to Francis of Angoulême, the insufferable Louise de Savoy's only son. She did not wish to see Claude's ducal inheritance of Brittany in Francis' acquisitive hands, should he one day become king.

Louis was careful to steer clear of Anne's territory, but would a future king of France prove equally as reasonable? The young dauphin Francis was in frequent contact with the king and queen at court. At age five, already Anne could see his dominant and ambitious nature. She guessed he would snatch Brittany from her delicate Claude before the dust had settled on their marriage contract.

Sending a silver rattle to Joanna and Philip for the infant Charles, Anne wrote to Isabella to let her know how happy she was to hear that her first grandson was born, and how delighted she would be to have her own daughter meet the new prince when they were older.

She rested her hand on her gently rounded belly as she stored away thoughts on the boy as a future match for Claude. Should it be a son she carried, Francis d'Angoulême would no longer be dauphin, but simply the count of Angoulême. Neither she nor Louis would wish their daughter, a princess of France, to marry a mere nobleman.

Caressing the small mound of her belly, she whispered a prayer to St. Anne d'Auray. "Let my child live and let it be a son." Yet, as she did, she felt the stern gaze of the wooden statue in the church of St. Auray upon her. No solace lay there.

Shuddering, Anne turned to her ongoing project: finding a marriage match for the princess of Naples.

She sensed that if she did not arrange a match soon, nature would take over and sway Charlotte from the rigorous training Anne had schooled her in over the past seven years since the princess came to her court. Already Anne had noted her distracted air, a likely sign that some young gallant had taken up residence in her heart.

"My lord, have you heard yet from Charlotte's father concerning a match for her?" Anne asked.

"My lady, I have heard and he leaves it to you." Louis returned to studying the map of Italy spread out on the table before him.

"As well he should." Anne breathed a sigh of relief. Charlotte had been a valuable addition to her court. With the princess' mother dead, Anne wished to choose a match for her herself. She would find a nobleman or a prince of the highest caliber.

Charlotte was high-strung, as was to be expected in a princess from as noble a bloodline as hers. Anne was aware that such a highly-bred young woman needed an especially refined lord who would handle her with kid gloves. God knew it was getting harder to find such a candidate with the likes of men such as Cesare Borgia now rising to power. The times were changing along with the centuries and Anne knew she must save the best from the past while letting go of customs and traditions that would hold her subjects back. It was hard for her, a traditionalist at heart, who held dear the ways of her ancestors.

"But in return for charging you with such an important mission, Charlotte's father has requested my visit to him in Naples," Louis fibbed. He hadn't requested any such thing, but Louis had aspirations there. Why should the dream of his predecessor not be carried out by him in Charles' honor?

"Husband, what business do you have with that sinful place?" Anne cast him a gimlet eye.

"It is the business of France to ensure that the kingdom of Naples is in the hands of its legitimate ruler."

"Legitimate by whose definition?"

"By inherited title, of course."

Anne's laugh was bitter. "Or whoever's claim to inherited title is backed up by a strong army."

"Madame, do not worry yourself with the affairs of men. They are my concerns, not yours." Louis' tone was lofty, overblown to hide his true intent. He had no good excuse to invite himself to Naples other than a desire to see if it might be feasible to take it for the crown of France.

"Do you not have troubles enough in Milan for the moment?" Anne pursed her lips.

"For the moment Milan is calm. Now is the time to make further inroads."

"But why, husband? Why do you wish to gain control of

a land where princes gain and lose control of their territories faster than seasons change? It is a godforsaken place!"

"*M'amie*, it is a beautiful place, lush and ripe with new ideas and new ways of doing things." A hint of exasperation tinged Louis' usually patient tone.

"New, rotten-to-the-core ways of doing things through ways and means that have no moral foundation."

"My lady, 'tis not that. 'Tis a new way of thinking, of being, that is different from the old, and therefore suspect to those who are used to the old ways."

"How well you state it, husband. And what's wrong with the old ways? They were good enough for my father and they are good enough for me," Anne huffed.

"Lady, just last year I was at your side on your progress through your own realm. I saw how carefully you listened to the dreams and practical needs of your subjects."

"Of course I did." Anne's voice rose in indignation. "I love my subjects."

"And you support them in their dreams."

"What are you driving at, husband?" She eyed him suspiciously.

"The dreams men dream these days have changed. Your subjects long to expand the industries of their regions, to trade their crops and wares abroad, and to increase the prosperity of their families and their towns."

"And why should they not?"

"They should. I saw how ably you understood their needs. Did you not appoint worthy men to grow their trade and find markets for their exports?"

"I did indeed."

"And did you find such men amongst your sparring Breton noblemen?"

"Not particularly." Anne paused, thoughtful. Not at all, in fact.

"No. You found those talents among men of the merchant class: tradesmen, weavers, cloth makers, linen and flax exporters."

"What of it?"

"*M'amie*, Italy is run by a similar class of people. It is a place composed of powerful city-states where the nobility comes and goes, but the merchant classes hold together the center."

"And what's that have to do with how beautiful the women are in Naples?" Anne gave him a baleful stare.

Louis threw back his head and laughed. "Ahh, now you've hit the heart of the matter." With a merry gleam in his eye, he took his wife in his arms. "Lady, when will you realize that your husband now is not the one you had before, God rest his soul?"

He gazed into her eyes. He had felt both affection and protectiveness toward his younger cousin and brother-in-law, Charles. Unfortunately, he had not been able to save him from himself. His predecessor's endless dalliances had distracted him from governing well and had angered his wife. Louis would not make the same mistake, nor did he desire to.

Upon returning from Naples in 1495, it was clear Charles had lost an alarming amount of weight. Some had whispered he suffered from the 'mal de Naples' so many of his men had contracted there. It had been said that the accident that had ended his life might have been exacerbated by him being in poor health to begin with.

"I don't want you going there," Anne complained.

"Wherever I go, *ma Brette*, you are in my heart," Louis soothed her.

"As long as no one is also in your arms," Anne countered.

"Who do you think you're talking to, *m'amie?*" Louis gave her a mock scowl. "Have you gotten your husbands mixed up?"

"No, Louis! It's not that! It's just that ..."

"You must let me do what I need to do, as I let you rule your duchy," Louis reasoned.

"But you will be there and I will be here!" Anne cried.

"I will be back soon, my lady."

"Best that you don't go at all!"

"Best that you attend to your affairs and let me attend to mine," Louis said, placing his hand on her belly.

"Then you know?" Anne's look was coy.

"Know what?" What else was his *Brette* intent upon? Forever planning, ordering, executing, he had married a woman who got things done. With or without his permission.

"That I am with child." She broke into a smile.

"*M'amie*, that is good news!" Louis' heart leapt. Would to God that his wife might produce a son and heir. Claude was healthy and blooming, although somewhat small. Why should his queen not produce a dauphin?

Two weeks later a tourney was held, at the king's behest. Louis was in great spirits at the queen's news. Seven knights from his side were picked to break a lance with seven knights chosen by the queen.

"I leave it to you, *m'amie*, to decide the award we shall grant to the most skillful knight from my side, when we win," Louis jested.

"I will think of something to grant my most valiant knight when our side prevails," Anne riposted.

"May the best man win." Louis left it, knowing what a happy distraction it would be for his glowing wife to organize the tourney's details.

"My best knight most certainly will." Her heart was light as she thought about which seven knights she would choose.

She would select both French and Breton knights, to appease the French as well as to valorize her own countrymen among them. What fun it would be.

The day of the tournament arrived on the first of May with the most glorious weather imaginable. After three rounds of jousting for each knight paired with the same opponent from the opposing team, Anne exulted to see her own side, all in black, get the best of the king's side, dressed in white. There had been one dark moment, with the prince of Navarre getting thrown from his horse; but once it had been determined that he would recover, the mood again turned to merriment.

The final round was between Pierre de Bayard from the king's side and Nicolas de Laval from the queen's. De Bayard was known for his jousting skills as well as his exceptional chivalry. A few years older than de Laval, he was one of the king's ablest soldiers.

That day, the mount of the chevalier de Bayard was spirited; it was clear the knight was having a hard time controlling the horse. But the chevalier de Laval did not take advantage of the situation, keeping his lance exactly at shield level and exchanging equally matched blows in the first two runs.

"Is the Sire de Laval not graceful?" Anne de Candale elbowed Charlotte of Naples next to her.

"I suppose so," Charlotte answered stiffly. Inside, her heart melted to see Nicolas perform so well, exercising skill as well as restraint. She rued her own lack of restraint in her dealings with him. Was restraint not the hallmark of a courtly knight as well as a Cordelière?

Feeling her face burn, she berated herself again. Why, oh why had she not followed her head instead of her heart when she kissed him at the end of the afternoon they had spent together?

Unable to keep her eyes off the graceful chevalier, she held her fan to the side of her face to prevent her friend from observing her gaze. It was the same as the first day she had become aware of his eyes upon her from the courtyard and she had been unable to stop staring at him from the window. How could she allow herself to be pulled against her will to him every time she saw him?

No good could come of such lack of self-control. Christine de Pizan would not approve, and neither would the queen. Charlotte had been carefully raised at the queen's court to school her emotions. Yet every time the young gallant with chestnut hair appeared, her heart rushed toward him.

Sighing, Charlotte turned her head from Anne de Candale, fan firmly in place, so that she could privately observe the object of her obsession.

The third and final run was about to begin. She watched closely as Nicolas charged down the list. Taking care not to deliver a mortal blow, his lance above the waist and below the neck, he aimed directly into his opponent's shield.

The chevalier de Bayard toppled from his mount, hitting the ground with a hard thud. After a stunned moment, he lifted an arm to signal he was unharmed.

The crowd roared its approval. How well Nicolas displayed the chivalric values she had admired so greatly in him until he had sullied their idyll with too close a familiarity with a kitchen maid.

She eyed the chevalier de Bayard, rising to his feet from the dust and saluting Nicolas, delighting the crowd. De Bayard was a great knight, but neither he nor any of the others held a candle to the future count de Laval, with his arrow-straight posture and leanly muscled lines. It was a pity that his chivalry did not extend to his behavior off the field.

Peeking over her fan toward Anne de Candale, Charlotte

satisfied herself that her friend was busy talking to Germaine de Foix on her other side.

At the end of the final melee the king signaled the conclusion of the day's events, then whispered something to the queen. It was evident that the black team had bested the white team, not only in jousting but in the final team scrimmage.

As the queen stood the crowd quietened.

"Let the winning team approach so that I may consider the dearest wish of its ablest jouster," she announced. Sitting back down, she gave Louis a sidelong smirk. She enjoyed winning. Louis knew she did, and she knew Louis enjoyed indulging her. Now, if only she could indulge him with a son and heir.

"All hail the queen's team!" the crowd cheered as trumpets and tabors heralded the approach of the victors, riding slowly to the queen's box.

The queen congratulated each of the knights in turn. Then she pointed her May wand at Nicolas de Laval.

"You may ride forward, Sire de Laval."

"Your Majesty." Nicolas de Laval motioned forward his reddish-brown destrier until he was directly under the queen's box.

The queen reached over the side and tapped him on the shoulder, then handed him the May wand. "As champion of the winning team, I will consider granting whatever wish is dearest to you." She leaned closer. "So long as it is a reasonable one," she whispered. Nicolas was a longtime friend. She trusted him not to ask for something she wouldn't consider granting.

"Your Majesty, I am greatly honored." Nicolas bowed his head.

"Anything you ask, I will consider. Think well, Sire de Laval." The smile Anne gave him held a warning in it. She depended on her countryman, who had stayed by her side during the siege of Rennes, to name a reasonable request, one that would conform to the chivalric values of their noble Breton ancestors.

A hush rippled through the crowd as all eyes turned to the young knight. He sat motionless on his horse for a moment. Then he turned his mount and rode a few paces past the queen.

"Where is he going? What is he doing?" could be heard as the murmur of the crowd swelled. The entertainment of sport had shifted to entertainment more appealing to the ladies, whose excited tones could be heard above those of the men's.

Nicolas de Laval stopped directly in front of the stand where the queen's preeminent maids of honor sat. Anne de Candale flanked Charlotte of Naples on one side, Blanche de Montberon on the other.

Nervously, Anne de Candale glanced at both Charlotte and Blanche, the latter of whom returned her questioning gaze. But Charlotte sat still as a statue, locked in her own thoughts and looking neither to the right nor left.

Reaching out with the May wand, Nicolas tapped her gently on one shoulder.

"Fair lady Charlotte, Princess of Naples and Aragon, it is my deepest wish that our queen consider granting you the one greatest desire of your heart." He stared directly into Charlotte's eyes, his thick chestnut hair riffling in the May breeze.

Charlotte sat rooted to the spot, paralyzed. He still cared for her. Was it not time to forgive him for an infraction to which she had perhaps overreacted, her sensibilities inflamed by overwrought emotions?

Rising slowly, she stood tall in the golden May sunlight. For the first time in months, she met Nicolas de Laval's eyes. They were as fervent, and questioning as they had been that fateful afternoon when she kissed him. Caught in his gaze, all

thought left her except one: the inescapable realization that she
had not been able to rid him from her heart or her mind from
the moment she first laid eyes on him.

She turned to the queen. "Is it to our Majesty's liking
that her knight may commute to me Your Grace's award to
him?"

Anne of Brittany smiled back. "I grant to the future count
of Laval permission to commute his award to you, *Madame la
princesse*. Think carefully then tell me the one greatest desire of
your heart, that I may consider granting it."

Charlotte searched her soul. Nicolas had wounded her, but
she had wounded him. Yet here he was, handing her his heart
on a May wand for all to see.

So he had known the kitchen maid's name. She forgave
him. Charlotte herself had been overly familiar toward him.
She forgave herself. It was time to reach for what she wanted.
If she didn't, the soft rustle of the May breeze warned her she
might never get the chance again.

Taking a deep breath, she glanced at Nicolas then back to
the queen.

"Your Majesty, it is the greatest desire of my heart that you
should grant me this knight as my lord and husband, should
he wish it."

A gasp resounded throughout the crowd, followed by a
groundswell of excited voices. Here indeed was entertainment
of the highest order.

"Do you wish it, then, Sire de Laval?" the queen asked
Nicolas.

On bated breath, every man, woman, and child in the
stands awaited the valiant young knight's answer.

"With all my heart," he declared in the clear, sweet, late
afternoon stillness. The firm ring of his words announced to all

that chivalry remained alive and well in fair France on that first day of May of the new century.

And that was the end of the princess of Naples' indecision about the future count de Laval.

On the tenth of June in the year 1500, Charlotte of Naples and Aragon married Nicolas de Laval. Only three days later, Guy V, the great count de Laval, died, undoubtedly a happy man to see his nephew and heir marry so fine and highborn a princess. Immediately Nicolas took his uncle's name in his honor, becoming Guy VI, Count de Laval.

Feeling her duty well done to her highest ranking maid of honor, Anne turned her attention to those next in line to be found suitable matches.

Anne de Candale was foremost among them. But for such an intelligent and well-reasoned young woman, she wished to find a partner among the highest ranks of princedom in Europe. Anne knew that her young charge was eager to marry, but she would have to wait. She would thank her queen ultimately because Anne of Brittany had it in mind to make a match for her that would equal her own.

The babe inside had begun to move, but Anne was careful to contain her happiness. Too many times before she had tasted bitter grief instead of the joy of welcoming a child into the world. Distraction was what she needed, and projects she could sink her teeth into.

The queen poured her energies into commissioning works for herself, her husband, and the renown of her order of the Cordelières. She ordered work to begin on a new convent in Lyon to be called Notre-Dame-de-la-Cordelière. For herself, she commissioned an illuminated book of hours, and for Louis, the delivery of something she had commissioned the year before for his upcoming birthday at the end of the month.

Anne's spending habits matched her appetite for beauty and luxury. As much as she distrusted Italian politics, she was deeply impressed by the new designs and techniques that were flooding into France from across the Alps.

But the special surprise she had for Louis neither came from nor was inspired by Italy. It was a work firmly rooted in the feudal era in which both of them had been born. She prayed it would be a masterpiece. Indeed, it would need to be, considering its cost.

The tapestries had arrived at an inopportune moment. She had wanted them hung before the king found out about them. Despite their being a birthday present to him from her, she knew her husband. He would balk at their cost. She had already taken measures to conceal the total amount, paying the designers in Paris separately from the still outstanding bill from the weavers in Flanders.

"*M'amie,* do you know what is on the carts that are being unloaded in the courtyard?" Louis turned from the window to his wife. She was forever acquiring things: artwork, books, bolts of cloth for dresses for her dames and maids, and God knew what else. Whatever it was now was a big delivery.

"It is nothing, husband. Something I ordered ages ago. Will you not hunt today?" she asked, her voice as innocent as the babe growing inside her. She took his hands and placed them on either side of her waist.

"I had not planned to hunt today. But it is not a bad idea. Perhaps tomorrow." Louis squeezed her sides.

"My lord, why not take a few days and enjoy yourself while the weather is fine and no crisis looms?" she suggested.

"Are you trying to get rid of me?" Louis scrutinized her.

Why was she being so accommodating all of a sudden? It was unlike her.

"I am trying to begin your birthday celebration by offering you a chance to enjoy yourself for a few days."

The king eyed her suspiciously. Usually she complained when he went off on overnight hunting trips. He knew it brought back bad memories for her of Charles' many dalliances, of which she had first become aware from his hunting trips.

But if she were amenable to him hunting for a few days, why not seize the chance? God knew it was rare not to have a desk full of troubles to address. He did, actually, but none were urgent. Why not enjoy himself for the final few days before he turned thirty-eight?

She needed to get the tapestries hung without Louis around. She had neither skimped on design, craftsmanship or materials, nor on size or scale. She imagined Louis' jaw dropping at first sight of them. Before he could blurt out some irritating remark about their cost, she would see to it that he was shamed into silence by the awestruck comments and compliments of his courtiers.

Besides, if Louis could spend money on campaigns in Italy, why could she not spend money on commissioning exquisite works of art? The six tapestries depicting a unicorn hunt would not only ennoble their thoughts, but also keep out the cold in winter months.

Anne had been clear on her choice of ladies to be depicted in the tapestries. She had not chosen lush, fleshy Italian beauties, but slim, elegant, and modestly dressed northern European noblewomen. Whenever Louis glanced at them she hoped he would forget all about Italy and whatever enticements it offered that drew him so strongly, as it had Charles.

Her Louis was a measured man, comfortable with the moderate climate and charms of France as well as Brittany. Such a temperament did not belong in Italy. If he couldn't see it for himself, she would open his eyes to his true sensibilities by surrounding him with reminders of who he was and where he came from. Then, if he insisted on trotting off to Italy, he would feel homesick at a certain point and come back, she reasoned.

Moreover, tapestries were a good investment, with a solid, functional purpose. Enormous ones, such as the six she had commissioned, would keep out the drafts back in Blois in the winter months ahead. If Louis complained, she would mention that having a warm castle would increase the chances of her safely delivering the son he sought.

"*M'amie*, do you wish to be rid of me so you need not trouble yourself with arranging a birthday celebration?" he joked.

"Husband, you have read my mind. Except that it is not because I do not wish to be troubled. It is because I know how well you enjoy such sport and I want you to do the thing you love most to celebrate your new year."

"To celebrate getting older? Perhaps this will be the last year I am able to hunt," Louis jested.

"Husband, you are not old at all," Anne protested, feeling a twinge inside. It was not the babe, but worry at the thought of what those three years in prison might have done to Louis in the flower of his manhood. He was still handsome, but the last seventeen years had aged him. She reached out and ran a hand through his silver-dusted hair.

How happy she was to remember the lush, straight, light brown hair and unutterably handsome face of the twenty-one year old duke d'Orléans. She had been so awed by him that she had barely been able to speak the first few days of his visit to her father's castle.

Now, when she looked at Louis, it was as if she looked back in time at the first man ever to take her breath away. How foolish of him it would be to spoil their joy in each other by quibbling over how much money she spent. Did she not spend it in order to increase the glory of their court and the admiration of their subjects?

She put a hand to her husband's face, smoothing the grooves that ran along each side from nose to mouth. Age had put them there, but prison had prematurely deepened them. If only she could erase every worry he would ever have.

"I have a surprise for you; that is why you need to hunt for a few days." She smoothed his forehead, hypnotizing him beneath her fingers.

"Wife, I am not one for surprises. I have had too many already in life." Louis' tone was muffled, his lips trapped under Anne's dainty hand.

"Was not becoming king of France a good one, then?"

"Not bad but filled with worries, truth be told."

"Then I guess marrying me is just another." She gave him a sly look.

Louis reached up and grabbed Anne's wrist, bringing her down on him.

"Lady, you try me," he laughingly murmured into her hair.

"Thank you. 'Tis my sport, just as hunting is yours," Anne riposted.

"I will not leave until you tell me what this surprise is."

"And I will not tell you unless you leave," she countered.

"But how can you tell me if you are here and I am away at hunt?" he asked.

"I will tell you upon your return or, rather, you will see for yourself what surprise I have for you."

"How much did this surprise cost, then?"

"Husband, you talk like an old man although you are a young one," Anne hedged.

"Wife, I am neither old nor young. I am a balanced man who likes a balanced budget."

Anne twisted her lips into a moue and scowled at him until he burst out laughing.

"Too bad you married me, then." She pushed herself off him and swished from the room. Behind her she heard his chuckle and her heart leapt. People said she was humorless. She was not. She adored hearing her neither-old-nor-young husband's laugh and she would do whatever she could to elicit it. When she was in the mood, of course.

Three days later the tapestries had been hung. Louis was back from his hunting trip and Georges d'Amboise was in the midst of smoothing the king's ruffled feathers over the imagined cost of the magnificent tapestries his queen had gifted him with. Nobody seemed to know the actual amount, and his wife refused to tell him.

"What do you think, Georges?" Louis' neck craned back, taking in the lushly detailed scenes on each of the six enormous pieces. Each featured a scene from the life cycle of a unicorn. The thin line of his lips indicated France's frugal monarch was miffed.

"I think your wife has presented you with a gift worthy of a king," d'Amboise answered judiciously.

"At what cost, Georges?" Louis asked crossly. "Could I not have outfitted my army and paid my mercenaries with the funds that paid for all this?"

"Not if those funds belong to the queen, Sire," d'Amboise observed.

"Well, do you know how she paid for these? I mean, they

are splendid, but how much could this possibly have cost? Did she tell you?"

"What do you think, Sire?"

"So we men are to be left in the dark, as usual."

"Sire, you see I have chosen the priesthood to avoid precisely these problems." The cardinal's eyes danced.

"I knew there was a reason driving you to enter the church, Georges. God's bells, it was a good one." Louis stared up at the magnificent scenes of the unicorn hunt before him, wrestling with his conflicted feelings. How dare she spend money so lavishly when he needed funds for his plans in Naples?

Scrutinizing a lord and lady staring into each other's eyes on the final tapestry depicting a unicorn being killed, he recognized his own long pointy nose on the lord.

"Georges, I wouldn't be caught dead in striped leggings. This has to be redone!" he railed.

"Sire, it is woven into the tapestry; I'm sure you would not wish to pay to commission the entire piece again," d'Amboise pointed out.

"Well, it's ridiculous; I would never wear such gaudy garments," Louis complained, thinking that the young Borgia had worn such leggings when he had shown up in Chinon. They had suited him, but Louis was cut from a different cloth. He was no dandy, certainly not at the mature age of thirty-eight.

"Sire, perhaps your wife is sending a signal that you might wear something more fashionable," d'Amboise suggested.

"A king does not need to be fashionable. He needs to rule. And to rule well, he needs money."

"Sire, to do most things well one needs money."

"Truth to that, Georges."

"I would say that your wife chooses artwork well." D'Amboise swung his head around the great gallery to take in the full set of tapestries. From the start of the hunt to the unicorn being killed and presented to the lord and lady, they were—inarguably—stunning. "Magnificently well, in fact."

"She does everything magnificently well, except stick to a budget," the king complained.

"Sire, begging your pardon, she is Queen of France. Would you have her decorate your royal residences to the tune of your own tastes?" d'Amboise brought a hand to his mouth to hide his grin. It wold not do to laugh at the king of France, no matter how close a friend he was.

"What's wrong with my tastes, Georges? What are you saying?"

"Nothing, Sire, it's just that … it's just—"

"Just what?" Louis stared indignantly at his lifelong friend.

"It's just that the queen understands that your subjects wish to be proud of their sovereigns. They crave pomp and ceremony, pageantry and bedazzlement, to make them proud to be French."

"As long as they have food in their bellies and are not being taxed to death to pay for our luxuries." The line of the king's mouth became even thinner.

"Sire, you are doing a fine job on both counts. Let the queen provide fuel to fire their spirits while you provide fuel for their bodies."

"Georges, why do you always take her side? Whose friend are you?"

"Sire, you know I have been yours first and will always be yours first to the very end. But your wife is a force of nature which none of us can rein in. As her judgment and taste are good, why not let her have her lead?"

"So I do, Georges. There is no other way to manage her. But I must have a say somewhere. I am king, after all." Louis' long nose jutted out as far as his lifted chin, making him look exactly like the lord depicted in the tapestry he stood next to.

"Then tell her you will not quibble over her art commissions if she stays out of your affairs in Italy." D'Amboise looked straight into the king's eyes.

"Do you think that will work?" Louis eyed him doubtfully.

"Will it not be a relief to get her off your back over Naples?"

"God's breath, yes."

"Then tell her every time she says you cannot afford further expansion in Italy, you will take one tapestry off the wall and sell it to one of the Medicis or the pope, in order to pay for it."

"Georges, she will never go for that." Louis shook his head, feeling a laugh form deep in his belly at the thought of her rage at such a strategy.

"Of course she will. She wants to keep her tapestries, and you want to expand France's foothold in Italy. Either you both get what you want, or neither does."

"Georges, are you sure you are meant for the priesthood? Your skills are far more suited to married life."

"God forbid, Sire. I have enough on my plate serving you. And our Lord, of course." Hastily, he crossed himself.

Louis looked up again at the tapestry of the unicorn being killed. He didn't know what to make of it, other than that it was huge and very well done. He didn't even care for unicorns; he had never given them a thought since he'd never seen any.

But he knew Anne did from a ring she had shown him the summer after Charles had died. It had been made of gold with a unicorn depicted on it. She had told him she had commissioned it for herself, just as she had evidently commissioned the tapestries before him for herself. At least he had gotten to hunt for a few days.

He sighed. What was he to do with her? Peering at the lord

and lady once more, he saw that the lady standing next to the lord that looked like him was nowhere near as beautiful as his lavish *Brette*.

Anne was extravagant, with a character and ambitions that were larger than life. She was also pious, devoted to him, a prudent confidante and as fine and fastidious a lady as any king could wish for as his queen. Could he really complain?

His hard feelings melted away. He would go find her to thank her for her gift. She might give him a son after all. And if she didn't, it didn't matter. He would marry their princess to the dauphin Francis and their bloodline would remain on the throne of France. It was enough to have a wife and queen who knew how to represent the glories of their kingdom at home just as he would soon represent them abroad.

CHAPTER SEVENTEEN

August 1500

Machiavelli Comes to Court

Two days after Louis' thirty-eighth birthday on June 27, French troops joined forces with the Florentine army to subdue Pisa, seventeen leagues west of Florence on the coast. Louis hadn't wanted to get involved, but the more time he spent in Italy the more he realized what a sticky morass he had gotten himself into.

Although traditionally an ally, Florence had not aided Louis in his successful bid to rid Milan of Sforza then capture him. Rather, the Florentine Republic had remained neutral, but then had entreated him for help in recapturing Pisa, which had revolted from Florentine domination in 1494. Louis had been vexed, but he needed Florentine support to cross its territory if he were to pursue his aims in Naples. Now he was doubly vexed as June turned into July, and news from Italy arrived that the siege had been unsuccessful.

Sire de Beaumont, commander of the French troops, had written him that he had been forced to retreat, heading north, and that the Florentines had been next to no help at all, sending neither additional men nor funds to pay their own mercenaries, who had mostly deserted.

"Fair-weather friends one day, double-crossers the next," Anne fumed, to which Louis reminded her of her own father's difficulties with the Breton noblemen who had sided with France, then returned to the fold in the three years of Brittany's Mad War with France.

"Husband, at least you knew the stripes of the tigers you were dealing with in my realm," Anne pointed out.

"I have the Borgias in Italy."

Anne crossed herself in response.

Louis stared at her then crossed himself, too.

Anne returned his stare until finally Louis broke his gaze. At that, they both burst out laughing.

Thank God Cesare Borgia was now on the other side of the Alps, she thought. His wife had delivered their first child, a daughter, just months earlier in May. Louis had told Anne that Cesare had no plans to return to France, intent as he was on seizing power in the Romagna, to the south of Milan. At least Charlotte d'Albret had the title of Duchess of Valentinois, as well as generous funds to support herself and her daughter. After what had happened to the Borgia's older brother, Anne thought it was for the best that her esteemed Cordelière remained safe at home in France.

"As you had Sforza until he turned against you," Anne reminded Louis. "And as Florence was your ally until you needed them to push Sforza out of Milan. Do you not think the Florentines will abandon you again, should it suit them?"

"They are sending two emissaries now to explain the situation and for us to hammer out an agreement."

"My lord, what weight will an agreement with the leaders of any Italian state hold, be it a duchy or a republic, when its leaders change? Or worse, remain the same but simply change their minds?"

"'Tis the way business is done, *m'amie.* Let us see what this delegation they are sending has to say. Meanwhile, Florence owes me for besieging Pisa for them and I need funds to pay my troops. I am sure we can come to terms."

Anne sighed. Why couldn't her husband, with his prudent, measured nature, resist the expansionary dreams in Italy her former husband had failed to fulfill? Was it because becoming king had turned his head, or was it because it was a king's prerogative to seek to expand his kingdom? In either case it was folly, in her opinion.

She lay a protective hand on Louis' arm. Whatever it was that pulled him eastward, she would use everything within her power to pull him home again to France. If only he could realize that his true gifts were his sense of moderation and willingness to forgive, his prudence and restraint, all of which the Italians would perceive as weaknesses and take advantage of the instant they took his measure.

Shuddering, she pictured the Borgia bull at Louis' side as he rode into Milan. No doubt, that raging opportunist had already sized up Louis and decided to avail himself of his support until he got what he wanted. Then he would likely chase the French king back across the Alps. She would be happy to have her husband home, but his pride would be battered, to have failed his mission in Italy.

Several weeks later the emissaries from Florence arrived.

"They are not as well-dressed as your Italian peacock friend," Anne observed as she and Louis peeked through the Venetian screen railing on the gallery above the great hall.

"*M'amie*, remember they come from a republic, not a wealthy kingdom," Louis replied.

"One of them seems terribly young," Anne remarked. Below them the two Florentines stood, surveying the new tapestries of the unicorn hunt covering the length of the hall. Were they as struck by their splendor as Charles had been struck by the wonders of Italy when he first arrived?

"It is said that he is a rising star in Florence's treasury," Louis reassured her.

Anne was not reassured. Peering closer she noted the younger emissary's close-cropped hair, giving him the appearance of a sleek cat. Energy poured off him, his movements quick but graceful. His head moved decidedly, as if with purpose, as his gaze traveled from one tapestry to the next. She sensed a wily adeptness in him not dissimilar to that of Cesare Borgia, but more polished, cloaked in a diplomat's veneer.

From the top of the staircase leading to the great hall Anne caught the eye of Georges d'Amboise, who was leading the two Florentines in her direction. With a slight nod, she indicated to him that she was ready to be introduced. As she descended the staircase, Louis stopped to receive a message that had just come in.

Anne continued alone, and as she did she met the eyes of the younger emissary. Shrewd inquisitiveness swam in them, somewhat impertinently upon her before he had been formally presented.

"Your Majesty, may I present to you Monsieur Francesco della Casa, special envoy from the Republic of Florence to the king of France," Georges addressed her at the bottom of the stairs.

Anne acknowledged the dignified senior emissary, breathing a sigh of relief. Although a republican, at least he had an aristocratic name.

"And this is his assistant, Niccolò Machiavelli, second secretary of the chancery of the Republic of Florence," Georges d'Amboise added.

"Your Majesty." The younger diplomat bowed low. As he did, a cuff emerged from one sleeve of his coat, torn at one corner and decidedly dingy.

Anne acknowledged him, thinking he was likely unmarried to present himself at court in such a state. When he lifted his head to meet her gaze, she noted his widow's peak was as deep as her own. Charles had always joked that he knew the adage of a widow's peak being a sign of high intelligence to be true because both she and his eldest sister had one and he didn't.

Observing the junior emissary's unusual hairstyle up close, she was struck by a sense of the new world meeting the old. She was younger than either emissary but it was the younger envoy, with his restless energy and close-cropped hair, who appeared to represent the new.

Turning her back to him, she addressed the senior envoy.

"Ahh, Sire della Casa. My husband tells me you are here on behalf of the great city of Florence," Anne remarked.

"Yes, Your Majesty, I represent the Signoria of the Republic of Florence."

"Who is the Signoria, then?" Did Florence have a female ruler she had not heard about? She had heard from Louis of Caterina Sforza, niece of Ludovico Sforza, who had ruled Forli, south of Venice, and defended it valiantly until Cesare Borgia had seized it and kidnapped her the winter before. Was there a woman now ruling Florence?

At a loss for words, the senior emissary turned to his assistant. In that instant, Anne knew who the power broker of the two would be.

"The Signoria is an elected council of nine men who manage the affairs of our city." Machiavelli gave the queen of France a tight smile.

"And where are these nine men drawn from?" Anne asked, noting the shape of the mouth on the man addressing her. His smile accentuated the mobile double curve of his mouth. She sensed he was a man of high complexity. She would keep a close eye on him while he remained at court.

"Your Majesty, they are chosen from Florence's guilds. Six from the major guilds and two from the minor," the younger envoy explained. "The final member is the Gonfaloniere, who presides over the council."

"And is he, too, elected every two months?"

"Yes, Your Majesty." The man's expression was unreadable, his dark eyes impenetrable. Her instincts told her to beware, that this man's inner and outer aspects might be as different as night and day; Louis would be putty in his hands. She would see to it that Georges managed him, keeping the king engaged with the senior envoy, who looked easier to handle.

"Then should you arrive at an agreement with my husband, who is to uphold it if Florence's leaders have all changed at a future point?"

"Madame, you ask a good question." Machiavelli bowed his head, as Georges d'Amboise hid a smile. "As Florence has been a republic since 1115, its leaders are bound by law to uphold the agreements they have made with neighboring realms."

"A republic with one family controlling it for sixty years?" Anne referred to the Medici family, even more powerful than the House of Sforza, that had finally been swept from power in

1494 with Charles' arrival in Italy. She narrowed her eyes at the junior emissary to let him know that her husband would not enter into any agreement without the shrewd assessment and counsel of his queen-consort.

"Your Majesty, you are correct that our republic was indeed somewhat in name only during that time which, fortunately, has ended."

Sensing his astuteness, she knew her message had been received. Her Louis was too nice a man to be entering into agreements with wily Italians seeking to take advantage of his innate decency. She would protect her husband's interests while this sharp second secretary remained among them.

As Louis' step sounded on the stairs above, all eyes turned. Anne gazed at her husband's handsome yet careworn face, feeling a fierce protectiveness well up inside. She knew behind her, the shrewd young Florentine would be sizing him up and determining sooner rather than later that France's king could easily be manipulated on the Italian peninsula.

Behind her husband's form the unicorn of the sixth and final tapestry shrieked out a silent cry for help as hunters and dogs ripped into his snowy white flesh.

Within three weeks of the arrival of the emissaries, Louis had gone from being mildly vexed to extremely irritated, then incensed. The bad news from Italy that Pisa had not been taken nor had his Swiss mercenaries been paid, combined with a minor hunting accident and the stifling August heat, had served to fire the king's rare temper.

"Do you think that France should recapture Pisa for you at our own expense?" he asked the Florentine emissaries. Behind him Georges d'Amboise rustled, his sizeable girth sweating from the heat as well as the sharp words being flung about, as both sides hurled blame at each other for the fiasco of the failure to take Pisa.

"Your Majesty, it is the Signoria's belief that if the French general had prevailed and not retreated, Pisa would have been taken," the senior emissary put as delicately as possible.

"Nonsense! It was your own hired troops who deserted, not even your own men, since you did not send any. Next time, fight your own battles!" Louis roared. He had heard from Beaumont that they had deserted because they had not been paid. It was precisely the same problem the French faced amongst their own Swiss mercenaries.

Nothing irked him more than dealing with allies even cheaper than he was. Judging by the threadbare coats and cracked leather poulaines of the two men before him, he could see that the Florentine Republic was not going to provide the sort of substantive support he needed to achieve his aims farther down Italy's boot.

But he couldn't move further south through Florence until he paid his troops—in particular, his Swiss mercenaries. The Swiss were devilish to work with when unpaid, almost as much trouble as they were helpful in battle when their wages were not in arrears.

"Your Majesty, it is of inestimable importance for our republic to regain its rightful possession of Pisa, for which we appeal to you to stand by your treaty obligation and aid us to accomplish," Machiavelli declared.

The king's ears twitched. Was he imagining things, or had the young envoy slipped a threat into his silky words?

"Aiding you is one thing. Doing the job for you is another!" Louis barked, slapping both hands on the trestle table he leaned on. "Tell your Signoria back home that not only must they repay me for the cost of the siege they caused us to lose, but they must pay the wages of my Swiss troops, too."

"Your Majesty, we will dispatch your conditions to the Signoria immediately," della Casa responded.

Louis felt better. If he could get the Florentines to pay for his Swiss mercenaries to do the job of returning Pisa to Florence, then he could get on with moving southward.

On both sides, the French and the Florentine, it came down to money. Without money, battles could not be fought nor kingdoms conquered. He would cough a bare minimum out of Florence, but it was becoming clear that he needed to look for a far more powerful and wealthy ally to accomplish his ultimate goal of taking Naples.

"It is of utmost concern that your interests and Florence's are aligned, Your Majesty," Machiavelli stated.

"Of utmost concern to who?" Louis shot back. Who did this young nobody from nowhere think he was? Even worse, why did he make him feel as if he must listen carefully to every word that came from his mouth in order to parse its true meaning?

"To Florence, Your Majesty. And I daresay to France, as well."

"I will speak for France, not you. Your job is to see that we are paid for services rendered to do the job your own country couldn't do for itself." Louis felt his face reddening again. Was it the content of their discussion or the maddening shrewdness of the young envoy before him that was trying his patience?

"To ensure we are sure of it, we will wait for your leaders to send the funds as soon as possible," Georges d'Amboise offered soothingly.

Louis eyed the young Machiavelli's shabby attire. It looked as if his leaders had not sent funds to cover even the most basic needs of their emissaries. He might manage to cough up compensation from Florence in return for delivering Pisa, but the city-republic was not in the league of the sort of allies he needed in order to establish a French foothold in Italy.

"Let your leaders know that we are eager to move south, but will not move until we have been recompensed by your treasury," the king spelled out.

"And does this mean that, while you are waiting, your troops will be making friends among others who seek your support and can pay for it immediately?" Machiavelli asked smoothly.

"It means that Florence puts itself in a precarious position until it has settled its debts. That is all," Louis answered, although the younger emissary had spelled out exactly what might happen while Beaumont's troops waited out the remainder of the summer, restless and unpaid, with nothing to do except make trouble until the march south could be resumed.

Dismissing both envoys Louis waited until they had left the room, then turned to d'Amboise, a dark look on his face.

"I will look elsewhere for support," the king said.

"Where is that, Your Majesty?"

"To Ferdinand in Spain."

The cardinal of Rouen's mouth fell open. When he shut it again, he realized that Louis was in no position to go it alone. As the French conquest of Naples hadn't worked for Charles he doubted it would work for Louis, who was far more cautious than his predecessor had been. But partnered with another powerful European ally, perhaps Louis' dream could be realized.

The Italian powers were too small and too untrustworthy. That left the Holy Roman Empire, England, and Spain. England had no interests in territorial expansion in Italy, but Spain did. Meanwhile, France's traditional enemy, the Holy Roman Empire, was tied to Spain through Ferdinand and

Isabella's second oldest daughter. Joanna of Castile was married to Philip, son of the Holy Roman Emperor Maximilian.

Vaguely, Louis remembered Anne telling him they had had their first child recently—a boy. She had sent them a gift. He didn't know why she had sent it, but it would serve to sweeten Ferdinand now with the request he would make of him.

"Do you wish to loosen the strings that bind Ferdinand to the Hapsburgs?" d'Amboise asked.

"Rather, I wish to strengthen the ties between France and Spain, so we have less to worry about from them," Louis told him.

"But, Sire, what manner of alliance do you wish to make with Ferdinand?" The cardinal looked concerned.

"One that will gain France the throne of Naples."

"Sire, at what cost to you will Ferdinand offer support?" d'Amboise asked, rubbing his chin.

"Whatever it is, there is only one way to find out." The king gestured to the attendant at the door. "Get me my writing tools."

By early September compensation from Florence had not yet arrived and Francesco della Casa had fallen ill. It was decided the senior emissary would return home, leaving his junior colleague behind until a satisfactory alignment of France and Florence's interests had been achieved.

D'Amboise found himself drawn to the nimble mind of the diplomat with ideas as sleekly modern as his hairstyle. He was far and away the most interesting person at court to talk with. Together they roved over subjects ranging from Europe's geopolitics to philosophy, to heated discussions on what constituted the essence of human nature. The Florentine's views on how a ruler should maintain power both fascinated and repelled d'Amboise, untethered as they were to any sense of duty to God or to one's ancestral mandate.

But however subversive the young emissary's ideas were, the cardinal of Rouen sensed that to support his king in Italy he would benefit from understanding them. If Louis wished to play on the other side of the Alps, d'Amboise would need to stay close at hand to advise him of the new rules of engagement. God knew he could barely make them out himself.

CHAPTER EIGHTEEN

Fall 1500

Anne as Royal Matchmaker

nne's son arrived that fall, too soon.

The babe was stillborn. During the numb weeks that followed, the queen's little princess filled her thoughts and frequently her arms as well.

Claude of France was her all; she was enough, Anne told herself. Thank God Louis was away in Melun, to the southeast of Paris. She could not bear to see his face upon hearing the news that a prince had been on his way, but sent back to Heaven before he had breathed his first. When she got to Heaven herself, she would ask why such hopeful expectancy followed by death's stony numbness should so frequently be a woman's lot. Why should any woman be asked to carry life for nine full months, only to see their dead child's face for a moment or two before burying it, along with every hope and expectation they had had for its future?

"Am I not to bear a son, then?" she whispered to Madame Dampierre, her closest companion since the death of Françoise de Dinan.

"Your Majesty, you have born a child who is alive and well, and so you shall again," her lady-in-waiting reassured her, smoothing her sovereign's furrowed brow.

"I have borne four sons and lost them all. 'Tis a sign, is it not?"

"Your Majesty, it is an indication that you should prepare yourself for the possibility that you are meant to be the mother of princesses and not princes."

"Although it is a queen's first duty to bear princes," Anne replied bitterly.

"Did not your own mother bear two fine princesses herself, one of whom now is duchess of her own country and twice queen of Europe's most glorious kingdom?"

Anne glared at her. "Glorious, but for the fact that it lacks a dauphin."

"But the young Francis, Madame—"

"Do not speak to me of that boy," Anne cut her off. "It should be my son on the throne of France, not the son of that— that woman." Anne hurled a pillow to the floor. She had wanted to say 'strumpet', but it didn't fit.

Louise de Savoy was no strumpet, but a woman of single-minded devotion to her children. She had joined a most unusual household at age eleven when she had been given in marriage in a dynastic alliance to Charles d'Angoulême.

Her husband had been seventeen years older, living a life of domestic bliss with his mistress and their two children at his ancestral home in Cognac. Finding no need to disturb his domestic arrangements, he had installed his mistress as his new wife's lady-in-waiting. Louise had been too young and too

unknowing to object, and they had all lived comfortably together until Charles' death on New Year's day of 1496.

Anne had heard of their arrangement when she first became
queen. Pious and faithful herself, she had been shocked.

"Your Majesty, if not your own son then why not your
daughter as his wife one day?" Madame Dampierre ventured.

"Never!" Anne exploded. With Francis having been raised
in such a highly irregular household, what would stop him
from installing his own mistresses under his wife and queen's
nose one day? She did not want her sweet Claude to be subjected to such a scenario.

"But, Your Majesty, would it not accomplish the same goal
of keeping your bloodline on France's throne?"

"It accomplishes one goal but would mean the end of
another." The bile rose at the back of Anne's throat to think
of it.

"What other, Your Majesty, begging your pardon?"
Madame Dampierre looked confused.

"One that is not your concern, but mine." Anne waved her
away. "Go now and bring me some broth."

"Yes, Your Majesty." Madame Dampierre hurried away
while Anne mulled over her dual role. As queen of France, her
aim was to keep her bloodline and Louis' on the throne. But as
duchess of Brittany, her goal was to maintain Brittany's independence from France by granting her ducal rights to a successor who would not hand them over to France.

If Claude were to one day become queen of France as Francis'
wife, Anne didn't doubt he would pressure her to hand over her
inheritance to him, or to a son who would succeed him as king
and would be eager to fold Brittany into France. Such worries
would not concern a Frenchwoman such as Madame Dampierre,
nor most others at court. Ahh, where was her beloved Françoise

de Dinan when she needed her? The Breton noblewoman would have at once grasped the dilemma the queen faced with her sole child a daughter.

Rising from her bed of misery, Anne put on her court face. She would show the impeccable self-possession she was known for, greeting her ladies-in-waiting and maids of honor with the dignity that befit her role as queen. Most of her forty-eight maids of honor would marry and bear children. More likely than not, every one of them would experience childbirth loss in the years ahead. It was her duty to show them how to step out from grief's shadows into sunlight once more.

Almost every woman she knew had suffered the loss of newborn. God knew, for all married women shadow phantoms of unborn or stillborn babes reached for them at night, clutching at their breasts, whispering to the mothers who had harbored them for too short a time of the reunion they would one day enjoy in Heaven.

Or not. Who knew the substance or nature of the hereafter? There was too much to get done in the here and now to dwell too much on mysteries none could substantiate.

Anne washed her face and called for her attendants to dress her while she downed a hearty cup of broth. She seated herself at her desk, eager to attack the large pile of letters and requests that awaited her. To begin, she attended to the administration of her duchy, then turned to granting bequests, commissioning works of art, and answering personal correspondence.

After several hours of satisfying immersion in the world of affairs, she summoned her ladies. She would show them how a queen reclaims her role after personal loss.

"Your Majesty, a letter from Hungary has arrived for you," Madame de Seneschale greeted her, holding out a missive stamped with the red and green seal of St. Stephen.

Addressed only to her and not the king, Anne's interest was piqued. She tore it open.

> 'To the most esteemed royal highness Anne, Duchess of Brittany, Queen of France,
> I am in need of a wife, to be crowned as my consort and to beget me sons and daughters. Could you find me one amongst your court of esteemed noble maidens? May it please you to send me the portraits of a few candidates, along with a word about each, that I may decide. I am, as always, your humble admirer.
> Vladislas, King of Hungary and Bohemia'

Anne laughed aloud as she finished the letter. It was her first moment of levity since the initial birth pang of her dead prince's delivery.

"Splendid!" she sang out, raising the heads and spirits of her Cordelières who sat on the floor before her.

"What news, my lady-queen?" Anne de Candale asked.

"'Tis a request from the king of Hungary and Bohemia to find him a wife," Anne said, delighted to have been entrusted with such a mandate. She guessed Vladislas hadn't bothered to write Louis on such a matter. Why should he, indeed?

"A wife? But does not the king of Hungary have a wife already?" Anne de Candale asked.

"My dear, there are times when I think I have done my job too well with you," Anne replied. Her lively charge always knew everything there was to know at court, far beyond the scope of her studies.

"Has he managed to get his marriage to the lady Beatrice annulled?"

"How in the world do you know about that?" Anne asked sternly.

"Your Majesty, it was talked about amongst the ladies. As you can imagine, what concerns Princess Charlotte concerns us, too," Anne de Candale explained.

"So you knew," Anne shook her head, wondering what else the court talked about in their free moments. At the top of their list, she imagined, would be her difficulties in childbearing.

"I know that the lady Beatrice is Charlotte's aunt, and that she was once the queen of Matthias Corvinus of Hungary, was she not?"

"Yes, my fountain of knowledge, she is and she was."

"Just like you, Your Majesty, she is twice crowned queen of her kingdom."

"But unlike me, she is no longer queen-consort, as her marriage has been annulled."

"Such a shame, Your Majesty!"

"It's time you got back to your studies," Anne chided her. "Have you been reading Madame de Pizan's book?"

"I have not quite finished it, Majesty." Anne de Candale squelched a smile to think of the latest book Charlotte had recommended to her by that greatly interesting author. *One Hundred Ballads of a Lover and His Lady* had not been on the queen's reading list for her Cordelières. It had proven an enlightening read.

"Then get back to it now. I must attend to business with my ladies-in-waiting. You are all dismissed." The queen waved them away.

Once the last of the demoiselles had cleared the room, Anne turned to Madame de Dampierre. Always up to date with the latest gossip, the queen guessed she would know something about why it was that Vladislas of Hungary was requesting her matchmaking services. She had not heard that he was recently widowed.

"So what do you know of this business of the king of Hungary's?" Anne asked, eager to be filled in on what had happened while she had been in childbed.

"Your Majesty, I am not sure of the details but I heard that he obtained his annulment based on the illegality of his marriage to the lady Beatrice."

"Why would it not have been legal?" Anne asked, intrigued.

"It was said that the king petitioned the pope that his noblemen had forced him, against his will, to marry the queen after King Matthias died. She was greatly supported by them and wished to be queen again."

"And did he not wish her to be his queen?"

"Perhaps he did at the time but no children came of it, so it is possible he no longer wished it after the years went by."

Anne raised her eyebrows. How precarious a childless queen's position was.

"There is more, Your Majesty." Madame de Dampierre cleared her throat. "It was found that the king had not obtained an annulment of his first marriage when he married the lady Beatrice of Naples."

"Remind me who he was first married to."

"He married the widowed duchess of Glogow, Barbara of Brandenburg, by proxy, but they never met."

So very familiar, Anne thought, breathing a sigh of relief that the annulment of her first marriage by proxy to Maximilian of Austria had come through just days after she wed Charles in 1491.

"And so, on the ground that he was not legally married to the lady Beatrice, he was able to obtain the annulment," put in Madame la Seneschale.

"But he sought it because the lady Beatrice gave him no heirs," Madame Dampierre added.

Anne thanked St. Claude of Besançon for her little princess. She could not honestly say that she hadn't wished herself to be queen of France a second time. Fortunately, she had her daughter to secure her position.

But would she ever have the son she sought? One who would secure not only her position as Louis' consort but Louis' and her bloodline on the throne of France as well. Her husband would seek to have his own line continued on the throne, one way or another, and if not with a son then with a daughter through marriage to a future king of France.

The queen thought back to the jest Louis had made at Claude's birth when Louise de Savoy had entered the room. 'Behold your daughter-in-law,' he had said to her. Never, Anne vowed once again, balling her fist in the folds of her gown.

"Have both annulments been granted?" she asked.

"Oh yes, Madame. The pope granted them both early in April this year and it is said that Beatrice is already back in Naples."

Anne nodded. Well she knew how easy it might be to obtain an annulment with Rodrigo Borgia on the papal throne. And well could she understand the longing of Vladislas of Hungary to have an heir. Who among her select maids of honor might she suggest?

"Tell my portrait artists I wish to meet with them tomorrow just after terce."

"Who shall we call, Your Majesty?"

"Jean Bourdichon, Jean Perréal, and the new one. The Italian." Anne's voice was crisp. How she loved spearheading a project.

"Monsieur Solario, Your Majesty?"

"Yes. That one." She would have each of them render a portrait of the two candidates she chose, then decide which one to send to the king of Hungary.

The attendant hurried off.

Choosing the artist for the portraits to be done was the easy part. Much harder was choosing the right candidate to be Vladislas' wife and queen. It was a great honor, both for the young noblewoman selected and for France's royal court. Whoever was chosen would serve as an emissary of French culture and values abroad for the remainder of her life and beyond, through her influence over her children and the royal court of Hungary. And if the candidate chosen had Breton blood, even better, Anne thought.

"Who amongst you knows anything about the king of Hungary?" she asked her ladies-in-waiting. Now that her maids of honor were out of earshot, much could be discussed.

"The king has no children, Madame."

"How old is he?" Anne queried.

"Your Majesty, I believe he is over forty years of age."

"How much over?" Slightly over and in good health would be fine. Closer to fifty and in failing health could mean whichever of her Cordelières she sent might have a short career in Hungary.

The ladies looked at each other, stumped.

"Get Sire d'Auton in here. We shall pick his brain."

"Will he know?"

"It is his job to know. And if he doesn't, he will know who to ask to find out."

Madame de Dampierre hurried off to find Jean d'Auton. Anne and Louis had appointed him to chronicle a historical record of Louis' achievements for posterity. The man was a wellspring of information, both historical and contemporary, making him an enjoyable conversationalist.

In a moment the royal court historian appeared in the doorway.

"Your Majesty, I have your answer," Jean D'Auton greeted the queen.

"You usually do, Sire d'Auton." With a slight wave, Anne bade him enter.

"Vladislas of Hungary and Bohemia was born in March of 1456."

"Forty-four. A good age." Anne approved. "What more can you tell us?"

Jean d'Auton cleared his throat. "Vladislas has lived a full life. By marrying Beatrice of Naples, he won the support of the Hungarian nobility and wrested the throne of Hungary from Matthias Corvinus' brother's claim to it. Unfortunately his marriage has not worked out, but his position on Hungary's throne is firm."

"A good starting point. Now tell us something more interesting." The queen's lips twitched.

"The king of Hungary is the eldest son of Elizabeth of Austria." D'Auton's eyebrows rose.

"Of the House of Habsburg," Madame de Dampierre added, moving into the room behind Sire d'Auton.

"Now that is more like it," Anne encouraged.

"The dowager queen-consort to King Casimir of Poland," d'Auton continued.

"As well as the mother of thirteen children, I have heard," Anne said. No one else would dare to mention such abundant childbearing success in her presence, so she would state it herself. It was time to clear the air in the wake of her prince's stillbirth.

"Eleven of whom are alive," put in Madame la Seneschale.

"Three of whom are kings," d'Auton followed up.

"A good pedigree," the queen approved. Would to God she herself could produce just one more child—a son. Briefly Louise de Savoy's image flashed through her mind. The woman thought of herself as the mother of two young gods. Spending time with her was insufferable, especially when she went on about the latest accomplishments of her little Cesar, forever her favorite topic.

"Your Majesty, it is my sense that he has not had a chance at true happiness with a wife, as he was compelled for political reasons to choose the two he no longer has."

"'Tis an old story, Sire d'Auton. We shall see if we can change his marital fortunes with the candidates we propose."

"Your Majesty, 'tis a great honor for any of our maidens to be crowned queen of Hungary," Madame la Seneschale pointed out.

"'Tis, Madame. So who would like to offer a suggestion?" Anne glanced around the room.

"Your Majesty, may I suggest Mademoiselle de Chabot?" Madame de Dampierre proposed.

"Your reasons?" Anne asked. Jeanne de Rohan-Chabot was as timid as she was beautiful. She would not hold up well in a foreign land.

"She is one of the fairest among your flock, Your Majesty."

"So she is, but that is not enough. I must choose someone sturdy and adventurous who will not be daunted by moving to a new land and establishing her own court at one with different customs and traditions."

"It is a tall order for a young woman," remarked Madame Dampierre.

"Perhaps Mademoiselle de Montberon," Madame la Seneschale offered.

"Why?" the queen challenged her. Blanche de Montberon

was another of the great beauties of her bevy of maidens. But she was as delicate as cut glass, rather in the mold of the recently-married Charlotte d'Albret.

"Well, she will, she is ..."

"Beautiful, like Jeanne," Jean d'Auton put in.

"Ahh, so you have noticed, Sire d'Auton," the queen teased. How wonderful it felt, if only for a few brief moments, not to be weighed down by grief at her latest loss. The king of Hungary's request for a bride had come at just the right moment. She would deliver a true gem to him in thanks for taking her mind off personal woes.

"Only in passing, Your Majesty." The court historian's face reddened slightly.

"Do tell who you think a good candidate might be," the queen encouraged.

"Majesty, I do not know your maids of honor as well as the ladies of the court do. In fact, I have only met one or two."

"Why have you met any of them at all?" the queen asked, feigning concern. She was careful to ensure that her Cordelières did not come into unsupervised contact with male courtiers at her court. Yet she was aware that her maids of honor were as eager to meet young gallants as most maidens beyond girlhood were. The only one she had ever heard of who was not had been Jeanne d'Arc, and look what had happened to her.

"Well, two of them came to me, together, in fact, to ask me what I knew of lands beyond France."

"And who were they?"

"Your Majesty, I believe they were the demoiselles Anne de Candale, and the king's niece—the one who is sister to the young Gaston de Foix."

"Ahh," Anne exhaled, filing away his information for further reflection. Indeed, Anne de Candale had the intelligence and sturdy constitution to embrace the good and withstand the bad in a strange new country far from France. And Germaine de Foix? God love her, the precious minx was as blithe and adventurous a spirit as any of her Cordelières. Both were excellent possibilities. She would think more on it.

"*Mes demoiselles*, how would you like to skip lessons for a few days while you sit for your portraits to be painted?" Anne asked Anne de Candale and Germaine de Foix the following morning.

"Yes, Your Majesty!" Germaine de Foix cried.

"Oh yes, Your Majesty," Anne de Candale breathed out.

"But you must bring a book to read while the portrait-master is working, so you don't waste your time." Anne's heart warmed to them both. She held an older sister's affection for both girls, but a queen's plans for their future.

"I have just the book in mind," said Anne de Candale.

"I hope it is by one of the great authors, then," the queen warned.

"By the greatest female author of them all, Your Majesty," Anne de Candale replied.

"Is it Marie de France, then?" Germaine de Foix piped up.

The queen turned to the younger one. "What do you know of Marie de France?" she asked sharply.

"Um, well, I—I heard she is a very fine poet," Germaine hedged, her face reddening almost to the hue of her strawberry-blonde hair.

"And have you read any of her poems?" the queen asked sternly. She didn't remember the head tutor mentioning Marie de France among the classic authors she had recommended for the girls to read. Marie de France was a greatly interesting one, especially with her *lais* recounting Breton legends. As fascinating as they were, Anne's sense of them was that her tales paid scant attention to moral grounding. In her view, they were not for the impressionable hearts and minds of unmarried maidens.

"I—I might have read one or two," Germaine replied, unable to lie to her beloved mistress.

"Germaine, you are thinking of Madame de Pizan, are you not?" Anne de Candale gave Germaine a piercing stare.

"I—I—"

"Madame de Pizan is surely one of the great authors, Your Majesty, is she not?" Anne de Candale cut her off.

"She is indeed." The queen turned back to Germaine. "And you, my dove, what do you plan to occupy your thoughts with while sitting for your portrait?" She fluffed the young woman's hair, glowing gold in the harvest season's morning light.

"I shall be thinking about why you are having our portraits done, Your Majesty," Germaine de Foix said gravely, or as gravely as she could for a high-spirited demoiselle of thirteen.

"That is for me to know and you to find out, *mes chères*." The queen hid a smile behind her hand. Leave it to either of the two before her to get straight to the point. Both young women were as sunny and straightforward as they were intelligent and sturdy. If they had been born men, they would have made fine knights. As women, they were among the most intelligent and best-educated of her Cordelières. But it was their fiery spirits that endeared them most to Anne, seeing herself reflected in them.

"When shall we find out, then?" asked Anne de Candale, curiosity swimming in her lively brown eyes.

"That is for me to decide. I will let you know when the time comes."

"But, Your Majesty, can you not offer us a hint?"

"It concerns your futures," Anne of Brittany replied.

"Do you mean our future husbands?" Germaine de Foix exclaimed.

"Lower your voice or you will not find a husband at all," the queen scolded, none too seriously. Then she leaned in close to the younger girl. "What do you think, little one?"

"I think it does, Your Majesty!" Germaine de Foix enthused as Anne de Candale looked just a bit stricken.

"And you, *ma chère*. Why the sad face?" Anne of Brittany took Anne de Candale's chin in her hand.

"I—I had thought of my own future."

"I'm sure you have, my dear one."

"And I had hoped to choose for myself." Anne de Candale's voice quavered.

"Had you, little one?" The queen studied Anne de Candale with grave but loving eyes as she stroked the young girl's chin with her fingers. "Do you not know that your sovereign will choose well for you amongst the ranks of kings and princes?"

"Kings and princes, Madame? Will we become queens or princesses then?"

"At least one of you will."

"Which one?" Anne de Candale asked, perking up as she usually did when a competition was announced.

"We shall see," Anne of Brittany teased, her tone mysterious.

"When shall we see?" Germaine de Foix asked, never one to back down.

"We shall see when the time comes. Now go to your lessons, and tomorrow at this time you will each come here with a book in hand." She chucked Germaine de Foix under the chin then glided from the room. She would dash off a short note to Vladislas to let him know she was working on his request. Then she would send a longer note to Louis to tell him of her commission and get his thoughts on her choices, which she would ignore.

She had already made up her mind.

CHAPTER NINETEEN

November 1500

Treaty of Granada

The king of Spain jumped on Louis' proposal for an alliance in Italy. With a reputation as one of Europe's wiliest rulers, Ferdinand II was eager to solidify his own aspirations in Sicily and the regions south of Naples. But the price was steep.

"It seems he wants Apulia and Calabria for Spain in return for leaving the Abruzzi and Campania in the north to you," Georges d'Amboise said, poring over the missive from Granada that had arrived in late October.

"Does my part include Naples?"

"Yes, Sire."

"Then let him take Apulia and Calabria. As long as Naples is mine, he can have the southern lands." Louis waved away both duchies with a dismissive hand.

"The wording about splitting the revenues seems problematic," d'Amboise mused, re-reading the letter.

"What's the problem? It seems perfectly reasonable that if one realm produces more revenue than the other, either Ferdinand will make it up to me or I to him." Louis looked satisfied. There would be no question he would take Naples with as powerful an ally as Spain behind him.

"Sire, what if there is a difference of opinion on the actual revenues each realm brings in? Will you be inclined to fork over a portion of Naples' revenues, should the king of Spain complain that his realm has not produced an equal amount?"

"Let us not quibble over details." Louis was overjoyed. Finally, Naples would be his.

"But, Sire, in the event that the southern parts do not produce the riches that Naples and your lands to the north bring in, you may chafe at having to hand over revenue to Ferdinand that you would prefer to see in your own coffers," d'Amboise reasoned.

"With Spain as our ally, we will gain our objective. I am eager to get my troops on the move, so let us sign and proceed, but secretly, so that Frederick does not catch wind of this."

Frederick IV of Aragon, cousin to Ferdinand and father of Charlotte of Naples, was now on the throne of Naples. Holding power only since 1496, after Charles VIII had lost it, Frederick had spent most of his life in France, married to two successive French wives from powerful families, before ascending the throne of Naples at age forty-four. Louis would offer him a title and a sizeable pension in France, once Frederick realized his claim to the kingdom was challenged by the king of France himself, supported by Spain, as well as the pope, to whom Louis and Ferdinand would appeal for support.

"Sire, is it not troubling that Ferdinand is so quick to sell out his own cousin to accomplish this aim with you?" d'Amboise's brows knit together as he faced his sovereign.

"That is his affair, not mine."

"But, Sire, if Ferdinand would trick his own cousin out of a kingship, might he not one day turn and do the same to you?" The cardinal of Rouen tapped his paunch lightly with his fingertips, his usual habit when mulling over a thorny issue.

"Georges, you are beginning to sound like my wife." Louis put his hands over his ears.

"Sire, I do not wish to dampen your spirits at the king of Spain's support, but is this truly an offer of support or a temporary alliance until he has established his own base in Italy, then turns on you and sweeps you out?"

"Fie, you are overthinking this. We cannot take Naples alone and Spain is powerful."

"That is precisely my worry, Sire." D'Amboise transferred his tapping fingertips from paunch to the edge of the table at which the king sat.

"The choices are bad all around," Louis pointed out. "Look what happened with Florence as our ally."

"What happened, Sire?" d'Amboise appeared puzzled as he scratched his head under his red cardinal's cap.

"Nothing!" Louis flung up both hands. "Nothing at all happened. Because Florence is small and insignificant."

"Not to mention short on funds."

"Speaking of which, has the money arrived yet from that ridiculous council they have?"

"The Signoria, Sire."

"Yes. Have the funds come yet?"

"I do not know, Sire."

"Then find that young man with the strange hairstyle and get an answer out of him."

"Right away, Sire." d'Amboise motioned to the sentry at the door then whispered to him.

The sentry turned and exited. Almost immediately he returned, startling both the king and the cardinal.

"Your Excellency, Sire de Machiavelli is already here, just outside in the corridor," the guard whispered to d'Amboise.

"Why did you not tell us he was here?" the cardinal demanded.

"I did not know myself, Your Excellency." The sentry looked uncomfortable. "I just saw him this moment."

D'Amboise turned to the king and frowned. "Do you think he has heard any of our conversation?" he asked, his voice low.

"I hope not," the king replied under his breath. "But if he has, he will keep it to himself. That one is as sly as they come."

"Sharp, too."

"Bring him in, so we can find out why he's here."

"Bid him enter," Georges d'Amboise ordered the guard.

Niccolò Machiavelli entered the room, looking as sleek as a ferret emerging from a pond.

"Your Majesty. Your Excellency." He bowed to both men.

Georges d'Amboise stared at him a moment, wondering how much of the conversation that had just taken place he had been privy to.

"What brings you here, Sire Machiavelli? We are surprised to see you so close by just when the king had cause to ask for you." D'Amboise frowned slightly at the younger man.

"I bring tidings from Florence, Your Excellency, from the council of the Signoria."

"It's about time," Louis grunted, his brows rising.

"Yes, Sire. It is indeed about time, as I myself have been waiting for additional compensation to wait upon your court."

"And is the news good?" Georges d'Amboise asked.

"It is good, Your Excellency. The Signoria has dispersed the promised 20,000 ducats directly to General Beaumont of the French command outside Pisa, to be used to pay your Swiss troops."

"Well done, Sire Machiavelli," Louis exclaimed. Once the agreement with Ferdinand was signed, his troops, rested and paid, would be ready to move south.

The Florentine bowed his head.

"Did you catch any of what we were just discussing, then?" Georges d'Amboise asked, his tone casual as he shook out the sleeves of his white vestment.

"No, Your Excellency. I was admiring the unicorn tapestries in the great hall when the sentry summoned me." He gazed at the bishop expectantly, his face as blank and smooth as a sleeping babe's. "Do you have news to share?"

"Nothing that concerns you," the king replied, feeling beads of sweat break out under the fringe of hair that covered his forehead.

"Very good, Your Majesty." The young envoy's expression gave away nothing of what he knew or did not know.

"You may go now," the king dismissed him.

Machiavelli left the room and, after a few moments had passed, d'Amboise bid the sentry at the door to enter.

"Did you say Sire de Machiavelli was out in the corridor when we asked for him earlier?"

"Yes, Your Excellency. He was just here, waiting outside the door."

"He was not in the great hall, but here in the corridor?"

"He was standing behind me in the corridor, as still as a mouse."

"Do you know how long he had been there?" the king asked.

"The sentry's face reddened. "Sire, I do not know, as I was facing inward to the room, as I am charged to do."

"So he may have been there for some time."

"Your Excellency, I cannot say how long he was there, as he

did not announce himself to me. I only noticed him when you bade me find him. He must have approached softly, as I did not hear his footsteps."

"Most unusual," Georges d'Amboise remarked.

"Your Excellency, am I—am I to be reprimanded?" The sentry shifted uncomfortably.

"Not at all, my man. You were doing your job and you did not know that you were not alone," the king interjected.

"That's it, Your Majesty. I'm very sorry. I—"

"Enough! You have done no wrong. Now go."

The sentry bowed low and quickly backed out of the room.

Louis and Georges d'Amboise looked at each other.

"Let's get the treaty signed and back to Ferdinand as soon as possible," the king said.

"Do you think he overheard details of it?"

"I think it doesn't matter if he did or not, as Florence is of no importance to us beyond being in our way." Louis made a flicking gesture with thumb and forefinger.

"And now it no longer is, as our men have been paid and are ready to march south."

"Get my signing pen."

"Yes, Sire." d'Amboise hurried to the anteroom where the king's writing implements were kept. Behind him Louis hummed a merry tune, one of the bawdy sailor tunes Georges recognized from time spent with his sovereign in Brittany.

The cardinal didn't join in. Something niggled at him about the alliance with Spain. He guessed that if the young Florentine had overheard what the king's plans were with Europe's most cunning monarch since the days of the spider king, he would feel precisely the same way.

On the same November day, missives arrived for both Anne and

Louis, the one for Anne from Buda in Hungary, the other for Louis from Granada in Spain.

Vladislas of Hungary wrote that he would be pleased to make Anne de Candale-Foix his wife and queen, if she would have him.

"Your Majesty, I am afraid to travel so far from home!" Anne de Candale cried, her emotions in a whirl. None of the other maids of honor were present. Anne had summoned her alone to receive such momentous news, so as not to incite the envy of the others.

"Nonsense, *ma chère*. It is a great honor to be chosen to be queen of a king from the Habsburg line. You will represent the courts of France and Brittany, and you will have the power and wealth to bring our customs to the court of Hungary to make it feel more like home to you."

Anne of Brittany was overjoyed. She would encourage the Austrian Habsburg connection in multi-faceted ways, so that Louis would look favorably on their daughter marrying Joanna and Philips' son Charles, who would one day become Holy Roman Emperor. Brittany's independence from France could then be preserved, a status likely to be threatened if Claude were to marry a future king of France.

"But, Madame, what if I don't love him? How can I agree to marry a man I have never met?" Anne de Candale was alarmed, yet excited, at the prospect of adventuring to a foreign land where she would be crowned queen. It was the stuff of which romances and *lais* were made, and in the event that circumstances didn't unfold perfectly, at least she would be queen of Hungary and Bohemia to compensate her for whatever else failed to materialize.

"*Ma chère,* you will love him because I have schooled you well, and you will know how to turn your heart to him when the time comes," the queen advised.

"Your Majesty, it seems to me that the heart turns where it wants to go, no matter how much schooling its owner has received," Anne de Candale declared in her usual forthright manner.

"My dove, I can tell you now as one who knows, that a happy marriage will prove the most reliable of all paths to the desires of your heart."

"Then I hope my heart will follow the path I am set on."

"I have a feeling it will. Your future husband is most enthusiastic about the qualities I told him you possess. He is taken with you already." *And certainly not because of that portrait.*

"Oh, Madame, what could you possibly have told him about me to make him choose me over Germaine?"

Germaine's portrait had been stunning, depicting her brushing her flowing reddish-gold locks. It seemed to Anne that Vladislas must have been decided by the description of Anne de Candale she had sent him because it certainly couldn't have been the portrait itself, which had made her look rather timid and docile.

What a shock Vladislas would be in for, the queen thought merrily, once Anne de Candale turned up in the flesh: lively, inquisitive, and bursting with ideas.

"I told him that you are a high-spirited intelligent girl who likes to read books outside of her prescribed reading list." A smile danced at the corners of the queen's mouth.

"But so does Ger—so do some of the other girls!"

"Do you, then? And what is it you spend your time reading?" The queen looked down her short nose at her favored maid of honor.

"Things I can't tell you about, but perhaps you have guessed," Anne de Candale confessed, confused to see the queen smiling at her.

"Yes, well, now that you are a betrothed future queen, you may put your extracurricular learning to work."

"I may?" Anne de Candale's expression grew even more puzzled as the queen's smile broadened.

"You may write to Vladislas and share some of your literary interests with him. It is a way to begin knitting him to you now so that, when you meet in person, both you and he will feel as if you already know each other."

"What an idea, Your Majesty!" Anne de Candale's eyes lit up at the thought. Then they dimmed again to think of the dull didactic sort of stuff she would most likely be required to pretend she found interesting.

"Why the long face?"

"Will I have to show Madame Leroux my letters before sending them?"

"*Ma chère*, you are the future wife of a king. You do not need to show anyone your letters to him. Develop some secrets between you!" Anne of Brittany let out a laugh that told Anne de Candale that a whole new world awaited her.

"Really, Madame?"

"You are on your way to becoming a wife. As a future queen you will have advisors, but your secrets with your husband are your own."

"Then I shall write him immediately!"

"He will be charmed."

"Perhaps not, Your Majesty." Anne de Candale put a finger to her chin, thinking of all the areas of interest she had that had nothing at all to do with what she had been taught in the queen's school for young ladies.

"Well, see to it that he is." The queen paused. "Just be yourself. I have already told him about you and he has chosen you, so write whatever you will to him, but send it soon so that he will send you a bauble or two along with the marriage contract." She kissed her charge on both cheeks then waved her away.

As the young noblewoman backed from the room, Anne remembered the other missive that had arrived. She got up to go find Louis.

"What news from Granada?" She admired both Ferdinand and Isabella, whose long and happy marriage since 1469 had brought stability and power to Spain.

Louis made a vague gesture. "Ferdinand sends his greetings."

"And not Isabella, too?" Anne looked at him expectantly.

Louis turned to the window, thinking fast. It would not do to mention the alliance he had entered into with Ferdinand regarding the partition of southern Italy. Isabella had not been a signatory to the treaty, and Louis doubted the king of Spain had discussed it with her.

"Of course Isabella sends her greetings." Louis swept Anne into his arms, tucking her head into his shoulder. Anything to avoid the knife-sharp gaze of his wife.

"Did they mention anything about my proposal for a match between Claude and their new grandson?" Anne's muffled voice emerged from his chest.

Louis' eyes widened. He had forgotten all about the idea Anne had come up with in the spring. She had proposed that their little Claude one day marry Ferdinand and Isabella's new grandson, he vaguely recalled. The child's grandfather on his father's side was Maximilian I of Austria, the Holy Roman Emperor. Should the boy live to adulthood, he, himself, would one day become Holy Roman Emperor as inheritor to the Austrian Habsburg dynasty.

"They didn't write anything, just sent a bauble for Claude." Louis stroked the back of Anne's hair, keeping her face pressed into his shoulder.

Catching the eye of Georges d'Amboise in the alcove, the

king motioned him away. It would not do to let the queen see the signed copy of the Treaty of Granada in his senior advisor's hands. It must be kept secret until the pope's support had been obtained and a papal bull issued to legitimize Louis' claim to Naples' throne. Then it would be time to proceed down the Italian peninsula.

God forbid that Anne catch wind of it. Aside from trying to persuade him not to return to Italy at all, she might mention something that would get back to Charlotte of Naples and Aragon, who, in turn, would warn her father that he was in imminent danger of losing his throne.

The cardinal of Rouen slipped from the room as the king held the queen tightly to him. Outside, in the corridor, d'Amboise glanced at the copy of the treaty in his hand.

The agreement between the king of France and the king of Spain had been signed by both monarchs and dated November 11, 1500. The note from Ferdinand stipulated that their arrangement be kept strictly secret until the time came to make their move into Naples and areas south.

D'Amboise rolled up the scroll, glancing around to ensure no one was near, most notably the young Niccolò from Florence. It would be difficult to keep such momentous news from him. The king of France's senior advisor recognized he had met his match in the perspicacious young diplomat.

Perhaps it was time to arrange having the Florentine recalled. It would be unwise to allow a foreign emissary as clever as Machiavelli to remain at the French court, uncovering and sniffing out Louis' secrets.

Continuing down the corridor, d'Amboise decided to hide the treaty safely away from anyone's eyes except his and the king's. Then he would go find the Florentine emissary to deliver a regretful message that the king had decided it was time to go home.

Back in the great hall, Anne pulled away from Louis. "We shall send another gift to Charles in return." She was delighted to hear they had thought of Claude, smoothing negotiations she would soon begin. Whatever it took, she was determined to prevent her daughter from becoming the wife of Francis d'Angoulême, as she suspected both Louis and Louise de Savoy wanted.

"Charles?" Louis asked, looking puzzled.

"The babe, *mon cher*. The one born to Joanna and Philip at the end of February. Who else?"

"Yes, of course. I leave it to you to choose something to send him." Louis felt the sweat pool under his arms, relief dripping off him at having gotten the secret treaty away from the queen's eyes. He wondered how Ferdinand, on his end, had kept wind of it from Isabella.

"Leave it to me to arrange everything. One day, when Claude is the most powerful woman in Europe, you will thank me." Anne smoothed a lock of hair from his eyes, looking pleased with herself.

"What do you mean, *m'amie?*" Louis scrutinized her.

"With a match with Philip and Joanna's son, she will one day be Empress of the Holy Roman Empire as well as Duchess of Brittany."

"*M'amie,* our princess is too young to be married off already," Louis smilingly protested.

"Nonsense. The sooner we begin talks, the closer our families will knit together in the years to come." And the sooner she could rest easy that Claude would retain Brittany's full independence from France, just as she herself had.

With the loss of yet another son, Anne sensed that the chance of Louise de Savoy's precious Cesar ascending the throne of France was strong. She feared that the masterful young Francis d'Angoulême might one day talk Claude into ceding her ducal rights over Brittany to him, should she become his wife. Anne would do everything in her power to prevent such a scenario from taking place.

"Talks are fine, but no contracts for now." Louis thought of the contract in Georges' hands at that moment: fully executed, fully confidential.

Anne would explode when she found out about it. God's bells, he was happy to think he would be safely on the other side of the Alps when she did.

"Talks will continue, but a contract must be drawn up within the next few years so that we all know what we agree to." Anne smiled at Louis, her eyes sparkling as she nodded in agreement with her own plan. She would make every effort to ensure the betrothal between Claude and Charles. It was the ideal solution to keep Claude's inheritance of the duchy of Brittany intact and independent from France.

Louis nodded back, returning his wife's smile. He loved her with all his heart. But if she failed to provide him with a son, he had no intention of seeing his bloodline slip from the throne of France. Claude must marry Francis d'Angoulême if he were to remain the heir apparent as he was now. It was the only way to preserve the Valois-Orléans bloodline on his kingdom's throne.

Arm in arm, Anne and Louis strolled from the room, each thinking entirely different thoughts concerning the future of their daughter.

Meanwhile, Princess Claude of France, future Duchess of Brittany, lay sleeping peacefully under her ermine coverlet in the royal nursery, oblivious to her parents' plans for her.

BIBLIOGRAPHY

Abernethy, Susan, *The Freelance History Writer* blog.

Baumgartner, Frederic J., *Louis XII*. New York: St. Martin's Press, 1994.

Beauman, Sally, *Destiny*. London: Bantam, 1987.

Bolton, Muriel Roy, *The Golden Porcupine*. New York: Avon Books, 1977.

Brock, Emma L, *Little Duchess*. Eau Claire, Wisconsin: E.M. Hale and Company, 1948.

Butler, Mildred Allen, *Twice Queen of France: Anne of Brittany*. New York: Funk & Wagnalls, 1967.

Chevalier, Tracy, *The Lady and the Unicorn*. New York: Plume, 2005.

Chotard, Pierre, *Anne de Bretagne: Une Histoire, Un Mythe*. Paris: Somogy éditions d'art, 2007.

Cushman, Karen, *Matilda Bone*. New York: Dell Yearling, 2000.

Davis, William Stearns, *Life on a Medieaval Barony*. New York: Harper & Brothers, 1923.

Eco, Umberto, *The Name of the Rose*. New York: Harcourt, 1994.

Evans, Joan, *Life in Mediaeval France*. Oxford: Oxford University Press, 1925.

Fairburn, Eleanor, *Crowned Ermine*. London: Robert Hale, 1968.

Fairburn, Eleanor, *The Rose in Spring*. London: Robert Hale, 1971.

De France, Marie, *The Lais of Marie de France*. London: Penguin Books, 1986.

Gobry, Ivan, *Charles VIII,* Paris: Pygmalion, 2012.

Greco, Gina L. & Rose, Christine M., translated by, *The Good Wife's Guide: Le Ménagier de Paris, A Medieval Household Book*. Ithaca and London: Cornell University Press, 2009.

Gregory, Philippa, *The Lady of the Rivers*. New York: Simon & Schuster, 2011.

Guizot, François Pierre Guillaume, *A Popular History of France from the Earliest Times, Vol. 2*. Charleston: CreateSpace, 2016.

Harrison, Kathryn, *Joan of Arc: A Life Transfigured*. New York: Anchor Books, 2014.

Jogournel, Thierry, *Anne de Bretagne: Du Duché au Royaume*. Rennes: Éditions OUEST-FRANCE, 2014.

Lesage, Mireille, *Anne de Bretagne: L'Hermine et le Lys.* Paris: Éditions SW Télémaque, 2011.

De Lorris, Guillaume, and de Meun, Jean, *The Romance of the Rose.* Oxford: Oxford University press, 1994.

De Maulde La Clavière, René, ed., *Procédures politiques du règne de Louis XII.* Paris: 1885, pps 915-16.

Mayer, Dorothy Moulton, *The Great Regent.* New York: Funk & Wagnalls, 1966.

Meyer, G.J., *The Borgias.* New York: Bantam Books, 2013.

Michael, of Kent, Princess, Her Royal Highness, *The Queen of Four Kingdoms.* New York: Beaufort Books, 2014.

Michael, of Kent, Princess, Her Royal Highness, *The Serpent and the Moon.* New York: Touchstone, 2004.

Morison, Samuel Eliot, *Admiral of the Ocean Sea: A Life of Christopher Columbus.* New York: Little, Brown and Company, 1942.

De Pizan, Christine, *Poems.* From *Christine de Pizan: Her Works* by Deanna Rodriguez, A Medieval Woman's Companion blog, 2013.

Reed, Joseph J., *Anne of Brittany: A Historical Sketch.* New York: Graham's American Monthly Magazine of Literature, Art, and Fashion, June 1858.

Rorimer, James J., *The Unicorn Tapestries Were Made for Anne of*

Brittany. New York: The Metropolitan Museum of Art Bulletin, Summer 1942.

Ross, Jack, *Marie de France: Laüstic (c. 1180)*, from Ka Mate Ka Ora, issue 11, March 2012.

Ryley, M. Beresford, *Queens of the Renaissance*. London: Methuen & Co., 1907.

Sanborn, Helen Josephine, *Anne of Brittany, The Story of a Duchess and Twice-Crowned Queen.* Memphis: General Books, 2012.

Sanborn, Helen J. & Bates, Katharine Lee, Anne of Brittany: *The Story of a Duchess and Twice-crowned Queen.* Trieste: Victoria, Australia, 2017.

Schoonover, Lawrence., The Spider King. New York: MacMillan, 1954.

Scott, Margaret, *Fashion in the Middle Ages*. The J. Paul Getty Museum: Los Angeles, 2011.

Seton, Anya, *Katherine.* Chicago: Chicago Review Press, 2004.

Siraisi, Nancy G., *Medieval and Early Renaissance Medicine: An Introduction to Knowledge and Practice.* Chicago: University of Chicago Press, 1990.

Tanguy, Geneviève-Morgane, *Sur les pas de Anne de Bretagne.* Rennes: Éditions OUEST-FRANCE, 2015.

Tourault, Philippe, *Anne de Bretagne*. Paris: Perrin, 2014.

Tuchman, Barbara W., *A Distant Mirror.* New York: Alfred A. Knopf, 1978.

Tudor Times, *Anne of Brittany: Life Story.* London: www.tudor-times.co.uk, 2018.

Vieil-Castel, Alex, *Je Suis ... Anne de Bretagne.* Paris: Hoche Communication S.A.S., 2015.

Warr, Countess de la, Constance, *A Twice Crowned Queen.* London: Eveleigh Nash, 1906.

Weir, Alison, *Eleanor of Aquitaine.* New York: Ballantine Books, 1999.

Wellman, Kathleen, *Queens and Mistresses of Renaissance France.* New Haven: Yale University Press, 2014.

Willard, Charity Cannon, *Christine de Pizan: Her Life and Works.* New York, Persea Books, 1984.

ANNE *and* CHARLES

Book One of the Anne of Brittany Series
The gripping tale of a larger than life queen
http://lrd.to/ANNEANDCHARLES

ROZSA GASTON

"An enchanting blend of royalty,
young love, and the French Renaissance."
—*Publishers Weekly*

ANNE *and* CHARLES

PASSION AND POLITICS IN LATE MEDIEVAL FRANCE
THE STORY OF ANNE OF BRITTANY'S MARRIAGE TO CHARLES VIII

"Historically sharp and dramatically stirring."
—*Kirkus Reviews*

ABOUT THE AUTHOR

Rozsa Gaston writes playful books on serious matters, including the struggles women face to get what they want out of life. She studied European history at Yale, and received her Master's degree in international affairs from Columbia University. She worked at *Institutional Investor*, then as a hedge funds marketer. Gaston lives in Bronxville, NY with her family and is currently working on *Anne and Louis: Middle Years,* Book Three of the Anne of Brittany Series.

If you enjoyed *Anne and Louis*, please post a review at http://lrd.to/ANNEANDLOUIS to help others find this book. One sentence is enough to let readers know what you thought. Drop Rozsa Gaston a line on Facebook to let her know you posted a review and receive as thanks an eBook edition of *Anne and Charles* or *Sense of Touch: Love and Duty at Anne of Brittany's Court.*

Visit her at rozsagastonauthor.com/anneofbrittanyseries
Facebook: https://www.facebook.com/rozsagastonauthor
Instagram: rozsagastonauthor
Twitter: @RozsaGaston

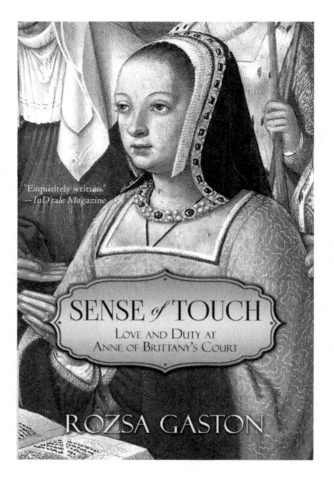

"Exquisitely written."
—InD'tale Magazine

SENSE of TOUCH
LOVE AND DUTY AT
ANNE OF BRITTANY'S COURT

ROZSA GASTON

"A romance and an interesting novel about a little-known French queen. It is a story with a strong sense of place and well-drawn characters, a story of heartache and forbidden love, of women in the 15th century French court, who fought with passion and determination for what they wanted. A striking story."
—*Historical Novel Society*

*An excerpt from Rozsa Gaston's prequel to the Anne of Brittany
Series, a 2017 RONE Award Finalist and 2018 TopShelf Book
Awards Finalist for Women's Issues*

SENSE *of* TOUCH

CHAPTER ONE

THE COURT OF
ANNE OF BRITTANY

"WHAT DO MEN KNOW of what we endure?" Nicole raged as she hurried down the hallway from the queen's bedchamber. Better to be angry than sad. The latest was beyond unbearable.

She slipped into the outer room of the king's quarters, catching the eye of Hubert de St. Bonnet, the king's head chamber valet. Quickly she shook her head and glanced away. He would understand. Silence spoke volumes. It always did at these moments.

Hubert hurried to Charles VIII at the far end of the room. Nicole watched as the men conferred, their backs to her. By the time her monarch turned to her she told herself he would be ready to receive whatever fortune had to deliver.

"The queen?"

"Fine, Sire. She is resting." Nicole couldn't bear to go on.

"And the dauphin Francis?" King Charles' posture held erect. His fourth son had been born three hours earlier. He had briefly seen him and given him the name Francis for his wife's father, Francis II, Duke of Brittany.

Nicole opened her mouth but nothing came out. The thought came to her that if she didn't say the words, they wouldn't be true. Finally, she spoke.

"The doctors would like a word with you if you can come."

"Does my son live?" the king thundered.

Perhaps he was less ready for the answer than she had thought. He had had plenty of practice receiving similar news in times past, but who could be prepared to hear it yet again?

"He—I cannot say, Sire. The doctor has asked only that you come," Nicole stammered. Better to let those more senior than she deliver the blow.

A tinge of gray passed over the young king's face before he turned from Nicole to his valet. At the age of twenty-seven, he had already sired four sons and two daughters. All rested under the earth, save the one who had just arrived.

Hubert de St. Bonnet nodded, almost imperceptibly. "I'm sure they are doing everything they can for—"

"Silence!" The king smashed both hands down on the wood table next to him. Then he overturned it. Courtiers scattered out of the way, the youngest running toward Nicole.

"Go now. The king will come when he is—when he is ready," he whispered, giving her a small push toward the door. The contact was comforting.

"Of course." She bowed her head but looked up through her eyelashes. For the briefest moment before Charles covered his long, angular face with one large hand she saw abject anguish there, a look of misery that made her heart drop. No such expression should cross the face of a man so hale, so fit and full of life as her monarch.

She backed out of the room, then turned and ran down the hallway to the queen's rooms. She could only imagine how the queen felt if the king's grief was that evident. Pray God Anne of Brittany was asleep, drugged with the sleeping draught the doctor had been preparing when Nicole had left. What comfort would the queen have when she woke up and found no small warm being snuggling at her side?

Oh, God, how could You be so cruel? Nicole crossed herself.

Who knew what was in the mind of the Master Creator? What point for a woman to hope, to suffer, then finally to labor in unbearable pain at the end of the better part of a year, only to deliver a child to die just hours after being born? No doubt God was a man with such faulty designs for womankind. She hoped one day she would get a chance to ask Him why He'd come up with this particular one. Catching herself, she crossed herself again and told herself to stop questioning what was beyond her ken.

THE STALLION HAD arrived the week before from one of the royal estates near Toulouse, in the region of Aquitaine in southwestern France. The queen was due to see the stunning new horse the king had gifted her with after the loss of their latest child. Six weeks had passed since the dauphin Francis had died, and Anne of Brittany, Queen of France, had seemed on the road to recovery.

But over the past week the queen had been out of sorts. Nicole hoped the combination of the glorious early September weather and the arrival the day before of the groomsman from Agen who would train the new horse would put her in better spirits.

"I am not in the mood today. Someone must go in my place," the queen said, looking sourly toward the cluster of maids of honor at her side. Her expression looked out of place on her young, fair face. Heart-shaped, with a charmingly pointed chin and rosy cheeks, such a face seemed ill-suited to wear such a world-weary expression. Losing six children by the age of twenty had had its effect.

Nicole discreetly scrutinized her royal employer. Her broad forehead glowed with health despite the downward curve of her mouth. Either all was not well or perhaps it was the best of all possible news. Whichever it was, she couldn't bear sitting around trying to coax the queen out of her doldrums any longer.

"Your Majesty, I will go," Nicole and Marie de Volonté offered simultaneously. Nicole looked at the younger girl next to her. The newest addition to the queen's ladies, Marie's head of lush, dark brown curls was beginning to be matched by the promise of an equally lush figure. At age fourteen she would soon be a candidate for the queen's considerable matchmaking skills, if she showed promise at court.

"Whoever." The queen raised a limp hand, and let it drop again in her lap. She breathed deeply then leaned back in her chair, closing her eyes. One of her attending ladies stepped forward and held a vial of violet musk perfume under her delicately upturned nose. It was the queen's favorite scent.

Nicole's heart leapt. She had seen that bone-tired attitude before. She would wager it heralded the first weeks of a pregnancy. A time when no one dared breathe a word but when all of the court ladies included the queen in their evening prayers and petitioned God for the child to grasp hold of its mother's womb and refuse to let go until the full time had come to enter the world. Later, the even harder work of keeping the newborn infant alive would begin.

Only once had the queen succeeded: she had given birth to Charles-Orland almost five years earlier. The following year, Charles Orland's brother, Francis, had been delivered prematurely, stillborn. Twice since, the queen had been pregnant, but delivered stillborn daughters. Then the worst had happened.

Just after his third birthday, the young dauphin, Charles-Orland, had succumbed to measles. Almost nine months to the day after that terrible event, the queen had delivered a new dauphin, again named Charles. The boy lasted several weeks before a sudden high fever sent him back to Heaven. After that, the latest delivery; again a son, again named Francis like his stillborn brother. The new Francis lived a mere three hours.

Some wondered if perhaps the queen had begun breeding too early, producing Charles-Orland just ten months after her marriage at age fourteen to the king. Most didn't, though, since it was common practice for royals to marry as soon as they reached puberty; especially if the marriage was one to cement an alliance for reasons of state. In Anne's case, she had agreed to marry Charles VIII in order to win her country's independence after the Franco-Breton war of 1491. The best way for her to secure her position was to produce a dauphin for France. If only any of them had lived.

SENSE of TOUCH

Available wherever books are sold or at

http://lrd.to/SENSEOFTOUCH

Anne *and* Louis: Middle Years coming fall 2019
Book Three of the Anne of Brittany Series
The gripping tale of a larger than life queen

Anne of Brittany and Louis XII
mosaic from Vannes train station, Vannes, Brittany, France
Courtesy of Wikimedia Commons

Acknowledgments

Aspecial thank you to Eleanor Fairburn, author of *Crowned Ermine* (Robert Hale Press: 1968), the most exciting historical novel on Anne of Brittany of all the books I read to research the Anne of Brittany Series. If I could pen a historical tale with one tenth the finesse of Eleanor Fairburn, I would feel that I have delivered to readers all that they had hoped for in a good book.

Thank you to Angela Loud Morris, Anna Words, Hilde van den Bergh, Donna Ford, Shon Tyler, Karen McCooey, Erick Negron, Laurence Siegel, Annette Bressie Jackson, Andreas Falley, Diana Cecil, Sheila Jodlowski and so many others.

With you, and readers like you, Anne of Brittany's story will flame alive once more.

Printed in Great Britain
by Amazon